T0265913

Advance Praise for *The Art of Pretend*

"Delicious and biting, *The Art of Pretend* probes the artifice of even our most intimate relationships. Lauren Kuhl's art world canvas is covered with the bold strokes of a wealthy New York family and the dark shading of an uneven friend dynamic. It kept me up way too late, with a sophistication that removed all guilt from the pleasure."

—**Avery Carpenter Forrey, author of *Social Engagement***

"This fun and twisty novel is a delicious take on class, friendship, and desire. Set among the super rich in the art world of New York City, Kuhl's cast of characters' ambitions inevitably collide in the ultimate pursuit of power, exposing the complexities hidden beneath the art of pretending."

—**Christina McDowell, author of *The Cave Dwellers***

"Spend a summer with the pretty young things as they traipse through the Hamptons, New York City, and Europe in Lauren Kuhl's compelling and beautifully written debut, *The Art of Pretend*. Kuhl explores the nuances of friendship and romance, while also capturing the absurd antics of the rich and Insta-famous. Poignant, funny, and elegant from start to finish, this artful book is a must-read."

—**Lauren Edmondson, author of *Wedding of the Season***

"*The Art of Pretend* is a compulsively readable, voyeuristic journey into the wealthy world of New York City, filled with unforgettable characters and razor-sharp dialogue. I devoured this page-turner."

—**Jillian Cantor, *USA TODAY* bestselling author of *The Fiction Writer***

The Art of Pretend

A NOVEL

LAUREN KUHL

GRAYDON
HOUSE

GRAYDON
HOUSE®

Recycling programs
for this product may
not exist in your area.

ISBN-13: 978-1-525-83153-9

The Art of Pretend

Graydon House
22 Adelaide St. West, 41st Floor
Toronto, Ontario M5H 4E3, Canada
www.GraydonHouseBooks.com

Printed in U.S.A.

To my parents, for everything

Art is a lie that makes us realize truth.

—Pablo Picasso

PART ONE

JUNE

1

The night started unassumingly enough, at a wine bar near Etta's apartment in Tribeca, a dark, cavernous room located down an inconspicuous flight of stairs, where the twenty-eight-dollar cocktails all had ridiculous names like "Juniper Berry Jubilee" or "Hazy Hibiscus Morning" and the sommelier waxed poetic about their natural wine selection that Etta complained was "undrinkable." That kind of place. When I arrived, she was sitting in the single booth in the back, wearing a thin lilac blouse that hung off her knobby shoulders like tissue paper, drinking a gin and tonic through a straw. She had already ordered oysters and a frisée salad.

Once the server took my order, Etta narrowed her green eyes at me and said, "Want to go to Brooklyn?"

"What's in Brooklyn?" I asked. Etta never left Manhattan.

Her eyes now on her phone, the bluish glare casting an extraterrestrial glow across her face, she said, "Nothing much." I waited. "Well, just a party. Thought it could be fun?"

"I don't know," I said. "I'm kind of tired."

"Sam's apartment is really cool, though."

"Who's Sam?"

"A friend of a friend." It was always a friend of a friend. "So? Is that a yes?"

Etta loved Thursday nights; she used to say they were "our" night, and I liked that, an evening belonging to us. But Etta was not plagued by the same realities that would greet me come morning. She would sleep in, wake up with the satisfaction of having nowhere to be, and I would suffer through my nine-to-five with a splitting headache and dry mouth, the residual price of last night's "fun." We had graduated from NYU four years earlier, and while the rest of us signed leases on cramped apartments partitioned by drywall and shared with four other roommates, slogged through entry-level jobs fetching coffee for bosses who were tired and stressed but all the while addicted to this elusive idea of importance, and worked our way up, up, up the corporate ladder, praying we wouldn't end up like the people to whom we reported, praying the whole time the figurative ladder might collapse, Etta played house in the apartment her parents had bought for her.

I smiled, but said nothing. I always agreed to go with her in the end, but sometimes, I enjoyed pretending there was an alternative world in which I said, "No, thanks, I'm good."

"Please!" she begged, then noticing a couple at the bar staring, more softly, "Please. It will be fun."

I took a sip of my wine. "Okay, fine."

We picked at our starters. When it came, I offered to pay the check, but Etta laughed and slid my debit card back across the table.

The party was hosted by the same hipster trust fund crowd and art cronies Etta knew through her family, or *friends of friends* to whom she always said things like, "Let's get a coffee soon!" knowing her words were empty, the suggestion a strategic means of ending a conversation already dead on arrival. I learned that from Etta, how to say things you didn't really mean while still convincing people of your sincerity. I learned a lot from her.

In the elevator, Etta buzzed "P" for "Penthouse," and we zipped to the top floor, where a tall man with thick, slicked-back hair welcomed us to a loft with wood-beam ceilings and brick walls, the smell of timber and sweat wrapping around us. The floors vibrated from the music booming through speakers, something by Daft Punk, and the traffic droning across the Brooklyn Bridge beyond the windows.

Etta immediately knew somebody, which meant I would cling to her, be introduced as her "best friend from college," smirk my way through small talk that did not really include me. When the same guy who had greeted us materialized with two vodka sodas, I swigged mine like I was afraid he might ask for it back.

"I heard your parents picked up that Pollock at Sotheby's," a girl with a pierced septum and long black hair said to Etta, who nodded before quipping it would probably end up on the bare wall in her own apartment.

"Oh, outside your bedroom?" I asked.

"Ren," she said, turning to me, "a Pollock would never fit on that wall. It's much too narrow." She rolled her eyes, as if to say, *This one, where did I find her?* and the other guests laughed, but then she pulled me close and squeezed my arm and so I laughed, too.

Etta was recognizable to these people; her parents were artists and collectors. They'd "revived modernism," whatever that meant, and apparently their signature sketches of glorified Venn diagrams could fetch upward of six figures, at least according to the internet. Sometimes, Etta liked to ramble about her parents, as if they were canonized saints, divulging the details of their days living in SoHo during the late seventies and early eighties, exaggerating their struggles and ignoring the fact that they had attended New England boarding schools and descended from families steeped in tradition, so their decision to live in SoHo when the neighborhood was an artists' enclave was one of free will and not circumstantial. To most people, Etta's deluded tone could be a turnoff, but to everyone else, to the other twenty people in this very room, it was normal, even cute.

It didn't take long for me to understand why Etta had insisted on the spontaneous sojourn to Brooklyn. We knew each other too well, could predict the patterns of each other's thoughts, knew which buttons to push, and when to stop, so when she floated across the room to a nondescript man with a thin, unironic mustache and greasy, dark blond hair and tapped him on the shoulder, I thought, *This makes sense.* This was the "new guy," the latest DJ she'd been texting. Just as quickly as we'd zoomed over the Brooklyn Bridge to get here, they veered down a hall and left me alone in an apartment full of strangers.

I crossed and uncrossed my arms, made small talk one beat too long with Sam, the owner of the apartment. I learned it was him not because he introduced himself, but because I heard someone shout "Sam!" and he responded. I thanked him when he reappeared with another round of drinks, noticed how he peered around, searching for my counterpart and the person explaining my presence here, and when I said, "I don't know where she went," he shrugged and downed the drink he made for her. I started to ask how he knew Etta, but someone else called, "Sam! Come here!" and soon, I was alone again.

It was in the kitchen area that I noticed Archer, approximately twenty minutes after I lost Etta, not that I was keeping track. Archer was Etta's older brother and a semi-established artist for someone who just barely scratched the surface of his thirties. There were his shows here in the city, plus Miami and Los Angeles and abroad. At one point it felt as if everywhere you turned, there was his photograph, or some article either praising or eviscerating his work, and then, nothing. Two years passed. He'd supposedly been living out in the country, followed by a friend's houseboat. Etta said he was "burnt-out," that it happened all the time with artists, this endless cycle of creation and expectation, feeding the public's appetite for something new, something exciting, something that had never been done before. But it had all been done before, that was the problem.

"Sounds intense," I had said, but she did not comment further.

Archer was still tall and thin, like Etta, with an angular face and pale green eyes that matched his sister's. The last time I'd seen him, his hair was long and he could tuck it behind his ears, like an imitation Kurt Cobain, but now it was cropped closer to his head. Of course he had a perfectly shaped skull, I thought, as he grazed his fingers across his scalp, eyes flitting about the room.

Then, his gaze landed on me.

I focused on my drink, mulling whether he could have any recollection of our brief series of encounters, whether he recognized me, or more realistically, thought I looked like someone he knew. I was always told I "looked familiar," or that I "looked like someone." It was always "that actress" no one could name, or a friend of a friend, though a few times, people said I resembled a young Jennifer Connelly and I thought, *Okay, I'll take it, thank you very much.*

When I glanced up from my drink, he was there in front of me, smelling of musk, or maybe that was his cologne, I wasn't sure. He looked tired, but tired in an appealing way, like his life was one big sleepless night, like he had stories and multiple lives and tonight, this moment, was only one iteration. I wished then that I'd changed after work, out of my black slacks and striped cotton-blend sweater and into something that didn't reek of corporate America and J.Crew.

"Have you seen Sam?" he asked. I wasn't even sure if he was talking to me, except that there was no one else around.

I said, "I think he went that way," and gestured behind me.

This earned a nod. "Oh, nice, I should say hi." I, too, nodded, thinking I was happy to help, happy to be here. He smiled and extended a hand. "Archer Crofton."

I stared at his hand, forgetting all social cues. "I know," I said, then regretted it, because of course he didn't remember me. "I mean, sorry, yes, I'm Etta's friend. Ren?" As I said my name, I sort of swallowed it, making a face as if gulping a vitamin.

He nodded again in that vague way, implying either faint recognition or a really good front, and I wanted to die a little when he said, "I thought you looked familiar."

Even though it was probably a lie, I smiled, but before I had the opportunity to respond, to insert myself in the conversation and ask, "What have you been up to? It's been a minute, right?" or attempt to sketch a convincing image of a shared world, one that found each of us as equals at the same party, his gaze slipped from mine and that was when I saw he was grinning at a woman with straight black hair lounging on a cognac leather sofa.

"Sorry, one second," he said, already walking off, but I knew better. I wouldn't be seeing him again.

I watched as Archer kissed the woman on the cheek, slid his hand down her back, this interaction between them so obviously comfortable and familiar. She was wearing a silk black shirtdress and platform sandals, sipping a pale-colored drink from a coupe glass with a sprig of something floating along the surface, rosemary or thyme or even dill, I had no idea.

I hung around for another twenty minutes, like some listless creature, waiting for Etta. When she returned, she'd say something like, "Shit, sorry, I hope I wasn't gone too long?" and I'd say, "Oh, no, not at all," and then we'd share a cab back to Manhattan and she'd tell me all about the DJ and his "avoidant attachment style," and I'd listen dutifully, grateful she hadn't forgotten about me.

But ten minutes after midnight, there was still no sign of her. When Sam reappeared in the kitchen, all slack-jawed and glassy-eyed and resembling, I realized, a hammerhead shark, I asked, "Have you seen Etta by any chance?"

He looked at me as if I'd spoken another language and reintroduced himself.

"Hi," I said. "I'm Ren. Etta's friend?"

He nodded. He didn't remember.

"Yeah, sorry, have you seen her, actually?" A pause—was I not making sense? "She's been missing for a while," I said. "I'm kind of worried."

"Oh," he said, breaking into a lazy grin, showing off the crooked keyboard of his teeth. "They left."

"They...what? Sorry, who's *they*?"

"Etta and Rex."

Rex. Of course that would be his name.

"Sorry, I've been standing here the whole time. Wouldn't I have seen them leave?"

"You're the babysitter?" he asked.

He was trying to be funny, I knew, but I had nothing left to give.

He pointed toward the windows on the other side of the loft, to the hall I imagined led to a slew of bedrooms or bathrooms or somewhere more private. "There's another elevator back there," he said, like this bit of information should have been obvious. Then he retrieved a glass from a cabinet and joined his friends across the room.

I chugged the rest of my drink. Archer's arm was still draped across the shoulders of the woman he had kissed hello, both of them visibly captivated by their conversation. Everyone had since gravitated to the far side of the apartment, and the music had become synthesized beats with no lyrics. The only other straggler in the kitchen was busy rummaging through a mostly empty refrigerator, thrilled by a discovery of animal crackers underneath the sink, so I was invisible as I slipped out the front.

Outside, I texted Etta: Hey, everything ok? I called twice, left

a voice mail, sent another message accessorized with five question marks. Should I just go home? But this last message wasn't
delivered and I guessed her phone must have died.

It was windy near the East River, and the buildings of the
Financial District twinkled like a distant dream across the black
water. I started to feel that last drink, the warmth concentrating
in my cheeks, and decided to order an Uber. The estimated price
for a ride home to the East Village, with a convenient surge for
the pool option, no less, was thirty-one dollars, equivalent to
an entrée and margarita, excluding tip, at a dive Mexican place
in Union Square that Etta and I liked. I made my selection and
sat on the curb, staring at my phone, willing Pyotr to arrive
faster so I could fold myself into the backseat of his red Toyota
Camry, suffocated by the artificial smell of a pine-scented air
freshener, and drive off into the night with three other passen-
gers desperate enough to share a car with complete strangers.

From behind, a door opened and shut. "Where are you?" a
voice asked. It was Archer. "Okay, yeah, yeah, I see you. Thanks,"
he said into his phone.

The app claimed Pyotr was four minutes away, but he wasn't
moving. The car looked like it was spinning in circles. It was
after midnight and there was definitely no traffic, so what was
taking so long? I tried calling, but his words were warbled by
static, drowned out by a thumping bass.

"Hello?" I said, pressing the phone to my ear and marching
down the block. "Hello? Hey, hi? Hi? Are you there?" A click,
then nothing. The line went dead. "Dammit."

"Where are you headed?" I heard Archer ask.

I kept walking, holding my hair back against the breeze, willing the car icon on my screen to move.

"Where are you headed?" Archer repeated, closer now.

I spun around. He was speaking to me. "Um, the East Village."

"Hmm." He diverted his eyes to a black town car across the

street. "Well, my driver is over there," he said, pointing toward it. "Want a ride?"

I recognized the town car, driven by Paul, their family driver; it made sense, then, why Etta had not asked him to take us to Brooklyn earlier. He had been reporting to Archer for the evening.

On the app, a notification appeared: Pyotr and his caravan of strangers were a minute away, but Archer had offered me a lift to Manhattan for free.

I hesitated. "Are you sure?"

"I mean, I'm offering."

"It's not out of your way or anything?"

"Positive," he said. "I'm already going to Chelsea."

I glanced at my phone again, and then up at Archer.

"Now or never," he said.

"Okay," I said, "thank you," and canceled the Uber. The five-dollar cancellation fee was nothing in comparison to the full price.

I followed Archer to the car, where he opened the back door, gesturing for me to go first before dipping in after me. He said hello to Paul, who eyed us in the rearview mirror. In all the years he'd chauffeured me and Etta, I'd never once heard him speak.

It was silent as we pulsed over the cobblestone and turned onto a main street. Archer asked Paul if he could put on the radio, and moments later, Van Morrison's voice murmured through the speakers. Archer drummed his fingers on the windowsill, humming along.

We crossed the Brooklyn Bridge and I was holding my breath now, when Archer asked, "So where do I know you from again?"

Before I could think about it too much, I said, "Why? You regret giving a ride to a perfect stranger?"

He laughed. "You're not a perfect stranger."

"Etta and I went to NYU together." He was still squinting, though, as if struggling to identify a mysterious artifact. "I was actually at one of your shows."

"I've had a lot of shows," he said, and I felt my face flush.

"Right. Well, this was like, a few years ago, I want to say."
In fact, it was exactly three years ago, but I didn't need him to
think I knew this. "Out in, I think it was East Hampton?"

He shut his eyes and snapped his fingers. "That's it," he said.
"I knew you looked familiar. You're Etta's sidekick."

"Guilty," I said.

"You were at the party after, at the house."

I nodded, practically beaming, then tried to act as if the re-
surgence of these memories was entirely insignificant to me.
Sure, he had probably forgotten the other times, but they were
minor run-ins. The most we'd ever interacted, up until now,
was at that party, when I'd congratulated him on the show and
he asked, "Are you having fun?" and I told him I was, because
what other answer could I have offered? People didn't ask if you
were having fun if they anticipated you might say something
like, "No, I'm bored," or "Not anymore." Being friends with
Etta, I'd gathered that sometimes, lying could be an expression
of gratitude.

With that same smirk, his mouth crooked, he leaned across
the middle seat so that our heads nearly touched. "Don't kill
me," he whispered, his breath brushing my lips, "but remind
me of your name?"

The headlights cut shadows across his face and his eyes were
so green, like an exotic body of water.

"Ren," I said.

"Nice to meet you again, Ren." He drifted back to his side
of the car.

━━━━

We were quiet the rest of the drive, another twenty minutes
until Chinatown appeared in the windows, restaurant workers
flipping chairs onto stacked tables in garish lighting, red and
yellow paper lanterns strung high above the streets. Archer said
my name again and it was like cutting back into lucidity.

"I don't know where you live," he said.

"Right. Sorry." To Paul, I said, "The corner of Seventh and Avenue B is fine."

Archer laughed and I realized I had screamed it. In the rear-view mirror, I could see Paul shaking his head, amused.

"Sorry," I said, trying to smile, but I was grateful the car was dark and Archer couldn't see I was blushing.

"So," he said then, "she ditched you."

"Who?"

"You know," he said, his gaze falling slowly on me again. "My sister."

"Oh," I said, "I think her phone died," and I pictured Etta, bursting into a pizza place back in Brooklyn like some midnight vigilante, asking the owner if she could borrow his charger, him obliging, gifting Etta a whole pie just because, and Etta nibbling on a slice or two while her phone revived itself.

"That's optimistic," he said.

"No, really. Do you want to see our messages?" I asked, and I found myself digging through my bag for my phone.

"No," he laughed. "It's okay. I trust you."

I caught Paul's eye in the rearview and he swiftly looked away.

"I'm sure you're going to miss her," Archer said.

"Uh, I think I'll be okay for one night?" I said, but I could tell he thought I was joking, the way his mouth curved into a smirk.

"Except it's more than one night," he said.

A pause. "Sorry, I think I'm confused. What are you talking about?"

"Etta didn't tell you?" He wasn't smiling anymore.

"Tell me what."

Archer ran his tongue over his bottom lip. "Etta's leaving soon, for Barcelona."

"Oh?" I heard my voice, floating, wispy, like a scrap of paper. "For vacation?"

"No, no." He laughed again. "She's taking classes there. Digital art or something."

"I didn't realize she was into digital art," I said. Why hadn't Etta mentioned any of this?

He clicked his fingers against the windowsill. "I really thought you knew."

"Yeah, well, I'm sure she's just crazed. She'll tell me soon. You know how she can be." I swallowed hard. "Forgetful."

"Of course," he said.

"So these classes? They're like a summer program?"

Archer hesitated. "I think it's a bit longer than that."

"How much longer?"

"A year."

I shifted in my seat, resting my head against the cool glass window, waiting for rationality to join us like another passenger, squeeze into the empty middle seat. But it didn't. Etta was leaving. No foreshadowing. No subtle hints. Just "Goodbye, so long, farewell, fuck you." And still, I hadn't broached the most obvious question.

"When does she leave?"

"In a week?" he said. "Two weeks? I forget."

I could feel Archer studying me, parsing my thoughts with a fine-tooth comb. "Wow, that's soon."

"Yeah, I think she's just been feeling sort of…lost, you know? New York is her home, but I don't think she's necessarily happy. I'm sure you know."

"Yes," I said, though I didn't because she had never mentioned it, the impending move or these alleged "feelings" of hers.

Archer fiddled with a button on his side of the car, opening and closing the back window, settling on open. I didn't want to talk about Etta anymore; I wanted to act as if he was wrong. It was easier that way.

"Thank you," I said. "Again. For the ride."

A wave of his hand. "No need to thank me."

But I did, when we stopped at a light on Allen Street, and again when we careened past a slew of drunk people funneling out of a bar on East Houston, and one final time, at the corner of Seventh Street and Avenue B, where I said to Paul, "I can just jump out here."

The car slurred toward stillness. Archer and I stared at one another for a moment and then I unbuckled my seat belt and said, "Well, good night."

Archer bowed his head. "Good night."

I scuttled across the street to my apartment, feeling more drunk now than I had all evening, or maybe it was my nerves. I jiggled the key into the first locked door, hyperaware that Archer and the town car were still at the curb across the street. The key's grooved head jabbed my palm; it was stuck in the lock.

"Need any help?" Archer called. He'd rolled down the window, his forearms resting on the edge as he watched me.

"All good! It just does this sometimes," I shouted back.

When I did, at last, succeed in unlocking the door, some thirty seconds later, I ducked inside the building and let the door shut. Through the double glass, caked in grime and years of fingerprints that no amount of power washing could erase, there was Archer, his green eyes flickering at me from across the street, the soft upturn of his mouth, as if pulled by an invisible string, laughing as the car drove away.

2

"You look like shit," Jeff said as I sat across from him the next morning.

Jeff was my coworker-turned-friend, and he wasn't wrong. All night, my mind had played a jingle on repeat: Etta is leaving, and then, Etta is *leaving*?

"I didn't sleep," I told him, tugging a tissue from the box on my desk. I wiped the excess mascara underneath my eyes as I logged on to my computer, skimming the emails that had clogged my inbox overnight.

"Ah, so your date went well?"

"No, I was out with Etta." I lifted my face just in time to catch his eye roll.

Jeff did not like Etta; he had strong opinions of people with trust funds who gave "nothing back to society," and could not understand why I continued to be friends with someone like her. "I just don't get it," he would say, and I would find myself defending her, as if by reflex. "She's better when you get to know her," I would counter, or "She doesn't trust most people," or "She's just lonely."

But it was me who would be lonely now.

Jeff asked if I wanted to get a coffee, and though I did, I needed to deal with an editor whose preferred method of communication was sending stream-of-consciousness emails, and also draft a press release for a B-list celebrity's perfume launch (because the celebrity fragrance market wasn't crowded enough). I was, in truth, relieved to have the work, a distraction that would keep me from dwelling on what Archer had told me last night, that Etta was possibly leaving, and more importantly, that she'd failed to tell me.

Jeff quickly stopped nagging about coffee, however, when our boss, Natalie, emerged from her office and appeared beside me, hovering above my desk.

"So Roger sent me a note," she said. She was not happy.

Roger was the editor behind the stream-of-consciousness emails, a veteran at *The New York Times* for over thirty years, one of those rare people who had earned the distinction of recognition by first name alone. He was simply Roger from *The Times*, and if you didn't understand the gravity of that statement, then you probably should be fired.

I tried to apologize, but she continued: "He's a pain but very important to the agency and we need to be very, *very* delicate with him, always. I don't care if he's calling you at eleven a.m. or p.m., you need to respond."

"I'm sorry," I said.

She held up her hand, didn't want to hear it. "Here's how we salvage it. Pitch him the exclusive for the perfume, make him feel special. Just be like, 'We'd love for you to break the exclusive on blah blah blah.' He'll probably see right through it, but sometimes brownnosing is the only solution." She gave me a look to make sure I understood.

I told her, "Sorry, yes. I'll call him right now," but she didn't budge until I picked up the phone.

Natalie smiled. "You're the best."

When she disappeared, Jeff rolled his eyes again. *"You're the best,"* he said, mimicking her.

The dial tone, that stale buzzing, drilled into my ears.

———

It was pouring when I left the office, so that when I got back to my apartment, my clothes were soaked and clung to me like Saran Wrap. I noticed the copies of *The New Yorker*, piling up on the small folding table off the kitchen, the dishes stacked in the sink, glasses ringing the coffee table. I'd told myself I would clean whenever a prospective tenant came to check out the second bedroom, as one was meant to this evening. Except they always canceled. Thanks, but I found something else, read a version of the same text, either a place closer to work, or the subway, or near their boyfriend/girlfriend/best friend, code for, *I found something better, I don't need you anymore.* And wasn't that what all exchanges were, meetings rooted in need? I padded into my bedroom, peeled off my wet clothes, and started changing into an old NYU T-shirt and sweatpants when the buzzer shrilled. I knew who it was almost instantly.

Etta had disappeared at eleven last night, and now she had resurfaced, fulfilling a pattern wherein she tended to show up, often unannounced, at my apartment. I was in the neighborhood, she would text, miming coincidence when we both knew better. Usually these arrivals came with gifts: an extra Rag & Bone T-shirt, vintage Celine sunglasses—"These were my mom's but they don't necessarily flatter my face shape"—even groceries from the market down the street when she was craving guacamole and asked me to make it for her. On one especially strange occasion, she'd lugged a full set of dinner plates, ordered on a whim from Roman and Williams, having decided that pale blue ceramic "wasn't her thing" and owed the impulsiveness of the purchase to both the waning moon and her menstrual cycle. But it wasn't the gifts for me; I didn't need them. It was that she thought I did.

By some miracle, Etta's pants, her hair, the white paper shopping bag she toted on her wrist, were all dry. She eyed me up and down, stopping at my wet hair. "What happened?"

"I got caught in the rain."

She peered out the window, as if unconvinced. I guessed this meant that Paul drove Etta here and she had been too engrossed in her phone to notice the weather, bypassing Mother Nature. She sat on the sofa, a basic white one from Ikea that had aged in the sun and since turned a shade of diluted mustard.

"Is it too early for wine?" I asked.

"No, it's almost seven," she said.

I remembered a bottle of Malbec on the counter. "Red okay?"

"Sure."

But I didn't move. I was watching Etta closely, looking for signs. She scrolled through her phone, her expression placid, relaxed—was she smiling? It was as if she didn't have a care in the world. As if she had nothing to hide. Perhaps Archer was wrong. Maybe she wasn't leaving.

I was trying to convince myself of this when she frowned. "You okay?"

"Yep. Didn't sleep great." I walked to the kitchen area and had just pried the cork from the bottle when she shouted from across the room.

"Ah, Ren?"

I stopped. This was it. "Yes?"

"Sorry. Do you have white?"

"Oh. Yeah." I left the bottle on the counter and instead retrieved an already open bottle of Pinot Grigio from the refrigerator door. With mechanical precision, I poured us two glasses.

"Thanks," she said.

I waited for her to say something, maybe the wine would loosen her tongue, but her eyes bobbed around the room, processing the congested apartment, which afforded just enough room for a tiny two-cushion sofa, one armchair, and an end table. Off the living space was a bathroom and two bedrooms, one partitioned by a fake wall, a standard procedure in the boxes we called "apartments." Etta liked to say the place was "cozy" and not "small," though to her, I understood that my apartment was like a recreational site she enjoyed visiting, but took solace in the fact that she was always able to leave.

I thought she was about to comment on the mess, and prepared to claim that I had a "deep clean" planned for this weekend. Instead she asked, "Whatever happened to your roommate? That girl?"

"She moved out two months ago," I said. Surely I'd told her this.

"Wait, why?"

"She's an actress. Or an aspiring one, I guess. She said there's more opportunity in LA. Commercials and stuff, I don't know."

All she said was, "That's sad." A pause. "So you're just living here by yourself?"

Wasn't that obvious? "Well, I'm looking for a new roommate. Why, do you want to move in?" I smiled, nudged her with my elbow, hoped I could coax her into telling me whether *she* was moving, but all I got was, "Ha ha, funny."

"I was actually supposed to meet with someone tonight. She was going to check out the apartment, but then she canceled."

"Huh," Etta said to herself. "That's annoying."

I half nodded and Etta drank from her glass, wincing, as if she tasted something bitter.

"Oh, wow," she said. "That's not good."

I thought it was tolerable, if not a little too sweet, but certainly not offensive. "Really? I thought it was fine?"

She set her glass on the end table, still grimacing. "Too fruity."

"Sorry," I said, then offered red, but she shook her head and insisted she was fine.

"How was the rest of your night?" Etta asked.

I swirled the wine in my glass. "It was okay," I said. "I was worried, though, when I couldn't find you?"

She searched her clutch for lip balm and smeared some on her lips. "Yeah, I'm sorry. My phone died. I didn't see your messages until this morning. Did you have fun, at least? I feel like Sam maybe liked you."

"Really? I didn't think that."

"Um, he was staring at you. Why do you think he was so frantic about getting us drinks?"

"I don't know, he was being a good host?" I said, laughing, trying to pretend I didn't care, that I was impassive to compliments.

She smirked. "You know he has some tech start-up, right?" I didn't. "He owns that apartment, and another one in Williamsburg, too." She raised each eyebrow playfully.

"I didn't know anyone there besides you."

"That's the point of parties," she said, "to meet people."

"Yeah, but then you left, and I just, I felt awkward. Out of place."

She shrugged, and I decided there was no real purpose to this conversation anymore. Etta had already made up her mind about her own lack of culpability and I would only end up mincing my words.

"I was just in a bad mood," I said. "And tired."

Her expression softened. "Understandable. I did kind of force you into going last night. And I'm sorry," she said, "I should have told you I was leaving with the DJ. That wasn't nice of me."

For the next twenty minutes we dissected the details of her evening. The DJ, her anxiety, the conversation she had with her therapist earlier; how she'd woken up at the DJ's apartment at 4 a.m., had a panic attack and took a cab to her apartment and

tried to meditate but her mind was racing too much for medi-
tation to be effective.

"I really wanted to cave and take a Xanax, but I didn't." She
shimmied in her seat. "You'd be proud of me. And we decided,"
she said, meaning she and her therapist, "that it's best I don't see
him anymore."

I said, "I didn't realize you liked him so much?" and Etta said
that her "liking him" wasn't so much the issue as her wanting
what she couldn't have.

"What do you mean?"

She dug her sandal into the floor. "Well, Ren, you see…he's
kind of married."

"Shit," I said.

She was quick to say, "But it's done now. I've blocked his
number. See?" She showed me her phone as proof. I'd forgotten his name was Rex and now all I could think of were dino-
saurs. "So you just Ubered home, then?" Etta asked, changing
the subject.

I took a mouthful of wine that burned its way down my
throat. "Yeah," I said, the lie giving me a little thrill. I could
have said I called an Uber pool, embellished the narrative. She
would have loved that, the image of me, smack in the middle
of the backseat of a Camry, cruising through the Financial District, suffering through the "long way home" in the name of
affordability, but I'd already whined about how she left me at
the party. There was such a thing as demanding too much pity,
and even I knew that.

Etta pouted out her lower lip. "Well, I'm glad you got home
okay. Sorry that I'm occasionally the worst."

"It's all good," I said. "No harm, no foul."

Etta was quiet. "You know, you can always sleep at my place,
if you don't want to come all the way over here? The doormen
know you, obviously."

"Well, I was closer to Brooklyn. Like, the East Village is closer to Brooklyn."

"I mean in the future." She lifted her eyes to mine. "Even if I'm not home. They'll always let you in."

This would have been the moment, I thought, to ask her, "What *about* when you aren't home?"

"Thanks," I said.

She gathered her things and squeezed my arm. "All right, I should get going. I'm meeting Plum for dinner." Etta referred to her parents by their first names.

"Just because?" I asked. She and Plum weren't especially close.

"She probably wants something," Etta said. "You know how she is."

"Well, what would she want?"

Etta stared at me. When she spoke again, her tone was strangely sharp. "I don't know, I guess I'll find out." She scrolled through their messages. "Look, she's already sending me pictures from that trip we took to Saint-Tropez last year. I was so miserable. All she talked about was..." I didn't respond and Etta's face froze. "Sorry."

"It's fine," I said, and really, Etta shouldn't have been sorry— I hardly spoke about my mother.

She opened her mouth, as if to say something, then elected not to, and I was fine with that. I didn't want to talk about it, either.

"Um, so anyway," Etta said, "Archer is introducing us to his new girlfriend this weekend. That's probably what Plum wants to talk about. To brief me on the 'run of show' or whatever. He's bringing her to Amagansett, which must mean it's serious."

"New girlfriend," I said, singing the words a little, and wondered if it was the woman he had kissed hello last night. Etta scoffed. "Well, it'll be nice to get out of the city?"

"I guess," she said, and I shifted my weight between my feet.

"Do you ever get like...tired of New York?" It was the perfect transition, natural enough that it wouldn't seem suspicious. She would say, *Yes, and speaking of...*

"Not really," she said. "Why? Are you tired of New York?"

"No," I said, too quickly. "Not at all." Then I got up and opened the front door for her. "Well," I said, "hopefully you'll get some nice family time."

She shrugged. "We'll see."

———

From the living room window, I watched Etta leave. It had since stopped raining, the ground glistening, puddles dotting Seventh Street. She looked like a pin among an army of other identical pins, no different from the dozens of other people speckling the sidewalk the farther away she got. As she jumped into the town car, I noticed she wasn't carrying the shopping bag she had toted on her wrist when she arrived. It'd been abandoned at the foot of the sofa.

I poked at it, considered if it was intrusive, then decided Etta wouldn't mind and opened the small box, brushed the tissue paper aside. Nestled between the layered sheets were two champagne flutes. I held one of the glasses, gingerly caressing my forefinger and thumb around the thin stem. I wasn't sure if these had been left for me, were perhaps her own personal purchase, or maybe had been intended for her mother. I set the flute on top of the tissue paper and drained the rest of Etta's wine into the kitchen sink.

3

That night, I couldn't sleep again. I thought about Etta and her dinner with Plum and how if Etta were leaving, that my life, my stake in this world, this city, would all be subject to change. It was funny, really, how I imagined we could stay like this forever, twenty-five and eternally youthful, and yet the truth was we were probably moving further and further away from this moment, the people we were now, every single day. And maybe Etta knew that; maybe Etta was ready for change.

I didn't like that.

In the morning the sound of my phone roused me from sleep. It had to be Etta, calling to download me about her "interesting" dinner with Plum. But it was Jeff's name that blared across the screen.

"Hello?" I said.

"Did I wake you?"

I sat up in bed and chugged the glass of water on my night-stand. "Kinda?"

"Did you forget about our plans? We said noon?"

It was 12:30 and I had, in fact, forgotten. I pulled the sheets up to my chin. "No, no. I'm just...moving slowly. I need to shower, and then I'll jump on the train."

"So you still didn't tell me about your night," Jeff said.

"What night?"

"When you went out with Etta."

"Oh, yeah, well—" I began, but he interrupted me.

"What is she up to these days? Still working reception at that gallery?"

"No...she hasn't worked there in a year."

"So she's unemployed."

"Well, no? I think she volunteers at a—"

"So wait, how long did she last there? Two months? Three?"

It was two and a half, and she quit because she didn't see how memorizing coffee orders and managing the schedule of a senior art director could teach her anything about life or art, but I didn't bother explaining this to Jeff. Instead I said, "All right, let's not."

"Nice life," Jeff said, and I felt it pertinent to add, "Well, her family is kind of weird."

Jeff laughed; it was difficult, if not impossible, for him to empathize. His dad was a principal at a school for gifted children, and his mom was a social worker. Although he could be overtly opinionated and contrarian, he was a good son who returned to his childhood apartment in Harlem for weekly dinners with his equally good parents.

"I mean," Jeff said, "I didn't exactly assume they were normal?"

"No, not like that. I don't know, I don't think they're so easy to deal with, based on what I've seen. Her mom is self-absorbed and her dad is..."

"Rich?"

"An asshole," I corrected, but he wasn't having it.

"Ren, please. She lives alone in a penthouse in Tribeca. Her family enables her. If they were so difficult, she wouldn't live there in the first place."

"Jeff," I said, "I literally just woke up."

He clucked his tongue. "Fine. You didn't ask about my date last night," he said.

I told him I was sorry, I forgot, but I was relieved he changed the subject.

"It was a bust. He works in ad sales."

"What's wrong with ad sales?"

"It's a tragedy, that's what. I mean, what do people in ad sales even do?"

"I don't know, Jeff. I guess people could say the same about us. Or any job."

"Huh. Yeah. Are you still talking to that guy?"

"Which guy?"

"The one who you matched with on that app? The lawyer?"

"Oh," I said. "I mean, not really."

"Did you even go out with him?"

"What? No."

"Why?"

Because that isn't how it works, I wanted to say. Because they were just pen pals, these men, strangers protected by their phones, shielded from any real intimacy, and maybe I was fine with that. Maybe it was a game to me, too.

I threw off the covers and said we could talk all he wanted about my dating life, or lack thereof, in an hour. I needed to shower first, and I'd meet him at his apartment around two.

But when I got out of the shower, there were two missed calls and three new messages from Etta. The first one read:

Just got to the house. Vibes are very weird. Plum and Lucy put out a whole lunch spread. It's overkill.

The next message, sent five minutes after:

What are you up to today? It looks like it might rain here. Can't imagine being stuck inside all day with everyone...

My hair was wet, droplets hitting the floor. There was a third and final message:

Ok I know it's last minute, but want to come out here for the weekend? Paul's already on his way to Manhattan...he could drive you back either late Sunday or even Monday morning. Miss you.

It was one—I could pack an overnight bag and get to Amagansett before dinner, which I think had been the whole point; I could be there to defuse whatever tension Etta had resigned herself to.

I texted Jeff that there was a change of plans. I did feel guilty, in a fleeting sense, but Etta needed me. And maybe, I thought, if Etta needed me, I could convince her not to leave. *If*, of course, she was leaving. There was still that possibility—that Archer was wrong.

Are you serious? Jeff said. That is so annoying.

I'm sorry, I said, but I wasn't.

———

Etta swung open the door before I could even ring the bell, and I understood that she'd been waiting for me, like a puppy pining for the arrival of its owner after being left alone all day, except I was definitely the puppy in this relationship. Etta wore a linen sundress the color of a Creamsicle and wrapped her spindly arms around me; she smelled like clean laundry and something floral, maybe tuberose? Like that expensive candle she had in her apartment. "I'm so, so glad you made it," she said, as if there was doubt that I might not. She took my bag and I followed her up the grand staircase, down a long familiar hallway, where she kicked open a door that had been left ajar. "You're okay with this room, right?"

"Yeah," I said. "Of course."

I'd slept in this room before, with its green toile wallpaper and rattan bed, its four windows punctuating the far wall and overlooking the grounds and navy blue Atlantic. She plopped my bag onto the bed and collapsed beside it, the duvet rippling around her like a fine current.

I sat next to her. "Oh," I said, and dug around in my purse, "this is for you." A croissant from her favorite bakery near my apartment.

She peeked inside the white paper bag and cooed at the pastry as if it were a small child.

"I was going to say we should go there soon," she said. "It's like you read my mind."

"Well," I said, "we can still go. Maybe next weekend?"

Etta smiled placidly. "Yeah, maybe." She returned the croissant to its bag next to her on the bed and I felt defeated, empty. "So lunch was chaos," she said. "Everyone was walking on eggshells with Jane."

"Jane?" I asked.

"Archer's girlfriend."

"Oh, I didn't realize that was her name."

"She *would* be named Jane," Etta said, tracing an imaginary thread on the duvet. "Plain Jane."

I wasn't sure why, but this insinuation thrilled me. "Plain?"

"Boring. Goody-goody." Etta sat up. "Everyone's obsessed with her. I don't get it."

I would try to play the compassionate card. "Maybe you have to get to know her better?"

Etta darted her eyes at me. I shouldn't have said that. But then she clapped her hands.

"So. Lunch. We had paella with lobster, shrimp. Just a lot." I nodded, as if I had been there. "Anyway, when we finished, my parents insisted on giving Jane a tour of the grounds, so we, you know, took our wineglasses with us and I think everyone was a little drunk and we were walking on this path when I heard this like, coughing sound?" Etta tilted her head toward the wall of windows, as if recollecting the scene, before turning back to me. "And Jane is fully vomiting."

"Vomiting?"

"Projectile. Everywhere. Plum is gasping, Archer is leaning over her, but I think is also too stunned to do anything about it. Warren is yelling to Lucy, who can't hear us from the house, and Jane is apologizing, obviously, but she can't catch her breath and that's when she tells us she is allergic to shellfish."

"But…she ate everything."

"Fucking everything," Etta said, swinging her legs over the edge of the bed like a child. "And I was like, 'Archer, how did you not know your girlfriend doesn't eat shellfish?' Apparently she didn't tell him, and she didn't realize her allergy was 'that bad,' whatever that means, considering she basically died."

I tried to invent something witty to say, but came up short. "She must be so embarrassed."

"See, I don't think she views it that way. I think she *wants* us to feel sorry for her. Like, she doesn't even carry an EpiPen?"

But I did feel sorry for Jane. I didn't know her, yet I could commiserate with the role of outsider, of wanting acceptance, and the consequences when things did not go as planned.

Etta peeled back the bag so the top of the croissant poked out and took a bite. "And you know Plum. She's afraid the acidity will do something to the soil—she's gotten really into gardening—so she's been on conference calls with the horticulturist and landscapers dealing with the possible fallout to the hydrangea."

"That's rough," I said, and then glancing around at what suddenly seemed so obvious, I asked, "So where is she?"

"Jane? Sleeping. She took Benadryl. She'll be fine." She jumped off the bed and walked to the window.

"Etta, are you sure it's okay I'm here?"

She was still chewing when she whirled around. "What? Of course it is."

"It sounds like your family has had a traumatic afternoon. I feel bad."

"Why would you feel bad?"

"Just my being here—it's not an imposition?"

She wrinkled her nose. "Not at all. Also, Archer brought Jane here, so I can bring a friend, too, right?"

I smiled. "Right."

Etta looked out the windows again, then her eyes snapped back to mine. "We're not going to eat for like an hour or two," she said. "Let's go for a swim?"

The two of us changed into our swimsuits and Etta grabbed towels from the pool house. She cannonballed into the deep end and so I did, too. The water was warm, the pool gleaming, the blue sky hazy and soft.

Etta climbed out of the pool, her long blond hair dark when wet, and hauled two pool floats from the pool house: hot-pink flamingos. She flung them into the water and jumped in again, hoisting herself onto one of the floats so it appeared as if she were seated on a throne. I held the neck of the second flamingo, preferring to stay in the water.

"My mom hates these. She thinks they belong at a tacky hotel in Vegas. All the more reason why I keep them around," Etta said with a wink.

"I've never been to Vegas."

Etta dragged a finger through the water. "It's terrible."

"Really?" I'd always thought of Vegas as an epicenter, the constant go-go-go and buzz of slot machines, glowing neon twenty-four seven. "It isn't fun?"

"It's tasteless," Etta said. Or that, I thought. "It feels like everyone there wants something they can't have. They're all sad or ugly, overdressed, and wearing too much makeup."

"Not everyone can be as naturally pretty as you are," I teased. That drew a small smile.

"No, but really. It's like all the worst parts of LA times a thousand. I don't know, everyone is trying too hard. It's painful to watch."

"All right, well, note to self—Vegas is off the list for your future bachelorette."

She flicked water at me, but she was still smiling. "I'm not getting married, you know that."

I couldn't help it and burst into laughter. "Sorry, what?"

"Well, why would I? Marriage is a terrible concept. Someone always has more power."

I considered Plum and Warren's marriage, the intricacies of it; they both hailed from old money families, but Plum more so. I wondered if this translated to anything tangible, if it meant *she* held the power.

"So what makes you think you won't be the one with more power?" I asked.

Etta was quiet; across the lawn, a door slammed and their housekeeper, Lucy, and another server lit votive candles, sparking little flames on the long wooden table.

"I don't know," she said finally. She craned her neck to look at me. "I'm really glad you're here, by the way. My parents have been acting weird since our dinner last night."

"Wait—I thought dinner was just with Plum?"

She shook her head. "Nope. Surprise. I got them both."

"Wow. Just because?"

She let her gaze drop to the water. "They brought up my 'stint—'" she glanced at me "—those were their words, at the art gallery last year. They were like, 'You know, that was our connection and you didn't take the opportunity seriously,' and 'You like living in your apartment, don't you?'"

I grimaced. "They said that?"

"I mean, not in those exact words, but I could tell those were the undertones." She sat up, her limbs screeching against the pool float.

"I'm sure they're just looking out for you."

She smirked. "That's the PC thing to say."

"I don't know," I said. "I'm trying to be supportive."

"Sure, sure." A moment of silence and I felt Etta staring. "Were your eyes always this blue?" she asked.

I turned from her. "Ah, it's probably just the light."

"They're like sapphire."

"Oh," I laughed. I was uncomfortable. "I've been using these new eye drops. My eyes are so dry. It's crazy."

Etta sighed. "We need to work on that."

"Work on what?"

"That," she said, pointing at me. "Why can't you take a compliment?"

I tried again. "All right, thank you, Etta."

"You're welcome," she said.

I pulled myself up onto the float. We reclined on the flamingos for another fifteen minutes, neither of us saying much, and I thought about how in a week, two weeks, I wasn't even sure, Etta was maybe moving to Barcelona and I wasn't supposed to know, was supposed to sit here and pretend that everything was normal and fine. I could feel my anxiety, activated like a virus, infiltrating all the healthy cells, wreaking havoc until all I could focus on was this series of pessimistic thoughts: *Etta is leaving. You are all alone.* I considered speaking up. I wouldn't admit I'd heard it from Archer; I could act as if the news found its way to me, at the loft party, perhaps, or that she'd mentioned it drunkenly.

"So, Etta," I started to say, but the clatter of plates across the lawn drowned out the sound of my voice.

"We should probably get out," she said, and jumped off the float, swimming to the edge of the pool. She looked over her shoulder, as if to say, *Are you coming?*

Standing on the pavement, Etta tossed me a towel. I wrapped it around me like a dress as I followed her across the lawn. We traipsed into the house, up the stairs, walked down opposite ends of the hall to our rooms. Once inside mine, I went to close the windows—it was humid and a colony of mosquitoes had gathered on the panes—but something stirred underneath the pergola.

Archer, stretched out on a lounger, a paperback tented over his legs.

Had he been there the whole time? Or had he just gone outside and we'd missed him, ships passing in the night? His eyes were squeezed shut, as if he was napping or in a deep meditative state, and it stunned me that, apart from a series of minor, ordinary interactions over the past eight years of knowing Etta, Archer had a whole life I knew almost nothing about, a reminder that you could meet people, even interact with them in some as yet undefined capacity, and they'd continue to go on with their lives, reading at their parents' house on an otherwise ordinary Saturday evening in June, and that you'd wonder if they thought about a three-minute interaction you'd had at a party at this very house years earlier, if they cared about the twenty-five-minute car ride you shared from Brooklyn to Manhattan, or if they'd automatically categorized you into the group of "ordinary activities and people in the never-read footnotes of someone's life."

Practically forgotten.

4

By the time we all sat for dinner, it was almost eight. We'd waited in virtual silence for Archer and Warren, Etta's father, who eventually thudded out from the house and assumed his place at the head of the table before beginning the salad course. He was the kind of person who liked being reassured of his importance, of learning other people found him intimidating. Well, he was intimidating. That wasn't so much suspicion as fact. He and I had met for the first time at college graduation, an underwhelming six seconds wherein he shook my hand and said his full name and didn't stick around long enough to hear mine. Each occasion after that was less enthusiastic, as if he were looking straight through me, but tonight he seemed to register my presence.

He leaned toward Plum and asked, "Who is that?"

What Warren lacked in social graces and general niceties, Plum compensated for in fluidity and tact. She didn't acknowledge his question, keeping her gaze on her salad, as if he hadn't said anything at all.

"Ren," she said then, raising her eyes to meet mine, "is that your full name?" Plum reminded me of a cat, green eyes matching Etta's and Archer's. Her lips were thin and pursed, her hair pulled taut in a chignon. She was fit, like a Pilates or dance instructor, her perfectly toned muscles hidden beneath the billowing fabric of her orange caftan.

I reached for my glass of wine and explained it was actually "Renata." I left out that it was my maternal grandmother's name, that it meant "reborn" in Italian. If I brought that into the equation, it would encourage discussion about families and lineages and other questions like, "What do your parents do?" and "Where were you born?" and "Can we all agree that California Chardonnay is, in fact, trash?" All attempts at unmasking a person, estimating your worth under the guise of meaningless small talk.

"And remind us where you grew up?" she asked.

"Connecticut," I said, casting a side glance at Etta, who was otherwise quiet.

Plum wanted to know where, and I said it was a small town, not far from Vernon. *Not your Connecticut*, I was thinking. Of course she insisted she knew Connecticut "very well" and asked again, but when I answered, she said, "Hmm, I'm not familiar."

I wanted to say, "Told you so." Instead I said, "Yes, it's very small."

Warren asked where Archer was, and Plum said he was checking on Jane. Plain Jane. Or not-so-plain Jane. I didn't know because I had never met her. A moment later, however, Archer was barreling toward us in a T-shirt and khakis splotched with paint. He kept his head down as he took a chair opposite mine. Plum asked if it would have been so much effort to get dressed for dinner.

Examining himself, he said, "Is this not dressed?"

Plum shook her head, almost playfully. Warren said nothing.

Archer smoothed a napkin onto his lap. "Jane isn't joining us, by the way."

Plum flagged one of the servers who was busy pouring water into Archer's glass, directing them to please remove that last place setting.

"How is she feeling?" Etta asked.

Archer scrolled through his phone. "Okay. Resting."

"Archer," Plum said, "no phones at the table?"

"It's work stuff," he said.

Plum looked to Warren, and then back to Archer. "Fine," she said. "It's a shame she's missing dinner."

Archer laughed, setting his phone on the table facedown. "Well, I doubt she has much of an appetite."

Etta cleared her throat. "Archer, you remember Ren, right?"

Archer squinted at me. I started to smile, said, "Nice to see you." He slowly nodded and it seemed as if he was about to respond and then...nothing. He picked up his fork and stabbed at the lettuce on his plate. Maybe he hadn't remembered me. Maybe he was in a bad mood. Maybe he was upset his girlfriend had food poisoning. *I shouldn't have come here*, I thought. I should have stayed in Brooklyn with Jeff. We'd be drunk by now, sipping cheap wine on his balcony, where we both didn't have to try so hard.

Behind us, the sound of clattering plates and rustling waves in the distance, the murmur of crickets growing louder with the thinning sunlight. The silence was awkward but at least the atmospherics were nice. I continued to eat my salad.

Plum sipped her wine, narrowing her eyes at me. She was going to ask me another question. "Are your parents still in Connecticut?" she asked, her tone swooping, the pitch of her voice higher at the end of every other word, as if the English language were one melodious song.

"Yes," I said.

"Do they come into the city often?"

"No," I said, praying she wouldn't force me to announce that my parents weren't together, that I didn't know where my mother was, that I had a strained relationship with my father, *strained* a generous adjective. I smiled. "They prefer the suburbs. More quiet."

"Siblings?"

This woman, I thought. "I have a sister."

"In college?"

"Northwestern." I felt Archer's eyes on me and focused on Plum.

A single raised brow, half-impressed. "And you're close?"

No, not at all, I wanted to say. We don't speak. Occasionally, I would message her on Instagram or comment on a photo of her backpacking trip through South America and she'd ignore me. Sometimes, if she was feeling kind, she'd throw me a like. Forget about the fact that I more or less took care of her after Mom left, right?

"She's studying in Peru," I said, and Plum opened her mouth to respond just as Warren started to cough, violent, heaving coughs that racked his body and interrupted the flow of conversation. He shielded his mouth with his napkin, pressing his eyes shut. Plum rubbed his back.

Etta and Archer stared at him, still chewing their food, and I waited for someone to really react, but a second later he exhaled and flung his hand to his chest.

"Walnut" was all he said, then he smiled for perhaps the first time ever.

———

Conversation eventually segued into two groups, one among Etta, Archer, and me, and the other between Plum and Warren. Archer led our discussion. He'd had two glasses of wine and was more chatty now, asking me questions like if the bars were "actually fun anymore" and whether I'd liked NYU. He said everyone he knew who had graduated from NYU was a "slashie."

"A *slashie?*" I asked.

He smiled. "Like a graphic artist *slash* DJ. Or a DJ *slash* model. Everyone has a side gig."

I said, "Well, I guess we're all just too ambitious."

He held my eye for another moment before glancing at Etta. "Well, you being the exception, of course."

"Hilarious," Etta said.

Archer was thirty-two, not thirty-one, as I'd thought. He'd attended Williams and majored in Studio Art, then spent time working on his own art in New York before he pressed "Pause" a little over two years ago, choosing to bounce around Corsica and Amsterdam and a friend's houseboat off the coast of Spain. He seemed so much more worldly than anyone I'd ever met, even Etta. I felt like a child, a little fish swimming upstream, trying to keep up, weaving in and out of the conversation and struggling to frame myself in some important light. When there was a lull between courses, he asked what Etta was like in college.

"Exactly the same," I said. I could tell she was watching me from the corner of her eye.

He laughed. "Meaning incredibly self-assured?"

"At least I have some humility," she said, gesturing to his phone, still facedown on the table.

"What do you mean?"

"'I'm just so busy with work,'" Etta imitated.

"Well, I am," he said, but his expression was suddenly serious.

Etta rolled her eyes, however, so that the interaction read as playful. "I know. I'm only joking." She sipped her wine. "Jane doesn't mind that you're always so busy?"

"She's pretty busy herself." He rested his elbows on the table, cradling his face in his hands so that he looked angelic in the candlelight. He was about to mention Barcelona, I could feel it, and Etta would be forced to come clean. I steeled myself for the reveal, cupped my wineglass and tensed in my chair.

"So," he asked, "how is your dating life these days?"

Apparently I was wrong.

Etta threw her head back and laughed. "Archer, what?"

"Too touchy?"

"Not touchy. Just…weird." She turned toward me and I thought I should smile. "For context, Ren, Archer and I *never* discuss dating."

"That's not true," he said, and Etta scoffed. "Sorry," he said. "I know dating in New York is brutal." He pivoted to me. "What about you, Ren? Anyone special in your life?"

"Don't interrogate my friend." Etta laughed again, splashing some of the water in her glass at him, and if I didn't know they were brother and sister, I'd honestly have thought she was flirting.

"So that's a no, then," Archer said.

I half turned to Etta, whose eyes slid toward me, as if to ensure I hadn't been hiding something from her, perhaps some secret boyfriend, which was of course ironic, given the circumstances.

"Yeah, nope, just…swiping until the day I die apparently."

"Oh," Archer said. "You're on the apps." He said the word as if it were alien.

"The whole city is on the apps, Archer," Etta said. "Except you."

"So tell me. What are they like?"

"It's online shopping," Etta said, "but you don't want to buy anything."

"Sounds promising," Archer said. "Ren?"

I considered the question. "I don't know, you can pretend to be anyone on those things. It's a haven for people looking to…"

"Looking to what?"

"Pretend they're someone else."

He leaned across the table and I pressed my shoulders into the back of my chair. "Is that what you do? Invent a persona?"

I tried to laugh. "No, I don't even think I'd know where to begin."

Archer traced the rim of his glass. "Maybe you'd have more fun if you did? Treat it like a game?" His lips turned up and I thought, *Wait, are we flirting right now?* But then he said, "You were so quiet the other night, Ren, I feel like I'm seeing a whole other side of you." I felt Etta's gaze drill into me.

She laughed faintly. "What do you mean, *the other night?*"

"Oh," Archer said, "I gave Ren a ride home. From Sam's place, when you—" he raised his glass at her "—abandoned her."

Abandon, that word. She would have to address the fact that she was leaving now, and maybe that was what Archer was doing, strategically guiding her there.

"You said you took an Uber."

"I… I called one. But then—" I looked to Archer "—it was taking too long, and it was cold…and so he offered me a ride."

Etta was silent for what felt like forever, and I realized she wasn't going to mention her possibly impending departure. No, the focus was on me—my wrongdoing, what a bad friend I was. She peeled her eyes from mine, sipped her wine. Her jaw was clenched.

I glanced at Archer, seeking direction for how to proceed, but he was studying her with this curious expression. Had he known she would be mad? Or had he assumed I'd told her?

"Well," she said at last, "that was really nice of you, Archer. You always show up when it matters most." I drank my wine as Etta swiveled in her seat. "But back to what we were just talking about. Dating apps, was it?"

"Yes," I said. I was practically euphoric. Back to our weird discussion of dating apps. I didn't even care that Etta was still potentially withholding a secret, anything to return to normal.

"Right," Etta said. "Well, Ren's never had a boyfriend before."

I understood then that she was livid.

"Sorry, what?" I asked.

She wiped her mouth with her napkin, so demure it seemed rehearsed. "Well, you go on all these dates and nothing ever comes of them," she said.

I'd dated someone for six months, I reminded her, after we graduated.

"That wasn't dating. That was fucking."

"Jesus, Etta," Archer said, and my face burned.

"Um, no," I said. "He came to my birthday dinner, remember?"

"Not really."

"Yes, you have to. You planned it. At Indochine?"

Etta laughed then. She remembered. "Oh, wait," she said. "Are you talking about Benji?"

"Yes. Benji. Exactly."

"Isn't he gay now?"

"What? No."

I could feel my heart racing, my thoughts becoming liquid. "What even *is* dating anymore?" I asked aloud, then I heard myself and concluded I was drunk or deluded or both.

Etta laughed again, said, "Oh, here she goes." Archer gestured for me to go on.

I said that everyone knew dating in New York was a sick joke. What even qualified as dating? Drinks? Being on the receiving end of a "u up?" text at 3 a.m.? Dinner, a movie, and a side of expectation? There were no parameters anymore. You could sleep with someone for a year and both parties would claim confusion at defining "what they were." Eventually, there would be some sort of mutual ghosting, or one party would coerce the other into doing exactly what they wanted. All dating was a quest for power, and the idea of equality in a relationship was a myth because someone would always have more.

"You're right," I said to Etta. "About what you said this afternoon. You're right."

Archer didn't say anything, as if taking it all in.

Etta twisted toward him. "Also, isn't it sexist digging into our dating lives? Like, there's lots of other things to talk about. How come men don't get asked these questions?"

Archer held up both hands. "Fair. Fair."

"I mean," Etta said, "we aren't snooping into your business with Jane. Are we?"

"No, I guess not."

"Or your business in general?"

Archer sipped his wine slowly, but kept his eyes on her. "I guess not," he said again.

Or your *business, right?* I'd wanted to ask her, but knew I wouldn't.

Etta pressed the rim of her glass against her lips. "Yeah," Etta said, "that's what I thought."

5

I was relieved when dinner was served: bison, rare, blood pooling on our plates, with truffles. Warren, I noticed, was again concentrating on me. Perhaps he'd forgotten my identity again and needed a reminder. "So, tell us what you do for a living?" he asked.

The moment, I thought, where they would really assess my value.

"I'm a publicist," I said, enunciating each syllable, as if to prove my own sobriety to myself. I'd lost track of how much wine I'd had.

Archer asked, "Did you study to become a publicist?"

I reached for my water and pressed it to my cheek, then realized everyone was watching me. "No, I was an English major."

"Do you like it?"

"Like what?"

"Your job," he said.

The answer to this question was complicated. Publicists were integral to the flow of things, the cast of unseen doers toiling behind the scenes, thankless creatures, mostly, who made things happen and accepted the fact that credit was never their due. Anytime you secured a story for a client, it became the client's reward, not yours. And this was simply the way of things, the terrain of the land, the primary edict of decorum: you did the work, then disappeared, a ghost. My boss, Natalie, liked to say, "The best publicists are invisible."

"Well, it's just a job," I said.

Plum and Warren had stopped listening, and Etta seemed to be staring off into the distance, but Archer was still engaging me. I wasn't sure if this was a good thing.

"It sounds miserable to spend your life doing something that's *just a job*."

Yes, I thought, *it is*.

And that was when I said, "But I'm also a writer."

Archer nodded, as if impressed. "What do you write?" he asked, and I immediately regretted it.

"Oh, just some short stories," I said. "A few essays." Archer, I was sure, had real artist friends. Poets and writers. He could see right through me. To be a writer, one had to actually write.

Etta said, "I didn't know you were writing again?" There was genuine surprise in her tone, that I'd been keeping something from her.

I shrugged and Archer was about to ask me something else when Warren interrupted. "So, Archer, I want to hear more about the show next weekend. We've rearranged our flights so we can be there."

Archer held my eye for another second before shifting his attention. I'd never been so relieved to be forgotten, an afterthought. I picked at the rest of the bison and thought it tasted metallic, as Archer's parents grilled him about his upcoming show. Lots of "Do you have a guest list to review?" and "Did Astrid cross-check her contacts with ours?" and "It's crucial that the right people, the right press, are there," and more mention of this Astrid person, whoever they were, and more "right" this and "right" that, and Etta just kept swirling the wine in her glass until our plates were cleared and I felt very alone, very ordinary, and like I might never amount to anything. Did all people feel this way? Like you might never be enough?

Dessert was a raspberry icebox cake, and though I'd lost my appetite, I kept eating anyway, shoveling spoonfuls of ice cream and crushed raspberries into my mouth.

Plum fixed her gaze on Etta. "This reminds me—have you given any thought to our conversation the other evening?" Etta picked at her dessert, and Plum said, "No thoughts on the internships at Pace? Or White Cube?"

"I haven't had a chance to think about it yet," Etta said, and I was thinking that perhaps there was some sort of confusion, and maybe Archer had his wires crossed. There were other options, like these internships, and she hadn't mentioned anything to me yet because she didn't want to be dramatic.

Plum set her fork next to her plate, as if disgusted.

"I'm just curious, though—what was Archer doing these past couple of years?" Etta asked.

Archer laughed, but I thought he seemed stunned. "Painting."

"For two years? And nothing to show for it until now?"

"I've been working on new material."

"For two years."

"Not everything reaps instant gratification," Archer said.

But Etta sighed, conceding. "I'm just proud of you is all. For not giving up."

I couldn't gauge what was unfolding, but Archer didn't flinch. After a moment he said, "Thank you, Etta. I appreciate that."

No one said anything else and soon our plates were cleared. Plum and Warren excused themselves and Archer left to take a phone call.

Etta said, "Sorry if that was weird."

"What? No. It wasn't weird," I lied.

She shot me a look. "It was weird. My parents are… They're on one." Etta darted her eyes at me, stifling a yawn. "I wish you told me Archer gave you a ride the other night."

What I could have said: *I wish you told me you were moving— are you?* What I actually said: "Yeah, well, it was stupid. It was literally a car ride."

"Nothing is just a car ride," she said.

———

In my room I changed into an old T-shirt and my old, ratty polka-dot boxer shorts and got into bed. The house was quiet, but I wasn't tired. I had the spins, slanted shadows on the ceiling creeping above me like the distorted mirrors of a fun house. I rolled onto my side. I thought I might throw up, but it was a false alarm. What I needed was water, something to dilute all the wine in my bloodstream.

I crept downstairs, toward the kitchen. I was sure Lucy or someone else would be cleaning up; they'd give me a water bottle or two and maybe even a bread roll if I was lucky.

But there was no clatter of plates, no sound of running water, only Archer alone at the kitchen table, facing the French doors out to the lawn. His chin rested on his fist, his knee bobbing up and down as he whispered into the phone: "I'll figure it out," and then "I'm not too worried."

I stepped back, but the floors creaked underneath my feet and he whirled around. "Okay," he said, watching me now. "Talk to you tomorrow. Have a safe flight." Gingerly, he slid his phone across the table and rubbed his temples.

"Sorry, I was just thirsty," I said, still idling in the doorway.

He didn't look up. "There's water in the refrigerator."

"Thanks," I said, but as I started to cross the room, he pushed out his chair to stand.

"Sorry," he said. "That was rude. Let me get it for you."

"It's okay," I told him, but he said, "No, no, it's fine."

He tugged open the refrigerator doors, his skin incandescent in the bluish light, and pulled two waters from a shelf, passing one to me. "Thank you," I said as he returned to his same chair. He took a long drink from the bottle, his throat moving as he tilted back his head, then flicked the cap across the table so that it fell to the floor.

"Well, good night," I said.

"This opening—" he was staring at his hands "—it's just a lot."

"I can imagine," I said, though of course I couldn't. I knew what it was like, all the pressure and expectations leading up to a launch or big event, but I was always emotionally removed. None of it really affected me because my work didn't belong to me. It was someone else's.

Archer laughed to himself. "It's just hard, sharing your work with perfect strangers."

I walked toward him so that I hovered near the table, but I wasn't sure if he wanted me to respond.

"I'm sure you get it, with your writing. It's so…personal."

I sucked at my teeth. "Yeah," I said, "it's terrifying."

"Art is weird like that. You bare a piece of yourself."

"Yeah," I said. Did I not have anything else to say?

"And even if you say it's not about you," he continued, "the work is *always* about you."

I was nodding when he considered me more intently. "So you're working on some short stories and essays, you said? What about a novel?"

To that, I laughed, then covered my mouth. I hoped no one had heard.

"That's funny?" he asked, but he was smiling now, too.

Quietly, I said, "No, no novel."

"Yet," he added. We were silent, and a sharp rattling noise made me jump. "The ice machine," he said.

THE ART OF PRETEND

"Oh," I said, and attempted a smile, but I was embarrassed and sipped my water.

"Sometimes, I think all art is the same," he said. "It's shouting, 'Listen to what I have to say,' louder than everyone else and hoping people listen. Or care." He chuckled into his lap. "I guess Etta had a point with the 'humility' thing."

"What?" I asked. "I mean, I feel like you're humble?"

He stood again. "That's because you don't really know me." He winked and headed toward the pantry. I wasn't sure if I'd been dismissed, but when he came back to the table, he was holding a bottle of dark liquor and two rocks glasses.

"Hibiki," he said, setting the bottle and glasses on the table. "Japanese whiskey. Do you like whiskey?"

I nodded. I'd had Hibiki before, at a tasting for a work event, but I acted as if I'd never heard of it. He poured us two glasses, neat, then slid one across the table in my direction. He drank his like a shot, tossing it back. I picked up my glass but didn't drink.

"I thought you said you liked whiskey?" he asked.

"I do," I lied. "I'm just tired."

"If you're tired, it might help you sleep."

"Nature's Ambien?" I said.

He smiled and I could tell he thought that was clever.

I tilted the whiskey into my mouth, slowly at first, then the entire pour, burning down my throat like lighter fluid.

"See?" Archer said. "Not so bad."

I gave a little laugh, my lips tingling, and thanked him again for the water and the nightcap, but he was quiet. He probably thought it was awkward I was still standing there, which it was.

"Well, good night," I said.

"Good night."

Upstairs in my room I locked the door behind me, and when I got into bed, I realized my heart was racing.

6

The next morning my head pounded as if a rock concert were being played inside my skull. Wine and whiskey, not wise, and though Etta had mentioned I could find Ambien in the medicine cabinet, there were no over-the-counter drugs, no Tylenol, aspirin, or Advil for average ailments like a hangover.

The pain radiated to my jaw, and my eyes stung from the white sunlight, so I was wearing Etta's Celine sunglasses, the ones she gave me, as I joined everyone outside for breakfast. Plum stood at the head of the table in another floral-print caftan that resembled a glorified shower curtain, leaning on Warren, who read the newspaper, his legs crossed at the ankle, two sticklike antlers sprouting from the trunk of a tree. Plum said, "Good morning," and directed me to the spread on the table: carafes of water with floating lemon wheels; hot coffee; tea; milk and cream; a bowl filled with at least two dozen hard-boiled eggs; a platter with sourdough, wheat, and rye breads; porridge; berries; yogurt; watermelon slices; what looked to be apricot and raspberry jams; scones; and butter. And yet, their plates were empty. They would eat none of it—the food, like everything, was just for show.

As I took a seat next to Etta, she leveled her eyes to meet mine. "How'd you sleep?"

"Okay," I said, and tried to eat a piece of sourdough.

Etta drank her coffee and asked if I was planning to stay the night, and I said I would probably need to leave, that I had work tomorrow, but I was cut off as the door to the main house opened and closed.

I turned around and there was Archer, his hand on the lower back of a woman I presumed to be Jane, and who I realized I'd seen before. Jane was the same woman from the Dumbo party, the woman whom Archer had kissed hello. So this was his girlfriend, Jane not-so-plain. She looked like a fucking Disney princess.

As she approached the table, she did this adorable thing where she buried her face in her hands and said, "I am so embarrassed about yesterday. I cannot apologize enough."

Archer pulled out a chair for her opposite me, and Plum told her there was nothing to be sorry about. Jane thanked her again, and I thought I recognized the soft lilt of an English accent. Everything she said rolled off her tongue, no harsh sounds the way Americans had butchered the English language. She clasped her hands on the table and I continued gnawing on the sourdough, which tasted like cardboard. How she apologized, how Plum didn't. How all was magically, inexplicably already forgiven.

Archer asked if she wanted coffee and she glanced up at him, casting beams of adoration that were truly nauseating to witness. But then he looked at me, as if recollecting that I was still here, at his parents' house, and I flashed to last night, the two of us in the kitchen, the illicit whiskey that was, in fact, not illicit at all.

"Etta," he said, sitting in the chair next to Jane, gesturing to me, "would you like to introduce your friend to Jane?"

Jane seemed harmless, wanting to make a good impression,

the same way I did. The difference was she didn't have to try as hard. I waited for Etta to intercede, to make the introduction, but she was occupied with her phone.

Archer said, "Etta," and she dropped her phone onto her lap.

"Sorry. Sorry." She assumed a formal, almost mocking tone. "Jane, it is my absolute pleasure to introduce you to my dearest friend, Ren."

I smiled but there was a crumb burrowing into my gum. Etta said, "You have something in your tooth." I dug it out while apologizing and Jane tilted her head benevolently.

Archer poured two cups of coffee and passed one to Jane. "It's wonderful to meet you, Ren," she said. "How do you two know one another?"

"College," I said. "We went to NYU together." I looked to Etta but she had since resumed texting.

Jane dropped a sugar cube into her coffee. "Nice. And you still live in New York?"

"In the East Village."

"Oh, I *love* the East Village," she cooed. "Such an eclectic neighborhood. I had a few friends who lived in a flat there years ago. It was my crash pad whenever I was in town. We had so much fun."

"Do you live in the city?" I asked.

She half turned to Archer. "I'm somewhat nomadic at the moment." She squinted at her lap, as if bashful, and Archer interrupted to say that she was finishing up her master's in London.

"Master's in what?"

"Oh, gosh. Economics. So boring, I know."

"Not boring. Um, that's amazing," I said, but I was really thinking what kind of psychopath could be so charming in their self-deprecation.

Jane started to wave her hand and Etta said, "Economics. Wow."

Jane peered into her coffee. "I don't know, I always wish I

was more artistic or something, but alas, I'm just boring old me. God, I mean, if I had half of Archer's talent. I can't draw to save my life. Not even a stick figure."

Etta said, "Oh, come on, Jane. Everyone can draw a stick figure."

"No, really. I'm miserable." I found this impossible to believe until Archer laughed and said, "It's sort of true." Jane's hand grazed his forearm and I looked away. "But anyway," she said, "I'm trying to stay stateside as much as possible. This one has a busy summer. Hopefully he can make a little time for me."

"Well," Etta said, placing her phone facedown on the table, "I'm sure he will do his absolute best. I mean, it can't be worse than last time."

Etta's words seemed to linger. Was this payback? Revenge for learning that Archer had given me a ride last weekend? No matter, because Archer was silent, instead idly drumming his fingers on the table as Jane hid behind her napkin.

When Jane realized Archer wasn't going to defend the situation, or respond at all, she said softly, "I'm not too worried."

Etta smiled, eyes still on Archer. "That's good," she said.

It was then I noticed Plum watching me.

"I love those sunglasses, Ren. Are those Celine?"

I forgot I was even wearing them. "I think so," I said, expecting Etta to say she'd given them to me.

"You know," Plum said, narrowing her eyes, standing up, "I had a very similar pair once. But that was a long time ago. I was probably about your age."

Plum was prowling around the table, hunting me as if I were her prey. I swallowed a mouthful of bread, the crust catching in my throat so that I started to cough, but Plum probably thought I was choking, and if I was, in fact, choking, she was unbothered, maybe even pleased. Everyone had stopped what they were doing to observe as Plum paused at my chair, towering over me. "May I?" she asked, and it wouldn't have mattered if I told her no because she slipped the glasses from my face and held them to the light.

"Vintage," she said, examining the frames at various angles.

I knew I should have told her that Etta had gifted them to me, but all I could do was wait, and I waited for what felt like an eternity but was more like thirty seconds, when she finally set the glasses next to my place setting and smiled. "Those are an excellent copy, Ren," she said, and of course, I knew they weren't a copy. That nothing Etta or her family owned was "fake." I was now aware of what everyone else already understood: Plum believed the sunglasses were, in fact, hers, and that I had stolen them.

But then it was as if nothing had happened. Plum returned to the head of the table; there was the familiar hum of conversation, slurping of hot coffee and tea, the rustling of Warren's newspaper as he flipped through its pages. Everyone's voices sounded far away but also as if they were closing in on me.

"Excuse me," I said, and pushed out my chair, but only Etta seemed to notice.

"You okay?" she asked as I backed away from the table.

"Yeah," I lied. "I just…" and held my stomach.

"Ah," she said, her mouth slipping into a frown.

Inside the main house, I marched to the nearest bathroom, locked the door behind me and stared at my reflection in the mirror, at the stupid sunglasses with the hairline crack on the frame, a barely there crack that Plum must have seen. The slight fracture that set this pair apart from all the other *copies*.

I splashed my face with cold water until my cheeks were bright red, until my face throbbed from the cold. *You don't belong here,* I told the girl in the mirror. *You don't belong anywhere.*

———

After breakfast Etta and I lounged poolside. Plum and Warren were both working somewhere inside the house, and Archer and Jane were strolling on the beach. Apart from the sound of sprinklers spitting water onto the lawn, it was quiet.

"So what's White Cube?" I asked.

"Hmm?" She didn't bother looking at me, still scrolling through her Instagram feed.

"Your parents mentioned something about White Cube and Pace last night?"

"Oh. They're galleries," she said.

"You would work at one of them?"

"They want me to. I just don't know if it's for me."

"Well, maybe you would like it," I said.

"Maybe."

So maybe she wasn't leaving. I was again reassured that life could remain exactly as it was. With Etta, my role was clear; she was the traffic light I would obey, and despite my occasional resentment, I feared her absence more.

"So what's this about your writing?" she asked.

I shifted in my seat. "What do you mean?"

"Just what you were saying at dinner last night? How you were working on stuff?"

"Oh. I mean, it's nothing."

"Obviously it's not nothing or you wouldn't have mentioned it."

I didn't want to admit that I'd fibbed to appear more important and interesting, so I said, "It's all preliminary," borrowing a phrase from Natalie, *preliminary* inferring that something was promising, but not up for further discussion.

Etta scratched her leg. "I used to love to read your stuff in college—" she eyed me playfully "—when you let me, of course."

It was how Etta and I had met, in a freshman writing seminar. I'd written an essay about my mother, a loss that wasn't exactly death but felt close to it. Etta said she was "moved" by the piece, asked me to lunch, and over mixed green salads, I learned that she wasn't like the rest of us. That Baby Spice had performed at her fifth birthday and her mom was friends with someone named

Alaïa. In time, these details would accrue additional meaning, like when I learned Alaïa was actually a famous designer, but back then, I'd just been happy someone cared.

"I'm sorry about breakfast," she said. "And this whole weekend, really. Plum can be such a bitch."

"Well," I said, "she thinks I stole her sunglasses."

Etta perked up in her lounge chair. "No, no, she doesn't."

Whenever anything upset Etta, she brushed it off, pretending like whatever terrible thing happened, had not happened at all.

"Yes, she does," I said.

Music blasted on the adjacent lawn. Samba, the tinkling sounds of a piano, a horn section.

"Why didn't you just tell her that you gave them to me?"

"Because they look better on you. Your features are smaller," she said, but that didn't answer my question.

"I don't think she cares if they look better on me. I feel like she wants them back." Etta was quiet. "I mean, you can say you found them or something, in your apartment or... I'm not attached to them. I don't want her to like, hate me."

Etta scratched her leg again, this time more fervently. "It's not just the sunglasses, Ren. She is this way with all her things. She let me borrow them and must have forgotten. And like I said, they look better on you."

"But she didn't say I could have them."

"Ren," she said, more agitated now, "it's a control thing, don't you see? I swear she genuinely forgot about those sunglasses until she saw them on someone else. Then it was like she needed to have them again."

"So she knows," I said. "That they're hers."

With her hand, Etta shielded her face from the sun, but kept her gaze straight ahead. "Don't overthink it," she said.

———

It was almost four when Archer and Jane came out to the pool to say goodbye. Jane's shoulder-length, jet-black hair was wet, so I gathered she had just showered, and she'd since changed into a pale blue linen jumpsuit that would become wrinkled in the car back to the city.

"We're heading out," Archer said, holding a small butterfly-print duffel bag that I assumed belonged to Jane.

Etta propped herself up on her elbows. "Paul's driving you?"

"No, we're taking the Land Rover," he said. "I want to drive."

"What about traffic?"

"We'll manage." To me, he asked, "Ren, will I be seeing you next weekend?"

"Next weekend?" I asked.

"My opening."

Etta said, "We'll see if we can stop by," and Archer said, "I was asking Ren."

Etta didn't react, remaining perfectly still, and when I realized he expected me to respond, I told him, "I hope so."

Archer nodded. "Cool."

Jane and I exchanged the routine call-and-response of "It was nice meeting you," and "You, too," and "Maybe I'll see you next weekend," and to Etta, Jane said, "I hope to see more of you this summer."

Etta's lips spliced into a half smile, but she stuck out her tongue the moment Jane turned her back.

When we heard the tires crunching over gravel and knew they were gone, Etta rolled onto her side so she was facing me directly.

"So," she said, "what do you think?"

"Of what?"

"Jane."

I shrugged. "She seems nice."

Etta clarified that "nice" was polite for "boring."

"I'd die if someone described me as *nice*. Like, oh, she's so *nice*. There are so many words to choose from." She felt around in her straw bag for sunscreen and dutifully applied it to her shoulders, her knees. "You must have made an impression on Archer the other night. I guess it worked out that I left you in Brooklyn," she said.

So she was still hung up on last weekend. The gymnastics of this conversation were exhausting, how we would pivot from Jane to Archer and back again. I couldn't keep up.

"Well, it was nice of him to offer me a ride, but obviously I would have rather *we* left together."

"He's been very friendly toward you."

"I feel like he's always been friendly? I mean, I haven't seen him in a long time."

"Yeah, I guess." She leaned in, bridging the gap between our two loungers. "So I picked up on some insecurity with Jane. Not that *she's* insecure, but more like she's insecure with Archer. With their relationship."

I felt like I was being lured into a trap. "Yeah, maybe," I said. "I don't know her well enough to make that judgment." She was quiet. "But I guess that comment you made at breakfast struck her a bit, though?"

She cocked an eyebrow, newly energized. "Which comment?"

I said, "Uh, the one, the one about like, their long-distance situation?"

"Ah, I thought so, too." Etta stood and dipped a toe in the shallow end of the pool, sending out ripples from where she'd pierced the water. "It'll be just like the last time with them. It's their pattern."

"Pattern?"

She twisted her dark blond hair into a bun at the nape of her neck. "They've dated before, more casually, but yeah, it's just the first time he's ever brought her home."

"I didn't realize that." A pause. "How do they know each other again?"

"Through friends," she said, drawing more circles in the pool. "Also, Plum and Warren know Jane's parents." That was it, I thought. It made sense now. Why Jane had earned expedited approval, despite yesterday's snafu and the "fallout to the hydrangea." Etta continued: "Her dad is some international businessman, and her mom is an ex-model who runs a nonprofit. You know."

I didn't. "Totally."

Etta laughed into her shoulder. "Yeah, I don't know what it is with Jane, really. Archer's a grown man. He can make his own decisions, but…" She looked to me. "He's too optimistic. With everything."

The samba music started to skip, the same two bars repeating over and over, a hopeful horn section cycling on a now-manic loop.

"Jesus," Etta said, tossing her eyes in its direction, "what the hell is with this music? It's driving me insane," and I understood that story time was over.

"Can't you ask them to turn it down or something?" I asked.

"I mean, in an ideal world, but no one's home."

"What do you mean?"

"It's a timer," she said.

"Why would they set a timer?"

"Oh, I don't know," she said, "to deter any possible intruders from ransacking their house while they sail the Mediterranean for the summer?" I nodded, but I wasn't sure I was following. "It's a decoy," she said simply. "You'd be surprised—security systems only go so far. They used to rent it out, but not anymore. Now it's just empty."

Etta wrapped herself in a towel and checked her phone, the music still skipping, sounding robotic and strange in the context of the nonexistent neighbors.

"Etta," I said, "do you think it would be okay if Paul drove me back to the city soon?"

"Why? Is something wrong?"

Yes, I could have said, *something is wrong*. I wasn't sure why I didn't just ask her about Barcelona. Perhaps a part of me didn't want to know, preferred ignorance, because as long as things were uncertain, I could still pretend. I could pretend nothing would change and everything would be fine.

So I rolled my eyes, gestured to my phone. "Yeah, I just have to deal with some stuff for work. My boss is texting me right now."

Etta nodded, as if she could empathize. "The people you work with are so needy."

7

The following Saturday I met my dad for breakfast at a Midtown diner, somewhere he would feel comfortable. He didn't like fussy places with too much "atmosphere," the snobbish hostess in the tight black dress, the trendy soundtrack, the table of aspiring influencers photographing their avocado toast. I hadn't seen him since Thanksgiving, when he took the train into Grand Central, something about the holiday evidently pinching a nostalgic nerve. We ate clam chowder at the Oyster Bar, enduring an hour of small talk and departing with the harsh knowledge that we had nothing in common and a reminder of why I never went home. But he had texted me Friday night, said he was in the city for a friend's retirement party, that he was staying at the Sheraton in Times Square if I wanted to grab breakfast? So we wound up in a sticky booth in the back, grease and burnt coffee wafting through the kitchen doors and Steve Winwood humming over the speaker. Across from me, my father, his puffy eyes, his thinning, gray hair. His sweatshirt and baggy jeans and New Balance sneakers. He asked for pancakes, bacon "extra crispy," and I ordered an egg white omelet with fruit salad. We both drank coffee, black.

"Jesus," he said at one point, "this is like rocket fuel. I'm going to be buzzing all day."

He wanted to know if I lived around here and I said, "No, in the East Village." His expression was blank. "Downtown, Dad," I said. He asked if I'd always lived there. "Yes," I said. "You've never seen my apartment."

"It's a haul to get into the city," he told me.

Excuses were our love language. It was two hours on the train and he'd made it in to celebrate a friend's retirement, a friend whom I'd never heard of, but no matter. I wasn't offended.

"Everything good with work?" he asked.

"Yeah, it's fine," I said.

"You like advertising?"

"I work in PR."

"Aren't they the same?" he asked.

I lacked the patience to explain the differences so I said, "Pretty much."

He drummed his fingers on the table and I looked out the window onto Seventh Avenue. "Have you heard from your sister?"

"No, have you?" I asked, but it came out accusatory.

"No."

"So I guess she's staying in Peru, then."

"I guess so."

The silence, painful. Why did I keep trying? Why didn't I just tell him I was busy this morning? He took out his phone to show me the birdfeeder he'd installed in our yard.

"You'll see it," he said, "next time you're home."

Wishful thinking, the words *next time* an assumption, but I nodded and said, "Yeah."

Thank god for fast service; our food arrived quickly. My omelet was wet, gleaming like brain tissue on the heavy white plate.

My father hunched over the table and dug in immediately, cutting into his pancakes with the side of his fork, chewing with his mouth open. I felt myself retracting into the booth, eyeing the few other tables, but no one seemed to notice his flaws except me.

He came up for air. "You don't like your food?"

"No, I do. I'm just not that hungry."

"You're not one of those girls with an eating disorder now, are you?"

"What? No."

He shrugged and returned to his pancakes. His friend, the one who was retiring, had plans of moving to South Carolina. He had similar aspirations apparently.

"You want to move to South Carolina?"

"Well, not South Carolina. Maybe Florida, I don't know."

"So you'd sell the house."

"Eventually," he said as I slid a piece of pineapple around my plate. "I don't get why you like it here so much. New York. It's filthy, loud. Weird people, too."

He carried on, something about the price of rent, the cost of living, and I picked at my eggs, having learned to drown him out. The man at the adjacent table asked if they had a high chair and from my periphery, I watched as he lowered a toddler into the seat. His stubby little legs, fleshy wrists. The man kept calling him "little guy."

My dad cleared his throat. "You're just like her sometimes, you know." I lifted my gaze. "Your mother."

It was weird of him to mention her; we preferred to pretend she didn't exist.

"She liked the city," he said. "She used to take you to see the Rockettes, do you remember?" I nodded, but he was staring out the window now. "I don't think your sister really remembers her."

I put down my fork. "Maybe it's better that way."

He didn't answer. If things were different, I told myself, I would have reached across the table, held his hand, told him it was okay, that it was okay to be angry or bitter or lonely or whatever, but there was an invisible force field and I couldn't cross it. So I picked at my food and waited for him to return to the present, to eat the rest of his pancakes and drink the last of his "rocket fuel" coffee, so we could finish this meal in silence.

And that was exactly what we did. When the server brought our check, we split the bill, and I felt a weight being lifted.

Outside the diner we did the familiar dance of uncertainty as to whether we should hug, ultimately resulting in an extension of both our arms. As he turned toward his hotel and me toward the subway, he said he would see me soon, but we both knew it was a lie.

━━━━━

Etta's apartment in Tribeca was situated on the top floor of a former sugar factory that had been converted into multimillion-dollar housing, with exposed wood-beam ceilings and hardwood floors and tall windows offering unobstructed views of the Hudson. A Swedish decorator named Nils had overseen the interior design so that it included clubby sofas, low to the ground so as not to block the views, and armchairs with perfect rolls resembling hot dog buns. There were multiple coffee tables constructed of marble and glass and textured wood, and of course, the art: sculptures and a prehistoric-looking chair that was, in fact, for show and not sitting, plus Etta's parents' own minimalist prints.

When the elevator doors opened to the foyer, I saw it: splayed boxes, everywhere, of all sizes. In the living room there were stuffed garment bags, clothing racks of expensive silks and linens and those textile-print dresses Etta liked from Italy. Snapshots of her summer wardrobe strewn across the furniture.

Either Etta was engaged in a rigorous round of spring cleaning, or Archer was right.

Etta rounded a corner from the hall in sweats and an old T-shirt, very unlike her, and clasped a stack of folded cashmere sweaters to her chest. "Shit!" she said, nearly jumping when she spotted me. "You scared me!"

I wanted to say, "What the hell is all this?" but instead as Etta flopped onto a sofa, I apologized. "Sorry I'm late," I said. "A train stalled at West Fourth. We couldn't move, it was awful."

"Ooof," she said. "The worst." She leaned over the coffee table, grabbing a box of crackers.

"What time is Archer's thing again?" I asked, still standing beside an armchair.

"Starts at seven. Why?"

"You aren't dressed."

"It doesn't take me that long to get ready." A lie, I thought. Another lie. "What did you do today?" She slid a cracker into her mouth.

"I saw my dad, actually."

She lifted her eyes to mine. "Really? Why?"

"He was in the city. He asked me to get breakfast."

"And how was that?"

"Weird. Depressing. He showed me pictures of this bird-feeder he installed in our yard. He said, 'You'll see it next time you're home.'"

She pushed out her bottom lip.

"We just have nothing to talk about," I said, crossing my arms. "I don't even know why I agreed to it."

"Because you have hope, Ren. That's why."

I started to laugh. "I do?"

"Yes. You have hope that things could be different between you two. That your next meeting might be the one that changes things." She bent toward me, aiming a finger at my face. "That's why you went."

I inhaled and exhaled. "Yeah, maybe."

"I would have come with you?" she said. "Maybe it would have been less awkward with me there to buffer the energy?"

I nodded. "Thanks, but it was probably better I went alone." Except really, the thought of Etta joining me and my dad for breakfast at a shitty Midtown diner sent chills up my spine. She'd met him only once, at graduation, where he was barely presentable in an old blue suit that looked as if it had been collecting dust in the back of his closet, because it *had* been collecting dust in the back of his closet. Luckily, the day had been chaotic and there was no room for actual conversation, no room for Etta to assess him or me or our fraught family dynamics.

"I get it," she said. "Sometimes we need to do things on our own."

I glanced around the room. "So what are all these boxes?"

Etta's gaze dropped to the floor and she brushed a crumb from one of the sweaters on her lap. "I've been meaning to talk to you about all this."

About all this. So this was it. So long, ignorance.

"After you left on Sunday, my parents and I had a 'talk.'"

I smiled, perhaps too much. "A talk about what?"

"More of the same. My life, its apparent lack of direction. How Archer's paved his own path, etcetera, because you know he can do no wrong. They seem to forget he hasn't done much of anything these last few years, but now he has this show, so—" She stopped short.

"So then what?"

"Do you want to sit?"

I'd forgotten I was still standing. "I'm fine."

"You sure? You're sweating."

"Oh," I said, and lowered myself into the opposite armchair, blotted my face with the back of my hand. I'd jogged the few blocks from the subway and my body sometimes operated on a delay wherein I didn't feel the physical ramifications of things until well after the moment of impact.

"So we had this whole long talk. But—" she popped a cracker into her mouth, chewing languidly, and I wanted to scream "—I think we've reached some sort of resolution."

"Uh-huh," I said, but I was already numb.

She stretched for her water glass on the table. "Well, I guess this might come as a shock, but... I'm moving to Barcelona."

And there it was. I'd known, of course, intuitively. In what world was Archer Crofton wrong? Certainly not the one I lived in.

"Moving!" I said, remembering I wasn't supposed to know. "Sorry, like, for good?"

"Well, for now."

I'd labored over my makeup, and now it was practically dripping down my face. Meanwhile, Etta was unaffected, refolding a cashmere sweater, looking as if she'd been ripped from the pages of a catalogue flaunting hot people with hangovers. The boxes, the clothes, the signs of her life in transit, perforated the present.

"But when do you leave?" I asked, trying to appear buoyant, optimistic, *hopeful.*

She said, "Monday," and I smiled even wider. She went on: "My parents have a friend who is on the board at the Academy of Art. I'm going to take classes there. They have a new digital art program."

Etta wasn't an artist. She'd studied English, like me. I'd edited all of her papers, combed for typos, made sure her theses were convincing, that she incorporated substantial evidence to back up her arguments. She sometimes still confused *your* and *you're.* Apparently, though, none of it mattered when you had friends in high places. Really, I should have been happy for her. A good friend, a better person, would have reacted differently, and I'd had all week to prepare for this moment. But still, the little, needy, menacing voice in my head kept begging to know, *What about me?*

"Barcelona, though," I said, as if in awe, wiping a stray eyelash from my cheek. "Can't you take classes in New York? I mean, why Barcelona?"

"My parents think it will be good for me. To get perspective."

"By moving to Barcelona."

"I don't know, they think my world is too small."

"I don't feel like your world is too small." She was silent. "Where will you live?"

"My parents have an apartment there, in L'Eixample—" this was supposed to mean something "—and they never use it, so I'll just stay there for now."

"You never mentioned they had a place there."

She narrowed her eyes. "I feel like I have?"

"Nope," I said.

"Huh, well, maybe because they never use it. Like I said."

"And you're there for how long again?"

"Jesus Christ, Ren. You're asking so many fucking questions. This is why I didn't want to tell you."

I'd pushed too hard. Etta stood and marched to the wall of windows, the gravity of her words landing on me. *This is why I didn't want to tell you*, as in she'd thought about it, as in she'd dreaded this moment, as in she'd been *avoiding* it. I wished I could have told her that I already knew, that Archer had mentioned it, but that would have only seemed vengeful, magnifying the fact that we had both been feigning ignorance.

"I'm sorry," I said, and I was. "I'm just going to miss you."

She was still facing away from me, her image reflected in the window. "I can't look at it as an 'ending,'" she said. "Endings are too finite and sad."

"It's not really an ending," I said.

"No, it is."

"Well, I'm excited for you," I lied.

Etta spun around. "I'm thinking I'll be back for Thanksgiving, maybe even before then, pending how things go?"

That's November, I thought, *five months from now—what will I do until then?* But I said, "Don't think so far ahead. This is good for you. Your parents are right."

"Well, hopefully you'll be able to visit. Maybe for my birthday?"

Her birthday wasn't until late September, *three* months from now. My life was regressing into a series of countdowns and Etta's would evolve in a new city. She'd have stories of new friends and faces and I'd be a relic from a bygone era, still working my same sad job and eating sad salads with Jeff on our lunch break and complaining about Natalie and the subway and the brown water coursing through the pipes in the kitchen because the building's infrastructure was old and then one day, we would all just die.

I squeezed my eyes shut. "It's so depressing, though, looking at all these boxes."

"Yeah, it's definitely weird. I'd almost rather skip this whole part and get there already." I didn't respond. "I didn't mean it like that. It's just messy. Packing."

"Of course not," I said. "Packing is the worst."

Etta stepped closer so that she was standing over me. "I'm sorry I didn't tell you sooner. I just knew that once I did, I couldn't take it back, you know? Telling you makes it real."

"No, I get it," I said. "I'm sure this is a lot for you. All this change."

She tugged a strand of my hair, stroked the top of my head. "Are you going to be okay here without me?"

"I mean, I'll miss you, but this is a good thing. A *great* thing. I'm happy for you."

Etta considered me, her eyes skipping across my face. "Okay," she said finally. "Well, I need to shower."

"We're still going?" I asked.

Etta rolled her shoulders. "Just give me a half hour."

I heard the water running behind the bathroom door and watched the sky's subtle darkening, pictured us as characters within the pages of a novel. I already knew the ending. Characters like me got "neat" endings, tidy resolutions. White-bread sandwiches with the crusts cut off. Characters like Etta would sail off into blood-orange sunsets, triumphant, full champagne flutes in hand. She'd think of me every so often, when the light conjured a specific emotion or the mood struck nostalgic, and remember me as someone she used to know.

8

We left for Archer's opening exactly twenty minutes after it started. "Just give me a half hour" turned into "I hate all my clothes" and "I'm on my period" and "Should we open a bottle of wine?" In the car, Etta said, "Honestly, it's better we're running late," but then we sat in traffic for a whole fifteen minutes on our way to Chelsea and didn't arrive until eight.

The room was packed, vibrating with conversation and the pulsating rhythms of an LCD Soundsystem remix, the white walls punctuated by imposing paintings that resembled Pollocks, in that familiar drip style. I'd read an article earlier that afternoon in which Archer had cited Pollock as a main inspiration. Apparently that hadn't wavered since his last show years ago.

Etta flung her arms around someone with a bright blond bob. "Lizzie," she cooed, acting as if this was her best friend, and maybe she was.

An almost comically handsome server, the model/actor type with a perfect jawline, floated by with a tray of champagne flutes. I lifted two glasses and handed one to Etta.

Lizzie said, "I can't even believe it. It's been like what, two years? Three?"

Etta pursed her lips, eyes wide, stunned by the passage of time. "I think you're right."

"I was hoping I'd run into you here, but I wasn't sure if you were in town?"

"Where else would I be?" Etta asked, and Lizzie said, "It's going to kill me—where were we the last time we saw each other?"

Etta paused thoughtfully, then squeezed her hand. "Ibiza."

"Yes. Sergio's birthday. How could I forget?"

"Poor Sergio," Etta said. They were both silent, as if in memorial. What happened to Sergio?

"But this show," Lizzie said, spinning around, "just *incredible*. I mean... I imagine everything has already sold."

Etta sipped her champagne. "We just got here. I haven't had the chance to properly explore."

Lizzie's eyes fell on me for a moment, then slung back to Etta, as if I wasn't really there. They started swapping names of people I didn't know, and would Etta be at Lisandra's wedding at Cap-Eden-Roc? While they caught up, I glanced around the room. There were a lot of older people, probably friends of Plum's and Warren's, and of course the requisite younger crowd: influencers and socialites, those "in the know" who wound up at these things through word of mouth. Speaking of, where was Archer? Maybe he'd already left? Decamped the scene, shook all the right hands, made nice with his enemies?

All of a sudden, Lizzie stuck out her hand. "Lizzie," she said to me. "I didn't realize you were with Etta." She laughed. "I thought you were just standing here. I was wondering when you were going to leave and then Etta told me she knew you."

Before I could respond, Etta said, "Yes, this is Ren. We're friends from NYU." She planted a kiss on my cheek. "She's the best."

"Cute." Lizzie swirled the wine in her glass. "This wine isn't very good." Etta asked what she was drinking and she told her, "It's a Riesling but…" She stuck out her tongue.

Etta laughed. "That bad? You should just stick to champagne."

"Or vodka," Lizzie said. She grabbed the bicep of a server as he passed and said, "This wine is carcinogenic."

He didn't bat an eye. "I'm sorry. Let me take your glass."

"Can you get me a vodka tonic, extra lime? A double."

He nodded. "Of course."

"Ketel One, please!" she called after him.

Etta refocused on Lizzie, touched her wrist, called her "Liz."

"Are you still in London?" she asked.

So Lizzie didn't live here. That explained why I'd never met her before tonight.

Lizzie licked her lips. She had a gap between her two front teeth that I hadn't noticed until now. "Correct."

"And? Do you like it?"

"I *love* it. I may never come back."

"Huh," Etta said with a smile. "How long are you in town for again?"

"Only the weekend. I leave Monday night."

"That's a quick trip."

"Well, Astrid's here for work so I tagged along."

Etta cocked an eyebrow. "Astrid?"

Astrid, I learned, was Lizzie's girlfriend. Their relationship was news to Etta, who kept repeating, "What? How did I not know about this?" I listened as Lizzie summarized the details of their fated introduction, the dinner party where she'd met Astrid three days before her scheduled return flight to New York.

Etta egged her on with comments like, "Unbelievable," and "So wild."

Astrid. Was this the same Astrid Plum and Warren kept referencing during dinner last weekend?

"Astrid works a lot," Lizzie said, "but I'm happy. We're good together."

They went on like this for a while, the conversation muffled by an imaginary droll, as if in a movie, the main character losing their grip on reality. I was still grappling with the fact that only an hour earlier, the rug had been ripped out from underneath me, and that in spite of this, I was supposed to be happy for Etta. Supportive. Reassuring. A *good friend*.

I heard Etta say, "Barcelona," and Lizzie made a face that implied she was impressed.

"When do you leave?" she asked, and I bit the inside of my cheek.

"Monday," Etta said. "I know, I know, it's wild."

Wild, I thought. *So* wild. It was so wild that in just two days, not even a full forty-eight hours, Etta would be halfway across the Atlantic Ocean, en route to a whole other continent.

I drained the rest of my champagne. "I'm going to the bar. Anyone want anything?"

Etta examined her glass. "I'm good," but Lizzie asked, "Oh, actually, yes, Rhianne—can you check on my vodka?"

I didn't bother correcting her. "Sure," I said.

I asked for two vodkas with tonic and lime, the way Lizzie had ordered hers, not that I liked vodka, but because there was less of a chance the bartender would screw up if I asked for the same. "Ketel One," I said, flattening my hands to the bar. "Please." The bartender nodded, but when I returned with our drinks, Lizzie was gone.

Like clockwork, Etta said, "Wow. Does she ever shut up?" Her eyes darted around the room, and it all came out: "I've known her since kindergarten. She's older than us, about thirty," and "Can you believe she's lesbian now?"

"No," I said, not because I couldn't believe it, but because I had never met her. I had no "before" for comparison. I drank my vodka tonic, which was really straight vodka, the tonic a whisper, a mere suggestion of something to cut the liquor, and Etta polished off her champagne, assessing the empty flute, as if considering whether she wanted another. "Who's Astrid?" I asked.

"Her girlfriend."

"Right, but like, *who*?"

"She's a director here. An art dealer. She works with Archer."

"So she helps sell Archer's paintings?" She nodded and I said, "Ah."

Etta laughed. "Why *ah*? Do you know her or something?"

"No, I just thought I heard Archer mention her once."

She frowned. "Really? When? In the car?"

So she was still fixated on the car ride.

"Last weekend," I said. "At dinner, I think."

She seemed to ponder this. "Huh. I guess that would make sense." She paused. "You know, they used to date. A long time ago."

"Archer and Astrid?"

Etta nodded. "And Lizzie had a thing for Archer, too, like a childhood crush. Classic."

"But Astrid and Archer work together. It's not weird?"

"No, not at all." Etta flagged a server to bring her another champagne, but I wasn't sure if he even saw her. "It *is* funny, though, their relationship."

"Archer and Astrid's?"

"No, Lizzie and Astrid's. Well, not funny. Calculated, I should say." Her eyes zeroed in on mine, and she lowered her voice. "Lizzie's dad is *crazy* wealthy."

For Etta to comment on someone's wealth, it usually had to be more than substantial. Money was taboo. No one in these circles—the people with money, *real* money—discussed it, and talk of it cast you immediately as an outsider, as someone who didn't belong and never would.

"He basically owns New York, and London, and has a shit-load of connections."

"Like he knows a lot of people?"

"He knows a lot of very *important* people."

"Like who? Archer?"

Etta laughed. "Archer isn't that important, though I can see why you would think that."

I smiled for effect, but bit the inside of my cheek again.

"So is her dad here?" I asked, casting my eyes about the room.

"No. No, he's almost never in New York, especially this time of year."

This made sense—if he was as powerful as Etta implied, and it seemed he was, he wouldn't summer in Manhattan. No, to stay in New York signified that you had nowhere better to go. People like Lizzie's dad migrated to the Hamptons, to Antibes and Mallorca and Umbria. New York was the center of everything, and yet come the warmer weather, the people who owned the city left it behind, shrugging it off like a second skin they didn't need anymore.

Just then, Etta's head jerked, as if by primal instinct. There were Plum and Warren, staring at us from across the room. Plum waved, a simple fanning of her fingers, and Warren sipped his drink, unemotive.

Etta grabbed what was supposed to be Lizzie's drink from my hand and took a swig. "Well," she said, returning the drink to me, "guess I better go say hi."

I began to follow her, but she turned around, told me it was better if I just stayed here.

Etta was gone for ten minutes, then fifteen and twenty. I ambled about, attempting to look occupied, examining Archer's paintings. In front of a purple-and-blue one with squiggly lines darting out from a circular blob that resembled the nucleus of a cell, someone with pigtails said, "It's magnificent, isn't it? So cerebral," and I told her, "I was thinking the same thing." I made three laps around the room, finished my vodka and headed back to the bar, but the area was mobbed and I couldn't get the bartender's attention.

As an older woman in a pastel twin set complained about her bourbon, specifically, the pour—"To the rim," she said—the crowd parted, as if making way for Jesus himself, and there was Archer, in his white T-shirt, plain jeans, an insult to the idea of "normal" because he so obviously wasn't.

I looked at him then looked away, but he already spotted me.

"Hi," he said.

I smiled, like I hadn't just panicked and tried to ignore him. "Congratulations," I said. "The show is great," though I didn't know if it was great; I had no real opinions to offer, but it seemed the polite thing to say.

He bowed his head. "Thank you." He motioned to the bartender and asked for a whiskey. "Where's your sidekick?" He meant Etta.

"Oh," I laughed. "She's over there somewhere. Talking with your parents."

His gaze traveled to them and then to my hand still holding a nearly full drink. "A bit aggressive to be at the bar when you already have a drink? Seems selfish," he said, but he was suppressing a smile.

"This is Etta's," I said, raising the glass, as if presenting the evidence, as if I was guilty of something.

"How is she?" he asked.

"Good," I said. "She just, um, told me about the move."

Archer tossed back his head. "Ah. How are you taking it? The wound still raw?"

So he suspected I would die in New York without her. Was it because it was partially true? I wanted to prove him wrong.

"Well, you already kind of told me about it, remember? So I was just waiting for her to tell me herself."

"Fair," he said.

I shrugged. "I'm happy for her. I think it will be *good* for her, actually."

"You should talk to our parents. They'd appreciate that sentiment," and when he saw me peek over at them, he added, "I'm kidding. Don't do that."

"I wasn't—"

He reached for my hand, brushed my fingers with his, and I stopped talking, nearly dropped my glass to the floor. His grip tightened and I realized he was only taking the drink from me. I watched him place it on the table behind us.

"What are you drinking?" he asked.

"Vodka?"

Without another word, he signaled the same bartender, ordered me a tequila soda with a twist of lime. He slid the drink toward me on the bar. "Enjoy," he said, before disappearing back into the crowd.

"What were you two chatting about?" Etta asked.

I jolted my glass so that some of the tequila sloshed onto the floor. I hadn't seen her reappear.

"You, actually," I said. "And how you're—" I couldn't bring myself to say *leaving* "—traveling. And then he got me a drink. How are your parents?"

"Oh, they're fine. They're happy to tell everyone about my plans. Something they can brag about now."

"I bet." Etta asked where her drink was and it turned out that the table Archer had placed it on had since been cleared. "I left it right there," I said, but she waved her hand.

She ordered another. "So how did he seem?"

"Who?"

She narrowed her eyes. "Archer."

"Oh. Fine," I said.

"Happy?"

"I think so."

"That's good," she said. "He's been so stressed lately. Did you notice the circles underneath his eyes?"

"No?"

"Like a vampire. I don't think he sleeps." When I didn't respond, she asked if I'd seen Jane at all.

I'd almost forgotten about her. "No," I said. "Have you?"

Etta craned her neck, scanning the room, then sipped her drink. "Nope."

"Weird," I said.

"Very."

━━━━━━

Around eleven, Archer vanished. The room thinned and the music died, and someone flipped a switch that sputtered like a strobe light, bathing all who remained in a sterile white glow.

Etta rubbed her mouth absently and searched in her bag for lipstick. "So Lizzie and Astrid are actually having a little thing at their place," she said, which didn't mean *little thing*, but rather a get-together with a DJ, open bar, substantial guest list, the works. That much I knew by now.

"I thought they lived in London," I said.

"They still have a place here. Well, it's Lizzie's dad's place, but that's beside the point. So? Want to go?" I really didn't, and it was like Etta could read my mind. "Do not say you're tired."

I said nothing, which was still saying something apparently.

"No! You can sleep when you're dead."

"That's dark, Etta."

"You know what I mean."

Lizzie and Astrid were lingering by the door, watching us, and I gathered that Etta would leave with them, whether I joined or not.

Etta swung my hands in hers. "It's only a few blocks away. We can *walk*. It's my last weekend, please?"

A pause; she was batting her eyes, practically pleading. "Okay," I said.

"Really?"

It was sort of endearing, how happy this made her. "Sure."

Etta squeezed my hand. "It'll be fun, I promise," she said, before excusing herself to say goodbye to her parents.

I sat at a table littered with empty glassware and used cocktail napkins, half-eaten pigs in blankets, and looked on as Etta kissed the cheeks of her parents' friends. I smiled at a server who collected the trash and wouldn't smile back. I understood why: he'd confused me for being one of them.

9

Lizzie and Astrid lived in a duplex near the High Line, the New Jersey skyline winking across the Hudson through floor-to-ceiling windows, but the first thing that caught my eye was the dining room table: suspended from the ceiling by metal chains so that it seemed to float inches above the ground. Around it, people sat on cushions, smoking cigarettes, doing lines, and in the corner was the DJ, who overlayed jazz synth with the voices of a children's choir. It wasn't necessarily music you could dance to, but it did create a certain aspirational ambiance.

In the kitchen, where Etta poured us two tumblers of vodka, I overheard a couple discussing their ayahuasca trip in Costa Rica, and did you know that if you ate nothing but toothpaste for two days, you'd lose five pounds? "Pure water weight," a marvel. And then, out of all the people in this city, there was Roger from *The New York Times*, reclining on a sofa, glowering at his phone. Roger with his curly gray hair, his scruff, his tiny glasses perched on the bridge of his nose. His black blazer and pilled sweater underneath it; his pants, two inches too short.

He wore his messiness like a badge of honor because he could be disheveled and get away with it.

Our phone conversation the other week had gone fine, not great, but fine. He always pretended not to know me whenever I called, and I'd be forced to explain after an exceptionally awkward pause, "I work with Natalie," and then he would understand, act as if he was doing a favor. He didn't want the perfume exclusive, said it was too "low brow," was annoyed I'd even offered. Natalie was pissed, but reassured me we could use him later, that if we played the game right, he would owe us a story eventually.

Though I didn't want to deal with Roger and his ego tonight, it would have been a missed opportunity if I didn't at least say hello. I told Etta I would be right back.

Roger's blank stare confirmed he didn't recognize me. I was no one.

"Ren," I said. Nothing. "We spoke the other week on the phone? About the perfume?" Still nothing. "I work with Natalie."

Bingo. "Oh, right. Yes. Ren." We exchanged "How are you's?" and he told me he had just come from a performance art exhibit nearby with a friend from *Vanity Fair* and was meant to meet another friend here who had opened a new restaurant in Red Hook that had Pete Wells raving—had I heard of it? "Of course," I lied, but the friend was stuck in traffic, how sad, and now Roger was here "waiting for Godot."

It was the most he'd said to me outside of a professional capacity, as he sipped from a glass I knew was filled with water. Natalie said he didn't drink because he might "miss something," but I thought he'd just crashed and burned a little too hard in the eighties.

"What brings you here?" he asked. His forefinger grazed the edges of his phone—he still used a BlackBerry.

It gave me some pleasure to say, "I was at Archer's show?"

intonating it as a question, so as not to seem too self-assured, using only his first name to infer familiarity. As if Archer was an old friend.

Based on Roger's expression, raised brows and vague nodding, I could gauge that this surprised him, that *I* had surprised him.

"Archer Crofton?" he asked.

"Yes," I said, feeling satisfied.

But he wasn't asking about Archer. No, Archer had materialized beside me, his hand resting on my waist.

"Oh," I said, my voice ascending an octave, "hi."

"Nice to see you," Roger said, standing. They shook hands. Did they know each other? "First show in a long time. Congratulations."

Archer studied Roger, a strange energy passing between them. "Thank you," he said.

Roger nodded, and perhaps sensing this same energy, added, "I'm a fan, Archer. Very much looking forward to seeing the new work." When Archer didn't respond, Roger laughed. "Sorry, do you not speak with writers unless it's off the record?"

God, Roger could be such a dick. He made it worse by saying, "I'm only joking!"

Archer was stoic. "I'm sure we can find a time for you to visit the gallery. I'll have someone in PR reach out to set it up?"

"No need," Roger said.

"No need?"

"No need. I'll plan to stop by when it fits my schedule. Have a nice evening." I watched as Roger stopped in the kitchen, grabbed a carrot stick from the crudités, then pressed the button for the elevator.

Archer kept his eyes on him, chewing his bottom lip, waiting until the doors opened and Roger disappeared behind them. "Excuse me," he said to me, his hand again on my waist before he walked away.

Back in the kitchen, Etta asked, "Who was that?"

So she had been watching me. "Someone from work."

"Like a coworker? He seems kind of old."

"No, an editor. He's with *The Times*."

"Huh, really. Archer knows him?"

"I guess. He's a legend, very old-school. We were just catching up."

She pinched my cheek between her thumb and forefinger. "Well, look at you, Ren! Making moves in the big old world."

———

I didn't want to tell Etta that she drank too much, but she drank too much. She continuously refilled her glass, each time with less and less ice so that eventually it was straight vodka. She'd started slurring her words, said, "Can you at least *act* like you're having a little fun?" and I said, "I am having fun," this after we had gotten stuck chatting with Ted and Tyler, twin brothers from San Francisco who said they were "angel investors," as Etta made mock halos above their heads. When Ted and Tyler suggested we go to this "great place near the water," Etta said, "We're already near the water." Tyler crossed his arms. "Well, princess, this is your town, why don't you show us around?" Etta blinked. "It isn't my town anymore," she said, and the two angel investors flew away.

"One more drink and we can leave," she told me, but of course Lizzie summoned Etta back to the kitchen. She was pouring tequila shots and Etta passed one to me and her face said, *I told you one more drink.* We tossed them back; the tequila was smooth, tasteless, refined. I had no immediate reflex to gag or cough. Lizzie must have registered my expression, and said, "It's good, right?"

"So, Ren," Etta said then, "I was thinking, how do you feel about staying at my place while I'm gone?"

My eyes skipped between the two of them. "Like, live there?"

Etta laughed. "Yes, like, *live there*," and then to Lizzie, she said, "Ren has this little apartment in the East Village, the tippy-top floor of a walk-up. I was thinking it would make sense if she stayed at mine while I'm away—" she turned to me "—if you want, of course."

If you want, of course, as if I had a choice. It was obvious Etta had expected me to jump at the chance.

Lizzie raised her brows, assessed me to see how I might react. "Wow. That's generous."

"I'm not asking you to pay rent or anything," Etta was quick to add. "You can literally stay there, no strings attached."

"No, of course, I just, I need a minute to think? My new roommate just moved in and—"

"You didn't mention you found someone to sublet the other bedroom?" Etta said.

"Oh, um, yeah. Sorry, I thought I told you? He moved in yesterday."

Etta didn't say anything and Lizzie chimed in: "Personally speaking, Rhianne, I wouldn't reject Etta's offer." She tapped the cocktail stirrer against the rim of her glass. "Think of it as playing house."

Of course, the prospect of living at Etta's was appealing. It was summer in New York and the AC unit in my apartment didn't exactly work and so I was always sweating. Meanwhile, at Etta's, the floors were heated or cooled in syncopation with the seasons, and light flooded every room, putting the two double windows in my living area, the pixelated view of the skyline, to shame. But living there would mean I'd owe Etta, more than I already did, and I could never repay her. Surely, she had to know this when she suggested it.

Etta sipped her drink. "What is it?"

"Nothing," I lied, but she knew me too well.

"You can't worry about your roommate," she clipped. "You don't even know him."

"I'm not worried about my roommate."

"You just said you were. How about if I pay your rent? Does that help?"

I laughed and Etta said she was serious.

My face flushed. "I can't ask you to do that. That's weird."

"But I'm offering."

Lizzie smacked her lips. "Rhianne, she's offering," and I said, "Etta, please. Not now?"

"Well, I leave—" she inspected her phone "—tomorrow, technically, so when, if not now?"

"I don't know, maybe if you'd given me more time to consider, instead of waiting until the last second to tell me that you were moving out of the country?"

Lizzie sucked on a lime, dragging the flesh through her teeth. I'd lost my cool, I knew, but it didn't seem to matter, because Etta had fixed her gaze across the room, her expression eerily placid. She pointed to a painting at the landing of the stairs. It was a chaotic scene, appearing to depict a circus, and in the middle of the ring was the painting's beating heart, a girl in a yellow dress, arms splayed, balancing on a horse.

"Lizzie, I love that one," she said. "It's a Chagall, right?"

"I think so. It just got here the other day." Etta nodded and plucked a cigarette from a pack on the counter. She only smoked when she was drunk, or furious. Perhaps she was a bit of both. "Listen, Ren, I know you're tired, you can leave if you want. I'll be fine on my own."

I tried to say, "I'm fine, too," but she had already begun to walk away.

Lizzie whispered in my ear, "Be smart, Rhianne," before trailing Etta up the stairs.

It was after midnight, and Etta was right, I was exhausted

and didn't want to be here anymore. But I couldn't leave. No, I sat on the couch. I would wait. I needed Etta to know that I could survive here, too.

———

I was trapped in conversation with a man who identified as a poet slash sculptor. He wore a heavy Celtic cross around his neck and asked if I was familiar with astral projection and when I said, "Not really," he responded, "That's a relief." He was busy rolling a joint, smoothing the edges of the paper with his tongue, when I spotted Archer again, cutting through the kitchen. He had since swapped his T-shirt and jeans for a pale blue button-down and black pants. I excused myself and made my way to him.

I didn't necessarily want another drink, but I reached for the bottle of tequila beside the sink. I wasn't sure what had come over me; perhaps it was Etta's leaving, her bizarre offer, or rather, plea, for me to live in her apartment. Or maybe I was simply drunk. Archer was several feet to my left, looking around, either ignoring me or not registering my presence. My hand shook as I filled a tumbler with ice. "Looking for this?" I asked, wielding the same bottle of tequila from earlier.

He laughed. "So you're a tequila person now? Did I convert you?"

"Maybe. This one is really good, though."

He smiled and poured a small amount into both our glasses, mixed in tonic, then sliced two wheels of lime with a paring knife.

"So how do you know that guy again?" he asked. "Roger, was it?"

I didn't want him to think we were friends; clearly, there was something weird between them. "Through my job," I said. "He's an editor."

"Right, you work in PR. I remember now."

"Yeah," I said. "So as much as us 'PR people' annoy him, he needs us so he can do his job."

Archer nodded to himself. "Makes sense. I'm just—" he hesitated "—careful with media."

I wanted to reassure him that we were on the same page, that I was an ally. "Well, he can be extremely annoying. And self-righteous."

"Sounds like a delight," he said.

"Between us, I only tolerate him because I have to."

Archer laughed. "Is that off the record?"

"Very." I started to smile, then thought of Etta—where was she? I hadn't seen her since she'd retreated upstairs. Did she really think I'd gone home?

Behind us, a group of girls in bandage dresses poured out of the elevator, hands clasped to their mouths, barely concealing their obnoxious laughter. Archer's eyes followed.

"Is Jane not here tonight?" I asked.

He checked his phone. "No, she had to fly back to London. Family stuff."

I tasted my drink. Archer's sat on the counter, untouched. "I hope everything is okay?"

"She really liked you," he said, which didn't answer my question. "She suggested drinks when she's next in town."

I grinned and told him that sounded nice.

Archer tucked his phone into his pocket. His gaze floated behind me, and a moment later, a tall woman slid beside him. She had long braided hair that fell to her waist, gorgeous in a way that was wholly intimidating, but it was also the way she spoke: the melodic fluency of her voice, how she held out her hand to accept the drink from Archer, expectantly, how she slipped her arm around his waist, fluidly. Like he belonged to her. She smiled primly, jostled the ice in her glass, taking a sip as her eyes landed on mine.

"Ren," Archer said, "this is Astrid."

Astrid, I thought, as in Lizzie's girlfriend, as in Archer's art dealer and former-girlfriend-turned-friend-turned-colleague.

I played it cool, said it was great to meet her, and then neither of us made the effort to shake the other's hand, instead settling on nods.

Her eyes said, *Who are you and why are you here?* but to Archer, she simply asked, "A new friend?"

"She knows my sister."

"That's sweet," Astrid said. This time I got a smile with teeth, but it read as an automatic response, not genuine. She turned to Archer again, fencing me out of their conversation, and whispered something about Chagall, or at least that was what I heard.

"Are you talking about the Chagall by the stairs?" I asked. There was a flicker in Archer's expression, a smirk from Astrid— they hadn't expected this from me.

"Why?" Archer asked. "Do you like it?"

"It's very cool," I said.

"Cool," Astrid said, as if judging. *Cool.*

Across the apartment, the DJ paused between sets; loud chatter and clinking glassware and the dinging of elevator doors opening and closing filled the vacuum. The girls in bandage dresses were still gathered near the entrance, texting on their phones.

"Did they say how much longer?" Archer asked Astrid.

She glanced at her watch, a band of gold glimmering on her wrist. "Midnight, but I guess they're running late. Why? Something better you need to be doing?" Astrid tossed her eyes at me and Archer rolled his and I felt small again.

Astrid's phone rang and she picked up almost immediately, though she acted unbothered, tracing circles on the counter while she spoke. "Excellent," she said, and "Perfect, we'll see you soon." She concentrated on Archer. "Should we head to the back?"

But Archer's gaze lingered on me.

"Astrid," he said, "you have my cards on you, right?"

"Of course."

"Give one to Ren." Astrid hesitated. "Please," he said.

Astrid pursed her lips, observing me and Archer, as if confused. One minute I was an accessory to their conversation and the next, a focal point.

Astrid crossed her arms, one hand gripping her phone. "Archer, they're going to be here any minute."

His eyes still on me, he said, "It'll take you two seconds."

A pause. "Fine."

While Astrid retrieved a stack from her purse across the room, Archer whispered to me, "In case you decide you want a tour of the gallery or something." He placed a hand on my shoulder and I watched him migrate across the room, behind the closed double doors off the living room.

Astrid returned and shot out her hand, a single card tucked between two fingers. "This isn't his personal number, so you're aware," she said. "It can only get you his work line."

I took the card, examining the fine print, the black ink etched into thick cardstock.

A possible tour of the gallery with Archer—was it the Chagall, the fact that I had demonstrated interest? Or a friendly gesture because I was his sister's friend? Whatever it was, Astrid seemed annoyed.

"So this Chagall," she said, and I angled my body to mimic hers, toward the painting. "Do you know what it's called?" I shook my head, but it wasn't really framed as a question. *"Circus Horse."* She circled me. "You should go check on your friend," she said, pointing to the second floor. "I think she needs you."

When she left, I studied the Chagall in question. *Circus Horse.* In the center of the ring, above the girl posing on a carousel horse, there were also people flying on trapeze. A minstrel. And in the corner, what resembled a dragon.

Entertainment for the crowd.

Upstairs I elbowed past those same girls in bandage dresses out-side a closed bathroom door. "You're cutting the line!" they said, and I told them, "My friend is in there. She *needs* me." A thrill because it was true. I knocked three times.

"Ren?" called a thin voice from behind the door.

"It's locked," I said. "Can you let me in?"

Seconds later the lock clicked and I shut the door behind us. There was Etta, hugging the porcelain throne. I filled a glass on the counter with water and said, "Let's drink some of this?" I got her to open her mouth, trickled the water onto her tongue. She gestured for me to lower my legs so she could lie in my lap.

"My head is spinning," she finally said.

"You have to put one hand on the wall, one leg on the floor."

"Mmm," she said, wriggling into position.

"Better?" I asked. She nodded. "So where did Lizzie go?"

"Asleep." Her voice was muffled in my lap. "Bed."

I stroked the top of her head, fielded her hair for knots. She lifted her chin and I pinched an eyelash from her skin, holding it between my thumb and index finger. "Make a wish."

She narrowed her eyes at me, and I blew on the lash, but didn't see where it landed.

"Ren, what am I going to do in Barcelona?" She said the name this time the way a local would, *Barthelona,* and I knew the move was getting to her, that she didn't *really* want to leave.

"Find yourself. Become an adult. Write your memoir."

"Fuck you," she said with a laugh.

"You'll be fine," I said, and she would be fine. Her family had an apartment there, and friends who would probably look after her. She wasn't starting so much a new beginning as she was writing a continuation of the same story elsewhere.

Etta sighed. "Tell me a story."

A story. She made it sound so simple, she always did.

"What kind of story?" I asked.

"I don't know, any story, just nothing sad."

I thought of a night in March, someone's birthday, a friend of a friend of a friend, a relative stranger, honestly. We'd found ourselves at this dive on the Lower East Side. Low ceilings, sticky floors, extremely strong drinks. The kind of place where all the "cool" kids lined up around the block in freezing weather for a chance to order the well tequila and be ignored by some hipster with a complex in an unironic beanie.

"You were wearing that bodysuit," I said, "and you had to pee so badly, but when we went to the bathroom, you couldn't."

Etta's eyes were closed, but she was smiling. "And you ran the faucet," she said. "And sang, 'Waterfalls, rushing waterfalls.'" She rocked back and forth in my lap and we were both laughing.

"Waterfalls, rushing waterfalls," I sang now in a dramatic falsetto. Someone knocked on the bathroom door and I yelled, "Still busy!" and Etta and I laughed even harder. Our capacity for forgiveness was generous. The truth was, and I didn't want to face it, I would miss her.

I was able to get her out of the apartment without attracting too much attention. I couldn't call Paul, because I didn't have his number, and of course Etta's phone had died; and yes, I was sure I could have waited for Archer, but that would have made me seem inept, too needy.

Luckily, we happened upon one of those blessed, spectacular New York unicorn moments because there was a taxi with its light on, idling at the corner of the street. I walked Etta over to it and tugged open the door. The driver took one look at her, her body bent at the torso like the wilted stem of a rose. "Oh, no, no," he said, flailing his hands. "Not in my car."

"She's fine," I told him, practically folding her into the back-seat myself.

"She's too drunk!" he said.

Etta seized several one-hundred-dollar bills from her purse and stuffed them through the opening in the glass partition.

The driver and I stared at one another, silent, on the verge of détente, I could feel it.

I spoke firmly. "It's just. Food poisoning."

Money talks, I reminded myself, as we sped down the West Side Highway, the June air coursing through the window, "Iris" by the Goo Goo Dolls on the radio. So melancholy, I thought, it was almost comical.

When we swerved toward the exit and our bodies pulled sharply to one side, Etta rolled over to face me. There was dried vomit on her dress, a last-minute *Oops, I'm going to be sick*, when I'd thought we were in the clear.

"Please stay in my apartment," she said.

"Of course, I'm not going to leave you like this—" I yelled so the driver would hear me "—with *food poisoning*."

She shook her head. "No. When I leave."

Play house, Lizzie had said. What was stopping me? Certainly not my new roommate; I barely knew him.

"Okay," I said, and she squeezed my hand twice, smiling as she shut her eyes.

10

Being in Etta's apartment felt illicit, as if I'd broken into some- one's home. No matter that I'd spent so many nights here over the years, revelatory Saturday evenings bleeding into hungover Sundays, passed out on the sofa, the sunlight stinging our red eyes until Etta clicked the remote to lower the blinds, shroud- ing us in darkness. It didn't matter because I'd never been there alone.

The first night I found myself tiptoeing, especially gentle with doorknobs and glassware, taking extra care to shut cabinets softly. I was scared of breaking things: the dishwasher, the sink, the garbage disposal, the refrigerator waterspout. The espresso machine with all its fancy levers and which I didn't know how to use without Etta's help. But eventually, the fear was replaced with something like curiosity.

Toward the end of my first week there, I pushed open the door to Etta's bedroom; the blackout shades were drawn so the space was pitch-black apart from a single shard of light stretching across the room from the hall. You could just make out Etta's king-size bed, its fluffy white linens, her dresser, her desk that she never sat at. I tiptoed inside; the room was cold, or maybe I was cold, I couldn't tell. I texted her, **Miss you, so weird being here without you!** It was 9 p.m. in New York, which meant it was the middle of the night in Barcelona. I didn't know if she would be awake, but I stared at my phone, willing a response. A minute passed and I saw the three dots appear and disappear in our thread of messages. She was typing, and then she wasn't.

I followed the sliver of light to her bedside table, where there was a bouquet of hot-pink ranunculus in a porcelain vase. They were dead now, the flowers wilted, practically rotted. Beside the vase was a note printed on a plain white square of paper. I flicked on the bedside lamp, and read the barely legible scrawl: *To your next adventure. Proud of you. Love, Archer.*

I eyed my phone again, its blank screen, still no word from Etta since she'd left. She'd asked me to stay here, and I agreed, and she hadn't even bothered to check in? Of course, she could have been busy, but she was still active on Instagram, still posting, still updating her followers on her evolving life; and her followers were growing, an anonymous army eager to know what she was up to.

Meanwhile, I was eager to get to work in the mornings, practically rushing out the door, even as summer temperatures swelled and I'd emerge from the depths of the subway practically drenched in sweat, my clothes sticking to me, my hair sticking to the back of my neck, my arms sticking to the arms of strangers as we made our way into the sunlight like a hive of bees. Work suddenly seemed like a blessing, where I would at least be with Jeff, my days a familiar pattern. It was the evenings when I didn't have plans—and that was most—that Etta's absence was magnified. No one to talk to, no one to entertain but my own thoughts.

It was at this point that I remembered Archer's business card, his number etched into thick cardstock. I located the number in my list of contacts—I hadn't remembered adding it; maybe I'd done so at Astrid's, just in case I lost the card. Just in case he meant it when he suggested I stop by for a tour.

Just in case.

Perhaps it was bold to ring his assistant at such an ungodly hour, but when she answered, I was reassured of the fact that those with "cool" jobs were almost always on call. Her tone was clipped, self-important, but it helped once I explained who I was, that I was Etta's friend, the connection a guaranteed in.

"And what is this in regards to?" she asked.

"Oh," I said. I hadn't gotten that far. "Archer and I were chatting at Astrid's place over the weekend—" she made an audible "ah" sound and I knew I really had her attention "—and he suggested I stop by the gallery for a tour?"

"He did," she said flatly.

"Yeah. Since the opening was so hectic."

"Hmm," she said. I considered if this was a line of Archer's, something he did often, doling out his card to a flock of women, offering tours like free candy, if his assistant was rolling her eyes right now. But then she added, "His calendar looks clear next weekend," and my stomach flipped.

"It is?" I asked. I cleared my throat, tried again. "It is."

"Yep. You're in luck. Next Saturday at noon work?"

Saturday at noon. A time and date made it real.

"Perfect," I said. "Thank you."

"Awesome," she told me. "I'll let him know."

When we hung up, I backed out of Etta's room, gently closed the door, left the flowers untouched.

I would still sleep in the guest room.

11

I was supposed to meet Archer at noon, and it was 11:15. My clothes were in a pile on the floor, suddenly every mediocre dress, skirt, and pair of pants all wrong for the occasion. Jeans seemed too casual, thoughtless, and all my blouses too prim, corporate, frumpy. I could wear a sundress, but that seemed juvenile. We weren't at the beach. I knew I was overthinking it, but it didn't matter—my thoughts made tracks of their own, and I couldn't outrun them.

But then, another thought: I pried open the door to Etta's bedroom. She had shipped most of her summer wardrobe to Barcelona: her shoes, blazers, pants, dresses, skirts, handbags, all of it gone. But in the walk-in closet, several items remained. My fingers grazed silk blouses and buttery leather skirts and a shelf of baby cashmere sweaters. Palazzo pants made of expensive Italian linen and the lapels of soft suede jackets. My phone buzzed in my pocket as I skimmed a pale blue knit minidress and entertained the faint hope that it could be Etta, reaching out, bridging the lapse in contact. She hadn't responded to my last message, my admission that I missed her either a text she had forgotten to answer, or a sentiment she didn't share.

I fished my phone from my pocket. It was Jeff. He was hungover and bored, and what was I up to?

"I'm going on a date, actually," I said.

He perked up. "An app date?"

"No," I said. "I met him at that art opening I told you about?"

Jeff cooed. "Oh, an organic meeting. We love to see it," and I laughed. "So how is living at Etta's?" he asked.

I'd wanted to say, *Fine, currently exploring her closet*, but refrained.

"Well, I don't live there. I'm *staying* there."

"Mmm, sure," Jeff said.

"But yeah, it's good. It's only been a few days."

"And the new roommate isn't annoyed?"

"Why would he be annoyed?" I asked, but I heard it, the defensiveness in my voice. "He'll have the whole place to himself at half the price. And I gave him my bedroom."

"You *gave* him your *bedroom*?"

"I mean, it makes sense, if I'm not living there. His room is a closet, and he's a big guy!" I tried to laugh it off, but Jeff was quiet.

"I have to go," I said finally. "I'm running late."

"Okay," he said. "Have fun on your little date."

"Thanks," I told him, then hung up and checked my Instagram, a nasty reflex. Etta had posted minutes earlier: "New digs," read the caption, accompanying the view from what I presumed to be the balcony of her apartment. Crystal-blue skies, not a single cloud, the roof of a coral-hued building across the street. I clicked to share a comment, but couldn't decide what to say, every word and emoji forced and fake.

I was about to leave the closet—there was nothing here for me anyway and I really was running late now—when in the far back, I saw it: a pristine linen jumpsuit the color of champagne.

I pressed it to my body and studied myself in the full-length mirror, then stepped into it. Etta was taller than me by a few inches, so the pants slouched in a puddle around my feet, but it was nothing a little heeled sandal couldn't fix.

Etta had taught me to appreciate nice things, to notice what was real or simply a cheap imitation, and so I smiled at my reflection. She would have been proud.

12

The door to the gallery was locked and I had to ring the bell. A snippy voice chirped through the intercom.

"It's Ren," I said. "I'm here for a tour with Archer?"

The voice was annoyed. "One second," it said. The line went static, then dead. A short, slender man in a black turtleneck—but it was June?—and capris unlocked the door, gave me the up-down, pointed to a white plastic-looking chair in the corner nearest the reception desk and ordered me to "Wait there."

And so I waited. I waited for five minutes. Ten became fifteen, then twenty-five. The man forgot I existed; his fingers clacked on a keyboard, his black spiked hair crowning behind the computer monitor.

"Archer is running late," he said eventually.

"Okay," I said. That much I'd figured.

"He should be here in—" he again glanced at his screen and back to me "—ten minutes."

"Great," I said, but I thought, *That's ten minutes too many; ten more minutes of anticipation.*

My palms slicked with sweat, I checked my phone, but there were no new messages. I opened Instagram: another post from Etta. She wore a billowing floral dress, gazing up at the bluebird sky on a wide, tree-lined street. *Rambling on La Rambla*, said the caption. The photo had almost four hundred likes in one hour and a bevy of comments, many of which she had responded to, and still, she had yet to answer me, to make contact.

I read some of the comments: *Pretty lady xx*, wrote someone named Jane Chen.

Jane Chen? As in, Archer's girlfriend? I clicked her Instagram handle—definitely Archer's girlfriend—but the page was private.

"Hey, Ren," a voice said.

Archer. He was standing in front of me.

"Sorry I'm late." He wrung a baseball cap in his hands, and his blue T-shirt was damp. Was it raining?

I bolted up from my seat. "It's okay. I was just catching up on email."

He walked toward the front desk, spoke to the man behind it, then to me said, "I took the 1 Train from Brooklyn and it stalled underground. Signal delays."

"So annoying," I said.

He rifled through a thin stack of papers on the desk, but said nothing else.

The gallery was one large room, more expansive, emptier, hollower without people to fill it like at the party two weeks ago. There was no music, no ambiance. It was funny how all those details could distract you, and when they were missing, how your interactions, your flaws, were magnified. Our footsteps echoed as Archer led me to the back, gesticulating. He was saying something about surrealism and Cubism, and I was nodding, as if I understood, but all I could focus on was the fact that he was wearing a T-shirt and khakis and Nike sneakers, and I looked like I was trying to cut the line at 1 OAK. As we crossed the space, toward an especially imposing canvas on the back wall, I heard the clacking of my heels against the floor, reminding me of women at job interviews, how you could clock their presence, how badly they wanted something, by the sounds of their stilettos.

"So," Archer said. He turned to me, clapping his hands. "Which is your favorite?"

"Sorry?" I asked.

"Do you have a favorite?"

I'd spent all last night googling Archer, educating myself on his inspirations—Pollock, of course, that I knew, also Rothko—but I hadn't anticipated this question. I felt my throat constrict and pointed vaguely to the canvas behind his head. "I did like that one a lot, at the opening."

Silence. Had I said the wrong thing?

After a moment I got an "Interesting."

Interesting? We moved closer to it. Splatters of dark blue and gray paint bled out at the edges, thick like string, and in the middle, a dense concentration of gray congealed like a bird's nest.

He swiveled toward me. "Why this one?"

I hugged my purse to my chest. "It seems sort of…ominous."

Archer raised a single eyebrow. "Ominous."

"Yes," I said, though I wasn't sure what I was getting at, and more so, what I had hoped to accomplish in coming here. I was in over my head. The internet had not given me the crash course on art I'd needed. I could talk Kafka and Wharton, but *art?* What was I thinking?

It was as if Archer had read my mind when he asked, "What are we really doing here?"

I blinked, a deer in headlights. "What?"

"What. Are we really. Doing here?"

"Um, you told Astrid to give me your card. To call if I wanted a tour. So I called." I chuckled nervously, waited for him to say something, but he didn't. I went on: "And I wanted to see your work. I mean, it's been a while." *It's been a while?* Was this an obligation to him? Had he been drunk or on something else when he directed Astrid to give me his card? Had he regretted it? I wished a sinkhole would open beneath me, swallow me whole.

"I think you know why you're here," he said. Why did he sound so calm?

"You do?"

"I remember what you said." A pause. "At my parents' house."

"Oh?" I really had no idea.

"You said you were a writer."

I started to laugh, shook my head. I could see the confusion splinter across his face. Playing with the chain on my purse, eyes burrowing into the floor, I said, "I mean, yeah, I *like* to write, but..." I stopped. The way he was looking at me now, as if I'd disappointed him. That the person he wanted me to be had fallen drastically short of expectation. I attempted a laugh again. "I don't know, I think I drank too much wine that night."

"Ren," he said, more firmly. "If you like to write, then that makes you a writer. It's relatively simple."

I nodded, too embarrassed for words.

He stepped closer. "I'm trying to be a friend. Maybe you can get something out of this."

What was *this*?

"If you want something, it helps to be near whatever it is you want."

I could see the stubble on his chin, the five-o'clock shadow. I told myself to breathe.

"Meaning if I'm around art," I said, slowly, carefully, avoiding his gaze, "I might feel inspired? Maybe I'll write more?"

"*Other* art," he said. "Writing is art, too."

"Right." I thought longingly of the sinkhole again, an instant escape route.

He shrugged. "At least that's the hope. I mean, it helps me. Even just being out in the world, noticing things, experiencing them—" he clapped his hands again and I jumped "—it gets me unstuck. It's why I gave you my card in the first place."

"It is," I said, flatly, but he said, "Do you think we should leave?" It wasn't a question as much as a declaration.

He looked over his shoulder, where desk man scrolled through his phone, oblivious.

"I'll do whatever," I said, and wasn't that the truth?

Archer rested his hand on my lower back, just like he did at Astrid's party, and again I held my breath.

"Let's go," he said, and I let him lead.

We walked around Chelsea, past the slew of other galleries, priceless art hidden behind glass doors. The streets were mostly empty this time of year, apart from the occasional pack of tourists searching for the High Line or a table at Cookshop. After eleven blocks, the humidity suffocating, Archer suggested we dip into a bar for "a beer and some AC," a dive where Chelsea met the West Village.

We sat on two stools at the bar. A jukebox in the corner blared Van Halen's "Dance the Night Away." It was just after two o'clock. An older woman with blond hair like an imitation Farrah Fawcett took our orders; Archer asked for a Guinness and I said, "Same," though I didn't think I liked Guinness. I drank it anyway.

Once she delivered the beers and floated away, he shifted in his seat. "So you live in the East Village."

I nodded. "But I'm staying at Etta's for now."

"Oh?" he said. Apparently he didn't know.

"Only while she's away."

"She asked you to stay there?"

"Yes," I said. "Why, is that weird?"

Archer winced. "Not weird, just… You want to live there?"

I thought of my new roommate, Abdul, how I hadn't heard

from him since I'd left. How I'd showed off the apartment, made a song and dance of the skyline view from the living room, how the light changed outside, reassured him that it wasn't always so noisy. Maybe he was happier without me there, viewed my absence as a gift. It kind of was.

"*Living* sounds very permanent," I said.

"You know what I mean."

"Well, it was nice of her to offer me the apartment. I think she hated the thought of it being empty, and I guess this whole moving thing has been hard on her. Like you said."

Archer rolled his pint glass between his hands. "Etta hates change. She also hates being told what to do." He shot me a side glance and I thought of the hot-pink ranunculus on her bed-side table, the handwritten note. They had their differences, but they were still blood.

"Have you spoken with her?" I asked.

He shook his head. "No, but we don't necessarily have that sort of relationship." He mimed texting, and I offered a laugh. "You have siblings?" he asked.

"A sister."

"Oh, yes. You mentioned at dinner. And you're...close? Not close?"

"Not close, sadly."

Archer nodded. "Does she know you're here?"

"Who? My sister?"

"No, Etta."

"No, no," I was quick to say, then for emphasis, a more firm "No. That would require her to answer my texts."

He laughed, throwing back his head. He angled his body toward mine. "You're allowed to have your own life, you know." He smirked, took a long pull from his beer.

"I do have my own life?"

Did I? "Etta's off in Europe, you're here. Don't worry if she isn't *answering* your texts. You're doing your own thing."

My own thing. Getting drinks with Etta's brother didn't exactly scream "independence."

"Right," I said. The Van Halen song had since ended and the jukebox hummed something by Simon & Garfunkel.

"So what made you move to New York?" he asked.

"School," I told him. "You grew up here, right?" I already knew the answer, but I was trying to reciprocate his questions. Archer and Etta, born and raised. Autumns in the city and summers in the Hamptons and winters split between Telluride and Anguilla.

"Born and raised," he said. "Your parents still in Connecticut?"

A bill of questions he already knew the answers to, I was sure—I'd divulged all these details at dinner—but perhaps we had nothing of real substance to discuss, and small talk was at least easy. I could have responded yes and dropped it, or drew a picture of normalcy as inspired by the scenes of my early childhood—Dad, Mom, baby sister, and me, trips to the beach and homemade waffles on Saturday mornings—but that seemed exhausting. And the Guinness was going to my head. And maybe, I wasn't sure, I wanted to tell him the truth.

I sipped my beer. "My dad is. My mom actually left when I was in high school."

He didn't break eye contact. "I'm sorry."

"It's fine, I don't really talk about it."

"Well, do you want to talk about it? We can, but I get if it's too personal."

It was, of course, too personal, but I went on to explain the details, adding a well-timed laugh every now and then so he didn't think I was trying to earn his pity, not dwelling too much on the fact that I still lacked the answers to this open-ended plot twist that had derailed a part of my life. How the summer entering my junior year of high school, when I'd returned home from a weekend in Rhode Island, Dad announced that Mom wasn't home, that she probably wouldn't be coming back. How I'd showered and combed my hair and made dinner and only when I marched into their bedroom to ask a question, realized she wasn't there. That when you called her cell phone an operator said, "This number has been disconnected," and that no matter how much I tried, or didn't, I would never be able to reach her.

"Damn," Archer said, and I shrugged, self-conscious that I'd overshared. "So I take it that you still don't know where she is."

I attempted to make light of the situation. "Nope. It's like a...soap opera, or something."

"And what does your dad do?"

I said he worked as a contractor, but left out the part where he built McMansions in what Etta had once described as "nouveau developments."

Archer asked if we were close.

"Not really."

"Well, I'm sure things got complicated, with your mom leaving? The dynamic changing?"

The bartender was cleaning glasses and I got the sense she was eavesdropping.

"He's just very... He hates New York, so he doesn't like to visit, and I don't go home a lot. But I'm fine. I have my life here, my *own* life—" I smirked "—and my job and..." I sensed I was rambling, or revealing too much, and slowed down. "It's really not that significant. No one died. No one... I mean, then there's the opioid crisis. That is serious."

"You're comparing this to the opioid crisis."

"Well, not comparing. But my point is—it could be worse."

He frowned. "I think you're discrediting your own experience, Ren."

I studied a half-empty bottle of Hendrick's on the bar shelf. "I don't want you to feel sorry for me."

"I never said I felt sorry for you?"

I wanted to say, *You don't have to; it's written all over your face.*

"It could be worse," I said again, but he became more animated now. I noticed a flush had blossomed in the apples of his cheeks, that he was the sort of attractive that bordered on wasteful because he seemed so unaware of it. Or if he was aware, he knew how to play it. I wasn't sure.

"But if we're being optimistic—" he pressed his elbows into the bar "—it is nice, how you're only accountable to yourself."

"What do you mean *accountable to myself*?"

"All I mean is family can be controlling."

I knew this, subliminally, about Etta's parents, and I recognized it in Etta, too, the genetics of character, but I wasn't sure why I'd imagined Archer to be impervious to it. Maybe because I'd only ever heard Etta's narrative, the carefully curated one emphasizing his perfection.

Archer's phone vibrated on the bar. He looked at it and groaned. "Sorry, I have to take this," he said. He answered the call and ducked outside.

I checked my own phone and saw that Abdul had texted me: a photo of what appeared to be the bathroom of the East Village apartment, the ceiling having split open so that plaster and bits of paint covered the tub and tile floor, like rubble after a natural disaster. Slight issue, the message read in reference to the eviscerated ceiling. Another message: I am not hurt, by the way, I was in the other room, but scary!!! I started to draft a response when Etta's name punctuated my screen. I picked up without thinking. "Hi, stranger," Etta said.

"Good," I said, and we both laughed. She hadn't asked how I was. "How are you?" I asked then.

"Wait, what?" Etta yelled.

"I said, 'How are you?'"

"Where are you?" she asked. "I can't hear."

I pressed the phone to my ear. "Sorry, sorry. Is this better?"

"Not really. There's like a weird echo and…music? Are you at a concert or something?"

I turned toward the jukebox, the song selection having since entered heavy metal territory. In the window, Archer paced outside, on the phone. "I'm waiting for Jeff," I lied.

"Where? In the bowels of hell?"

"No," I laughed. "At a bar in his neighborhood. He's having boy problems."

Etta didn't respond to that, simply said, "I'm going out tonight with some friends from school, so I'll get the chance to scope out the cool places for when you come visit. And my parents' friends are hosting me for dinner tomorrow. They live outside the city, so they're sending a car to pick me up."

"How nice," I said, but I was really thinking, *Of course.* It was exactly as I'd predicted—Etta slotting herself into a new life with relative ease. It was why I hadn't heard from her until now. "I've missed you," I told her.

"What?" she asked, yelling again. "Ren, I cannot hear you."

The door opened. Archer walked toward me, and I told Etta I had to go, though I wasn't positive she'd heard me, perhaps owing the end of our call to a bad connection and nothing more.

As Archer sank into the bar stool beside me, he sulked into his glass.

"Is everything okay?" I asked.

He didn't look at me. "*The New Yorker* published their review. *Artforum*, too."

"Of your show?"

"Yep." I intuited his curtness as a sign that the reviews were not favorable. "Sometimes it's hard to…" He trailed off. "You know, it reminds me why I took time away. How can these 'critics' assess anything when they've never, not once, tried making art themselves?" He shook his head. "Doesn't seem right."

All I could say was, "I'm sorry."

He went on: "There are critics for everything these days, fashion and art and film and literature, but how can they conclude what's 'good' or 'bad' if they've never done it?" He swiveled in his stool, eyeing me expectantly. I told him I didn't know, but I also got the sense that what I said didn't necessarily matter. "It's like a critic turning her nose up at a film when she's never made one, never acted in one, never even been on a film set. Why does *she* get to have a say? That's what is messed up about the world, besides a lot of things—we look for validation from the wrong people, and then we act like their thoughts are the only ones that matter."

Gently, I said, "They're just opinions."

"Well, art is a canvas for *everyone's* opinions apparently." The bartender returned with Archer's second pint and collected his empty glass. "Lu?" he said. She spun around, flopped her palms onto the bar. Her skin was tanned and leathery, and there were wrinkles around her mouth, but her brown eyes were kind.

"I was waiting for a proper hello, Archer."

So they were acquainted.

"Lu, this is Ren. She's a friend of my sister's."

"Hi, sweetheart," Lu said. She turned to Archer. "What brings you in here on a day like this? Shouldn't you be outside?"

"You're shooing me away already?"

"Never shooing you." She pointed to the lone window. "But look at that sun! Why would you rot in here, by choice?"

Archer instead asked, "How are the boys?"

Lu's face lit up. "They're upstate with their dad for the weekend. I'm planning them a birthday party for when they're back. It's a surprise."

"A surprise," Archer said, smiling. "How old are they now?"

"Six."

"Wow."

"Yeah, our neighbor is letting us use their backyard. I'm making the cake, we'll order pizza, but the balloons you know, the, uh, the helium ones?" She looked at me. "The helium ones are *so expensive*. It's crazy, but—" she shrugged "—I guess I can get like, the regular kind. Kids don't really know the difference."

There was a lull in the conversation. Lu kept smiling, and Archer was watching her. He dug in his pocket, flipping through a wad of cash, almost effortlessly. All one-hundred-dollar bills. I lost count as he slipped at least five of the bills onto the table. He pressed them with his hand so they were flat against the bar, though still curling at the edges.

Lu's eyes went wide, and I wasn't sure what was happening. She nudged the money toward him. "I haven't even given you your bill yet," she said with a laugh, but Archer pushed the cash toward her.

"No, I know. This is for you."

The words seemed to clot in Lu's throat. "This is more than… more than the bill, Archer. I…"

"Take it. Please?" Archer said. "Really."

A moment of consideration. I could tell Lu wanted to take the money, and Archer nudged it toward her, again, for good measure, as if to say, *It's okay. I want you to have it.*

Lu accepted the cash. "Thanks, Archer." She whirled toward me. "I'll bring you both a shot on the house. Whiskey? You like whiskey?"

Archer gestured to me.

"Sure," I said.

Lu disappeared, and I whispered to Archer, "That was really nice of you."

"Her kids want helium balloons," he said softly. "She should be able to get them."

I studied Archer's profile and was overcome with unexpected emotion. I told him, for what it was worth, I really did like his show.

"You have any interest in becoming the art critic for *The Times*?"

"Sorry?" I asked.

He fumbled with his phone. "It was a joke."

"Oh," I said. "Well, I think you're brave to keep putting yourself out there."

He half smiled. "Brave or stupid?"

"Brave," I said, more definitively. "Braver than me. Than most people. I think that's why I'm afraid."

"Of what?"

"Writing. Rejection. Uncertainty. I don't know, PR is the easy choice because I can be detached. None of it really belongs to me. I guess a part of me likes getting up every day and knowing what's expected. It's just like, do your job. Don't screw up too badly. Be polite, be respectful."

"I would hate that," he said. "Someone else being in control."

Our eyes were locked, our knees touching underneath the bar.

"Well," he said, "I guess we all pay a price. I can control what I make, but not what people will think."

PART TWO

JULY

13

The Fourth of July came and went. I had no plans, no hours of my life lost in traffic en route to the Hamptons, or worse, standing on the LIRR, watching the retired frat bros drink their six-packs, the warm-up for a weekend spent at summer shares in Quogue and Montauk. Jeff invited me to Fire Island, but I passed, something about cramming into his cousin's friend's house not exactly appealing, and then it rained on the Fourth and the city fireworks were canceled. I hardly left the apartment except to get groceries, and was reminded of the fact that without Etta, I really was alone. I read Didion's essay "Goodbye to All That" three times and couldn't imagine the moment of arrival she described: falling out of love with New York, or knowing it was "entirely possible to stay too long at the Fair." I was still riding the carousel, I thought, and I wasn't ready to get off.

I hadn't heard from Archer. I wasn't sure why this shocked me—it happened all the time. He wasn't a stranger I'd met at a bar or another passing profile on an app, but he still probably wasn't thinking about me, and if he was, it was likely as a fleeting thought, a blurry image in the background.

Meanwhile, I decided to give Evan of the app-verse a try. Evan, who was twenty-eight and worked as an operations analyst at some midtier bank. Evan, who suggested we meet at Tacombi in Flatiron because it was near both our offices, except it wasn't near mine. Evan, with his thick, gelled hair like a helmet and who more resembled Ross Geller in person than a young Michael Corleone, as his profile had encouraged me to believe. Evan, who recommended we split a pitcher of sangria, and Evan, who after one too many drinks said he would fuck our waitress, on a dare of course. Evan, who claimed to be five-nine, but was definitely five-six when he stood to use the restroom. Evan, who told me I would make an "excellent trophy wife" and couldn't understand why I would find his comment sexist. Evan, who recalled the details of how he and his buddies got "so wasted" after their company holiday party, the drug dealer he had scored blow from outside a bar on Bowery and the freshman girl from Pace he brought home that night and later learned was an especially mature sixteen-year-old student at Chapin. And Evan, whom I still brought home to Etta's and who tried to kiss me, or whatever he thought kissing was, until I said I was going to be sick. Still, once he'd gone, I wished he had stayed, not because I liked him, but because I hated the sound of silence.

———

On the fifth, Jeff made me promise to get drinks with him after work. It was a no-frills pub near our office, frequented by finance guys in ill-fitting suits, a place Jeff wouldn't have been caught dead at under normal circumstances, but he said he needed a drink to calm his nerves before his date later that evening.

"We met over the weekend," Jeff said. "He does PR for Louis

Vuitton." He queued up a photo on Instagram and showed it to me. "Doesn't he look like Troye Sivan?"

He did not.

"I can definitely see that," I told him.

Jeff set his phone on the table. "So what are we drinking?"

"Ah, just water for now," I said, and when he fixed his death glare on me, I added, "Please."

"Seriously? What happened to solidarity?"

"I have a headache."

"You always have a headache."

"What? No, I don't," I said, but Jeff had already marched to the bar. When he came back, he stretched out his legs on his side of the booth. "Your *water*," he said, pushing my glass toward me.

"Thanks."

He twirled the straw in his drink. "I don't think we're getting dinner," he said, his eyes searching mine. "Does anyone get dinner on a first date anymore?"

"I don't think so. Well, Evan and I ate tacos but that doesn't count because…" I realized Jeff wasn't listening. "Forget it."

"Should we get an order of fries?" he asked.

"If you're hungry," I said.

Jeff peeked at his phone. "Hmm. He mentioned something about a cocktail bar? In SoHo?"

"You hate SoHo."

"Well, I think it's where he works? Or he lives down there?" I could tell Jeff liked this guy from how he intonated his sentences, posing them like questions, almost defensively. How his nerves perforated all his words, so that he didn't sound so self-assured anymore.

After a few minutes Jeff got up to use the restroom. There was a message from Archer on my phone. Archer, risen from the dead. What did he want? I'd stopped anticipating, stopped hoping for contact. I had given up, and now, here we were.

I opened the text: Hey what are you up to tonight? Sorry I've been off the grid.

Yes, he had been off the grid, but what was the subtext? Did Archer want to see me, tonight?

I strategized; Jeff would be meeting his date in an hour. I could see Archer after he left. I typed furiously: Hi, I'm just getting a drink with a friend near work.

The rolling ellipsis: Where's work?

Midtown, unfortunately lol

Too funny, I'm in Midtown. Where are you?

He was in Midtown? Voluntarily? Jeff reappeared, slipping into his side of the booth. I was still staring at my phone. I responded to Archer with the location of the bar. Should be done here soon, I wrote.

"Oh! Fuck *me*!" Jeff said.

"What?"

He pouted, slid his phone across the table. "He just canceled."

"Ugh, I'm sorry, Jeff," I said, returning his phone to him. I didn't read their conversation.

"He said he's working late. He's definitely lying."

"Or he really is working late. We work late sometimes." Jeff shrugged and got up. "Where are you going?" I called after him.

He spun around. "To get another drink. And one for you, too, bitch. We're drinking tonight."

"Just one, Jeff!" I would play the desired solidarity card for a minute. If I stuck around for another round, I could be a little late to meet Archer and at least pleasantly buzzed.

Except then Archer texted, I'll be there soon, and it was too late to reply with *No please don't*, and that was how Archer, Jeff, and I wound up crammed into a booth in a shitty Midtown bar on a Wednesday night sharing an order of fries.

"What are you drinking?" Archer asked when he arrived.

Jeff watched as I said, "Gin and tonic," and I sucked down the rest of my drink through a straw.

Archer turned to Jeff. "I'm fine," Jeff said, but when Archer departed for the bar, Jeff leaned across the table and whispered, "So *now* you're drinking?"

"Well, I was going to meet Archer anyway."

Jeff saw right through me. He always did. "Were you just waiting for me to leave?"

"No," I said. Yes.

He leaned even closer, a wild smirk spreading across his face. "You texted him."

"No," I whispered, glancing over my shoulder at Archer, who was thankfully oblivious to this conversation.

"You are a liar."

"No, Jeff. He just texted *me*." I shoved my phone in his face, as if to say, *See?*

Jeff scoffed. "*Off the grid?* Where was he?"

"I don't know, Jeff. Maybe he's been busy."

"Classic," Jeff said, slinging his eyes to Archer, who was paying at the bar. "I can't believe you went out with Etta's brother."

"As friends," I said, but I thought of Jane and wondered if she would find *as friends* a convincing argument.

"Okay," Jeff said. "Sure."

Archer was approaching our booth.

"Jeff, please," I whispered. "Don't make this weird."

As Archer set two G&Ts on the table, Jeff beamed at him, and my heart raced.

We toyed with proper introductions first: "Archer, this is Jeff, by the way. We work together," I said, and Jeff asked, "So what brings you to Midtown?" as if it were no-man's-land, and Archer said, "I met with a client for dinner."

Jeff said, "Well, we work in the area."

Archer caught my eye as I sipped my drink, letting the gin rinse my throat.

"I think Ren has mentioned that," he said, and I added, "Yeah, our office is only a few blocks away."

"Midtown is a disaster," Archer said.

Jeff laughed. "Really? I rather enjoy it." My face said, *What the fuck?* but he'd already moved on. "So," he continued, "Ren tells me you're an artist?"

"I am. A painter, mostly."

"Mostly?" Jeff brought the straw to his lips and drank.

"I mean, I've done some sculpture, but painting is my main medium."

Jeff said, "Ah," and I was suddenly incapable of speaking.

"And you were off the grid, Ren says?"

I wanted to kill him. In cold blood. Right now. I kicked him under the table, but he did not react.

"Yes," Archer said, coolly. "In Mykonos, funnily enough."

Funnily enough. I laughed on cue. "Mykonos!" I said.

"Vacationing?" Jeff asked.

My eyes flitted between the two of them as Archer rattled the ice in his glass. "You could say that," he said.

"So you were working," Jeff said. Would he quit the interrogation already?

"I'm always working. Even when I'm not in my studio—" he pointed at his head "—I'm working things out up here."

The lights dimmed and a group of middle-aged men in suits flooded through the front doors. They smacked their briefcases onto the leather bar stools and promptly loosened their ties.

I focused on Jeff, still swirling that straw, as if trying to glean the missing context, though there was none. When Archer dipped out of the booth, I felt myself turning to him, expectant, as if to ask, *Where are you going?* and *Will you come back?*

But he announced, "I'm going to find the restroom. Please excuse me."

I smiled. "Okay," I said, as the smile, my performance, melted off my face. "What the actual fucking fuck, Jeff? *Off the grid?* You made me look like a stalker!"

Jeff craned his neck, following Archer across the room. "I don't like him," he said.

"You don't like anyone." I chomped on a mouthful of ice.

"No, Ren, you don't see it?"

"See what?"

"He's kind of...cagey."

"*Cagey?* No, Jeff. He's..." I stared down the length of the bar. Archer was waiting for the restroom in the back. "He's probably upset about his reviews."

Jeff seemed unconvinced. "Still?"

"Of course, still. It's not...it's not something he can brush off so easily. His work is his life."

"Our work is kind of our life," he said.

"It's different. His work is so personal. He said it's like baring his soul."

Jeff pretended to gag. "He did *not* say that."

"Yes," I hissed. "He did."

"So he loves himself."

"What? No. I think he just takes a lot of pride in what he does. And he should—it's brave." I could tell Jeff thought I was drinking the Kool-Aid. Maybe I was, but I couldn't stop. I wanted to be right.

"I don't know, what's so great about him? Besides the fact that his parents are rich?"

"That's crass."

"Like you care."

"What does that mean?"

"You're living at Etta's. You're not precious about any of this."

What was Jeff saying? "You think Etta buys me, don't you." Jeff was silent.

"I'm not like that. You *know* I'm not like that."

"Okay," Jeff said, the sarcasm gone from his voice. "Okay, I'm sorry."

As I finished the rest of my drink, one of the older men from the corporate group at the bar migrated to our booth. He placed his hands on the table—a gold band on a swollen ring finger—and in a thick, booming voice, said, "Fuck, marry, kill: Tom Cruise, Donald Trump, or Bill Clinton."

Jeff and I said nothing, avoiding eye contact, hoping our silence would send him away.

"So?" the man asked. "Thoughts?"

"I think we're good," Jeff chirped, but the man said, "I wasn't asking you," and he wasn't. He was looking only at me.

"We're fine," I said.

"So that's a no," he slurred.

I peered up at him, noticed his jowls, the spot where he'd no doubt nicked himself shaving, the sweat glistening on his forehead. I wanted to know if he had daughters, how he might have felt if someone had leered at them like he was leering at me.

"Yes," I said, my voice calm, too kind. "I mean, we're okay for now. But thanks."

He crossed his arms, resting them above his gut. "We just wanted to include you in our game. You aren't being very nice."

"I'm sorry. We're just in the middle of something right now." I smiled at him through tightly closed lips, but the guy didn't budge.

"Ah, see that?" He inched closer. "When you smile, how much prettier you look?"

Fuck you, I thought. If I was brave, or perhaps more chaotic, I would have given him the finger, but I waited it out, still with that same smile, like I was taught, like a good girl.

And it worked: another moment of ignoring him, his agitation bearing down on us. He seemed to get the picture. "Bitch," he mumbled, and walked away.

Archer returned from the bathroom but did not sit back down, skating a hand across the top of the booth, behind my head. He was going to tell me he was leaving, he had to take a call or make a call or Paul was outside to shuttle him to Brooklyn, or he had to paint—"Inspiration just hit me over the head like an anvil!"—or Astrid called, I didn't know, and I'd be stuck here, in Midtown with Jeff, riding the wrong carousel.

But Jeff stood. "I'm gonna get going," he said.

Suddenly, I couldn't stomach the idea that Jeff might be mad at me. "Is everything okay?" I asked.

He slung his bag over his shoulder. "I'm meeting friends in Brooklyn," he said. "Why? You wanna come?"

Archer scrolled through his phone, offering minimal acknowledgment, and Jeff searched my face, reassuring that the opportunity still belonged to me: I could come, too. I could leave, now. He was giving me that.

Instead I said, "I'm good, you have fun."

When Jeff left, Archer lowered himself next to me, pressing his knees against mine, and I thought, *I guess we are staying, then.*

His eyes fell to my empty glass. "Should we have another?" he asked.

"Sure," I said, but I was distracted; Jeff had won. He'd gotten in my head.

Archer said, "Only if you want. No pressure."

I picked at a wood chip on the table. "Yeah, we can stay, whatever works."

"So you work with him? Jeff?"

I glanced out the window, but Jeff was gone. "Yeah. For the last five years. We joke that we're trauma-bonded."

"I like him. He's an interesting character."

Archer's approval relaxed me. "He used to be a child actor."

"It all makes sense now." A pause. "I was wondering, though, how he knew about my being off the grid?" He cocked his brow and I winced.

"Sorry, yeah. He was...going through my phone. My messages."

"You allow him to do that?" Archer asked, but his tone was more impressed than judgmental.

"Sometimes, I don't know. He just like, takes it." I couldn't admit that I'd shown him voluntarily.

"So you were talking about me?" he asked.

"Well, not 'talking, talking,' but...yeah, you came up."

"What else came up?"

I could have invented a stock response, offered a litany of unimportant topics, like Jeff's canceled date, some anecdotes about work, the stress of it all.

"Just that I hadn't heard from you. And I wasn't sure why."

He tilted his head, not missing a beat. "Yeah, I am sorry about that. Work's been a lot. That's why I went to Mykonos. Needed to decompress. Poor me. Sorry. That sounds awful."

"No, not awful," I said. "Sometimes, you need to forget about life."

Archer nodded, his eyes tracing mine. "Yes, exactly."

At the bar, I caught the man we'd rejected from our booth earlier sneering at us, and I refocused on Archer. "Hey, want to play a game?" I asked.

"I like games," Archer said.

I popped an ice cube in my mouth. "Fuck, marry, kill."

———

An hour later Archer walked me home. Well, he paid for a cab, no Paul tonight, I guessed, and we got out near King Street because Archer said it was too nice of a night not to walk. It was warm but not humid, "a unicorn summer night," I noted, and he laughed.

We strolled the rest of the way to Etta's. He told me about new paintings he was working on, that he wasn't going to let the reviews affect him so much. Also, that a friend of his was the assistant DP on a David Lynch film in Morocco; he was maybe going to visit him in the fall, that he'd never been and visiting new places always helped his work.

I nodded, kept nodding as if my life depended on it. Occasionally our hands would brush and neither of us pulled away, but he never bridged the gap, either. No lines were crossed. I wondered again about Jane. What their relationship was like, whether she cared that Archer and I were "hanging out." Were we hanging out? Maybe he didn't see it that way.

After a half hour we found ourselves in front of Etta's building. I thought about the man in the bar, how I could have reacted differently, more boldly, and if this aspirational version of myself were resurrected right now, how she might behave. She would invite Archer upstairs, mix a mean martini, or possess impressive knowledge of Spanish wines all in the name of practiced seduction. But I wasn't that girl, because that girl already existed, and currently she lived in Barcelona.

Archer turned to me. "This was fun," he said. "Let's talk soon?"

I watched him go, my eyes trailing his figure north, toward Chelsea, or the West Village, or wherever it was he was headed, I didn't know, because he didn't tell me. Even once I lost sight of him, I stood there, stunned into stillness, and surveyed the passing cars, their golden headlights swimming in the cool dark, fantasizing that he would come back and say he had forgotten something.

14

"Did you hear about Archer's reviews?" Etta asked the next day.

It was after work, and I had been sitting on the sofa in her living room, picking my cuticles. It was the first time we'd spoken since our stunted conversation weekends ago, which made me feel both unimportant and elated to hear from her again.

"No," I said, too quickly. "Why? Are they okay?"

She sucked at her teeth. "Not exactly."

"Oh, no," I said, and listened as she explained the details I already knew, pretending it was the first time I'd heard. "How is Archer handling it?" I asked.

"Fine, I think. He just got back from Mykonos."

I almost said, *Oh, yeah, I heard*, then caught myself. "That's nice. On vacation?"

"He goes every year with some of his artist-y friends. They stay on a boat and do like, mushrooms."

"Interesting."

"I really have to call him," Etta said. "I haven't been a very nice sister lately."

I thought of the flowers in Etta's bedroom and wondered if I should throw them out.

"Well, you've been busy, right? Adjusting? I mean, I haven't heard much from you." I added a laugh so she didn't think I was hurt, but Etta didn't bite.

"Ah, I don't know. He's got a lot of things going on at the moment. I want to make sure he feels supported. My therapist and I talked about it. Have you seen Archer at all?"

I swallowed, was about to respond, *A little, here and there*, but when the words materialized, they were a resounding "No. Not since you left."

"Oh, was just curious," she said. "I told him to look after you."

A sinking sensation, like rocks tumbling off a cliff and into a pit. That pit was my stomach.

"You did?" I asked.

"Yes. I figured if you need anything or whatever, it's nice to know he's around. Someone you can call?"

"Thanks," I said. "I appreciate that."

"All right," Etta said, "well, I'm going to try to sleep."

"Oh, okay." I'd be lying if I said I wasn't relieved.

She yawned. "Sleep tight. I love you."

"Love you, too," I said, but the line was already dead.

———

I invited Jeff over later that week, an overdue apology, an "I'm sorry I left you in Midtown for Archer" gesture of goodwill. As the elevator doors to Etta's apartment parted, the entrance flooded by golden light through the living room windows, he said nothing. I set my purse on the counter, watching as he walked in circles.

"You live here," he finally said, as if stunned by this fact.

"Well, technically."

"You. Live. Here." He spun around to face me, his mouth weaving into a smile.

We ate sushi and split a bottle of white wine, *The Real House-wives* muted on the TV.

Jeff studied the label on the bottle. "Is it bad that I can't de-cide whether this is supposed to be good or not?"

"No, I can't tell, either," I said. "But I'm sure it is. I mean, Etta doesn't drink bad wine."

Jeff polished off his glass and leaned back against the sofa cush-ions, his gaze drawn to the windows. "I still think Etta's a bad person—" he turned to me "—and a brat, but..." He trailed off.

"But she means well."

Jeff relented. "Yeah, okay. Fine. It was nice of her to let you stay here. There, I said it."

"She can be really generous," I mused, and I remembered what she'd said about Archer on the phone, how she'd asked him to look after me.

Jeff stretched his arms above his head, taking stock of his sur-roundings. "This place is like, a *real* grown-up apartment," he said. "I mean, there's no Ikea in here."

I laughed. "You should see her closet."

I led him down the hall, past a slew of brightly colored paint-ings, each under an individual light, as if they belonged in a gallery, which they probably did, and pushed open the door to Etta's bedroom, then her walk-in closet.

Tall and thin like Etta, Jeff slipped on a sweater and skirt, wedging his feet into a pair of heeled Manolo sandals. "Holy shit!" he kept saying at his reflection in the full-length mirror.

"Be careful! Don't rip anything!" I tried to smile, tried to gently lift the sweater back over his head, but he skimmed past me, strut-ting across the length of her bedroom, toward the speaker, raising the volume so that Prince's "Let's Go Crazy" seemed to ricochet off the walls. "Jeff," I whined, but he was in bliss, twirling around, a silk Hermès scarf now coiled like a serpent around his neck. "I said you could *see* her closet, not try on everything! You're going to break her shoes."

"Babe," he said, "I think her feet are bigger than mine. I'm not going to break anything."

Still, I imagined Etta's reaction; she'd claim it was a breach of her trust; she didn't even know Jeff. That this was *her* bedroom, *her* apartment, where I was staying *for free*, and I'd have no argument to offer because she'd be absolutely right.

As the song ended, he flopped beside me onto Etta's bed, out of breath. I reached for the remote and lowered the volume.

"How much do you think her parents' art sells for?" Jeff asked.

"I don't know, a lot, I'm sure. Can you get changed now?"

Instead Jeff whipped out his phone. I should have known there would be a corresponding investigation. The image on his screen: sculpted hands protruding from an otherwise blank wall with tongues like Gene Simmons's sprouting from their palms. "Frieze LA," Jeff said.

"I don't like that one," I said. "It's creepy."

Next he showed me an image of a set of concentric circles set against a white background, their typical Venn diagram sketches. "Two million," he said, his voice eerily devoid of emotion. "Sold to some Swiss countess."

"Damn," I said.

Jeff tossed his phone across the duvet. "This shit is so tasteless, but people with money like it."

I shifted toward him so that I was propped up by my elbow. "Did you see that painting in the kitchen, though? Above the table?" Jeff shook his head. "It's a Picasso."

"Of course it is. Picasso and pancakes. Must be nice."

"Must be," I said. A shrill noise rang out and I jolted upright. "Do you hear that?" I asked.

Jeff's eyes fluttered shut. "Hear what?"

I killed the music and twisted toward the windows, but couldn't see past the blackout shades. "Listen. Is that rain?"

"I don't think so?" He made a face, as if straining to hear. "I think it's the buzzer."

I bolted up and out of the bedroom, down the hall. On the intercom, the doorman told me it was Archer, and could he come up?

Oh, the irony of Archer having to request permission to come up to his sister's apartment. Didn't he have access, or a key? Or had Etta sent him, like she'd mentioned on the phone, to check in on me? I scanned the apartment, the scraps from dinner in the living room, white sushi rice and a cube of avocado on the rug, empty takeout containers on the coffee table, the bottle of wine next to it, empty, two glasses.

"Yes," I said. "Of course."

Jeff had since emerged from Etta's bedroom, having wrapped the scarf around his head, tying it in a knot underneath his chin so that he looked like an old Hollywood film actress.

"What's going on?" he asked.

"Archer's coming up," I whispered.

"Now?"

"Yes, now."

I leapt across the living room, grabbed the wine bottle, our plates, scooped the food on the floor into my palm, threw the dishes into the sink, glasses in the dishwasher.

Jeff crossed his arms. "Did you know he was coming?"

"No," I said.

He laughed. "I don't believe you," he said, but I was too preoccupied searching for the recycling.

Jeff started to go off on a tangent and I spun toward him and said, "Jeff, sorry, but you can't be here right now." He gave me a look, his brown eyes shrinking, and I pointed to the hall. "Just go hide in Etta's bedroom. Please?"

A minute later the elevator doors opened: "Hello?" Archer asked.

I said I was in the kitchen, where I sat at the counter, staging the scene of a quiet evening: half-drunk glass of wine, Eve Babitz's *Sex and Rage* beside it. The image convinced that I was a respectable person, with respectable interests, and that my friend was not hiding in his sister's bedroom wearing her clothes.

When he saw me, he said, "I hope it's okay I'm here?" I told him of course it was. "I called," he said as he approached the counter, "but you didn't answer."

My phone, I thought. I hadn't looked at it in half an hour. The one time it mattered. "I'm sorry," I said. "I've been bad with my phone tonight."

He was beside me now, glancing over my shoulder. I felt his breath on my neck. He placed his hand on mine and there was a moment of hesitation, but then he shifted my hand so he could examine the book.

"*Sex and Rage?*" he asked.

"Eve Babitz," I said. "I really like her."

"I know Babitz." Of course he did. A vein pulsed in his forearm and I forced myself to look away. "What do you like about her?" he asked.

"She's a great writer."

"She's inconsistent. But I guess all artists are." Archer ambled around the kitchen until he arrived at the sink. He took a glass from the cabinet and filled it from the tap even though there was filtered water available from a spout on the refrigerator.

"I don't know," I said. "She doesn't really give a shit what other people think. She kind of does whatever she wants." As Archer drank, I thought I could make out a smile. "I admire that about her."

Archer nodded to himself and I realized I wanted him to say something, to agree. Perhaps we could discuss it further, and I could prove that sometimes, I actually knew what I was talking about.

He cleared his throat. "So I'm sorry to intrude."

I guessed that conversation was over. "You're not intruding," I said.

"But I stopped by because I need to pick up a painting. It sold today and I have to get it back to the studio."

"Oh," I said, and then registering the dejection in my voice, added, "Congratulations. That's exciting," and gulped my wine.

"Thanks," Archer said. "It's just in the hall, outside of Etta's bedroom. I'll be quick."

Etta's bedroom. He strode toward the opposite end of the apartment, past the living room to the wing of bedrooms, where Jeff was hiding.

"Let me help you!" I called after him, but he said, "It'll take two minutes. It'll be like I was never here."

I jogged after him, clipping his heels. "Are you sure?" I asked, eyeing the slightly open door to Etta's bedroom, envisioning all the clothes and shoes in puddles on the floor.

At the entrance to the wing, I could hear my heart beating in my ears.

"That's it, right there," he said, and when he continued down the hall, toward the painting, I shut Etta's bedroom door.

The painting was on the smaller side, larger than a foot but not comparable to a Pollock or most of the paintings at his show last month, which is to say, he did not need my help. It featured two orange-and-yellow rectangular shapes with blurred edges. I could guess that it was an oil. I looked on as he gripped either side, the muscles in his back flexing and releasing through his T-shirt as he dismounted it.

"That one looks different," I said, as I followed him into the foyer, "than your other ones, I mean," but he must not have heard me.

"Can I borrow a sheet?" he asked instead.

"A sheet?"

"Or a tarp? If you have? I forgot mine." I eyed him blankly. "A sheet is fine, actually," he said.

I rounded the corner, then returned with a pale gray fitted sheet from the linen closet.

He thanked me, loosely wrapping the painting in it. "All done," he said, pressing the down button next to the elevator, resting the painting against the wall. He clenched and unclenched his hand. "Sorry for the imposition. I'll let you get back to your reading."

I opened my mouth to respond, to say, "It wasn't an imposition," but the elevator arrived, so I said, "Have a good night," and began to walk away. I didn't need to internalize another image of him leaving, the rejection.

"Also, Ren?" he said then. He had propped the elevator open with his foot, the painting now tucked underneath his arm.

My eyes said, *Yes? What? Anything?* but my voice said, "Yep?"

"There's an art show in East Hampton this weekend, at my friend's gallery. I thought you might be interested." I nodded, not sure what he was getting at. "Anyway, the show is Saturday morning. If you can get there Friday, I'm having a small dinner. Paul can pick you up."

Paul can pick you up.

"That sounds fun," I said. Had Etta put him up to this, too?

The doors threatened to close and he pushed against them so they sprung open again. "Meaning that's a yes?"

He was inviting me to his family's house to attend an art show. Something told me this wasn't Etta's doing.

I nodded again before I was conscious of it. "Sorry, yeah. Yes."

After Archer left, I sank into the sofa, heard the door click open down the hall, the sound of footsteps. For a moment I'd forgotten Jeff was still here. He sat beside me, still in Etta's clothes, and crossed his legs at the ankle so I could see he hadn't taken off her shoes. I could predict his next words, his judgment; I didn't want to hear it, or explain. But as I turned to Jeff, I noticed that he was studying the floor and frowning, pointing at his foot, where the strap of Etta's sandal had snapped cleanly in half.

———

"I'm craving fried chicken," Natalie said at work the next day.

I glanced up from my computer monitor and realized she was speaking to me. I said, "That's funny," because it was such a specific request and I didn't know what else to say, but then she told me there was a cart serving fried chicken on the corner of Seventh and that we should go. *We*, as in *Natalie and I*, and apparently also, *We should go* now. At least it was a good opportunity to ask her about taking Friday off, or leaving early.

Natalie and I had never gotten lunch together. She usually ate alone in her office, in between calls and meetings, shoveling sad salads just like the rest of us. But at the chicken cart, she ordered a bucket, twelve pieces, "extra crispy, extra spicy," and when we sat at a bench near the entrance to our building, said, "Shoot, Ren—I forgot sauces!" So I scurried back to the cart and asked for ketchup, mustard, hot sauce.

I returned triumphant, glad to prove my usefulness, hoping it would help my request. "Sorry, doll, one second," she said.

I watched as she fired off a flurry of emails, three minutes' worth, and rehearsed the conversation in my mind: I would remind her that I hadn't taken any vacation days this year, that I'd be available on email, always, of course, forever. It was just one day, the Wi-Fi was perfect—it wasn't, but I would figure it out.

Natalie slammed her phone onto her lap. "I want you to pitch Roger," she said. "For the sock story."

We had recently signed a new client who made crew socks that had become a symbol of "arrival" for the young downtown crowd. Now an up-and-coming street artist named Ubi Dub, deemed the next Banksy, was designing his own capsule collection of socks for the brand. "PR gold," Natalie had said. "This will sell itself." Except for the fact that the socks were hideous, neon-yellow with a swish mimicking the insignia of another distinguished brand. Ubi Dub wasn't known for his originality, I guessed. Still, there would be a big launch, queued up for Fashion Week in September, when everyone would clamor for a pair anyway.

"Okay," I said. "I'll call him today."

She was eyeing the fried chicken, but still hadn't touched it.

"The exclusive, I mean. Give him everything. Interviews with Ubi Dub and the designer, in person, on the phone, whatever. Visits to the factory. We'll brief the client and tell them, 'Nix the child labor that day.'" I laughed but she glared at me and I understood she wasn't joking. "Make sense?" she asked. I nodded. "Great," she said. Back to her phone, she pushed out her bottom lip, brows knit together as she typed.

"Natalie," I said.

"Yeah." She didn't look at me.

"Would it be okay if I took Friday off?" She was silent, still texting. "I have family in town," I lied. Still nothing. I opted for an anxious plea. "I haven't used any of my vacation days, but I can be online, of course. Or you know, I can leave early, if I can't take the whole day?"

Her phone rang again. "Ugh, my husband. He's killing me, I swear." She stood. "I have to take this."

"Um, sorry, so I can take Friday, then? I'll still be—"

"No, sorry, love. I heard you the first time. We are too, *too* busy these days."

Love. The cherry on top.

I could have argued, could have asked for something like a compromise, but I knew she wouldn't bend.

"Of course," I said. "Makes sense."

She pressed the phone to her ear and her gaze landed on the bucket beside me. "I hope you're going to eat," she said.

The fried chicken was hot, and steam billowed from the bucket, but it smelled gross, almost artificial, like the bathrooms at Burger King on a middle school field trip. I wanted to gag.

This was your idea, I'd wanted to say. Instead I asked, "You're not going to have any?"

"I don't have time for this," she said into the phone, and then to me, "No, I have another meeting in five." She pursed her lips, pointing again at the bucket. "But seriously, enjoy. My treat."

15

When I woke up Friday morning, six hours before Paul was set
to whisk me away to Amagansett, I sent Natalie an email, explaining that I was not feeling well, that I had a migraine, a specific sort of pulsating pain. That it felt like my head just might
explode. She responded with one word: Ok. There was no *I hope
you feel better*, no miming of well wishes even if they were empty,
though I wasn't sure why I'd expected them in the first place.
Jeff texted, I know you're not sick, and I responded with a flurry
of emojis: a crystal ball, a pink heart, the winking face, and the
one laughing so hard that it cried. He sent me a middle finger.

———

Lucy was waiting at the front door. She led me up the stairs, to
the same bedroom I'd stayed in last month, and placed my bag
on the chaise longue, then smoothed the duvet with her palms.

Lucy spoke first, her Irish accent inflected with hurried syl-
lables, that familiar singsong melody. "Too hot?"

"Sorry?"

"Is it too hot in here? I can lower the temperature."

"Oh, no, it's fine, thank you."

We studied one another. I knew her only peripherally; Etta said she'd been employed by the Croftons for thirty years, but I could count on one hand the number of times they had exchanged words apart from general requests of "Can you please" and "I'd like."

"Archer is busy working," she said. "Would you like to wait for him downstairs?"

"Sure," I said, though it didn't seem there was another choice.

She took me to the great room, with its three sofas and multitude of glass surfaces, wall of windows and French doors that framed the lawn. She told me to sit, and when she offered water, I said, "Yes."

As I perched on one of the porcelain-colored linen sofas, I wiped the sweat from my hands on my dress and remembered an article I'd read that said you could trick yourself into translating your anxiety into excitement, that they were virtually interchangeable. The rapid pulse, the hot and cold flashes, an occasional wave of nausea. All excitement, I reminded myself.

Lucy marched back into the room and handed me a glass of ice water, a single lemon wheel floating in it, watching me as I drank.

I offered a smile. She crossed her arms.

"So he's working...in the house?" I asked.

"Upstairs. His studio is upstairs."

"Oh, I didn't know."

"Your friend isn't here this weekend," she said.

She meant Etta. "No, she's in Spain," but surely she knew this? Lucy smirked. "I didn't know you were friends with Archer?"

"Oh, yes," I lied.

She nodded again, as if to herself, then turned to leave before looking at me over her shoulder. "Don't worry," she said.

"About what?"

She shrugged. "I won't say anything."

Archer made me wait for almost an hour. I finished my glass of water and Lucy brought another. I played with my thumbs, caught up on email, realized I was sweating through my dress.

Pots clanged in the kitchen. Archer had mentioned a small dinner when he invited me, and I considered what constituted *small*. Friends? Acquaintances? Just the two of us? I checked the time on my phone: it was nearly six o'clock and the light outside was shifting, sketching shadows across the walls. I examined my hands: my cuticles were ragged. I should have gotten a manicure.

A door slammed, followed by footsteps on the stairs.

I stood as Archer walked toward me, wiping his hands on a rag. There was paint on his jeans and T-shirt.

"I'm so sorry. I hope I didn't keep you waiting too long," he said.

I smiled on demand. "Not at all."

He gave me a hug, his T-shirt damp, and asked how the traffic was.

"Just the usual," I said, as if I were a seasoned visitor.

"So four hours spent luxuriating in bumper-to-bumper traffic."

"Yes, it was a great time for dissecting my existential thoughts."

"Well, we could have chartered you a helicopter, but I didn't think of it until now," he said, and I laughed because I couldn't tell if he was joking.

"I'm excited for the show tomorrow," I said. "Thanks again for inviting me."

"Me, too. Lots of local artists will be there. I think you'll really enjoy it."

I nodded. He nodded. He was still holding a paintbrush, and when he lifted his shirt to clean the bristles, I saw a hint of his stomach. I clasped my hands together and concentrated on the floor.

"Lucy showed you to your room?" he asked.

"Yes," I said, "the same room I stayed in last time." I wasn't sure why I shared this; he probably didn't even know which room I'd stayed in.

But he was gracious. "That's good. Do you like that room?"

"Uh-huh," I said. "It's great."

Footsteps then from behind: Lucy barreled past us, pursing her lips at Archer, before opening the French doors out to the lawn. A breeze slipped past and a man followed behind her, carrying stacked dinner plates. They were setting the table. I imagined the two of us, eating together at the obnoxiously long table, like the king and queen of something, he at one end and I at the other, neither of us speaking apart from the occasional remark about the sky or the wine he detested and which I thought was "fine," or the steak, "too rare," and neither of us touching, because we were too far apart to reach one another.

"So dinner," Archer said.

I refocused my attention on him.

"A few friends are coming over tonight."

"Perfect."

"Great."

"Can't wait to meet everyone," I lied.

"It'll be casual," he told me, and I could almost guarantee that much was false. I knew enough by now how these things went: the introductions and cocktails, the three-course dinners, maybe four, with wine pairings. The conversations that I would drift in and out of, my opinions entirely irrelevant, and the people they'd talk about whom I didn't know. Come the end of the evening, Archer would ask if I'd had a nice time and I'd say yes, because that was the right answer.

Archer pointed to my glass on the cocktail table, and my immediate thought was shame that I hadn't thought to use a coaster. I scooped it up and apologized.

"For what?"

"I couldn't find a coaster," I said.

Archer brought his hand to his forehead, as if amused. After a beat, he said, "That's not what I was going to say, but thank you for your diligence." I smiled but I was gritting my teeth. "No, it's the lemon, see there?" He pointed again. "How it's sort of drooping?"

I raised the glass above my head, as if to examine it, but he took it from me, ran his finger down the length of its side. The single lemon slice was draped over a mountain of melting ice.

He said, "It reminds me of Dalí—*The Persistence of Memory*. Do you know it?"

The image of the soft melting clocks. I did know it, which didn't feel like an impressive feat because didn't everyone? Regardless, I said, "That's the one with the melting clocks, right?"

Archer laughed. "Pocket watches, but yes. And it's what everyone thinks of when they hear the word *surrealism*." He went on: "Anyway, with the pocket watches, or clocks, Dalí was alluding to the perception of time while people dream. That it doesn't seem to exist."

That was how I felt right now, as if I were dreaming. That being here felt like a dream, a strange dream, bittersweet. I wanted to be here, but there was the doubt, the anxiety, saturating each thought. Was it Etta? That she'd asked Archer to *look after me*? Was it that I hadn't told her I was here? Then again, Etta hadn't told me about Barcelona. In fact, she'd withheld this information until the last possible minute, until her apartment and life were neatly squared away into moving boxes. I was the final loose end she'd needed to tie up.

"That's very cool," I said. "I didn't know that."

He laughed, his chin dropping toward his chest.

"What?" I asked.

"Nothing, just…is it really *cool*?"

"Sorry?" I asked. Archer was smiling and I was getting more flustered. "Well, do you recommend I find another word?"

"No, no," he said. "You don't—" Archer collected himself. "It's just something I noticed is all, you using that word a lot."

"Well, yeah, you're not wrong," I said, though I was also thinking, *What else had he noticed?*

Archer shifted on his feet while he played with the bristles on his paintbrush. I pictured his knee, bobbing uncontrollably at the bar weeks ago. Without warning, he moved closer. There was paint, hunter green and yellow, stuck to his forearms. He continued toying with the bristles on the paintbrush, but his eyes were on me.

"Ren," he said, "what I wanted to say is *you* are also interesting."

"Am I?" I asked, but it came out flat. *Am I.* Disbelieving, incapable of accepting a compliment, like Etta had said.

"But you're also afraid." I started to frown. "Sorry. I didn't mean…it's just…you *seem* afraid? Uncertain, maybe? Are you?"

Afraid of what? Uncertain of what? Everything?

"I mean," I began to say, "yeah. I guess it's fair to say I'm afraid *and* uncertain. Isn't everyone, though? To some degree?"

Archer shrugged, but he was still smiling as his eyes examined mine. I didn't move as his gaze dropped, first toward the floor, and then to the sofa behind us.

"Your phone," he said.

My phone? I turned around. My phone. The home screen lit up: Natalie.

I said, "It's nothing," but Archer had already twisted from me and was walking away.

"Go sit by the pool," he called over his shoulder, "or stay inside. Whatever you want. I should shower. I'll be down soon."

I was alone again. "Dammit," I said under my breath, then answered Natalie's call. She didn't want to know how I was feeling; she didn't acknowledge that it was after six, on a Friday, in mid-July, when most of New York had stopped responding to emails for the weekend. It wasn't that she'd "forgotten." No. She

was reviewing a report, had I brought my laptop? Could I help
her pull a few stats, she was locked out of Cision. The numbers
for *The New York Times* seemed "inconsistent," and who was
managing the intern, was it Jeff? I thought, *Isn't there someone
else you can ask? Why me?* And then, *of course me.* She exercised
control, and that was the whole point.

———

Archer's friends piled into the foyer around eight: three guys
and one girl. "This is Ren. She's friends with Etta," Archer said,
again and again, reciting it like a line from a poem so that by
the last person, I did us both a favor and said, "I'm friends with
his sister."

I would remember Sandeep, he was shorter and less preten-
tious than the others, but the other men looked the same, each
average, around five-ten, though I could almost guarantee that
if pressed they would argue they were six-foot. Sandeep's girlfriend was named Claire and she had straight long brown hair,
pale skin, a pointed noise, wide forehead. Very patrician.

Lucy made everyone cocktails; Claire asked for a scotch, Sandeep
a tequila on the rocks, and the rest of us G&Ts. We migrated to
the great room, and I sat on a sofa by myself as the others crowded
onto the other two. Everyone was debating the outcome of a recent
Formula 1 race—apparently Sandeep's brother was in attendance—
and which I knew nothing about, so I started to contemplate how
Archer knew these people. They grew up together, I would learn.
Besides Claire and Sandeep, there was also a "Chip" and a "Rob";
well, I thought it was Rob; but then I heard one of the guys say,
"Bobby," so it could have been "Bob," or it could have been a
private joke. They were lawyers and bankers in khakis and loafers, and Claire was a psychologist in a pink floral wrap dress with
a tie at the waist, graduates of Princeton and Amherst and Penn,
surprisingly straight-edged for all the slashies Archer supposedly
hung out with. The one I believed to be Chip kept patting Archer

on the back and saying, "So how's that art thing working out for you, buddy?" but Archer was good-natured about it, so I figured he wasn't serious.

After ten minutes Archer led us through the French doors and toward the gardens. Everyone seemed self-involved or busy catching up, and I awkwardly trailed them, following the sound of their voices and the clinking of ice in their glasses to a circular wooden table with six chairs. Sandeep pulled one out for Claire and sat beside her. I sat between Sandeep and Chip, and across from Archer. The sun had lowered over the horizon and a golden haze settled around our heads like soft halos.

Archer asked Lucy for another drink and Sandeep said, "So tell us more about this opening, Archer. I'm sorry we couldn't be there."

Claire added, "We were in Yosemite."

"It was last month, don't worry about it," Archer said, as if he wanted to drop it, but Sandeep said, "Well, my parents said it was great."

Archer concentrated on his glass. "You're so diplomatic when you want to be, Sandeep."

Sandeep said, "Um, I was being genuine, Archer. My parents really did like it. I think they bought a piece for their place out in Napa?" but Archer had already shifted his attention to Claire.

"So. How was Yosemite?"

"Very eventful," she said with a flourish of her left hand. A diamond the size of a grape sparkled on her ring finger.

There were congratulations. Even I said, "Oh, that's great," though I'd never met them until tonight.

Chip said, "Did you post to Instagram, C?"

Claire clicked her tongue. "What is it with you and Instagram lately?"

"I'm just curious when you're going to share the news with all your followers!"

"Oh, please. My followers? Sounds like a cult."

"Well, you're telling us now," Chip said, mocking how she had waved her hand moments earlier.

"Because you're my friends? Would you rather I *not* say anything?" she asked. "Because that seems more hurtful."

I thought of Etta, the fact that I was here, surrounded by Archer and his childhood friends, wondered if she'd find the circumstances weird, then knew she would.

Chip's nostrils flared. "I'm joking. I didn't mean to get such a rise out of you," he said, but it seemed like he did.

Sandeep held his drink in front of his mouth. "I deleted my Instagram," he said, and Archer added, "I never had one."

"Classic Archer," Chip said. "Always the mysterious one. Part of your charm?"

Archer shrugged and Claire chimed in: "Okay, but meanwhile, Etta looks like she is gaining *quite* the following."

Archer seemed annoyed. "What do you mean by *following*?"

She absently twirled the ring on her finger. "Just posting lots of content. Getting lots of likes."

"Oh, you mean on Instagram," Archer said.

"What did you think I meant?" Claire laughed. "Her pictures are gorgeous, I will admit. Makes me want to drop everything and join her, to tell you the truth. Must be nice, having no responsibilities."

Archer said, "Well, she is taking classes."

Chip queued up Etta's Instagram page and asked why I wasn't in more of Etta's photos, if I was such a "good friend."

I opened my mouth to respond when Claire interjected, "She's obviously curating an image."

"As in Ren doesn't fit that image?" Chip challenged.

"That is not what I said."

"Sounds like it."

"Oh, leave her alone," Claire said, acknowledging me for the first time all evening. "You don't need to talk to him, you know. We only tolerate him because he knows our darkest secrets."

"Well," Archer said with a wink, "most of them."

Chip groaned before setting his phone on the table, an image of Etta sipping a cappuccino at a café on the screen. Her hair looked blonder, or maybe it was the filter.

He said, "I swear I am not the bad guy here."

"No one said you were," Claire told him.

I assessed Chip's profile. He had angular features, like Claire, with a Chiclet-smile, his teeth so neat and small and perfectly white. "So," he said, facing Rob/Bob, who hadn't spoken much since we sat, "how does Tracy feel about Instagram engagements?"

Claire said, "All right, let's not pick on Tracy."

Chip raised his glass. "I'm not picking on her."

Rob/Bob knocked back the rest of his drink. "She's fine."

Chip asked, "Fine as in 'manic'? Or…"

Chip contributed to the conversation with lots of hand gestures, compensation, it seemed, reassurances to Claire that he was only repeating what he'd heard: that Tracy might threaten to end it if Rob didn't propose. That was how I confirmed his name was Rob, not Bob.

Archer and I locked eyes for a moment, then he asked, "So is this what you guys talk about when I'm not around?"

Chip said, "Meaning when you're finger painting in the basement? Yes." Archer flicked some of his drink at Chip, who elbowed me by accident. He spun around, said, "Shoot, I am so sorry." I told him it was fine, and Sandeep said, "This is why you're single, man."

Everyone laughed except Rob, who pushed his dark hair from his face.

"All right, though, that's not what happened," he said. "Tracy didn't threaten to *end it*."

Claire placed a hand on Rob's shoulder, as if in sympathy, but Chip had less tact. "She left Saint Lucia early when she found out you didn't have a ring. I mean. Let's just leave it there."

Rob said, "No, she had a work emergency."

"She works in PR."

"Ren works in PR," Archer said, but no one seemed to hear him.

"But she left," Chip said. "I mean, she boarded an aircraft and *departed* the island." A pause. "Am I right?" He turned to me. "Ren, what's your take? I'd love an outsider's perspective."

Claire said, "Ren, you don't have to respond."

"She can answer if she wants, Claire."

"You're *pressuring* her," she told him.

"I don't know her," I said, and everyone fell silent. "Tracy, I mean. I don't know Tracy."

"But you *get* the situation," Chip said, leaning forward.

Archer started to speak but Chip held up his hand, as if to silence him.

Slowly, I said, "Yeah, I mean, it sounds like, I don't know, maybe Tracy had expectations. That she wanted something and...she didn't get it. So she didn't know how to react, and it was easier for her to leave than deal with the consequences."

Everyone seemed to absorb my words, or perhaps they didn't know how to react, or more realistically, they hadn't been listening. But after a moment Chip said, "See! Told you," and slung his arm around me. "Always helps to get an outsider's opinion."

"Ren isn't exactly an outsider," Archer said, and Chip threw him a look. "What?" Archer asked. "She isn't. I've known her for years."

"No, your *sister* has known her for years," Chip corrected.

I kept my eyes on my place setting, at a gnat fluttering around my wineglass.

Claire sighed. "Chip, why do you have to be such a contrarian? Can't we ever have a nice time together?"

Chip drank hurriedly from his wineglass and grabbed the bottle in the center of the table for a refill. "I am having a nice time. You aren't?"

"You call this a nice time? You're acting ridiculous."

Sandeep laughed. "This is a shock to you?"

"It's sexist and pathetic, honestly. You're acting like Tracy is desperate, like she needs to be someone's wife or something."

"Well, doesn't she?" Chip asked. He was grinning now.

"No. She's a successful lawyer. I'm sure that's what Rob loves about her. Her—" she searched for the word "—independence."

"Guys," Rob said, but Chip cut him off.

"I only speak the truth."

"Okay, then," Claire said, "let's just change the subject. We're going to have a nice night. No arguing." She brought her drink to her lips. "Ren?" I looked up from my place setting. "I can call you that, right?"

"That is my name," I said, smiling, and she smiled back, warmly, so warmly that I couldn't tell if it was sincere.

"Perfect. Ren. I wasn't sure if it was a nickname. I wouldn't want to overstep."

"You're not overstepping," I said.

She clasped her hands in front of her, her nails perfectly oval and painted a demure shade of pale pink. I hid mine in my lap so she wouldn't see the mess they were.

"So you're a friend of Etta's, yes?"

This question, again and again and again, but I kept on smiling, acted unbothered, gracious, like a good guest.

"Yes, we went to NYU together."

"Oh, wow. College friends. That's a special bond. You must really miss her."

Archer drank his wine, watching me over the rim of his glass.

"It's been an adjustment," I said, "obviously, not having her here."

"Of course," Claire said. "But luckily you have Archer, yeah?"

Archer and I exchanged terse smiles. "Yeah," I said.

"Lucky you." Claire smiled.

"Lucky me," I said.

"But it looks like Etta is having an *incredible* time," Claire said, and Sandeep began to say that social media couldn't be an accurate barometer for gauging one's true happiness, that plenty of people with supposedly "great lives" were actually miserable. Claire pressed a finger to his lips and, glancing between me and Archer, said, "So you and Archer met through Etta, correct?"

Archer said, "Yes. Years ago. Didn't I already say that?"

"But Etta's not here?" Chip interjected.

"No, she's in Spain. Which we already know," Archer said.

"Well, you two must be very comfortable spending time together like this, right?"

Archer cleared his throat. "Ren's into art. She's going to a show tomorrow, in East Hampton."

I noticed Claire's eyebrows rise and fall. "That's fun. So you're staying here? At the house?"

"Just for tonight," I said, though I wasn't sure why I'd defaulted to lying, that it was better they imagined I was only here overnight versus an entire weekend, like one night made such a difference.

"Got it," Claire said, before shifting toward Archer. "I was going to say, it would be kind of weird, no?"

Archer asked, "What would be weird?"

Her eyes met mine. "Being alone here, without your friend. But it's not like you're strangers."

16

We ate mashed potatoes and rib eye. I drank three glasses of wine and Chip scraped all the mashed potatoes from his plate with a fork, reminding me too much of my dad and our breakfast last month I wanted to forget. Claire and Sandeep said the wedding would be a civil ceremony, maybe an intimate brunch afterward, but they weren't into "weddings for the sake of weddings," whatever that meant. Somehow, between dinner and dessert, strawberries and cream, Chip's arm had found its way to my back, and I would catch him looking at me from the corner of my eye.

After dinner we crossed the lawn to the pool, illuminated by a bluish-green light and appearing like a portal to another world. It was fully dark outside now, the crickets murmuring all around us, cementing the fact that it was peak summer. Archer ducked into the pool house, returning with a six-pack of Modelo and a bottle opener. Archer and Rob shuffled the shoes off their feet, sat down at the edge of the deep end, and submerged their calves in the water. Chip and I sat corner to them, while behind us, Claire and Sandeep curled up on a lounge chair.

Chip scooted closer and asked me, "Want to see a trick?" *No*, I thought, but I watched as he cracked the top off the bottle with his teeth, spitting it onto the pavement. His mouth was red from the wine and when he looked at me, expecting recognition, I said, "Wow, impressive."

"Chip never left college, unfortunately," Claire said.

"Hey, she thought it was cool."

I started to shake my head to the contrary while Archer laughed softly.

Rob raised his beer to Archer then. "Hey, did Jane ever get my email?"

"Email?" Archer asked.

Chip's hand had gravitated to my knee and I pretended not to notice, but Archer apparently had. He was peering at us, as if unsure what he was seeing. Did he care that Chip's hand was on my knee? I inched closer.

Rob said, "Yeah. She asked about job opps at the bank, in New York, and I told her I'd connect her with my MD?"

Archer fixed his attention on the pool. "Honestly, I'm not sure."

Rob laughed, an annoyed laugh. "Well, can you ask? I forwarded her information to my boss. I don't want to look like a flake."

"When is she visiting again?" Claire asked.

"Not sure," Archer said.

"Oh, well, we talked about getting lunch the next time she's in town."

The next time she's in town. Archer had said Jane wanted to get drinks the next time she was in town, and I pictured the three of us around a table and considered whether Jane knew Archer and I were spending time together, if she cared, or if I was such a non-threat that none of it mattered.

Finally, Archer said, "Yeah, I don't know."

"Sorry, I don't mean to pry," Claire said, "but is everything okay with her dad? I know he's been sick."

Archer stood abruptly and disappeared inside the pool house. Claire whispered something to Sandeep. Rob said, "What was that about?" and Chip asked me, "So where do you live in the city?" I didn't answer.

A moment later Archer reappeared with two more Modelos. He gave one to me and opened the other for himself, then sat back at the edge of the pool and scratched his head.

Claire said, "Archer," as if rousing him from a daydream.

"Yeah?" he asked.

She smiled. "Is everything all right?"

"Everything's fine."

"Archer," Claire said again, this time more sternly.

He tipped his head back and drank his beer. "We aren't together anymore."

I gripped my own beer by its neck until my knuckles turned white.

"Oh, no," she said. "What happened? I'm so sorry to hear."

"It's fine, just wasn't working. Not more to it."

Archer looked up, catching my eye, and I quickly stared down at the pool.

"It was the distance," Rob said, "wasn't it?"

Archer laughed. "Yeah, the distance wasn't ideal."

I took long, concentrated glugs of my beer, though I was full and my throat burned. I noticed Archer's eyes had slid to Chip again, specifically the placement of Chip's hand now on my thigh, his other on my back. I could have shifted from him, created some space, but I didn't. A part of me liked wondering if Archer was jealous.

Chip pointed to Archer. "Listen, my sister's got some hot friends. We'll all go out soon."

"Chip," Claire said, "isn't your sister in college?" Chip's eyes said, *So?* and Claire sighed. "Archer needs someone his own age."

Chip scoffed and asked why she cared so much, and I drained the rest of my new beer so that I was sucking air at this point.

Claire acquiesced. "Fine. Twenty-eight. Minimum."

Chip said, "Okay, *mom*."

"No, I'm not being a *mom*. Archer just needs someone on the same page as him. And I'm sorry to say—Jane was a good match."

"Was she, though?" Archer asked.

Claire flattened her hands to her chest. "I mean, *I* adored her, but you obviously have to be happy. It's your relationship."

"Claire," he said, smiling placidly, "if you really feel that way, you wouldn't be sitting here right now telling me who I can and cannot spend my time with."

Claire stiffened and Sandeep said, "Archer, come on."

"Just being honest," Archer said, "about what it looks like from my perspective."

"And what does it look like?" Claire asked.

"Like you're another person in an already long line of people who claim to have my 'best interest.'"

A muscle in my thigh twitched, I could see it quivering underneath Chip's hand.

Claire sat up on the lounger, scrunching her facial muscles, as if she was about to argue.

"I'm sorry," she said instead. "I don't know, I liked her."

"Well," Archer said, "I'm sorry to disappoint you."

———

Around eleven, Sandeep and Rob announced they should get going. They were in the Hamptons for a bachelor party—Claire was not thrilled, but "boys will be boys" were her parting words—for the same friend from their Princeton days, and they were heading out to Montauk for the rest of the weekend, where they would flirt with the twenty-two-year-olds at The Sloppy Tuna as if they were still twenty-two and day-drink themselves into oblivion and be betrayed by their thirty-three-year-old livers, which, regardless of their enthusiasm and the fact that it was easier to get girls now when you had fat pockets and, for some, a Juris Doctor at the end of your name, did not work with that same speed and agility, and they'd end up puking in the parking lot, or blacking out, or both, just like they did when they were twenty-two, paying the price for pretending they still were.

In the driveway Chip and I stood next to his dad's hunter green Jaguar, the car he liked to drive best when he was "out here." I half listened as he blabbered about his summer plans, a few weddings in Europe, and did he mention his brother's daughters, whom he loved so much? He just *had* to show me a picture. I smiled as he scrolled through his camera roll; men were always invoking children as a means of appearing more desirable.

Chip's phone was open to a photo of his two-year-old niece, her face covered in strawberry ice cream, when he shouted to Archer.

"What?" Archer asked from the other side of the car.

"So this art thing tomorrow," he said, glancing back at me as if to say, *I have all the good ideas*, "do you have room for one more?"

No, nope, too much, rewind, reverse. This was supposed to end, whatever this was, tonight. Now. Preferably, two minutes ago.

Archer crossed his arms. "Aren't you heading to Montauk?"

"No, that's just Rob and Sandeep. I'm free as a bird."

"Oh," Archer said, as I wobbled on my feet and leaned against the car and Chip said, "Whoa, easy there," and I said, "I'm fine," but I wasn't.

"Well?" Chip asked Archer.

"I don't know, I have to check."

Chip smacked the roof of the car so that I jumped. "Really? You don't have like, people who can do your bidding for you?"

"No, what do you think I am, a rock star?"

"If I said yes, would that boost your ego?"

"It's not my show," he said, and started walking away.

I told Chip I should get going, but then he placed his phone in my palm. "Add your number," he said.

I considered skewing the number by one digit, but Chip would be the type to call before he left the premises, so I played it safe. Satisfied, he kissed me on the cheek and dipped into the driver's seat. I waved goodbye, the dust gathering around my feet, as the Jaguar disappeared down the driveway.

Archer was waiting for me on the lawn near the back of the house. "I'm not really tired. Are you?" he asked.

I looked back at the house. All the windows were dark apart from a dim light on the second floor. I shook my head and Archer guided us back to the pool. I sat at the ledge, dipping my legs into the water, while Archer gathered the empty beer bottles. After he disposed of them inside the pool house, he asked if I wanted anything else to drink and I was quick to say, "No, I'm okay."

He flicked on another light, casting a weak beam across the pool and pergola, and sat beside me, nursing another beer. "Sorry about Claire," he said. "And Chip."

"What do you mean?" I asked.

He held the beer in front of his mouth. "I don't know, they can be a lot."

"I didn't mind." He didn't say anything. "I mean, I don't disagree. She and Chip really seem to go at it."

"And me, I guess. Sometimes."

"Yeah, but you guys are kind of sweet. How well you know each other. I don't really have many friends from growing up. We all sort of—" I waved my hand in the air "—lost touch. And then I came to New York and I didn't really go home much anymore."

I was just drunk enough that I felt like I could tell him anything. In truth, I almost always felt like I could tell him anything.

All he said was, "Mmm."

I kicked my legs in the water and Archer drank his beer. In the window of the pool house, I spotted the sinewy neck of one of the flamingo floaties, as if it were watching us. I shuddered and Archer asked if I was cold.

"No, I'm fine," I said.

"You sure?"

I nodded. "Yep. All good."

"So speaking of Chip..."

I stiffened. "What about him?"

"I feel like he likes you."

I angled toward Archer, but his gaze was fixed straight ahead.

"As in, 'like-like,'" he clarified.

"What is this, elementary school?" I asked. Archer shrugged, suppressing a smirk, which annoyed me, that he thought any of this was funny or entertaining. "I think he's just a flirt," I said, swatting at a mosquito on my shoulder.

Archer shrugged again. "I can text him in the morning."

"Text who?"

"Chip." He said this matter-of-factly, simply, infuriatingly.

I'd been too convincing in giving Chip attention, and now it seemed Archer was testing me, taking the temperature of the situation. "Oh," I said. In truth, I'd hoped he would forget what Chip asked, about joining us at the show. Desperate to change the subject, I asked Archer if he had a water or seltzer? I was suddenly thirsty.

Archer retrieved a water bottle from the pool house, tossing it to me before he sat down again. "Yeah, so about tomorrow," he said, "I figure we can leave here around eleven? Sound good?"

I noticed Archer was looking at my lap and I sat on my hands.

"Yep," I said. "Well, wait, sorry, do *you* want him to come? Chip?"

"It's up to you."

Of course he would put this on me; we were playing a game. I volleyed the potential resolution back to him, played the indecisive card: "Well, I guess if you want him there, it's your friend's gallery," and "I'll do whatever."

Archer said, "I don't know what that means. *Do whatever.*"

"I'll do whatever you want." It came out more harshly than I'd intended.

Archer's eyes flashed to mine, and I churned my fist into the pavement.

"Saying you'll *do whatever* is faking ambivalence."

"What?"

"Ambivalence. It means—"

"I know what ambivalence means, Archer."

"You must have a preference. So what is it?"

"Well, I don't want to tell you what to do with *your* friend."

"You're not. You're making it more confusing."

I wanted to say, *No,* you're *making it more confusing.* Instead I was quiet.

Archer lolled back his head to finish his beer. He set the empty bottle beside him.

"It's just funny is all."

"What's funny."

He motioned with his hands. "Forget it. It's nothing."

Obviously it was not *nothing.*

I whirled toward him. "Can I ask you a question?" Archer nodded. "Did you invite me here this weekend because Etta asked you to?"

"What?" I was silent and Archer was frowning. "Etta doesn't even know you're here. Am I missing something?" he said.

Was he pretending, or did he really not know? It was hard to tell with him sometimes.

"She said she asked you to look after me."

He said nothing and I kicked my legs, making a slapping noise in the water.

Finally, Archer spoke. "She asked me to check in on you, yeah."

A pang in my chest. I wasn't sure why I found this confirmation so defeating. Etta was being thoughtful, but her actions felt rooted in something else. Something like control.

"But no," Archer said, "she did not tell me to invite you this weekend."

I opened my mouth to respond but hiccuped instead. At first, I thought it a singular event, but the hiccups became rhythmic. My body shook with each one.

Archer said, "You have to drink for nine seconds, then swallow three times. Hard."

"What?"

"To cure your hiccups."

I tried the prescribed remedy. He counted aloud for nine seconds, then three swallows. It didn't work. I tried again, continued drinking water, my body pitching forward every few seconds as if it were glitching.

"So you and Jane," I said, between hiccups.

He tilted his head to the side, rubbing his jaw. "Yeah?" he said.

"I'm sorry to hear," I said. Another hiccup. "That you broke up."

He laughed into his lap. "Are you really, though?"

Somewhere on the lawn, I heard sprinklers, a distant whispering.

"Wait, what?" I asked. Hiccup. "Of course I'm sorry."

"Mmm," he said, and I could feel my face burning.

"I feel like Claire," I said, "thinks it's weird I'm here."

"What makes you say that?"

"She kind of said so? At dinner?"

"I don't remember that."

Another hiccup. "I mean, we aren't really friends. You and

me." I twisted toward him and he alternated his gaze between me and the pool, as if he couldn't commit to either.

"You came here to see the show," he said.

The show.

He went on: "I know you talked about wanting to write. I find I'm more inspired when I'm exposed to other art."

I started to laugh, this menacing, pathetic laugh. Archer was too stunned to respond.

"I haven't written a thing in ages. I mean, *ages*. And sometimes at work I'll be writing a press release or some, I don't know, 'document,' and I will wonder, truly, if I've forgotten how to write. Like, really write." Hiccup. "Not this corporate bullshit. Not emails." He was silent. My thoughts became words, and the words became liquid, slipping from my tongue, and I couldn't catch them anymore.

"I'm sorry if it's weird for you that I'm Etta's friend." Hiccup. He flicked his eyes toward me and I thought, *I have gone too far*, but also, *Now I really have him*. In my mind, I sounded impassioned and eloquent, but it was all a facade. Loose thoughts strung together in unconvincing arguments.

"I don't find it weird," he said.

I kept going: "But also I haven't told Etta we've been 'hanging out' or whatever this is. I mean, I could tell her, obviously. Do you think I should? Is it strange if I don't?" I couldn't be sure because he didn't answer. "Also, I know you and Etta have this weird relationship and I can't figure it out…so maybe it *is* weird that I'm here, even though she asked you to *look after me*. She'd *hate* me for this. She hated that you gave me a ride from Brooklyn that night, even if she doesn't want to admit it. But also, she didn't tell me about Barcelona. Well, she *did* tell me, but only when it was like, too late. You know? Because she was leaving already. I don't know, I don't know what I'm saying. Ignore me."

Archer did. He rolled the empty beer bottle between his

palms, and I realized my dress was damp and I could see the bug bites dotting my legs, raised bumps that would mean itching and raking at my skin until they bled. Perhaps I deserved it, a flurry of sleepless nights.

Archer dragged his finger through the water. It left no trace, just a faint ripple, as if he hadn't even touched it at all, and I thought, *It's like we aren't even here.* I saw *The Persistence of Memory,* the warped perception of time, those wilted clocks. I saw my own delusion. Archer's eyes were glassy and pale green. Below them were dark circles, I noticed now, pale purple rings. Etta was right, maybe he didn't sleep.

"Your hiccups are gone," he said at last. I gave him two thumbs but wouldn't face him. He stood, crossed to the pool house, and reappeared with another bottle of water. "You should drink this."

I took the bottle from him without meeting his eyes, and he reached for my hand to help me to my feet. I helped myself up instead.

"It's late," he said. "We should call it a night." He placed a hand on my back, ushering me toward the house.

The grounds were dark and limitless, the grass damp beneath my feet. There was no moon. Once we were inside, he locked the French doors behind us. The house was cold from the AC and my skin prickled as I continued through the great room, then up the stairs. If I stopped moving, my mind would start and I'd regret everything I said, I was sure of it.

"I'll tell Chip we couldn't get him in." Archer's voice cut through the stillness. I froze, gripped the railing. "But I'll text him in the morning, so it doesn't seem obvious."

"Okay," I said. I walked up the stairs and found my way to my room. Minutes later I heard a door slam down the hall. Neither of us said good-night.

17

The show was at this little gallery in East Hampton and it started at eleven, though we got there for noon. Archer drove us into town in his old Land Rover and I noticed there were all these receipts in the center console. I tried to make out what they said but the text was faded, aged past the point of comprehension. The car was also so old that the AC didn't work; all the windows were open and my hair whipped around my face. Archer wore a white linen button-down, the collar flapping up with the wind. Every so often I'd glance over, as if about to apologize for last night, to say, *Sorry, I was drunk*, but I think he understood as much, and didn't mention Chip. Instead when the silence became too much, I said, "God, the bugs destroyed me last night," and pointed at my legs, which were itchy and swollen, and come to think of it, why had I drawn attention to them?

"There was Off! in the pool house. You should've said something, I would have gotten it for you."

"Thanks," I said, but I wasn't sure why I'd thanked him. It was too late, the damage already done.

———

Archer's friend Priest ran the gallery. When we arrived, Archer waved at him, and Priest half nodded, half smiled. He wore a practically sheer black button-down, matching cigarette pants, and these thin gold necklaces. "I should go say hello," Archer said to me, before he jogged after him, but I saw it, the millisecond wherein Priest tried to escape, to jump into another conversation, to feign preoccupation.

The room was full, but not packed, and people in pastel-colored suits and florals and full faces of makeup paraded around with flutes of champagne and mimosas, fussing over the art. Toward the back of the room, Priest and Archer were huddled in conversation now, their mouths moving quickly as they spoke. After a moment Archer beckoned me over and said, "Ren, this is Priest." I waited for the obligatory "She's a friend of my sister's," or "She knows Etta," but he'd smartly eliminated that addendum.

No matter, Priest did not acknowledge me. He was watching Archer, tight-lipped, his matching gold septum ring glimmering in a bar of sunlight. His eyes shuttled back and forth between us. "Your friend?" he asked Archer, then proceeded to look me up and down. "Find me later," he told Archer, before excusing himself.

I counted twelve paintings on the walls. "Like a Monet," a voice from behind said. They did sort of remind me of Monet, lots of pastels, pretty landscapes, very pleasant, supremely calming, proof that art could be nice to look at and nothing more. That not everything possessed "meaning" or "complexity" or "connectedness." But Archer didn't seem to be paying much attention, instead texting on his phone, eyes shifting around the room.

"So that was your friend?" I asked. "Who owns the gallery?"

"Yes," he said. He dropped his phone into his pocket, his eyes landing sharply on mine. "I mean, no. Sorry, he doesn't own it, he oversees the programming. Some of the sales."

"Ah," I said. "Remind me how you know each other?"

"Williams." Archer leaned in. "And his name isn't actually Priest."

"What is it?"

He lowered his voice. "Peter," he said, stepping back, smiling. I laughed, relieved we could be normal again. "But I guess *Priest* is more fitting in these circles." Archer pressed a finger to his lips. "Shh, don't say I told you."

"Secret's safe with me."

Archer started walking ahead and I followed.

"He gets overwhelmed at these events. Sorry if he was rude."

"I didn't find him rude," I said, but I guessed I was becoming immune.

"Well, I did. It's like, sometimes he forgets how to treat people."

Just then, a woman with long red hair down to her waist tapped Archer on the shoulder and said, "Archer Crofton, as I live and breathe?"

Archer's face lit up. "Sorry, Ren, excuse me for a moment," he said, and that was how we passed the next half hour, him coming and going and me making laps around the room. I drank one and a half mimosas, which had a shampoo effect, only a small amount of alcohol necessary to revive my buzz from last night. I checked my messages as I walked, but apart from a series of emails from Natalie, no one was looking for me. It was a strange feeling, my own unimportance. While I waited in line for the restroom in a back hallway, however, my phone started ringing, as if I'd summoned her, except it turned out she had butt-dialed me. She didn't bother apologizing, just hung up.

Fine by me, I thought. The hall was short and narrow, with linoleum floor and three closed doors past the bathrooms. One was slightly ajar. From behind it, a man's voice said, "I understand, but you know our summer programming is full," and another voice that sounded like Archer's said, "You can't make an exception? Just once?" A long pause and I strained to hear more. The first voice said, "We could consider winter?"

"Winter," the second voice said, as if in disbelief. "Listen, Archer," the first voice said, "you know I'd help if I could. But my hands are tied."

I felt like a child, eavesdropping on a conversation intended for adults. In line, only one woman stood in front of me now. I checked to see if she was listening, as well, but she was staring at her phone, blissful and oblivious.

Archer said they both knew winter shows didn't have "that same buzz," and the other man said that it wasn't a matter of "fit" as much as it was "timing."

"I don't make the rules," he said, and Archer laughed.

"But you *can* make an exception."

The woman in front of me ducked inside the bathroom as the door that was previously ajar flung open. Priest stood in the doorway, hands on hips, staring back into the room. "I'm sorry, Archer," he said, "really, I am, but I can't keep talking in circles." Then he hurried down the hall, out toward the gallery, and I knew this was an exchange I wasn't meant to have heard.

A moment later Archer came out, head bowed. I tried to seem absorbed with my phone.

"Ren?" he asked.

I looked up. "Oh, hey! I'm just waiting for the bathroom."

He eyed me a second too long. "Okay," he said. "Another ten minutes or so? Then we'll go?"

"Sure," I said, and nodded.

———

"Are you hungry?" Archer asked, opening the refrigerator and examining its contents. We were back at the house after another silent car ride.

"I could eat something," I said.

He'd given Lucy the day off, since it was "just the two of us," and made us sandwiches. Turkey and avocado and the best heirloom tomatoes served on sourdough with waffle-cut potato chips. "The only respectable potato chips," Archer said, snapping one in half.

We hardly spoke while we ate, except when he said, "You hum when you eat, you know that?"

I wiped my mouth on my napkin. "I never noticed."

He took our empty plates, rinsing them in the sink before loading them into the dishwasher. I stood and poured myself another glass of water from the pitcher and leaned against the counter beside him.

When he was done, he tossed the towel onto the counter and, studying the lawn, said, "It's sunny—should we sit outside?"

I followed him to the pool; he sat in a chair underneath the pergola and I reclined on a lounger a few feet away.

"So I have to admit," Archer said, "my wanting to go to the gallery today was selfishly motivated. If you couldn't already tell."

"What do you mean?" I would pretend I hadn't overheard his conversation with Priest.

"I was hoping to connect with Priest, about work stuff."

"You mean… Peter?"

Archer smiled. "Yes. Peter."

"And? How did it go? Any luck?"

"Not exactly. It seems like the gallery is booked out, which I should have guessed. The season is almost over."

"Maybe you can do something with them another time?"

"Yeah, maybe." He seemed especially glum. "I don't really know if my work is a fit, though. I mean, what do you think?"

"What do I think? I mean, I liked the show and everything, but…" Archer was watching me and I felt that my choice of words was suddenly important. "I don't know, everything there looked the same. I'm happy you invited me, but your show was different. Better, I thought. Like the caliber of work. Everything today looked like an imitation Monet. Like something I'd seen before."

Archer smiled so that his eyes crinkled this time. "Thank you for saying that."

"I mean it," I said. He turned away, blinking up at the sky, and I told him, "I'm sorry, by the way, about what I said last night."

"What did you say last night?" Archer had since gravitated to the foot of the lounger next to mine so that I could see him in my periphery. "You know, after everyone went home, and I was rambling by the pool."

"Oh, yes. Yes."

"I'm really embarrassed. I didn't mean any of it. Obviously."

"It's fine. You were overserved. Chip made sure your glass was always full."

I didn't want to talk about Chip.

"Well, I am sorry," I continued. "I was not myself."

Archer was quiet. "Yeah, I should also apologize. I should have told you about Jane."

"No, it's okay. That's your business."

"I just… I really didn't want to talk about it, with everyone. Relationships, friendships…you know the only people who know the truth, right?" I shook my head. "The two people living it. So as much as Claire likes Jane…we just weren't a fit." Archer wiped the sweat from his forehead, looked up at the sky. "Maybe some relationships are better in theory than actuality."

"Oh," I said, softly.

"You meant it, though. What you said last night."

I glanced back at him. "Meant what?"

"You're really scared of Etta, aren't you? Of what she might think?"

"I didn't say I was scared of her," I said, but his expression, brows knit together, told me he knew I was lying. "And it's not what she might think. It's that, I don't know, she doesn't know I'm here and it's weird."

"Define *weird*."

"Okay. Being here without her, for example. That she doesn't know. It's like I'm keeping a secret." A pause. "Can I be honest with you?" Archer nodded. "I'm afraid that Etta and I are drifting."

"What makes you say that?"

"I know it probably sounds stupid, and maybe I'm paranoid, but we don't talk as much. Obviously, she's busy and there's a time change so it's hard to like, align schedules or whatever, but…it just feels like our lives are moving in different directions."

"So tell her," he said.

"Tell her what?"

"I don't know, that you're here. If it will make you feel better."

Of course, that was the logical solution, to confess the truth.

"Oh, no," I said, and laughed. "I can't do that."

"But you just said you don't like keeping things from her."

"Yeah, I don't."

I smiled into my lap, but still this conversation was confusing, and I couldn't decipher the subtext—if there *was* subtext—or if I was inventing things in my head.

Archer stood, stretching his arms toward the sky. "If you'd prefer not to say anything, that's fine with me, too."

He was towering over me now, casting a shadow.

"I think that would be best," I said, looking up at him, "for now. If that's all right."

"All good with me. Are you all right if I go do some work?"

I said of course, it was no problem, he could work as long as he wanted. I was an "easy guest," totally happy and content, and he smiled and said, "Okay, great."

18

I wasn't sure how long I had been floating in the pool when I heard a door slam and noticed the music had stopped playing next door, that same manic samba gone eerily silent. I saw the black town car first, its trunk propped open near the garage. Paul lifting suitcases and setting them on the gravel driveway. The hum of voices and the back of a woman wearing an emerald-colored turban and matching caftan. The woman turned. It was Plum, and I knew with absolute certainty that I was not supposed to be here.

Warren's voice added to the mix and there he was, too, in a wrinkled white button-down, beige suit jacket slung over his arm. Paul dragged a suitcase toward the house.

So they were back early from Europe. Did Archer know? Surely he would have told me; but if they discovered me here, in their pool at three o'clock on a Saturday in July, then Etta would find out, too.

I pushed myself out of the pool and hopped across the hot pavement, grabbed my phone and towel from the lounger and scurried into the pool house, where I shut the door, sank to the cool tile floor, and gagged.

The pool house was really just one room, unusually modest for the size and scale of the property. There was a white two-person sofa and pale blue armchair, a coffee table and porcelain sculptures that were probably meant to resemble coral but reminded me of heart valves instead. Down a short, narrow hall was a bar with a mini refrigerator and off the bar was a bathroom with a walk-in shower. I could have survived for a few hours—there was a frozen bar of Swiss chocolate in the fridge and several liters of Evian to tide me over.

Still, I texted Archer: Your parents are here, then when thirty minutes passed and still no response, I am in the pool house btw lol.

LOL, that I'd tried to make a joke of the fact that I was hiding in his family's pool house. LOL that he either didn't know or hadn't thought to share with me that his parents were returning early from Europe. LOL that Etta had no idea I was here. LOL that I was a liar, and LOL that I would likely continue to be one.

But Archer wasn't answering. Did he not check his phone while he worked? Probably not, I thought. He was likely one of those artists who shut out the world, acted as if it didn't exist. And meanwhile, the pool house was freakishly cold.

An hour passed. I watched the sun etch shadows across various points of the room and a deep golden light reflect off the mosaic tile floors. Finally, a message from him:

They weren't supposed to get here until Tuesday.

As if this made it any better. Well, they're here, I wrote.

Five minutes later Archer was hovering over me with this bemused expression on his face.

"It's really not funny," I said.

Archer kneaded his fist into his cheek. "What do you want to do?"

"I can't stay in here?"

He scanned our surroundings. "I mean, you *probably* could…"

"Archer!" I said.

"Sorry. It was a joke." He turned toward the windows, as if thinking, and then back to me. "Do you just want to leave? I can drive you back to the city?"

No, I thought, *of course not*. I shrugged. "Probably, yeah."

Archer shuffled back and forth. "All right, let me get your stuff."

"This feels dramatic."

"It is dramatic," he said. "You're hiding in a pool house." But he wasn't smiling now, and I realized that the situation was perhaps more annoying than funny to him at this point. "Let me get your stuff," he said again.

"Thanks," I said, and I felt like a runaway, ambling from one place to the next, each experience, each destination shockingly impermanent. As he pivoted toward the door, I asked, "What will you tell them?" He stared at me. "Your parents."

"That I have a meeting tomorrow in Manhattan, I don't know. It's fine. I'm strategic."

Strategic meant sneaking my bag into the trunk of his car. It meant returning to the pool house under the guise that he'd forgotten something and bringing me a clean towel and a black cotton dress of Etta's to change into. It meant waiting for his parents to head upstairs to wash up for dinner, before guiding me across the lawn.

We were quiet on the drive back to the city. I leaned my head against the windowsill and the motion lulled me to sleep; when I came to, we'd stopped for gas somewhere in Commack. Archer settled into the driver's seat again and passed me a bottle of Dasani. We split a KitKat.

The traffic on the Cross Bronx was miserable, per usual, and Archer said, "I really didn't know. That they were coming back."

I licked the chocolate film from my teeth.

"I would have told you," he said. "Believe me. I was just as surprised as you were." His eyes bounced between me and the road. "Sort of funny, though, imagining you in the pool house like that. Pretty clever."

"Well. It was either the pool house, or drown." I saw I made him smile.

"I don't know if I should be concerned that you would rather drown than be seen by my parents."

"It would get back to Etta."

Quietly, he said, "I figured that had something to do with it."

It started to rain, droplets ricocheting off the windshield. Archer turned up the radio and that song "Unforgettable" crackled through. "I hear this song everywhere," he said, and went to change the dial.

"No, wait, I like it," I said, and reached for the dial, too.

Our hands brushed and I saw from the corner of my eye that his jaw was tensed as he returned it to the steering wheel, where he obviously thought it belonged.

The George Washington Bridge rose in the distance, like a mirage in the fog, and I knew we were almost home. The song ended and an overenthusiastic voice announced, "And that's number four in our Summer 2017 Hottest Songs Countdown." I didn't remember numbers three or two or one.

We curved along the West Side Highway and then over the cobblestones of Greenwich Street. Archer pulled into an open spot outside Etta's building and I said, "Thank you for the ride."

"You're welcome," he said.

The moment was reminiscent of that night in Brooklyn at the loft party, over a month ago, and when we'd gotten drinks in Midtown. How he dropped me off and left. Night over.

"I'm sorry," I said again.

He smiled at his lap. "You've got to stop with that. Always apologizing."

"Well, I feel bad making you drive me back. Like I'm a... criminal or something."

I peeled my eyes from his and watched the rain streak the windshield.

"It's fine," he said. "I have errands to run anyway."

The conversation died, as had the music, and the car was hot and sticky from the lack of AC. *Good night,* I heard myself say in my mind, *thanks again.*

"Do you want to come up?" I asked instead.

He said nothing. The wipers groaned against the windshield. He was going to say no, invent an excuse as to why this was a bad idea, and didn't I think it was a bad idea, too? I waited a moment before the silence reassured me of this.

"Sorry," I said, "have a nice night." I tugged the handle on the passenger-side door and stepped one foot into a puddle on the street.

Archer killed the engine.

"Wait."

———

The apartment was dark apart from the faint white glow of the building lights across the street.

"Can I get you anything? A glass of water?" I asked.

"Sure," he said. "Water's great."

I was aware he was trailing me into the kitchen as I stretched for two glasses in the cabinet, pressing them underneath the spout on the refrigerator. I offered one to him.

"You like living here?" he asked between sips.

"It's nice, yeah."

He smirked. "It's nicer than where I live."

"Okay, sure."

"Nice to have friends in high places," he said.

"Etta's really good to me," I said, and it was as if I'd voiced this as a means of mitigating my guilt, or magnifying it, I wasn't sure of my logic anymore.

Archer chuckled under his breath. "You know," he said, "it's not often I become friends with my sister's friends."

"Ha, well, maybe that's because Etta doesn't have a lot of other friends?"

"That," he said. "Or—" he drank his water "—I just like you."

"You just like me," I said.

"I did invite you out east this weekend."

I laughed. "This is true."

"So I don't despise your company. In case you were uncertain."

"Hmm," I said, but I wasn't sure what he was getting at, whether we were flirting or not. I needed a drink, something to quell my nerves, my impulsive decision to invite him up here, to his sister's apartment, but Archer was nodding to himself now, smiling, and I ordered myself to relax.

"What do you like about me?"

His eyes fell to the floor, then floated back up to mine. "I'm not sure exactly."

Not the answer I was hoping for. "You aren't sure," I repeated.

A pause. "Well, I feel like it's an energy thing."

Too vague, I thought. *Too vague.*

"Sorry," I said then, shaking my head, "that was a weird question, I—"

He held up his hand. "No, I'm thinking now."

This was an opportune moment to suggest opening a bottle of white, or a summer red. I could have sworn there was a Lambrusco in there that Etta liked.

I pointed to the wine cooler behind him. "Shall we open something?"

He checked over his shoulder. "No, I'm good with water. Thanks."

What was happening? "Okay," I said, and forced a smile.

Archer went on, now gesturing with his half-drunk glass. "You have a lot going on underneath the surface, but then... I don't know, you're also funny, but in a self-deprecating way. And you're smart, very perceptive. I guess I like talking to you."

"Well, I guess I like talking to you, too."

We nodded at one another.

"Can I ask a question now?" Archer asked.

"Go ahead."

"Why did you invite me up here?"

"Because I like talking to you," I said, too quickly.

Archer cocked his brow. "That's all?"

I nodded fastidiously, smiled, and positioned my glass on the counter behind me because my hand was suddenly trembling and I didn't want him to see. "That's all."

"I don't know, Ren," Archer said. "I don't know if I believe you." He downed the rest of his water without breaking eye contact.

"Well, you said you liked me."

"Ah," Archer said. "I did."

"But...this kind of feels like an exchange we'd have in middle school. So I don't know, I guess I was curious if it was like a 'friend' thing, or...something else."

Archer was silent, and there was my answer: obviously a "friend" thing. My cheeks felt hot. Gingerly, he placed his empty glass on the table. He would choose his words wisely, succeed in providing a definitive nonanswer that wouldn't satisfy my question, but still manage to address it. I wanted to say, *Well, what about this weekend? And what about the dive bar?* but really, what about any of it? We were friends, or friends of friends. Why did I have to complicate everything? Why couldn't I accept the compliment, like Etta had warned? I turned around, yanked a dish towel from the counter and pretended to mop up an invisible mess. I didn't want him to read the hurt on my face when he responded.

Except suddenly there was a sensation on my waist. His hands gripping me, twisting me toward him. His lips were inches from mine and he spoke against my mouth.

"I don't look at you as a friend," he said. "And I think you know that, otherwise why would you have invited me up here?"

And then Archer kissed me. Things moved both quickly and in slow motion as I led him down the hall, toward the guest room, like I was in my body but also disconnected from it.

Coming up for air, he said, "I just think it's funny you're so worried about Etta and my parents, but Paul drove you to the house."

I pushed him away. "Do you think he would say something?" I asked, and Archer gave me a look as if to say, *You are losing it*, and clearly, all things considered, I didn't care that much, or at all.

I stood very still for a moment until he pulled me to him again, and I thought, *We are kinetic.* There was an ease in the syncopation of our bodies finding their way to one another, and a carefulness, our bodies conforming gently, silhouettes melting in the darkness. After a while, once we were lying on the bed, I asked if he had a condom. We both sort of stared at one another, realizing that he would be forced to search for one in Etta's bedroom.

When he came back victorious, he said, "Not something I had on my bucket list—discovering a box of condoms in my sister's bedroom."

I buried my face in my hands.

"But," he said, "I guess we're in luck, right?"

I nodded as he lay beside me again. He tucked a strand of hair behind my ear. "You sure about this?"

For once, I didn't allow myself to overthink. "Yes," I said.

After, he curled next to me in the bed, tracing the crest of my collarbone. The room was shadowy, as if in sepia tone, as if we were actors in an old movie. On the ceiling, I noticed a stain, slightly darker than the cream-colored paint. I hadn't seen it before—was it new?

Archer asked, "So are you happy that Chip didn't come with us to the gallery?"

"Funny," I said, smiling. "To be clear, I do not like Chip."

Archer nudged my ribs with his elbow. "It seemed like you did."

"I only wanted you to think that." I turned onto my side so that we were facing one another. "Did it work?"

Archer laughed into his pillow. "I didn't take you as someone who could be so calculating."

"I'm not calculating."

"You invited me here so that I would get into bed with you."

The rain had started up again, prattling against the windows.

"Well, it didn't take much convincing."

Archer laughed again, ran his finger down the length of my arm. He kissed me and said he was going to get water. "Need anything?" he asked.

"No," I said, "all good."

When he left the room, I shifted onto my back again, examined the ceiling. I couldn't tell if the stain was growing in size, an amorphous blob, or if my eyes were playing tricks, catastrophizing. I hugged the sheets to my body, reassured that I could simply notify maintenance. If only real life were the same, I thought, all our problems met with the promise that someone would always be there to fix them.

19

"The mole people of Midtown," Jeff said, browsing bags of popcorn, eyeing the fellow patrons of Starbucks in their corporate-best. "Do you ever notice all their suits are like, gray?"

"I do." I paid for my five o'clock coffee and banana muffin.

"It's incredibly depressing."

"So I think Natalie hates me," I said. All morning she'd pretended I didn't exist, even when she called us into her office for a department meeting so we could meet Jasmine, the new account executive. Jasmine, with her frosted blue eye shadow and painstakingly applied eyeliner. Her gross enthusiasm that I knew would tarnish and turn into resentment with time.

Jeff returned the popcorn to its shelf. "Hates you? No. She's *disappointed*." He enunciated the word.

"She definitely knows I lied. About Friday. I wasn't sick."

Jeff crossed his arms. "You? Lying? But I thought you had a migraine," he said, knocking me gently on my head.

I swatted at his hand. Someone behind the counter shouted, "Tia, we're out of the Colombia roast!" as Jeff fielded in his pocket for his vape. "So," he said, "are you planning to enlighten me about this illustrious weekend of yours?"

"I thought I was sparing you."

"That's thoughtful." He pinched a piece of my banana muffin from the paper bag and popped it into his mouth. "But I still want to hear."

The espresso machine whirring in the background, I turned to Jeff. Once I told him, I couldn't take it back.

I was about to begin, but then he said, "You had sex, didn't you." When I didn't answer, Jeff flung his hand to his mouth and some of the banana muffin he was chewing fell to the floor. "Oh. My. Sweet. Lord. I can't believe this. I mean, I *can*, he's got this weird like sultriness thing going on and that was definitely the reason he invited you out there but—" he dragged on his vape and fluttered his eyelids "—wow. Wow, wow, wow. So you *did* do it, right?"

I would be stoic; I would be calm. "It was beyond," I said, and giggled like a teenager. It felt more real now that I'd told someone.

"Huh. He looks like he would be good at sex." I gave Jeff a weird look and Jeff shrugged. "What? It's true. Are you going to tell Etta?" he asked.

"What? That I slept with her brother? Absolutely not."

Jeff sucked at his teeth. "Yeah, I guess that would be awkward."

Or a total betrayal, I thought. I couldn't decide.

The door opened then, letting in a gust of warm air. Natalie walked past us, texting on her phone, oblivious to our presence. She ordered a coffee, black, but her card was declined. She tried another, examining the popcorn display while the cashier completed the transaction.

"I didn't see that email go through," Natalie said. She cupped her phone in her palm, as if midtext or email, but she concentrated on me. She was speaking *to me*.

I smiled. "Sorry, what email?"

"To Roger. About the exclusive. For the Ubi Dub collab?"

Shit, I had never sent it. She'd asked me to do it last week and I called out sick and now I would be crucified for my negligence. Ignore the fact that I'd helped her with that report on Friday evening; she had already forgotten or didn't care.

"I'll do it right now," I said.

"Don't bother." Her words overlapped with mine and I felt it: the fangs of her frustration, sinking into me. "I already did it. You're in copy. Did you not see?"

"Not yet," I said, which I knew sounded bad. "Thank you. I'll follow up if we don't hear back."

"Don't do that. Roger hates being chased."

"Okay, sorry, I won't then."

"Give him three days. Then call. You know better. It's all about timing. We don't want to seem *desperate*."

She held my eye for a moment longer and I tried smiling again before she returned to her phone. Jeff was quiet through the whole exchange, didn't nudge me with his elbow or whisper in my ear. We got our coffees and made it as far as the door before Natalie called after me.

"I'd like to see a draft of the press release," she said.

I spun around. "I thought I sent it to you?"

"Not the perfume, Ren. For the collab? I'm still talking about Ubi Dub."

I nodded. "Yes, sure thing, no problem."

"Before you leave."

"Today," I said.

"Uh-huh. Client is asking for something to review, and I want my eyes on it first."

Impossible, I thought. It was five o'clock and I had yet to start it, but the official end of the workday was a loose suggestion, not fact.

"Of course," I said. It was the only appropriate response and we both knew that. There would be no pushback. She wanted me to know: I could call out sick or lie about a migraine and she would *still* have me. She wanted to remind me she held all the cards.

———

It was after eight when I got around to the press release. Jeff left around six and I'd procrastinated for two hours, followed up with editors who wouldn't respond to emails after five, all of Condé Nast screening my calls, skimming my messages in their inboxes, choosing not to answer. Being ignored had become like second nature.

How to make socks sexy, I thought. Well, if I were to write the document from an honest perspective, it would have gone something like: *You will want them because it means you've made it and it will serve as a token of relevancy to your friends and the maître d' at the cool downtown restaurant or the bouncers at the clubs and bars with a strict door policy, reassuring them of your "worth," but after a month or so or whenever the next "it" item announces itself, you will be shut out, thrown out, cast aside. You won't matter anymore and guess what? You never did.*

I thought of Etta then—she would have laughed about the release with me, the particularities of my job, of "marketing cool"—and missed her as if I were grieving a premature loss. I thought of how I'd worried about us growing apart, but that I hadn't made much of an effort to contact her, either. I thought of Archer and what we'd done. Of the breakfast we had at a no-frills diner in Tribeca that was somehow so much better than the Midtown diner I'd gone to with my dad. Archer had a thing about egg yolks, said they freaked him out, so he ordered scrambled egg whites and finished the rest of my toast, and I didn't remember what we talked about specifically except that the conversation was easy, stupidly easy, so that I felt like I was living in a daydream.

The sun was starting to set, glimmering off the buildings in Midtown like obsidian. My stomach grumbled and I finished a bag of pretzels I kept in my drawer. I considered ordering a real dinner with the stipend earned when working late: twenty dollars and proof of a receipt that the food was delivered after eight. Instead I opened a fresh search window and typed in my mother's name, something I occasionally did, but all the websites still listed her old number that had long been disconnected, our address back in Connecticut where she didn't live anymore. Beside my keyboard, my phone lit up with a message from Chip.

What are you up to? he asked. It was a Monday. What did he think I was up to? Where's your office? he wrote next. We can meet for a drink? I didn't respond and deleted his texts. He would get the hint. Big egos could only persist for so long.

I spun around in my chair, my eyes dancing across the office: apart from an intern several rows behind me, I was the only person here. On my desk, my phone flashed again, and I thought of Chip and his stupid face, his stupid Chiclet smile, his stupid self-assuredness, but it wasn't another message from Chip.

Hi, Archer said. The ellipsis signaled he was still typing, and I waited. I waited and realized I had stopped breathing. He shared an address, which I plugged into Google Maps. It was far west, near Tenth Avenue in Chelsea. Near the galleries.

What is this? I asked.

Where I live, he said. I'm working and would love some company?

I stared at my computer screen, the only disruption to the stark white Word document two sentences about socks, one with a typo that spell-check hadn't detected.

———

Archer's apartment did not align with the picture I'd drafted in my mind: not a duplex like Astrid and Lizzie's place, or something at least remotely mimicking Etta's, with its floor-to-ceiling windows and parquet floors. No, this apartment was one generously sized room, floorboards with hairline cracks that creaked when you walked. Exposed pipes and light bulbs dangling from fine wires like spaghetti. There were windows, yes, but they were blocked by blackout shades so time did not seem to exist. A desk, like one you might find in a precinct, stacked high with papers and a filing cabinet in the corner. A mini-fridge; a folding table with plastic forks and knives still in their wrappers. Canvases lining the floor. Tarps, buckets of paint, buckets of brushes, rolls of toilet paper. That was where Archer was when I arrived, on the floor, dripping purple paint from a turkey baster onto a large canvas.

"It's open," he yelled when I knocked, but he didn't get up to greet me, only smiled from a corner of the room, told me to make myself at home, except there was nowhere to sit apart from a desk chair besieged by a pile of laundry.

In the opposite corner was a twin bed. Unmade. Beside it a simple wooden nightstand with a digital alarm clock, a tiny lamp with a navy shade. No, I thought, he didn't *really* live here. Surely he had a place nearby, near Lizzie and Astrid's, or maybe a pad in Brooklyn, with panoramic views of the Manhattan skyline and East River.

As we waited for our Chinese food, I ambled around the studio. I couldn't help but ask, "Sorry, you live here?"

He didn't look up, didn't register my question as invasive or inappropriate. A string of purple paint flew across the canvas.

"Yes," he said, standing, scrutinizing his work. "Why? Not what you were expecting?"

"No," I said.

He grabbed a tool that resembled a metal spatula, and again kneeled to the floor. "I lived somewhere else. Not far from here. Near Lizzie and Astrid's, actually. Until fairly recently. I really liked that place. The light was great. There was a, uh, claw-foot tub in one of the bathrooms. Not that I ever used it. Shame."

"So why did you move?" I asked, taking a seat on the floor in the middle of the room.

"The lease was up, and I needed change," he said. His eyes snapped to mine from across the room, and my expression must have given me away. "I told you Etta's was nicer."

"I wasn't comparing," I lied.

"Yes, you were," he said. "Subliminally. It's okay, though." His back was to me now. He threw a rag over his shoulder and started smudging the paint with his fingers. "I would be doing the same thing. It's not a bad life, the one Etta chose, but it's not for me."

"What's not for you…"

"You know, being indebted to my parents. You accept too much of their generosity and it will only hurt you."

I swallowed hard and thought of Etta. Had I accepted too much of *her* generosity over the years?

"Do you think it's hurting Etta?" I asked.

He rose to his feet once more, eyes still glued to the canvas. "Well, it *could* have hurt her, but she's doing what they want, so no, I think she'll be just fine."

"Your parents made her go to Barcelona, didn't they…" I knew this, but I'd wanted Archer's perspective.

"My parents can't make anyone *do* anything," he said, looking to me. "But yeah, their ultimatums certainly help. I think she's happy, though, so maybe it wasn't a bad idea after all."

Archer tugged one of the blackout shades and cracked a window as the whine of sirens filled the room.

I didn't want to talk about Etta anymore. "So," I said, standing again, "what are you working on?"

He squeezed one eye shut, assessing the canvas. "I'm not sure."

"Not sure?" I asked.

"Nope, no idea. You don't know if what you're making is any good until you finish it. Art is all just one big gamble." He turned around to dip a brush into a jar of cloudy water, then went back on the floor.

"But," I asked, "what if you don't like it? Or it's not *good*?"

He shrugged. "Then it's not good and I start again."

"That sounds..."

"Exhausting?" I wasn't sure if he was humoring me. "It is," he said. "But art is a risk. And risk is inherent to anything you truly care about. I mean, you don't think I would be doing this if I didn't care, do you?"

"No," I said quietly, but I was thinking, did that explain what I was doing here? Going behind Etta's back with her brother? If I was really afraid of risk, I would have stayed at the office, done my work, not slept with Archer, not gone to Amagansett at all.

"You know," he said, "it's like that with everything. Art, life. You can't be so afraid of failure."

I laughed. I didn't realize I had walked into a therapy session. Archer glanced up at me, as if to say, *Is something funny?* He was so consumed by his preaching that it hadn't occurred to me he might be serious.

"Sorry," I said, but I was embarrassed, afraid I'd insulted him. "I guess I can't imagine living with that level of uncertainty. You know, devoting so much time to something and it not... working out."

Archer tapped a brush against the rim of a paint can and it made a hollow, tinny sound. "Yeah," he said after a moment, "but in fairness, nothing in life is a guarantee. It's not only limited to art."

"Uplifting," I said.

"Optimism is my specialty," he said.

He began to clean up his workstation, tidying his desk, and I said I had some of my own work to do.

"Writing?" he asked, seeming genuinely affected by the possibility.

I shook my head, knowing my answer would disappoint him. "No, my boss asked for this document weeks ago. She's going to kill me if I don't get it to her by tomorrow."

"Ah," he said. "Well, I'm going to jump in the shower." He

gestured to his bed, his desk, told me I could work wherever I wanted. He moved the pile of laundry onto the floor, then squeezed my hand in his. I started to turn around when he pulled me toward him and kissed me. His hands were damp with paint and left purple fingerprints on my biceps. We both smiled before he made his way to a door that I assumed led to the bathroom. "Oh, if the buzzer rings—mind answering it?" he asked. "It's probably our food."

"Sure," I said.

The sound of a faucet squeaking, shower water beading against a plastic curtain. I glanced at my arms again, tried to rub the paint off, then decided perhaps I didn't mind being branded. I sat on Archer's bed. It was firm, but not too firm. His sheets had little sailboats on them and I smirked. He was a grown man with sailboat sheets. On the nightstand was a paperback copy of *The Catcher in the Rye*. Was Archer reading it, right now? I picked up the book and flipped through; the cover was wrinkled, a deep crease like a fault line down its center, and many of the pages were dog-eared, as if he'd returned to the story many times. Gently, I set the book back where I'd found it and reached for my laptop in my bag. I propped it open on the bed, and there lay the duplicity: Archer made art and I chose the easy way out. I was writing about socks.

I attempted to draft the release again, really, I did, but a smoke alarm blared somewhere in the building and I forgot my headphones and so I perused Instagram instead. Etta had posted a photo several hours ago, the Barcelona skyline captured from a hilltop, blue skies and swirls of cotton candy clouds.

A moment later there was a notification in my messages. It was her. It was almost nine o'clock in New York, making it almost 3 a.m. in Spain.

hiiii stranger miss your… she said. Miss your? Miss you?

Miss you, too, I said. How are you?

How are you; the most monotonous question in the book. I had nothing else to say, our conversations already rare these days, and when we did speak, the content was bland, limited to a series of "What's new?" In fact, it felt like we'd actively started excluding one another from our lives. Etta was likely keeping things from me, too.

I watched my phone screen—Etta was still typing, the ellipsis appearing and disappearing. What was she thinking? Did she know about the weekend, was waiting for the opportune moment to catch me in a lie? I stood, paced the room. In the shower, Archer sang Neil Young, poorly and out of tune, and when I checked my phone again, there was a new message.

Greeeaatt, Etta said, meeeeet Michael Jordan.

Sheer relief, she knew nothing.

As in Michael Jordan? I replied.

She sent me a photo. Etta, her arm wrapped around a man that was not Michael Jordan, at least not the Michael Jordan most people would recognize. This man was bald, with wrinkles and a lip ring. Both their eyes were lifeless. They looked fucked-up.

Lol that's not Michael Jordan, I said.

Hesss pa romorter.

A what?

Promotro

I waited.

mmy promoter.

I studied the photo again. Etta's lips were cracked and dry, fading in the middle where she'd applied red lipstick, like a sad porcelain doll.

I said, Are you ok?

She sent me another photo. Michael Jordan was gone now, and she was giving me the middle finger. Before I could reply, she followed up with a winking emoji and then a red heart. She didn't know what she was saying. The buzzer sounded and I remembered our food delivery.

Sdflwkejrwioerw, she said, and I exited the app.

I wasn't so hungry anymore.

I pressed the green button next to the door, letting the delivery person into the building, and tried to will the thought of Etta from my mind. There was a heavy knock on the door. I turned the knob, but it wasn't our lo mein or wonton soup. It was Astrid in a coral-colored pantsuit, thin gold hoops dangling from her ears. She leaned against the door frame, evidently not recognizing me based on her blank expression.

"Hi," she said, peering over my shoulder and into the room. "Is... Archer here?"

"He's in the shower," I said, then realized how horrible that seemed, what it signaled. I wanted her to say, *I'll come back*, or *Can you tell him I stopped by?*

She didn't do either.

"I can wait," she said. I stepped aside and she entered the apartment. "Ren, was it?"

So she did remember me. "Sorry, I thought you were our Chinese food." She was nodding, but not looking at me as she crossed the room. "Archer's food," I was quick to correct. I'd reverted to walking on eggshells. I had a feeling it wasn't good that Astrid knew I was here.

"Uh-huh," she said, sitting on Archer's bed, crossing her legs, placing her tote on his nightstand, sending Archer's copy of *The Catcher in the Rye* to the floor. She eyed my laptop and I slammed it shut, apologized, said I was answering a few emails.

"Uh-huh," she said again.

I wrung my hands. "I didn't realize you were in New York?"

"I'm back and forth frequently. It's a quick flight from London. Easy."

"Oh, that's nice."

"Very." Her eyes skated around the room, and then to me, to Archer's fingerprints on my arms. I hugged them to my chest. "So I guess you enjoyed your tour with Archer, then?"

"What tour?" She made a face that accused me of being facetious. "Sorry, yes," I said. "The tour at the gallery. It was great."

Her mouth fixed itself into a little smile. "And now you're doing...?" She held up her hands and shrugged, expecting me to fill in the blank.

"I asked Archer if he would paint something for Etta's birthday. From me." It was the first thing that came to mind. I hoped she wouldn't ask more questions.

"And?"

"He said he would do it," I told her, and smiled.

She smiled back. "Of course he did. He would do anything for her." A pause. "How is she, by the way? Enjoying Spain?"

"I think so, yeah," I said.

The shower water had since stopped. I heard the scraping of the curtain across the metal rod. A moment later the bathroom door swung open. Archer had wrapped a towel around his hips.

"Is our food here?" he asked, then he saw our guest.

"Hey, Archer," Astrid said, smug.

I wanted to slip out of my skin, but if Archer was concerned, I couldn't tell.

"Oh, hey, you," he said. She tipped her chin up to his and he kissed her on each cheek. "When did you get in?"

"Late last night. Had a day from hell, or else I would've stopped by sooner. But I've been catching up with Ren. She told me all about Etta's painting."

"For her birthday," I was quick to add.

Archer was squinting at me, then started nodding. "Yes, for her birthday."

Astrid said, "That's really nice, but don't you have other things you should be working on?" She raised an eyebrow, but she was smiling, so I guessed this was their banter, somewhere between sarcasm and gentle teasing.

"I'll figure it out," Archer said, still watching me.

I stood up. "All right. Well, I guess I should head out, then."

"Okay," Archer said.

Astrid didn't seem to care, whether I was leaving or staying or where I was going. She leaned back on her elbows and gazed up at Archer. "So what did you order? Ren said you got Chinese. Anything I would like?"

As I slid my laptop into my bag, Archer said, "Um, wonton soup, lo mein, egg rolls."

"Oh, you love your egg rolls," she told him.

"Okay, well, nice seeing you both," I said, but they didn't respond. I avoided looking at either of them as I slipped out.

In the hallway the lights flickered, like a fucking horror film. I heard Astrid's voice slithering behind me. "I hope you got dumplings," she said as I pushed the button to call the elevator one too many times.

When the metal grates locked me in, I lost it. I did. I cried all seventy seconds, the whole ride down.

20

"Wow, I finally got you," Etta said on FaceTime. It was late Saturday afternoon, and I was sitting in her living room. I'd had two and a half glasses of wine, an especially aromatic Pinot Noir from California that stained my mouth red. I hadn't eaten much all day except for two slices of toast, a banana and a handful of pistachios, so I was already a little drunk. My appetite wasn't great this past week; Jeff owed it to stress, but I knew it had more to do with the fact that I hadn't seen or heard from Archer since I fled his apartment on Monday.

"What do you mean?" I asked, and Etta burst into laughter.

"You look so concerned. Just that every time I call, you don't answer. Aren't I supposed to be the busy one?"

"Well, we talked a few days ago?" I said, but Etta came back with a resounding, "No, we didn't?" She had forgotten our Instagram exchange, the incoherent messages. Maybe they didn't count. I decided not to press the issue.

"It's work," I said. "I've been crazed. It's actually annoying."

"That's not sustainable. You're going to burn yourself out."

She adjusted her hair, which was fastened on top of her head in a high ponytail, its long mane swinging from side to side as she traipsed the apartment. She settled on a clubby sofa not so different from the one I was sitting on in New York.

"So funny story," Etta said. I was grateful for the change in subject. "Astrid said she ran into you?"

That gratitude was replaced with a pit in my stomach. I didn't know how to respond, if it was better to admit I had been at Archer's or attempt lying again, but then she added, "Outside of the gallery? I don't know, Lizzie told me."

"Oh," I said, trying not to smile too much, "yeah, earlier this week. I was, um, leaving a work dinner. Of course."

It was startling how easily these details came to me, but they seemed to convince Etta. She leaned back so that her head was cushioned by an especially plush cream-colored pillow.

"Was she nice?"

"Yeah, she was fine," I said.

"But she didn't seem stressed or anything."

I frowned. "No, I wouldn't say so. I mean, I probably spoke to her for thirty seconds."

Etta nodded slowly and the screen froze for a second.

"So a lot has happened since we last spoke."

"Has it?" I asked, and she broke into a smile.

"I may have met someone."

I threw back my head, matched my smile to hers.

"His name is Erik. He's a graduate student. Assisting our professor. He's from Girona." The way she said *Girona* implied she found him exotic. "He created a GIF that went viral here. Hold on, let me see if I can find it." She paused the screen so all I could see was her blurred outline. She went on: "Digital art is sort of lowbrow, though, all things considered. I haven't said this to Erik. He'd think I was a snob, but between us, I'm kind of shocked my parents suggested I do this program in the first place. I mean, digital art is challenging the integrity of what art really means, in terms of its being a commodity. Yes, it provides job opportunities for people that need them, but I don't know, my parents said that one day, in the near future, digital art will *ruin* real art. Devalue it."

"Oh," I said, though I had no idea what she was talking about.

"No, really," Etta said. "Eventually, people will call anything they want *art*. It cheapens it. Digital art is not art."

"Sounds complex."

Her face shot onto the screen again. "I can't find it. Sorry."

"Well, another time, then," I said.

Etta was silent. It felt as if she wanted to say something else, was perhaps withholding, or considering the best approach. A wave of anxiety roiled through me and I had the sudden urge to end the call, but then she said, "You should come visit me."

Another performative smile as I told her, "I'd love that." Sometimes, when you told someone you would love to do something, you didn't have to mean it, only hint that you cared enough to entertain the idea.

I laughed. Etta laughed. Then she stopped laughing.

"You can stay with me. We'll get tapas and I can show you La Boqueria. I guess we could go to Park Güell, too. Oh, and the beach. You have to see the beach. We'll cover all the touristy spots. And I can host everyone for dinner one night. Erik will cook—he's an *insane* cook. He taught me how to make this dish called *pan con tomate*, which is basically just bread with tomato…" She carried on, how the beach clubs were a "shitshow," but we would have a table and not to worry.

Maybe it was the wine or low blood sugar, but my mind was spinning, her generosity like a gag shoved down my throat.

"Etta, sorry, I can't just come to Europe right now," I said.

"Not right now," she said, as if it were obvious. "I'm talking like September. For my birthday."

I remembered the lie I'd told Astrid, the painting I'd supposedly asked Archer to make for Etta.

"Right," I said. "But aren't flights so expensive? At the moment?" I was clawing for excuses—money seemed like a legitimate one, and maybe Etta would understand.

"I'll book your flight for you," she offered.

I explained I had a job, and a boss, though I didn't mention she was a boss I had lied to so I could go to Amagansett with Etta's brother, and that it was a job I was ambivalent about, but which imbued my days with clear purpose and meaning. "Etta," I said, whining, smiling, "thank you, but I can't just request days off to travel to Europe, as much as I'd love to see you."

"But I'm giving you enough notice." She pouted.

Without warning, she flipped the screen so I could see her surroundings: high ceilings, sleek, brightly colored art on the walls offsetting a creamy marble coffee table, pale blue bouclé sofa, two matching suede armchairs. She led me to a pine-green shuttered door and pushed it open, stepping onto a balcony. I heard the din of traffic below, a cluster of voices floating up from the street. Across the way was a row of apartments with individual Juliet balconies framed by a dark purple sky.

"Does this make you want to visit? Just a little?" she teased.

I wasn't going to win. "I'll think about it," I said.

Etta slammed the shuttered door behind her. "Okay. Now show me the view from my apartment."

My apartment. We were treading on delicate ground, an inevitability that she would remind me I was living in her apartment, for free, that I "owed" her. She wasn't wrong.

I got up from the couch and padded across the room, pressing the phone to the window. Here in New York, the sky was unusually foggy, clusters of clouds masking the sun. In fact, I hadn't seen the sun in days, and I couldn't even comment on the temperature because I hadn't been outside, instead choosing to mope, watch Bravo, scroll mindlessly through my phone.

Etta issued the perfunctory "I miss New York," and I told her, "New York misses you."

"Do you just tell me what I want to hear?" She arched a single brow, but before I could react, she chuckled and asked me to show her around the apartment; she was homesick.

Easy enough. I began with the living room, pointing out familiar objects, narrating the furniture she knew she had, the views with which she was all too familiar. She said, "Flip the screen. I don't need to see your face."

"Okay," I said, continuing the tour. "On to the kitchen…"

She called out the pistachio shells on the counter, the sparse roll of paper towels, the dirty dishes stacked in the sink, the dish towels on the island, and one draped over a bar stool. "Well, someone has made themselves at home," she said, and I flushed red. She asked me to open the wine cooler. "Now show me—" Laughter funneled through the phone. "Ren, have you been helping yourself to my wine?"

I could have said, *Not only your wine.* "Guilty. Is that okay?"

She laughed even more. "Of course. I'm glad someone's enjoying it. There are some really good bottles in there! Champagne, too."

I wanted to say, *I'm well aware,* but instead I smiled.

From the kitchen we crisscrossed to the dining room, housing a long glass table with twelve seats, set for no one, a cabinet offering a glimpse of Laboratorio Paravicini china. We traversed to the bedroom wing, and at her request, I pushed open the door to hers.

"Can you do me a favor?" she asked once we were inside.

"Yeah?"

"Those flowers on my nightstand. Do you see what I'm talking about?"

Of course I did. "I think so?" I said.

"They're dead. Weird Cora didn't throw them out." Cora was the woman who cleaned the apartment. "Can you do it?" she asked.

"Yes, absolutely," I said, and dutifully grabbed the bouquet, the vase of murky water.

"They were from Archer," she said. "Congratulating me on the move. It was actually really thoughtful of him."

"Aw." I examined the flowers again, now growing mold, and pitched them into the trash in the bathroom. "Etta," I said then, flipping the screen back, "your parents know I'm staying here, right?"

"No. Why?"

"They wouldn't be mad?"

"No. They're hardly in New York during the summer anyway, and if they are in town, they're in the Hamptons." She saw my panic. "Ren, they aren't going to show up at the apartment. They literally have no reason to."

"But what if they do?"

"Trust me, they won't."

"How can you be sure?"

"I just am," she snapped. "They didn't when *I* lived there, so why would they now? Regardless, they don't care about you or what you're doing there or why. None of it makes any difference to them."

She'd made it sound so simple, so matter-of-fact, but I knew it wasn't. I remembered what Archer had told me, about Etta being indebted to their parents, that comfort came at a price.

"I'm sorry," I said.

Her face softened. "You worry too much," and I thought, *If only you knew.*

I walked back toward the living room. Our conversation was reaching its inevitable end. She'd say she was tired, or had to run, or was hosting friends for a late dinner, I didn't know, and I'd be relieved and could continue whatever it was I was doing before she called: more wine, more takeout, more ruminating on my choices and whether I would hear from Archer. It was pathetic how much of my mental space he'd taken up. If it were any other person *but* Archer, I could have confided in Etta, but I'd relinquished that option several weeks ago, when I called his assistant.

Etta yawned and I was about to say, "Good night," when halfway down the hall, she said, "Wait. Stop. Go back." She made a motion with her hands. "Like back. Walk."

I retraced my steps and Etta instructed me to rotate the screen so she could see.

"Hmm," she said. "That's weird." She closed her eyes, as if trying to remember something. "There used to be a painting there."

"Where?" I asked.

"On that far wall."

She was right. There had been a painting there, the one Archer had stopped by to retrieve when Jeff and I were playing dress-up in Etta's closet.

"It was like orange-y," she said.

"I'm sorry," I said, "I don't remember."

She pursed her lips. "That is so strange."

Was it strange? I didn't want her to jump to conclusions, to imagine that I was keeping something from her, well, apart from the obvious. Better to be honest now, I thought, when I needed to lie again later.

"Wait, sorry," I said. "Brain fart. I'm pretty sure Archer picked it up."

"He stopped by the apartment?"

"Yeah, a few weeks ago. He was here for like, five minutes. I honestly forgot until you reminded me. He said he sold it."

"He did?"

I nodded, but I was sweating through my T-shirt.

"Wait, that's exciting. Did he say to who?" I was about to say no, but she said, "Forget it—I doubt he went into that much detail with you." I wasn't sure if she'd meant it as an insult, that I didn't matter enough to warrant explanations. The muscles in her jaw relaxed. "Sorry, I got kind of panicky there. I thought someone had like, stolen it."

I continued toward the living room and sank into the sofa. Through the window, a bolt of lightning split across the sky. This summer, with its impossible heat and bursts of precipitation, and still, nothing could cut the humidity.

"Well, I'm sorry, too," I said. "I should have mentioned it when he stopped by in the first place. I didn't think anything of it."

"It's okay," she said. "It would have gotten back to me eventually, one way or another."

I forced a smile. "Right."

"So," Etta said, "what else is going on? Any boy stories? I told you mine."

I studied Etta's face. Her eyes were slightly puffy, but her expression was peaceful, open. She sincerely wanted to know.

"Well," I began, "I have been talking to someone, kind of."

"I knew it," Etta said. "You're always so coy with this shit. Go on."

I wiped my palms on my thighs. "Well, it's early, obviously, we've only gone on a few dates."

"How'd you meet? The apps?"

I swallowed. "Mmm-hmm."

"Nice."

"Yeah. Um, we had a good date the other day but I think I… I may have said something weird, and ruined it."

"What did you say?"

I stalled, said it was nothing in particular, come to think of it, that I probably was only acting strangely. "Distant," I said, "you know how I can get."

"I do," she said. "Your defenses are always up."

I shrugged. "So yeah, anyway, I haven't heard from him."

"Ren," she said, as if staring deep into my soul.

Uncomfortable, I started to laugh. "Yes?"

"Why don't you just text him? Maybe he doesn't know where you stand."

I avoided her gaze. "You think that's a good idea? It isn't too forward?"

"Get out of your head, Ren. Do you want to text him or not?"

I hesitated. If only she knew the truth, the details I'd omitted.

"My advice is pointless," Etta said. "You already know what you want to do anyway."

21

Later that evening, as Etta had predicted, I caved and texted Archer.

He responded immediately. Well it's nice to hear from you.

We agreed to meet in Washington Square Park tomorrow afternoon. It was almost too cliché, congregating in not only one of the city's most iconic places, but a focal part of my old NYU stomping grounds, too. In the early stages of my friendship with Etta, when it was still warm outside, I'd find her sitting on a bench between classes, wrapping up a call with her therapist before therapy had become both mainstream and cool. How she'd look at me and roll her eyes, miming that she'd just be "one second," but it was never just one second. Inevitably, I'd end up waiting for much longer than she'd promised.

At 1 p.m., the park was crowded, people cutting through the pathways, sitting on benches shaded by leafy green trees. Tourists and families lined up for the ice cream truck near the Arch, a man blew bubbles—always a man blowing bubbles—and two gentlemen played the tuba and trombone. A cacophony of children's laughter as they splashed in the fountain. A woman, about my age, maybe older, frowned at a paperback, tossing annoyed looks over her shoulder at some noise or another. I thought, *Why come here to read?* She was probably a grad student at NYU, or someone who took herself too seriously. She wore a long black tank dress and Birkenstocks, a dark leather satchel propped beside her on the bench, as if to say, *Yes, you can sit here, but my bag and I would prefer if you didn't.* I wanted to say, *Do you want attention for reading your book in a very public place? An award, even? You want people to admire your self-professed intellectualism, your "dedication" to whatever it is you're doing?* And then I realized, I was jealous. I was jealous of her independence. I was jealous that she didn't care what people thought of her, their assumptions. Etta once said that the things we didn't like about others were the very things we lacked; ironic, considering she was perhaps the least self-aware person I knew, and yet, she did know people. She could read a room, recall important details, facts, entire conversations. It was her superpower.

I only stopped eyeing the woman with the book because I'd spotted Archer, seated across from her, near the center of the park. I recognized his back, the slope of his long torso. I called his name but he didn't turn around. As I got closer, I saw his headphones, their thin white wires hanging from his ears. I tugged on one and it fell to his knee.

"Hi," I said.

He looked up and smiled, then gestured for me to sit, handing me a hot coffee from a cup carrier beside him.

"I didn't know if regular milk was okay?" he asked.

"I'm not picky," I said.

"Well, you know, everyone with their 'milk alternatives' these days. Etta's a complete milk snob, I'm sure you know."

"Almond milk or nothing," I said.

"Go figure."

Small talk first, each of us sharing updates about our week, though I was too in my own head to even comprehend what either of us was saying, but when I heard him mention Astrid, I must have made a face.

"Astrid didn't ask about you," he said, "if that's what you're worried about."

"Sorry, what?" I wished I had been paying better attention.

"When you left on Monday. Or is *bolted* perhaps a better word?"

"Was it that obvious?" I asked.

"No, I really don't think she cares. But apparently I'm painting something for Etta's birthday? Care to tell me about that?"

I peeled my eyes from his and stared across the park. "Sorry. It was the first thing I thought—I panicked when Astrid showed up."

Archer sipped his coffee, watching me as if unconvinced.

"So Etta and I caught up the other day," I said.

"And all good? You're feeling better about things?"

I recalled the lie I'd told her, about the guy I'd been supposedly seeing from the apps, and how in actuality he was seated beside me, tilting his head and drinking a coffee, that there was a small scratch on his chin from where I guessed he had nicked himself shaving.

"I think so," I said. "She wants me to visit her. In Barcelona."

He didn't hesitate. "You should do it. Have you been? It's great."

I shook my head, and a filament of thought registered that he was getting rid of me, sending me away. "Yeah, maybe I'll go for her birthday."

I wanted to disappear, to thank him for the coffee, to go home, wherever that was, and start over. Press Control-Alt-Delete on my life, up until he said, "So is this why you texted me?"

I turned toward him. "What do you mean?"

"To tell me it was fun, but we shouldn't see each other again?"

I drank my coffee and burned my tongue. "Why, do you think we shouldn't?"

Archer pressed his finger to his lips. "I guess I was concerned I hadn't heard from you and then I realized I wanted to hear from you, which meant that I wanted to see you again. So. I don't know. You tell me."

Archer knocked his knees into mine and I smiled with relief.

"I would like to keep seeing you," I heard myself say, and it sounded as if my voice were hovering above me, like my life was being narrated by someone else. No matter that sometimes I felt like a puppet, my emotions mastered by strings I didn't control. I decided that in this moment, I would choose happiness, or whatever I thought happiness was.

Across from us, I again noticed the woman with the book, her eyes tracing a clear line to me and Archer, her book propped open in her lap, the pages flapping in a light breeze. Minutes ago I'd envied her. The statement she made by choosing to sit alone in a crowded place. But maybe she saw me and Archer, looking blissed out with our coffees and our smiles and our touching knees, and she thought, *I want what they have,* as if we were the best item on the menu. And maybe, she envied me, too.

———

We ate lunch at a bistro on Sullivan Street, narrow tables on a stretch of sidewalk and where the chef owner was an "old friend" from somewhere. This was his city, I thought, old friends tucked away in every corner, waiting to rush to his assistance. We ordered eggs and French toast and more coffee and these little ricotta toasts with raspberries and honey, and when the check never came, Archer laughed and said, "They must be comping us," meaning we didn't have to pay, but Archer still tipped two hundred dollars cash from the wad in his wallet anyway.

"So," he said, "I did leave out one detail about my week."

"Oh?" I asked, and I felt my throat constrict, the familiar sensation that the other shoe was about to drop.

"I went back to Amagansett for a few days."

Oh. That was all. No falling shoe, no real drama.

"To see your parents?" I asked.

He brought the mug of coffee to his lips. "I don't know if Etta has told you, but they do these parties. Their 'summer series,' they call them." He rolled his eyes as he sipped and I laughed.

"Yeah, she's mentioned it. They invite a bunch of their friends, right?"

"Friends, colleagues, acquaintances. It's just like, an opportunity for everyone to get together and brag about their lives, but—" he gestured so that some of the coffee leapt out of his mug "—tastefully, of course. Always tastefully. There's a real art to the humble brag."

"Lovely," I said, but Archer became more serious now.

"Well, anyway, I went to one of these 'parties.'"

"And how was that?"

"Fine. I mean, it would be ignorant of me to avoid *all* of their connections. Some of their friends are pretty important. Big collectors and whatnot."

"So can they help you at all?"

"Hopefully. One of their friends is affiliated with a pretty significant gallery abroad. He says I might be able to show there. Not until next summer, though."

"That's exciting," I said.

He rubbed his face in his hands. "Yes, but it's funny. I want these 'things,' these 'opportunities,' but it's still work. It can subtract from some of the joy that comes with making art. The commodifying aspect."

Quietly I said, "I guess that would make sense. Art is still a business."

"Oh, don't ever doubt it. That's the fucked-up thing about it all. There is no art without money. There is no art without people like my parents' friends. I would be happy just making things. Who needs the rest of it?"

I stared at him blankly. "But what about compensation?" His eyes didn't acknowledge my question. "I mean," I said, "if you're going to make a living with your art…" But then I heard myself, remembered people like Etta and Archer pretended money didn't exist, and regretted asking at all.

Archer scratched at his cheek. "That's part of the issue. I could have chosen another path, couldn't I?"

"I guess?" I said, though I didn't think he was really asking my opinion.

He tapped his fist against the surface of the table. "I've thought about taking a break, like a real break, not 'living on a friend's houseboat and still working out ideas in my mind' break, but every time I've come close, I'll get a flash of something and start the cycle again. And I'm honestly afraid I'd go crazy without it."

"I get that," I said, but I was thinking of my job now.

"But it is what it is," he said. He tipped his mug on its side so it looked as if the coffee might spill, and asked, "Do you ever think seriously about your writing?"

"What do you mean by *seriously*?"

He tried again. "Do you feel like you need to write, or it's more of a hypothetical?"

"I still don't know what you're saying."

"This other job of yours," he said.

"My actual job, you mean. In PR. Yes?"

"I guess what I'm saying is you have to ask if you're content with your life, or if a part of you will always wonder if you sold yourself short."

I laughed, which seemed to surprise him.

"I don't know," I said.

"That's a good answer," he said.

"Most people don't make it, Archer. So it's kind of like, why bother?"

"That's the gamble with everything. You should still try."

I wanted to say, *Easy for you to say; gamble is a loose term, a suggestion; your parents have already ensured some level of your success*, but I knew I couldn't. I'd seen his reaction when the first reviews were published, when the people whose opinions mattered most more or less vilified him for not being good enough, original enough, "avant-garde" enough. That was life, wasn't it? There would always be an antagonist reminding you of your shortcomings.

"Yeah, maybe. I don't know. I'll get around to it," I said, but my brain dissolved of all its logic when I saw my father striding toward us in wrinkled cargo shorts and a pale red short-sleeve shirt. Those same New Balance sneakers, nauseatingly pristine in juxtaposition to the rest of him. What was he doing here?

When he got closer, I realized he wasn't alone, accompanied by a busty blonde woman. Or maybe it wasn't him, my eyes were playing tricks on me. The stain on the ceiling, and now this.

"Ren?" he asked.

So it was him.

They paused at our table and I felt all the blood draining from my face, all the coffee I'd drunk rattling my insides. "What are you doing here?"

I felt Archer's eyes flitting among me, my dad, and the woman I presumed to be his girlfriend. The confusion pooling between us, spilling onto the sidewalk.

"Archer, this is my dad," I said, looking down at the table.

Archer stood to shake his hand and I felt like I was having an out-of-body experience.

"Shari," my dad said, turning to his companion, "this is my daughter, Ren." He still hadn't answered my question about what he was doing here. Shari gave me a passive little wave, flaunting her French tips.

"What are you doing here?" I asked again.

He glanced at his hands. "We're here for a...long weekend."

A server came by and asked if we wanted more coffee and Archer whispered to him, shaking his head.

"Just because?" I asked.

Shari said, "My daughter just moved in to a studio on Thompson, around the corner?"

"I know where Thompson is," I said, and Dad shot me a look.

"We're helping her get settled. On a quick break right now, our hotel is just that way." Shari pointed past Houston Street.

My father, who'd never seen my apartment, whose sole charitable act was meeting me for breakfast at a Midtown diner, where we split the check, was helping someone else's daughter *get settled*. I focused on Shari and smiled wide. "How exciting. She's new to the city?"

My question was the gateway to information I didn't need: where her daughter worked—at a consulting firm that meant nothing to me—and her boyfriend who had, so sadly, accepted a job offer in Tulsa after graduation. "But you know," she said, "they're young, and I told her there's so many fish in the sea." Shari was doing that thing where people rambled during uncomfortable situations, as if their verbal diarrhea might offset the awkwardness.

So it was serious between Shari and my dad, I guessed, serious enough that he'd helped her daughter move in to her apartment. Meanwhile, I'd hired movers on my own; I didn't bother to ask for his help, and he didn't offer.

"You live here?" Shari asked me.

I said, "The East Village," at the exact moment my dad said, "Uptown."

Our eyes caught; my dad broke away first.

"I'm just...so shocked to see you," I said to him.

My dad cleared his throat. "I think we'll be back in..." He searched Shari for an answer.

"August," Shari said. "The sixth. My daughter's birthday. We have a dinner reservation at this Mexican place she loves, not too far from here?"

"Hmm," I said, but I was thinking how many times could this woman reference her daughter in one conversation, and of the tacky Mexican place where they likely had a reservation and where I'd been once, with Etta, when it first opened and before it devolved into a haven for the Bridge and Tunnel crowd.

Archer's face was a blank palette; it wasn't often there was no place for him in a social situation.

My dad said, "You should join us," newly cheerful, trying to win me over with mediocre tacos and margaritas at a glorified tourist trap. No, thank you.

"I'll have to check my calendar," I said, and I wished they would just leave.

Shari spoke with her hands. "Well, you know, if not then, we could meet for lunch or something. I'm retired now and have a lot more free time."

I remembered how my father had conveniently been in the city for a friend's retirement party last month, when he stayed at the Sheraton and met me for breakfast. So this was the *friend*. I should have known.

I eyed my dad, as if to say, *I know*, but he was ogling the sidewalk. "That would be nice," I said, though it wouldn't, and if they asked me to grab a meal or coffee or participate in any degree of mediation, I would say, *I'm busy*, every single time. "Well, it was great meeting you…" I looked to Shari, inferring that I'd already forgotten her name.

"Shari," she said.

I nodded. "Shari. Anyway, good luck with the move."

My dad seemed weirdly hesitant to leave, as if he wasn't sure how this revelation had landed with me (poorly) and if he should really depart on this sour note (yes), but Shari tugged his arm, pulling him down the street. She glanced at us over her shoulder as they made their way to the far end of the block.

"I'm sorry," I said to Archer once they'd gone, "that was so weird."

"It wasn't weird," he said, but I could sense the lack of conviction in his voice, that he was only telling me this to make me feel better. "They seemed nice." Code for "boring," I thought, recalling what Etta had said. "So this was the first time you met his—" he seemed apprehensive "—girlfriend?"

"Yeah," I said.

Shari and my dad were now waiting for the light to change at the crosswalk. His shorts were wrinkled, as was the back of his shirt. He looked like someone I barely knew, maybe because I didn't know him. Not anymore.

PART THREE

AUGUST–SEPTEMBER

22

I started spending most weeknights at Archer's, walking from my office in Midtown to his studio in Chelsea. After a month, we had something of a routine: he would paint and I would read. Lately, it was *Goodbye, Columbus* and Didion's essays in *The White Album*. Reading made me feel closer to the act of writing. We'd order takeout because Archer's place only had a mini-fridge so cooking was impossible. While Archer showered before our food arrived, I'd cross the street to the liquor store and select a bottle of wine, which we would drink from plastic cups. He didn't have a television so we would stream Netflix on his laptop, perching it on his lap and pressing our bodies to one another in his twin bed. One evening I brought over an electric kettle from Etta's so we could make tea. Archer said, "It's August," and I countered, "But it's freezing in here." So at night he would hold me and I'd feel his heart beating against my back and he'd say, "Are you warm now?" and I'd say, "Very."

———

"Do you only choose to spend time with me when your boyfriend isn't available?" Jeff asked. We were at Etta's apartment on a Thursday after work while Archer was out of town at some artist retreat in the Catskills.

"No," I said.

"I don't believe you," Jeff said.

"Also," I corrected, "he isn't my boyfriend."

"Oh? Then what is he?"

"I don't know. We're taking it slow, I guess. Labels ruin things."

Jeff sneered. "Yeah, they all say that."

"Who's *they*?" I asked.

Jeff stood to use the restroom and over his shoulder said, "Everyone."

———

Archer invited me to a thing at the MoMA, which meant I would need a dress. I borrowed something of Etta's, a beige vintage slip and Gucci heels that were a little too big on me but still passable. Of course, Natalie had a last-minute dinner; our client from London was in town and they'd never met, only existed to one another as voices on a conference line. The dinner was at Carbone, an Italian place on Thompson and far away from the MoMA. Natalie asked if I could somehow get to the restaurant before her, find out from the maître d' who else was seated at their table, and text Natalie this information while she was in her Uber from the office, and then, if I wouldn't mind, if I could escort Natalie to the table and introduce her to our client. To be "introduced" conveyed your importance. Naturally, Natalie's perverse use of *if you could* and *if you wouldn't mind* were all designed to trick me into thinking I had a choice, that I could say no, when both of us knew I wouldn't dare.

I texted Archer that I would be a bit late, changed into my

dress and heels at the office, then took the train downtown. It would be relatively painless. A quick train ride, maybe a cab uptown if I was feeling fancy, or my feet hurt.

At the restaurant, however, the maître d' was perturbed why I would ask for such determinedly "private" information about a reservation in which I wasn't included, that he couldn't share information about their guests, or where they were seated. When I explained the situation, that my boss had sent me there to introduce her, he seemed to feel sorry for me, probably believing I'd gotten all dressed up for the occasion. He said, "I can't *confirm* they are seated there, but if they're a larger party, they might be at the round table in the back."

"Thank you," I whispered.

Moments later Natalie arrived, commenting on my dress, asking where I was headed since I looked "so nice," as if I'd never looked truly nice before. When I told her I was going to an event in Midtown, not so far from our office, she clicked her tongue and said, "Oh, how annoying of me that I asked you to come all the way down here."

I smiled. "It's no problem. I'm happy to help." I held the door open for her and locked eyes with the maître d', a silent exchange of sympathies.

"So where are they?" she asked, and I responded, "In the back."

Natalie stomped ahead and I chased after her, feeling like a court jester as I said, "This is Natalie," then announced her title and how long she had been with the agency—fifteen years.

Our client stood and kissed her on either cheek, said it was the "greatest pleasure" to meet her, then everyone inspected me, as if wondering what I was doing there, and why. Natalie whispered, "Okay, you can go now," and I sort of bowed my head and left.

I hailed a cab to the MoMA and in the car texted Jeff what had happened. He wrote, **You better expense that cab, bitch,** except I knew I wouldn't.

It was a donor event, a "thank-you" from the museum to its patrons in the form of an open bar and passed bites, and because
Archer's parents were out of town again, though their exact
coordinates were vague, he went on their behalf. I recognized
the format well: not black-tie, but formal enough that people
had put on their faces. Like usual, everyone knew one another,
clustering in groups across the museum, and I found myself on
edge, eyes skating around the room, watchful of a photographer or someone who might want to get a photo of me. *Don't
flatter yourself*, I thought.

Around nine, Archer asked if I wanted to leave and get pizza.
When he went to use the restroom downstairs first, I sat on a
bench in the hall and kicked off my heels. The leather straps
had cut into the side of my foot, as if someone had taken a dull
knife to my skin. In my purse, my phone vibrated with a text
from Chip. At Spring Lounge—what are you up to? he asked.
The fact that he was still trying implied boredom or a bruised
ego, that he couldn't *accept* that I wouldn't give him what he
wanted: attention. I wouldn't respond.

Minutes later Archer reappeared, rolling up the sleeves of his
white button-down. He looked almost like a stereotypical finance guy when he dressed the part, except for his sneakers, old
Nike ones that he wore with everything and which made him
seem both like he didn't care at all or as if he'd only cultivated
a specific persona of not caring.

"Ready?" he asked.

I slipped my shoes on and hooked my arm through his. Paul
was off tonight so Archer hailed us a cab, but when we slid into
the backseat, he gave the address of the gallery in Chelsea.

"I have to pick up something first," he said, and wove his
fingers with mine.

In my lap, my phone pinged with another message from Chip,

then another. Archer noticed and I flipped the phone so that the screen was facing down.

"You're talking to Chip?" Archer asked, surprised.

"No," I said. He dipped his chin in my direction. "I'm pretty sure he drunk-texts me when he's bored. I don't answer or anything."

"You can answer if you want," Archer said with a shrug.

A distinct sense of disappointment, that Archer didn't care.

"Well, do you *care* if I answer him?"

He took a moment to respond. "I mean, I'd prefer if you didn't."

An opportune time to ask, "What are we?" or "What is this?" but I didn't want to ruin whatever was happening between us. I'd learned that assigning meaning and titles to things could often make men squirm, and it wasn't like I was interested in Chip anyway; he was a clown.

"So I'm not going to respond then," I announced.

Archer squeezed my hand in his and my mouth stretched into a smile.

———

The gallery was closed but Archer had a key. He punched in a code and beelined for the offices in the back. The quiet was almost eerie as I walked around the main room, where his paintings were still on display, assuming an almost ghostly presence in the half light.

"They're coming down this week," he said.

I spun around as Archer crossed the room to the front desk, unlocking a closed drawer.

"What is?" I asked, walking closer until I stood just behind him.

He rifled through the drawer. "The paintings. The show is over. It ends Thursday."

"Oh," I said. *The show is over.* The general passage of time, summer's denouement, read like an omen. "That was quick."

"Well, it might have lasted longer if the reviews were more favorable." When I was silent, he looked up and said, "I'm kidding. The show is over because the dates in the contract say so." *Of course*, I thought. "But it's okay. It means I have time to think, to attempt to reinvent myself again. Everything here sold, too."

"That's amazing," I said.

"I guess, yeah. So maybe I should stick with this general direction? People seem to like paintings that resemble a mess."

"Ironic," I said.

Archer laughed—the sound surprised me. It was higher pitched and echoed around us.

"Sorry," he said, "let me find this sheet of paper, then we can go. I know I promised pizza and I like to be a man of my word."

"All good," I said as Archer focused on the task at hand. Outside, an ambulance whirred past, red flashing lights flooding the room like a crime scene. "Archer," I said.

"Hmm?"

"Do you think there is such a thing as being 'ready'?"

He stopped what he was doing. "What do you mean? Like, you're ready to go?"

I laughed. "No, I mean in terms of like, life. Being ready to *do* something."

He resumed searching the drawer, but I could see his brow was furrowed. "I'm not sure," he said. "Can you elaborate?"

I considered the errand I'd run for Natalie tonight, how I'd always been so eager to please. How I'd bent to Etta's whims and demands without ever really pushing back until now, when she was far away, when I didn't need her as much. I wondered if I would ever shed this version of myself, or if it would only strengthen with time.

"I think sometimes," I said, "I'm scared of change."

"That doesn't make you defective. It makes you human." He paused. "It's why we have to push ourselves to do the uncomfortable thing, but—" he scanned the room "—I do believe that sometimes we are not ready for certain experiences. That there is such a thing as divine timing."

"Oh, god," I laughed. "What did they teach you at that artist residency?"

Archer laughed, too, but he was squinting past me now, as if in deep thought. "However, I *do* think that the notion of being ready is also an excuse. There are things that we may never be *ready* for, and avoiding them reads more like fear."

His words confirmed what I hoped they wouldn't. That in avoiding Etta, in refusing to challenge the status quo of my life, whether that was in work or personal or whatever, I was making a choice—one rooted in this exact fear he described. Ambivalence would only get me so far. Still, it was the evil I knew.

I turned away from him, gravitating toward a particular painting on the far wall. It was smaller than the more imposing canvases, and different in style, too. In the pseudo-darkness it seemed blue, but it could have also been black or gray, I wasn't sure, with a single white line cutting across the center, almost like the line of a horizon, a clear separation of something, a new beginning, or ending, even. *A before and after,* I thought. Once you crossed that line, you could never go back.

Footsteps behind me then and Archer's shoulder brushed mine. He asked what I was thinking.

Startled, I said, "Nothing."

"No one ever thinks about *nothing*."

I paused. "I was thinking of my mother. Actually."

"Do you think about her a lot?"

"Not really. I mean, I used to, but it wasn't helpful. All that dwelling."

As if on cue, he asked, "Is that why you avoid writing? Because you're afraid of what you might have to say?"

Yes, I thought.

"Did I tell you about how I used to google her?" He shook his head. "About a year ago there was an obituary. So I clicked on it, but it wasn't hers. Just a woman with the same name, in her eighties, in like, Oregon. Not my mom." I lifted my chin to his and saw he was frowning. "The worst thing is, in the seconds before the page loaded, there was still a chance it could be her. I was disappointed when it wasn't. Obviously, I didn't want her to be dead or anything, but at least it explained her—" I struggled for the word "—absence."

"That makes sense," Archer said, and I inhaled. Once I said this next part, I couldn't take it back.

"It was almost like I could face her being dead more than the fact that she had rejected me."

Archer was quiet; I'd shared too much. He was going to accuse me of being a monster, self-absorbed, a psychopath, and maybe I was. Maybe that was what I was avoiding, too—my own innate ugliness. I buried my eyes on the floor when he pressed his thumb into my shoulder, and then there was his hand, pulling me toward him. I started to cry.

"I'm sorry," I said into the collar of his shirt. "That's so fucked-up."

"It's not," he said, but it was.

23

"Remind me," Jeff said, "when do you leave for Spain?"

Etta's birthday, I thought. I'd nearly forgotten, had pushed the trip so far from my mind. I'd allowed her to book my flight, because she'd insisted and knew I wouldn't spend over a thousand dollars on airfare, yet each time we'd spoken over the past few weeks, she'd failed to mention it, almost as if it wasn't truly happening.

"Not until the end of the month," I said. "And it's only for a few days. A quick trip."

Jeff nodded, *quick trip* being a consolation to myself that I wouldn't be there very long. That I could play the part for a long weekend, forget about the details I'd hid from Etta these past few months. And it would be fine—a short burst of togetherness until I could return to New York and resume my life.

We were sitting on our usual bench outside the office with our iced coffees and a front-row view of the construction across the street, the men working all summer on a project concealed by scaffolding. Several feet from us, a man in a baggy suit waited at a hot dog cart, though it was only 11 a.m., and I wondered when we'd all allowed our lives to become so monotonous.

"How is Archer handling it?" Jeff asked.

"Handling what?"

"You. Going to Barcelona to see his sister."

I said, "We haven't discussed it?" as if it was a question.

"So you still haven't said anything to her about it, then."

"*It?*" I asked, though his eyes told me, *You know what I mean: you and Archer.* "No," I said.

"I guess I'm just concerned that you seem to be getting more—" he hovered over the word "—*serious,* and you aren't planning on telling Etta? At all?"

"It's not that I don't plan on telling her. I just don't think I can handle it at the moment."

"You don't think you can handle it."

"You don't know Etta," I said. "If she finds out... I'm afraid she might..."

"*Afraid she might* what?"

I changed the subject, knew if I let Jeff in on some other intimate update, he'd forget all about my avoiding Etta. So I indulged him in the details of my conversation with Archer at the gallery last night. I went on to explain how I was afraid of writing because I was afraid of writing about her.

"It's like he knew, without me having to say it. I don't know. It's weird. Like he was reading my mind."

In my periphery, I could see Jeff watching me. "You want me to say that it means something, right?"

"No," I said with a scoff.

"Well, I was going to say I agree." I considered him. "Obviously, you feel comfortable enough to share these things with him. I mean, it's heavy stuff!"

"Yeah, well, I woke up this morning and found myself googling her all over again. It's like a compulsion. I'm better off when I don't think about her."

"I believe they call that a defense mechanism. You keep brushing things under the rug. Eventually, the problems only get bigger. Learned that in therapy."

I examined my straw; I had chewed it so much that I'd perforated the plastic.

"I already know what a therapist would tell me," I said, "that I need 'closure.' That I should write a letter to her and not send it, something cheesy like that."

But I'd be lying if I said I'd never imagined it, the hypothetical conversation. Ideally, I'd be much more established, a version of myself that could argue my success and independence. *Maybe when I'm thirty*, I thought, as Jeff scooted closer.

"Did you ever try her maiden name?" he asked, queuing up a search on his phone.

I took his phone and with a just a few taps, there it was, all laid out for us in painfully small, sterile font. Age, address, a link to a website. She had reinvented herself as an interior decorator, how cute! No, she wasn't dead. In fact, she lived twenty minutes from where I'd grown up.

Slowly, I lowered Jeff's phone onto his lap. A man shouted expletives at the construction site across the street.

"We should go back to the office," I said. "It's late."

"We have another ten minutes," Jeff said, but I'd already gotten up.

The man from earlier ate his hot dog outside the building's revolving doors, and the air, I realized, suddenly smelled of manure. The seasons were changing and so were the trees that had been transplanted into perfect plots of soil, lining the perfect promenade near our building. And it did look perfect, until you noticed all the trash lining the gutters, until you peeled back the layers. Bags of Cheetos and soaked brown napkins and a plastic Starbucks cup, rolling and rolling until it crossed someone's path and they crushed it under their foot.

24

On a Friday night I met Archer at the Angelika to see a Japanese film his friend had written. Apparently it had shown at Cannes, and it was only his first film, too. I said, "Are all of your friends such high achievers?" and jokingly, Archer told me, "Only the sociopathic ones."

Afterward, we walked to the Lower East Side to get ice cream at Morgenstern's and sat on a bench facing Rivington beside a blur of taxis honking their horns in standstill traffic. Eventually, I said, "So I found my mom. Well, actually Jeff found her." I focused on swirling my spoon in my cup of strawberry ice cream.

Archer was watching me, his spoon frozen in front of his mouth. "You waited all evening to tell me this?"

"She lives in Connecticut," I said. "Twenty minutes from our old house." I flicked my gaze to his. "She doesn't use her married name anymore. It's why I could never find her."

Archer was quiet. We'd reached a place where we could say nothing and my insides wouldn't fear that we had somehow run out of things to talk about. He set his hand on my leg.

"I'm sorry" was all he said.

"It's fine, just weird." He wiped a droplet of ice cream that had dripped onto my knee and I squeezed my eyes shut. "She was a good mom," I said.

"I'm sure."

"No, really," I said. "She was. She proofread all my papers. Helped me with my math homework—I hated math. Made dinner. She was a freaking Class Mom. She just...she did everything." I heard the emotion catch in my voice. "I don't understand what happened. I guess you never know what people are really thinking."

Archer was quiet again, his hand still resting on my leg.

"I don't think my parents are good people," he said then. "Well, they aren't *bad* people, but they aren't great, either. They didn't—" He collected himself. "Sometimes I don't think they understood what it meant to be parents. They never really changed their lives for us, made 'sacrifices.'"

"What do you mean by *sacrifices*?"

"Okay, for example, we went a whole summer once without seeing them because our dad had a show in Hong Kong, and Plum went with him. Me and Etta... It feels like we raised ourselves, a little bit. I—" he removed his hand from my leg and scrubbed at his eye with his fist "—could have probably been a better brother. In retrospect."

"Because you were always the favorite?"

Archer threw back his head. "Is that what she tells you?"

I shrugged. "She doesn't have to. I saw it myself."

Archer ran his tongue along his teeth; he was probably surprised I'd defended Etta. "Yeah, you're not wrong. There's always been a strange double standard with us. Probably because of our parents, how they more or less pitted us against each other. We should have been allies, not..." He trailed off.

"I don't want to be like my parents," I said.

"You won't," he told me, but there was no way he could be sure.

"My dad hasn't called. Since that day we ran into him. Not that I was expecting him to or anything, but still. Just sucks. My mom was my person."

Archer kissed the top of my head and I relaxed into his torso. "Do you ever think of, I don't know, reaching out?" he asked.

I angled my body so I was looking up at him now.

"I mean, you found her new number. You could call her."

"That's insane." I sat up, brushed a bug from my thigh.

"I'm not saying you have to, but *if* you wanted to, if you wanted *closure* or answers, I don't know, maybe it would help?"

I imagined what it might feel like to hear my mother's voice again after all these years. Would it sound the same? Would I recognize it? Would she recognize *me*? But what kind of person abandoned their family? I wasn't sure I wanted to know, if the version of her that existed was better left untouched, protected and preserved by memory.

"Maybe," I said.

Archer clasped my hand in his. "You have to ask yourself what it is you want."

What did I want? I pictured Archer's painting at the gallery, the blue one with the line down the middle. I'd crossed the line; I'd been crossing lines all summer, and crossing lines meant there would be consequences. I couldn't go back to the way it was.

"What I want is to go back to your place," I said, and Archer smiled.

"It's nice out," he told me. "We can walk."

25

It was Ubi Dub's sock collaboration launch party and no one ate lunch or dinner—it wasn't that we wanted to starve, but there was no time. At six, I consumed half a tin of Altoids as we piled into Ubers to the venue, a raw space on Kenmare, all us publicists decked in our "event black," as if we were attending our own funerals. Black meant we blended in, yet could still be easily identifiable should someone need something: to borrow a cell phone, a charger they would never return, or a Xanax, perhaps.

Minutes before doors opened, Jeff tucked an iPad in the crook of his elbow, eyes misting over the long line of guests already snaking around the block, weathering the heat wave all in the name of being seen. Someone passed around headsets so we could all communicate effectively, meaning no one would communicate effectively because everyone with a headset would spend the evening talking over one another, attempting to drown out the static of the competing voices in their ears. Jeff and I secured our headsets, fitting the accompanying radios into our back pockets. Showtime.

The photographer for the event was a man named David. A forty-something-year-old eternal bachelor type with a year-round suntan and perfect veneers. He knew everyone and everyone knew him, so each time I attempted to point out someone of significance, to say, "Oh, there is Countess Anne Grenova," he was already three steps ahead of me, sauntering through the crowd. No matter that I was meant to shadow him for the evening, to ensure he photographed all the most important guests, it was obvious he didn't need, or want, my help.

Within an hour, the room was bursting at the seams, guests sweating off their full faces of makeup, the AC and additional fans nothing more than a placebo against the temperature. Still, people shimmied as a DJ spun a remix of Tears for Fears' "Head Over Heels" while a visual of Ubi Dub reciting T.S. Eliot's "The Hollow Men" projected onto the bare walls. There were the fashion and party editors, exchanging hellos and here on assignment; short, bald men, likely collectors; hedge fund guys and other investors on the arms of their much younger girlfriends and socialite wives; C-list actors clinging to their singular thread of fame from a starring role in a cult teen film over twenty years ago; a niche cluster of eighteen-year-old activists boasting seven-figure Instagram followings and taking advantage of the free champagne; the son of an Oscar winner and his disciples; and finally, the models, swaying their lithe limbs above the heads of everyone else. The excellent turnout confirmed that enough people cared about socks and Ubi Dub, that enough people cared about being seen, and that being seen would always matter.

"Roger not here yet?" Natalie asked. Roger was meant to interview Ubi Dub for an event-specific piece, a favor since he'd passed on the exclusive. He was known for being notoriously picky, earned through decades of reporting for *The Times*.

I shook my head. "I haven't seen—"

"So no?"

I stopped. She wanted certainty. "No. He isn't here."

Natalie's forehead was a smooth, shiny plane, the Botox still fresh, and while I couldn't read her emotions, I sensed her aggravation.

"Great," Natalie said. "So we're waiting on Ubi Dub *and* Roger now. Perfect."

"Wait, Ubi Dub isn't here, either? Where is he?"

She shrugged, her mouth in a knot. "Stuck in traffic? At his hotel? Smoking the biggest *fucking joint* in this whole fucking city?" On the headset, someone's voice crackled: "PR? Can we get someone else at the door? PR? PR?"

"Should have just pitched the story to someone else. You know—" she wagged her finger at me "—if he wasn't with *The Times*, he would be irrelevant. Thank god he's retiring. All this walking on eggshells. He's so persnickety, too."

"Who is? Roger?"

She shot me a look, as if I should have already known, but then softened. "I've worked with Roger for twenty years. He's iconic and his retirement means the end of an era, but it's like shooting a tired horse, cruel but necessary if you want to win."

I was afraid I didn't understand.

"There's always someone younger," she said, "more 'on the ball' who can do his job, and for less, I'm sure. We're all just numbers." Natalie pressed her phone to her ear—she was too senior for a headset, the lone unicorn galloping the floor with only a cell phone. "His publicist, I swear to god, I—" She was smiling serenely now, lowering the phone from her face. Ubi Dub's publicist stood in front of her, meaning Ubi Dub's arrival was imminent.

A voice seared through the headset: "Someone on PR, come to the door *now!*"

Outside, David the photographer smoked a cigarette with an heiress to the "new alternative to ketchup"—she swore you "seriously couldn't taste the difference"—when Jeff shoved his iPad into my arms.

"Thank *god*," Jeff said. "I am literally going to pee myself!"

"Wait," I said, "that was *you*?" but he had already darted inside, leaving me at the door. I wiped the sweat from my forehead as I checked in a couple of writers from *Nylon* and Ubi Dub's friend from art school, a wiry type who'd experienced a sliver of success when an A-lister purchased one of his prints last summer.

A sprinkle of raindrops fell from the sky and I ducked under the awning. I overheard Jasmine the new girl telling someone that she didn't see their name on the list, that she was "so sorry" but she "just didn't see it." I was checking in two influencers in matching pleather dresses when I noticed with whom, exactly, she was speaking.

"Roger," I said, smiling my biggest smile, my biggest *I am so sorry please accept this as our humblest apology* smile. Despite his supposedly imminent retirement, he had promised us a story and we still needed to treat him with care.

He was not having it; he scowled in his faded corduroy jacket, baggy khakis, worn around the knees, and scuffed loafers. Of course Jasmine wouldn't have recognized him, or gleaned his importance—he appeared too ordinary, and she was still too green, having yet to memorize all the faces and names of the right editors, the right party guests, her grasp on this world too tenuous.

I sidled up to Jasmine, peering at the list on the screen, and there it was, a typo. His name had been misspelled. "Roger is an editor with *The Times*. He's interviewing Ubi Dub," I told her.

Awareness set in. Her cheeks flushed red. "Ohmygod. I am *so sorry*."

I said, "It's fine," and asked her to please escort him to VIP. I'd gifted her with a task, as I announced into my headset that Roger had arrived and was being "delivered to Natalie ASAP."

I smiled to myself. The adrenaline rush of navigating a crisis, the satisfaction of solving a problem. I continued checking guests' names off the list, denying those who weren't on it. David was now smoking another cigarette—wait, was that a cigarette?—with the condiments heiress, shielded from the rain by a rando's umbrella, and Jeff had apparently died when he went to use the restroom.

There was a distinct sensation of a hand gripping my wrist. It belonged to a man, tall, broad-shouldered, and wearing a white button-down and dress pants. Gold cuff links winking at me. John Lobb loafers. "What's happening in there?" he asked, glancing past me at the door. Not American. Was he Russian? There was definitely a discernable accent. He had chemically whitened teeth. Hair plugs. I estimated that he was middle-aged, but shot up with Botox that made Natalie's look modest.

I offered him my best PR smile, practically reciting from the press release: the event was a celebration between our client and the lauded street artist Ubi Dub, a limited-edition sock with limited availability.

A second man entered the frame, shorter with a reddish-blond comb-over. He asked, "So how do we get inside?"

"I'm sorry," I said, adjusting my body to block their view, "this is a private event."

The one with the accent stepped closer. "So how," he asked, "do we get inside?"

I started to laugh, gently, of course. Usually, that would do the trick. You'd pad their ego and then they'd get the picture and leave you alone. I said, "I'm really sorry, I do believe we're at capacity."

They were laughing now, pressing in on me, personal space no longer existent. I could smell the alcohol on their breath, the steaks, rare, that they'd had for dinner. My stomach was suddenly burning because all I'd eaten was half a tin of mints, and where the heck was Jeff?

An editor I recognized from *Vogue* sashayed to the front of the line and I checked her in effortlessly.

"At capacity?" the friend with the comb-over asked.

"She's on the list," I said. "She's a writer." My patience was wearing thin; a single droplet of sweat slipped down my back. The air was thick, but the rain was picking up, and the two men huddled closer so they, too, were protected by the awning.

"Well, how do you know *we're* not on the list?" the friend asked.

Because you're not, I thought, *because you're no one*. I knew their type: middle-aged men who worked in finance. They lived in certain enclaves of Connecticut or Westchester or New Jersey. They were drunk following a client dinner and not ready to return to their wives, their lives, which seemed so much more alluring three decades ago when they were young and hopeful, the very life from which my own mother had escaped. But they'd go back, like the good and dutiful husbands their mommies raised them to be. They'd go back because they convinced themselves that their sins were a slate wiped clean when you were a gentleman.

The man with the accent adjusted his sleeves. I could see the diamonds floating in the face of his watch. "Are you absolutely certain?"

I checked over my shoulder. Usually, I wouldn't have budged, but I heard someone inside squeal that Ubi Dub was here and David had stomped out his cigarette with the sole of his sneaker, and I didn't have time for their antics anymore.

"Fine," I said, stepping aside, "you can go."

The friend thanked me, but the man with the accent winked. He whispered in my ear, "We weren't taking no for an answer anyway," and pinched my ass. I froze as they disappeared inside the party.

"I'm sorry," Jeff said then, panting and visibly sweating, his hair matted by rain.

I served him with the iPad. "Where were you?"

THE ART OF PRETEND

"Ubi Dub arrived through the back and apparently the needs for his rider weren't met, so I had to run to the Duane Reade and get six liters of Evian. *Six.* He's here for five fucking minutes."

"He didn't walk the carpet?" I asked, looking around.

"I guess he decided not to."

"I hate this," I told him, but I was still thinking about the gross men with their gross entitlement, when I realized David had vanished again. "Shit," I said, "I keep losing the photographer," and darted inside.

Grainy footage of Ubi Dub jumping on a hotel bed and close-up shots of his socks played on the walls. A line of editors, hopeful to obtain a quote, had formed around the VIP section, recorders at the ready; and there, at the center of the madness, was Ubi Dub, sipping a Red Bull and texting. He was tinier in person, with delicate features, his hair in pigtails. He seemed unfazed as someone adjusted the frilly collar of his blouse, which resembled the pirate's blouse from that episode of *Seinfeld*, except it was probably Gucci and retailed for two grand. His publicist whispered in his ear and he shrugged, then spat a wad of gum into her open palm.

Despite the initial chaos, the interview went seamlessly. David snapped photos, and Ubi Dub and Roger hit it off. When the interview concluded, he shook Roger's hand, and that was when I spotted the man with the accent and his friend, flirting with the pleather-decked influencers in a corner of the room.

"Who are those guys?" Natalie asked me.

"I'm not sure."

She cranked her head in my direction. "You aren't *sure?*"

I had clearly said the wrong thing.

"That's a problem," she said. "We should recognize every single person here. Who's manning the door?"

I sputtered out, "Jasmine?" Natalie's gaze shot toward the entrance and I added, "Jeff, too. I think."

If the Botox had not frozen the muscles in her forehead, something told me she would have been frowning, but she seemed to forget the issue when she recognized a familiar face at the bar and left to greet them.

The beauty of good timing, I thought, and speaking of, Roger appeared, asking if I could send him a comprehensive guest list?

"Sure, of course," I said.

"Well," Roger went on, "it would have made more sense if I spoke with Ubi Dub *before* the first piece came out, and not those garbage quotes you publicists draft and attempt to pass off as 'original.'" I laughed awkwardly and Roger's eyes bobbed around us. "Definitely an interesting crowd tonight," he said. "It's gotten steadily more bizarre over the last few years. I'll tell you, I have just about seen it all."

"Yes," I laughed, and for a moment I saw Roger not as a titan of the PR and reporting world, but as a person. Did he have a partner, someone he loved? Maybe kids or grandkids? A cat or dog? I realized I knew nothing about his life, and he knew nothing about mine. We were strangers, names clogging each other's inboxes when we wanted something. Feeling sentimental, I said, "I'm sure you'll miss these sort of events, though, right?"

He pushed his glasses up his nose. The lenses were smudged, and I thought he had perhaps not heard me—the music was, after all, suddenly too loud.

I smiled. "Well, just, with your retirement."

Roger took a step back. "I didn't realize I was retiring?"

"Oh," I said, scrambling. "It was something I heard, but sorry, are you not? Retiring, I mean."

Roger's eyes flitted around my face and I thought of how Natalie had compared him to a tired horse; but were tired horses still this sharp?

"Hmm," he said, "I'm suddenly parched," he said, as the back of his head, the tuft of gray curls, disappeared into the crowd.

Out of nowhere, David surfaced again, another drink in hand. "I haven't seen Archer Crofton at one of these things in ages."

And there he was, looking a little lost. He'd traded the T-shirt and jeans for a pale blue suit and his signature sneakers. He glanced at his phone, then toward the back, the cameras blinking around the DJ booth. He smiled, but he wasn't smiling at me. I watched as he crossed the room, stopping to greet the two men I shouldn't have let in. He shook both their hands, hugged the one with the accent. "You know him?" I asked.

"Once upon a time," David said.

"Well, should we get a picture?"

David laughed. "Yeah, good luck with that."

"Isn't that your job?" I asked, but David didn't like that, me questioning him.

"I can try," he said, "but he's not exactly the approachable type."

"He's not?" I decided I would indulge him.

David's eyes went wide. "Nooo. No, no. Guys like Archer—" he flung his hands and some of the ice in his glass tumbled to the floor "—they like to fade into the background. Not one for the spotlight, you get my vibes?"

All night I'd wanted David to understand that I wasn't some joke of a person, and now was my chance. "Oh, well, it shouldn't be a problem," I said. "Archer is my boyfriend."

David rocked back and forth on his heels. The lift of his brows, the half smirk of his mouth, made it worth it. He was impressed. We stopped three times en route to Archer; first, so David could finish his vodka; a second, so David could get a new vodka; and a third so David could shovel two more mini hot dogs into his mouth. But when we approached Archer, David said he had to "dip for a second," and pointed to his phone. Apparently it was important.

A moment later I was wrapped in Archer's arms. Over his shoulder, I clocked the nameless men. The one with the combover was occupied by his phone, but the one with the accent was watching me with this bemused expression.

Archer turned to him and I stepped aside. "Sorry," he said. "This is Ren."

"Your girlfriend?" the man asked.

"We met earlier," I said, and went to shake his hand. His grip was strong, his palm sweaty and hot.

"Oh, yes," he said, his accent suddenly thicker, even more commanding, "the door girl on a power trip."

"Door girl?" Archer asked.

The man said, "You know, she let us into this place."

Archer eased his hand from my waist and smiled. "Oh. Too funny."

To his companion, the man said, "It's getting too hot. I need to leave. My driver will get us around the back," and then to Archer, "Nice seeing you, as always." Neither of them looked at me as they walked away.

After he left, Archer grabbed two of whatever the specialty cocktail was from a passing tray, a mojito, I guessed by the look of it, gave one to me, and when I told him I couldn't drink while I was working, he placed it on the table behind us.

"Who was that?" I asked.

"Oh, just a friend of my parents'."

Of course, I thought. Always a friend of a friend. Every room we entered, it was almost a guarantee Archer would know someone, or vice versa. It was the same with Etta. I laughed to myself, recalled the incident at the door, how the man had pinched my ass, and understood I'd overreacted. Middle-aged men on a power trip, a little drunk, a little sleazy. It was textbook; I shouldn't have been surprised.

"It's kind of random," Archer said, "running into him here."

"Maybe he's stalking you," I said, laughing, feeling lighter now.

Archer squeezed my side. "Funny."

I made sure Natalie was preoccupied—she was, shimmying with an old *Vogue* acquaintance, evidently more relaxed now—

so I cozied up to Archer. He placed his hand on my back; I wanted to have a drink, to feel like I wasn't working, but knew I couldn't, so I popped a stick of gum into my mouth. My phone vibrated in my pocket and I stepped aside as Jeff's voice cut through the headset: the line outside had thinned; were we at capacity?

"Everything good?" Archer asked. He tucked a strand of hair behind my ear and I flinched, not from his touch, but because we were in public and I wasn't being exactly professional.

"Sorry, yes," I said.

"So this is your work?"

"It's weird, right?" I said.

Archer smiled. "Seems kind of fun?"

"That means we're doing a good job, making it all look so seamless."

He tugged at my headset, considering me. "Look at you, so official."

"I'm what they call a 'photo shadow.'"

Archer tilted his head. "That's not a real thing."

"It is. Come on, you know what a photo shadow is," I said, and tried to explain it from his perspective, as the person being photographed. "It's important that we get photos of all the 'right' people at an event. It's good for our client, good for press, we can use the images when we pitch the news to media, and it cuts through the clutter of a crowded landscape."

Archer suppressed a smile.

I sighed. "Photos of important people prove that our event matters. That's all."

Archer nodded, drained the rest of his cocktail, and reached for the other on the table. He bopped to the music, a pop rendition of "We Are Family."

"So basically," he said, "you lurk around all evening scouting the most important people in a room, and then beg them for a picture?"

"Uh, when you say it like that…"

"Well, is that not what it is? At its core?"

"At its core?" A pause. "I feel like you're judging me or some-thing."

"Judging you? No, of course not. I'm just making an obser-vation."

His eyes drifted from mine, in the opposite direction. He seemed different somehow, unusually contrarian. Was he drunk? A voice hissed through the headset. Ubi Dub's car was out front; should they send it to the service entrance around back, and could someone please get ahold of Ubi Dub's assistant? I changed the channel on the radio, cutting off the chatter.

"Are you okay?" I asked him.

"Fine. Why?"

"I don't know. You seem…different."

"All I'm saying," Archer said, "is that for someone who is supposedly dissatisfied with their work, you're pretty content."

"Archer," I laughed, "I don't know what you want from me."

"It doesn't matter what I want from you. You don't know what you want for yourself."

Heat surged in my cheeks and I scanned the room for the fans stationed in all four corners. An insurance plan, in case the AC stopped working. This job, I thought, this job was an in-surance plan. The backup. Except it wasn't so much a backup anymore as the lone front-runner. A backup meant you had an-other plan, and I didn't.

"That was rude," I said softly.

"I'm sorry," Archer mumbled, rubbing my back, his touch a mild consolation. "Are you excited for Etta's birthday?"

"I am. It'll be good to see her."

"I know she's very excited to see you. Only one week until you're reunited," he said.

"Yeah," I said, but I felt it, the sudden shock of anxiety like an electrical charge.

"So do you remember that show I was telling you about?" he asked.

"Which one?"

"The one next summer." I said that yes, I remembered, and what about it?

"It's in Barcelona," he said. "The gallerists want to meet with me, actually. The end of the month."

"In Barcelona."

He nodded again. "Since you're already going to be there, I think I'll join you."

"For Etta's birthday?" More nodding. "The whole weekend?"

"You don't seem excited."

I wasn't. I was nauseated. I'd excelled in maintaining a clean separation between Etta and Archer all summer, and now that seemed poised for change. My worlds colliding.

"Does Etta know?" I asked.

"It was her idea."

Had Archer forgotten about our conversation? Or was I being unreasonable? I'd dug my own grave, waited too long to confess, and now it was weird, almost deceitful. Correction: it *was* weird, it *was* deceitful.

"Are you...concerned or something?"

Yes. "No," I lied.

"Okay, because, it's probably getting a bit strange, don't you think? That Etta doesn't know?"

Yes. "I mean, sure, I guess a little, but..." I trailed off. Where was David? Could we take the damn photo already?

Archer rattled the ice in his glass. "Can I ask what, exactly, you're afraid of?"

If I were being honest, I would have said I was afraid of what Etta might do if she found out I'd kept this secret from her, after all she'd done for me, her displays of generosity, forced and otherwise. Etta was my best friend, but in getting involved with her brother, I would be too close to her equal. She wouldn't like that.

"I don't know," I said, "I'm afraid of a lot of things."

He didn't like that answer. "Ren, she is my sister, you are her friend. I mean, we met at a party she brought you to."

"What does that mean, *we met at a party she brought you to?*"

"It means we met because of her."

"No, we didn't."

"Sorry?" he asked.

"We didn't meet because of her," I said again. "We're talking about that night in Brooklyn, yes?" He half nodded. "You introduced yourself, but then you saw your friends or whatever and left. You then offered me a ride in your car, which I accepted, because I didn't feel like waiting for my Uber. We didn't meet because of Etta. She wasn't even there. She had already gone."

"Well, you know what I mean."

"No, I don't know what you mean, because I can't read your mind."

There was a lull, and we both checked our phones. I didn't know why I was behaving this way—maybe because I wanted them both. I didn't want to choose.

"Sorry about that," David said, waving his phone in the air, and in his other hand, yet another flute of champagne. "So we ready to take a photo?"

I looked to Archer, but his eyes were on the floor, and I could tell David had likely picked up on some residual awkwardness between us, like a child intruding on an argument between their parents.

I chimed in and tried to be professional, hoping Archer would agree to our ask.

"So Archer," I said, "David and I thought it might be good to snap a quick photo?"

David was newly submissive, knocking back the rest of his drink. "If you want, man. I know you're private."

"Now?" Archer asked.

Please, I mouthed.

Archer put down his drink. "Okay," he said.

"The light is better over there, right?" I asked David.

David lifted his camera and instructed Archer to smile, and Archer smiled, then David said, "Relax," and Archer simply crossed his arms. David said, "Now, jump!" and Archer asked, "Seriously?" David said it again: "Jump!" He counted down from three and Archer was airborne, his Nike sneakers hovering above the ground, as if he were floating.

26

The cab drivers in Barcelona were on strike and so I took the bus from the airport, then another to Etta's neighborhood. It was nine in the morning and the sun beamed down as I tugged my suitcase across the cobblestone and toward Etta's building, a pale yellow structure eight stories tall. Everything seemed so bright, almost in Technicolor, the sky this perfect shade of robin's egg blue. I buzzed Etta's apartment and a thin older man in uniform unlocked the gates in front of the door, leading me through a small marble-floored lobby, past a mosaic of mailboxes. He slid open the grates of an old elevator and accompanied me to the top floor.

There were only two doors on the landing, each bookending either side of the hall. The doorman said, *"A la derecha,"* and pointed to the right before climbing back into the elevator.

I knocked on the door, then rang the bell, and a shiver snaked down my spine. Would we hug? Would she say she missed me? Would I echo that I missed her? Would I mean it?

From inside, I heard a voice say, "One second," and I thought, *I could vomit right now*: the cheese plate, the two miniature bottles of red wine, a bag of Doritos I'd eaten on the plane. Right there, on the white marble floor.

The door opened. Etta wore a floral silk robe with loose bell sleeves, her hair in a messy knot on top of her head, long blond strands framing her face. She looked the same, and if she looked the same, then everything was the same between us, right? Etta shrieked, drawing me close for a hug. She smelled of powder and soap, and as she led me inside, sunlight poured in from generous windows, that dense golden light described in near-death experiences. Blinding.

"I can't believe you're here. How was your flight?" she asked over her shoulder and I followed behind, dragging my suitcase, heart racing.

"Not bad," I said. "I passed out for most of it."

"No delays?"

"No, luckily. But apparently the cab drivers are striking so I had to take the bus here."

"Welcome to Barcelona," she said, turning to me, "the land of petty inconveniences."

I laughed, but I could feel the sweat ringing my underarms, wondered if I could shower or at least freshen up. "Etta—" I began to say.

"I hope you're not too mad we started breakfast without you. I was starving."

We. The word passed over me, not registering, until I saw Archer, sitting at a table set for four, wearing a white button-down, looking expensive and oddly untouchable with his hair combed back. I hadn't expected to see him here, so soon. I was still in my leggings and sweatshirt, my hair matte and greasy from the plane.

Etta whirled toward me and I flinched. "Sorry, let me take that from you," she said, and reached for my suitcase. "I'll pop it in your room."

"Thank you," I said, as she rolled the suitcase down another

hall, leaving me and Archer alone, obviously not thinking anything of it.

Archer gave me a small wave. "Coffee?" he asked.

I nodded and watched as he poured from the Chemex into
a porcelain cup, setting it onto a matching saucer. Behind him
was a wall of stained glass windows and, to the right, what appeared to be a sitting room, with the pale blue sofa I'd recognized from FaceTime, the green shuttered doors leading out to
what I presumed to be the Juliet balcony.

"Thanks," I said, and pulled out a chair opposite his.

"So," he said, "how are you?"

I shrugged and sipped my coffee. "A little jet-lagged." I examined him. "Your hair."

He laughed slyly, patted the top of his head. "I have a lot of
meetings, so trying to look more important than I am."

"I think you're important," I said quietly.

Archer glanced at his lap, then back up at me. "She's really
happy you're here. She's been talking about it for days."

I smiled, but was plagued by a sudden suffocating guilt as Etta
reappeared. She stood in the door frame, clapped her hands.

"Ren, I'm so rude. You remember Archer, right?"

"Of course," I said.

Etta took a chair next to mine and explained that Archer was
in town for business, but the timing worked out "so nicely"
that we could both be here for her birthday. "Feels like fate,"
she said cheerily.

"It does," Archer said with a smile.

"God, I feel so old," she said.

"Old? You're only turning twenty-six."

"Twenty-six is closer to thirty."

"How do you think I feel?" Archer asked. "I'm almost *thirty-
three.*"

"Same age as Jesus when he died," Etta said. "Or so they say."

"Should be a good year for me, then," Archer said.

I swallowed a mouthful of coffee, my gaze flitting between the two of them, and Etta looked at my plate, which was still empty. She told me to help myself to the food on the table: a bowl of fresh fruit, bread rolls and pastries, whipped butter and jam. She peeled the lid off a small jar of yogurt and dug her spoon into the mixture.

"This apartment is gorgeous, Etta," I said. Though on Face-Time it had seemed modern, in person the ceilings were grand and ornate, festooned with intricate floral details.

"Yeah, it has a lot of character," she said. Her eyes floated about the room before landing on me again. "So what have you been up to?" She turned to Archer. "I think this is the longest Ren and I have gone without a proper catch-up. What has it been, a month?"

"No," I said. "A few weeks."

"A few weeks is a month," Etta said with a laugh.

Had it been that long? I brought the coffee to my lips, but didn't drink. "No," I said again, "we spoke the other day."

"Yeah, but that was to confirm you were still coming."

"Of course I was still coming." Out of the corner of my eye, I noticed Archer watching us.

"Well, anyway," Etta said, "I feel like I know nothing about your life."

"Everything's the same with me," I said, perhaps too quickly, before going on about the unseasonably humid New York weather, how busy work was, and had she heard of Ubi Dub?

"Everyone's heard of Ubi Dub," she said. "His installations are all over Instagram. Archer, you know Ubi Dub, right?"

"Of course," Archer said. "Everyone says he is—"

"The next Banksy, I know," Etta said. "Ren, sorry—what were you saying?"

"Just that our client partnered with him."

Etta nodded, as if processing this fact. "So how's the apartment?"

"It's good," I said, reaching for a croissant. Etta told Archer I was staying there.

"But you already know that," Etta said to him. "Ren mentioned you dropped by a while back to pick something up?"

Archer hesitated. "Yes, I did," he said.

"That painting of yours, right?"

"Yes," Archer said. "Sorry—do you two talk about me behind my back or something?"

Etta chuckled. "Don't flatter yourself."

"Archer," I said, "are you staying here, too?"

He shook his head. "I'm over at Soho House."

I was relieved. "Is that far?"

"Across town. Closer to the beach."

"But I convinced him to join us for breakfast this morning," Etta said. "He's been so busy."

"Yeah, I'm sorry I bailed on dinner last night. My meetings ran long and then one of the gallery owners wanted to take us out, so…"

"I get it," Etta said. "Business first."

Archer glanced at me. "I have a show opening next year. Well—" he dabbed at his mouth with a napkin "—potentially."

"It's why his hair looks like this." Etta mussed it with her fingers. "It's his 'professional' look." Archer recoiled and lightly elbowed her. "What do you think, Ren? Do you like his hair like this? Or do you prefer how he normally wears it?"

My stomach flipped as if I were on a roller coaster. "Um," I said, "I don't know what you mean."

"Well, you liked when it was longer, right? You were always saying he looked like, who was it, Kurt Cobain?"

Archer cleared his throat and my face stung from the blood pooling in my cheeks. "Maybe that was it, I don't remember," I said. I turned to Archer, attempting to pivot the conversation. "Congratulations. On your show. Well, 'potential' show. That's really awesome."

Archer smiled. "Thanks, Ren."

"So how long are you in town for?" I asked.

He poured more coffee. "Until Tuesday. You?"

"She leaves Monday," Etta answered. "Ren, you've hardly eaten."

I glanced at my plate, the untouched croissant. "Sorry. I'm like half-asleep."

She pointed at my nearly full cup of coffee. "Well, drink up. You can't nap. It'll only make the jet lag worse." She focused on Archer again. "You're going to join us for dinner tonight, though, yes? I want you both to meet Erik."

Erik. Illustrious Erik, the possible boyfriend.

Archer said he was planning on it.

"Astrid knows she's invited, right? Maybe I should double confirm with Lizzie," Etta said.

I lifted my eyes to Etta. "Lizzie?"

"Her father docks his boat here for a week every summer. Well, not a boat exactly."

"I was going to say, Etta," Archer said.

"Yacht, I know." She shifted in her seat. "We're going to spend Saturday on the *yacht*."

"Sounds fun," I said.

Etta shrugged. "Lizzie's less on my nerves these days. She just needs a lot of coddling, a lot of attention. I don't know if things between her and Astrid are so good right now. Has Astrid mentioned anything to you, Archer?"

Archer covered his mouth while he chewed. "No, but we also don't really talk about her personal life."

"Oh, that's weird," Etta said.

"Weird?" Archer asked, but I noticed it, the annoyance edging into his tone.

"Well, you guys used to date, right?"

Archer flapped his hand. "A long time ago."

I sat up in my chair reflexively.

"Anyway," Etta said, but she was still staring at Archer, "guess who's been sliding into my DMs these days?"

Archer asked, "Who?" though he sounded distracted.

"Your friend Chip."

I almost choked.

"Hmm," Archer said, now concentrating on me. "That's odd. What does he want?"

"Just asking what I'm up to, when I'll be back in the city. He was in Umbria a few weeks ago for a wedding and thought I would have recommendations. I was like, 'Chip, I'm in Spain, not Italy,' though I am familiar with the Amalfi Coast..." Obviously, Chip hadn't mentioned me, then; maybe because I had rejected him. Maybe his ego was, in fact, bruised. "He didn't tell you?" Etta asked.

Archer spoke in a measured voice. "No, but we also haven't spoken in a minute, so that could be why. Or maybe he knows it's weird to harass my sister."

"He isn't harassing me," Etta said. Archer exhaled but said nothing. "Wait, are you annoyed? Is this weird for you?"

"Not at all," Archer said. "It's your life."

Etta swiveled toward me to explain that Chip was a friend of Archer's as I took a bite of my croissant.

"From New York?" I asked, alternating between the two of them.

Archer said, "Childhood. Known him too long to get rid of him at this point."

Etta pierced a slice of kiwi with her fork. "Yeah, well, we all have those people in our lives. You just can't get rid of them." She leaned toward Archer then, resting her head in her hands, angelic. "I know it's probably too weird for you if I were to date him, but maybe Ren would like him? What do you think?"

Archer knocked his cup into its saucer so that coffee leapt onto the table. He blotted the mess with his napkin, and I focused on chewing my croissant, turning the dough over and over in my mouth.

After a moment Etta said, "Archer?"

"Yeah?" he asked.

"You didn't answer my question," she said.

"What question?"

Etta gave him a look, as if to say, *Come on.*

"Oh," Archer said, "yeah, I don't know."

"What do you mean you don't know?" Etta asked. "You've known Chip since you're like, twelve."

"Exactly," Archer laughed, "that's what I'm saying," but Etta was still fixed on the idea, said she was shocked she hadn't thought of it sooner.

I started to laugh, which sounded more like one long syllabic "Ahhh" when Archer chimed, "I don't know if he's really Ren's type."

"Ren can decide what her type is," Etta said, and I tried to stay neutral by asking if I could see a picture before we made any "sudden movements."

"Yeah, sure," Etta said, and began to scroll through her phone.

But Archer pushed out his chair and stood. "Okay, well, I think that's my cue. Thank you for breakfast, Etta."

"You're leaving already?" she asked.

He snatched a black blazer from the couch in the adjacent room. "My meeting is at eleven."

"It's not even ten," she said.

"I'd rather be early than late."

"I didn't realize the Spanish were such sticklers with punctuality."

"They're not. The people from the gallery are English. From the UK, I mean."

"Oh," Etta said. "That's weird."

"Not really," Archer said. "There are lots of expats in this city."

"Like me," Etta said.

Archer paused in the door, his attention on his phone. "Yes, just like you."

Etta looked at me, made a face, mouthed, *Sorry?* and I mouthed back, *All good.*

"All right, well, I should go. Ren, it was good to see you again." He kept his head bowed as he left.

Etta called after him, "Don't forget, dinner's at nine. Eight for drinks!"

The door slammed.

"He is so weird sometimes."

I shrugged and picked the crumbs from my napkin.

———

The rest of the afternoon with Etta: walking La Rambla, or "the city's Times Square equivalent." We stopped at La Boqueria, the famous food market, smelling of the ocean and fried fish. Stands stacked with bright yellow lemons and perfect green limes and whole coconuts, chili peppers braided together and necklaces of garlic. Legs of jamón hanging from pegs. Chocolates and gumdrops and creamy hazelnut gelato and blush-pink raspberry sorbet and freshly squeezed fruit juices in clear plastic to-go cups arranged like a pyramid atop sheets of crushed ice. Etta insisted we try the churros, coated in sugar and cinnamon, and which we dipped in melted chocolate, licking our fingers clean. She then bought us two strawberry smoothies. We drank them as we strolled, until there in the clearing appeared the beach at La Barceloneta. Like a postcard with its palm trees, people splashing in the blue Mediterranean. Music blaring and stacks of sunbathers slicked with oil lying on beach towels, their umbrellas rippling in the breeze.

We sat at a touristy sidewalk café overlooking the beach and ordered glasses of cava and chips, guacamole, and salsa. The wine went straight to my head and I felt warm and whole.

"So," Etta said, eyes closed, leaning back, "how are you? Really?"

I forced a laugh. "What do you mean *really*? I'm good."

"I don't know. I feel like you didn't want to talk in front of Archer this morning."

"What makes you say that?"

"You were so—" she opened her eyes then and I saw the freckles sprinkling her nose "—quiet."

"I was tired. I did just fly eight hours."

Etta pitched herself forward so our faces were almost pressed together, and I panicked at what she might say. Instead she smiled. "Sorry, I'm like, kind of drunk."

I exhaled. "Oh, yeah. Me, too."

"But I still feel like every time we speak it's so…"

"So what?"

"Surface-level. You only want to talk about work and the weather. Are you sure everything is okay?"

"Yes, of course, everything is fine."

She shot me a look, as if to say, *Really?*

"Genuinely," I said. "It was a weird summer. It was weird without you in the city."

"That's what I'm talking about," she said. "I worry about you."

"Well, I worry about you, too."

She screwed one eye shut and asked why I would be worried. "Everything is great with me," she said, emphasizing the word *great* so it possessed a certain forcefulness.

"That night," I said, treading carefully, "at the club. When you were messaging me." She didn't seem to remember. "You sent me a picture. You were giving me the finger."

"What? When? I don't remember that."

"Months ago."

"Months ago. Exactly."

"You were incoherent," I said, but I wasn't sure why I was pushing the issue, maybe to distract her.

She didn't like that. "Oh, like you're the Virgin Mary? You threw up in the sink at 1 OAK."

My twenty-first birthday; she'd never let me forget it. Bottle service and too many tequila shots. I'd passed out in Etta's bed by one and spent the next afternoon on her couch drinking blue Gatorade and slurping Katz's matzo ball soup. I wore Etta's clothes to class on Monday.

"That was college, Etta," I said.

She removed her sunglasses. "Okay, forget it. We've all had our moments. I don't want to argue." She gripped my hand. "What I do want to say is that I am beyond grateful that you came all this way to celebrate with me. I've missed you."

And there it was again: the guilt, like the tide rolling in, pulling me under.

"I've missed you, too," I said. "And thank you. For paying for my flight and everything."

She made a face, as if to say, *Why are you thanking me?* The server reappeared with our second round of drinks and Etta asked for more chips.

"I'm really lucky to have you," she said once he left. "Coming here, starting over, I guess I've been lonely, too, and…" She stopped midsentence. "I was thinking about you the other day. How you're like a sister. I know we have our moments, but I feel like you are always so…honest. And want what's best for me. I can't say that about everyone in my life."

The guilt, a riptide now, white water foaming at the lip of the shore and filling my mouth, my nose, my lungs. Eventually, I would drown.

"Well, what about Archer?" I asked. "I mean, he's here for your birthday, too."

She clicked her tongue. "Yeah, but it's different with him.

He doesn't get it. He tries. I mean, he's been trying *really* hard these last few weeks, calling me constantly."

I swallowed hard. "Do you not usually talk?" I asked, though I knew they didn't.

She laughed. "It's like my being here or something has triggered his brotherly instinct. I think he hopes that I'll figure things out, that he can guide me or whatever." Etta glared at the sky, then back to me. "I just feel this weight lately. Maybe it's this birthday. Like suddenly every decision we make matters."

"I mean, I guess every decision has always mattered."

"I know. I know that. But it's the first time I've really had to think about what I want. Or what's next after the program ends." The reminder that the program would end and this period was finite. That Etta would return to New York, that this charade, the intricate double life I'd constructed still bent to Etta's timeline. That she still exercised control. "I mean—" she flicked her head back to me "—I have a year here, but still. Sometimes, I have no idea what I'm doing."

"Etta," I said with a laugh, "no one our age knows what they're doing."

"Yeah, and Archer had already sold a painting for a quarter of a million dollars."

"Well, he's just the exception."

She traced the rim of her glass; moments ago she'd argued that everything was "great," but her words didn't seem so convincing anymore.

"Brands have been messaging me on Instagram," she said, "wanting to 'collaborate.'"

I tried to be uplifting. "That's good, right?"

"Yeah, they love my 'content.'"

Etta's content: strategic shots of cappuccinos at sunlit cafés, winding cobblestone streets in dimly lit alleyways; Etta, smirking at the camera, an untouched plate of olives and her wineglass on a small, circular table. The tone could be summarized in one word: *aspirational.* She was cultivating a lifestyle, an ideal; of course people would buy into it. Technically, I already had. I'd been her first follower.

She sighed. "Everyone must think I'm living some dream."

I scanned our surroundings: the Mediterranean flashing gold in the sunlight, half-drunk glasses of cava, our sunburnt cheeks. "Well, aren't you?"

When she was quiet, I feared I'd overstepped, but instead she asked, "Would you say you're happy, Ren?"

This question struck me as odd, as did this entire conversation. *"Happy?"* I asked.

She nodded. "Yes. Like a happy person."

"I mean, I'm happy right now. I'm happy to be here."

"But I mean in the greater sense."

Our server set down another basket of tortilla chips and a small bowl of salsa. Etta dipped a chip and snapped it in half with her teeth, her eyes never leaving mine as she chewed.

I spoke carefully, enunciating my words. "I think happiness comes and goes. I don't think anyone is truly happy all the time, unless they're bullshitting you."

She licked salsa from the corners of her mouth. "Are you bullshitting me?"

"What? No, of course not."

"You said you're happy. Is that a lie?"

What was she getting at? "Well, I'm happy right *now*," I said. "Not all the time. No one is, that's what I'm saying."

I waited for Etta to interrogate me further; part of me felt like she knew something and was trying to catch me in a lie. But she didn't say anything else and started absently scrolling through her phone.

"So there is something I haven't told you."

She lifted her eyes to mine.

"I found my mom's number. Online."

"Your mom? But isn't she missing?"

"Not *missing*," I said. "She left us."

It was the first time I'd said the words aloud: *She left us.* The onus was on her, not me. I was not to blame, but if I wasn't to blame, why did I feel so terrible?

"That's what I meant," Etta said.

"Yeah, well, she lives twenty minutes from our old house."

A long pause, as Etta registered the gravity of this fact. "Shit."

"Yep."

"I'm sorry," she said, grabbing my hand from across the table. Her palm had the texture of sand, a graininess from the salt of the chips. As she tightened her grip, I saw my knuckles turn white. "So what are you going to do?"

"Nothing. It's not like I need her in my life. She hasn't been a part of it for years," but when I said it, my eyes stung.

Slowly, Etta looked away, removed her hand. "This is heavy, Ren. I'm sorry, I don't know if I can take it on right now."

"Of course, yeah, sure." I should have known better than to bring up such a *heavy* topic when she was already down.

On the beach, two middle-aged women massaged a couple lying facedown on towels in the sand. A policeman in uniform patrolled the boardwalk and the two women exchanged panicked looks before darting to the sidewalk. Once he had gone, the women returned, resuming business, telling the couple, *"Lo siento."* I am sorry.

Etta must have seen me concentrating on them, the strangeness of the situation, when she said, "It's illegal."

"What is?" I asked.

Etta laughed, nodding in their direction. "Offering massages on the beach. That's why they had to run off like that."

"Oh," I said. "Funny."

Etta's phone vibrated and her entire face illuminated. She said it was Erik, and I zoned out while they spoke, a mixture of English and broken Spanish on Etta's end. I again focused on the masseuses on the beach. It wasn't devotion to their work or any purity of practice. They had one goal: money. What was my goal? Was I supposed to have one? Archer had asked what I'd wanted, and apparently I still didn't know, was only biding my time until the inevitable unveiling of the truth. Eventually, I'd have to tell Etta about Archer, but maybe it would be okay. Maybe she'd understand.

And yet, it seemed impossible. Someone would lose, and that someone would probably be me.

27

Erik wasn't coming. It was seven thirty and he was supposed to have been here at seven to prep the fish. Etta stood in the kitchen, back pressed against the counter, arms crossed. Ten minutes earlier we'd decided to open a bottle of wine, "just to taste," but which really meant we wanted an edge before everyone else arrived. To feel light and tipsy as we greeted her guests, which was fine by me. I was nervous to be reunited with Archer again, nervous to see Lizzie and Astrid, especially after our run-in at the studio over the summer, and I could tell Etta was nervous, too. She had talked about Erik on the metro back to her neighborhood—Etta, on the metro, a refreshing surprise—and as we perused the wine selection at the bougie liquor shop around the block from her apartment, and while she braided her long, wet hair, and when she called me into her bedroom to choose which outfit she should wear of the three displayed on her unmade bed. I'd voted for the black A-line linen dress with a scooped back, watched as she'd painted her lips an orange-red, but wore no other makeup.

I watched the disenchantment splinter across her face when he texted her and she realized the night was over before it even began.

"What did he say?" I asked.

Etta clamped her hand around her phone. "That something came up, he can't make it."

"But he already dropped off groceries."

Etta scoffed. "What does that matter? He still isn't coming."

I would think on my feet. "We can go out to eat? If you don't feel like cooking?"

But Etta wasn't listening. She texted furiously, then set her phone on the counter and reached for her wineglass. "I told everyone dinner's off," she said. "That I ate bad paella."

"Oh," I said. "Okay. If that's what you want."

Etta had clutched her wineglass to her chest, her other arm wrapped around her torso; she wasn't looking at me.

"When did I get like this?" she asked.

"Get like what?"

Etta was silent.

I stepped closer. "It's normal," I said, "to be disappointed. I'd be disappointed, too."

Etta rolled her eyes, ran her tongue along her teeth.

"Do you need me to get you anything?" I asked.

She drained the rest of her wine. "I need to lie down."

When I heard the bedroom door slam, I poured myself another glass. There was a whole fish on the counter resting on a bed of parchment, its single shiny eye staring at me.

———

A text from Archer ten minutes later:

So dinner's off?

Yeah, Etta isn't feeling well.

Are you ok?

He must have assumed Etta and I both ate the same "bad paella."
I'm fine, I wrote. I didn't eat as much. Only one prawn.

Oh. Ok. That's good at least.

What are you up to? I asked.

I was about to leave my hotel but now, idk...

It was almost eight, and the sun still punctuated the sky. I
was sitting on the pale blue sofa in the living room, restless, my
internal clock stuck somewhere between exhaustion and de-
lirium, the reason I'd traveled across the Atlantic passed out in
her bedroom.

We could get a drink somewhere? I said.

I watched the ellipsis appear and disappear as I drank my second glass of wine. Perhaps I was too brazen; we were in Etta's
territory, after all, and weren't we trying to be quiet about things?

Finally he said, I'll come to you.

I knocked on Etta's door and when she didn't respond, I
turned the knob. The blinds were drawn, but I could make out
the shadow of her clothes on the floor, like dark puddles, the sil-
houette of her body underneath a mountain of blankets. I stood
in the doorway and whispered her name. On the nightstand, her
phone vibrated angrily. I tiptoed toward it—Erik was calling.

A muffled voice said, "Can you turn that off?"

"Oh, sure," I said, startled that she was awake. As the phone
powered down, the screen cutting to black, I asked again if she
needed anything. She said she was fine, she just needed to sleep.
I told her to rest, that I was going on a walk, but I would be
back soon. She gave me a thumbs-up.

I left a glass of water on her nightstand and shut the door behind me.

An hour later I met Archer at a restaurant around the corner, quaint with warm yellow lighting and brick walls, candles flickering on the bar. Archer was nursing a beer at one of the few small tables in the front, near a row of open windows. I sat across from him and ordered a glass of white wine.

"You look nice," Archer said.

I smiled and said something self-deprecating about the dark circles under my eyes. "I haven't slept in… I've lost count at this point. Maybe it's better I don't know."

"I like them," he said.

"You like the fact that I look tired."

He nodded. "You look mysterious. Any particular reason you're not sleeping?"

You. Etta. Everything. "Oh, you mean apart from flying across the Atlantic for a long weekend?"

"Ha," Archer said, "of course."

A man with narrow hips and a dark mustache deposited my wine onto the table, along with warm bread, a bowl of olives, and a plate of tomato spread. Archer asked what I did today and I told him about my touristy afternoon with Etta, the men dressed in costume on La Rambla, the beachside café and our glasses of cava. Archer mentioned the terrorist attack there last month, and I said, "Wait, where? On La Rambla?" He said it was an extremist group, that they drove a van into the pedestrian walkway, that people were killed.

"You don't read the news?" he asked. "It was everywhere."

I frowned, but I was also embarrassed. "No, I must have missed it."

Archer noticed the change in my voice. "Sorry, I didn't mean to make you feel bad."

"It's fine. It's just Etta never mentioned it," I said, and I started to feel sick. "I'm glad she's okay."

He popped an olive into his mouth. "Me, too. So you had a good day, though? With her?"

"Yeah, but—" I glanced around the restaurant. "I didn't realize she's not doing so well."

"What do you mean?"

"I think she's a little…lost. Maybe she's feeling the weight of this transition, I'm not sure."

The server came around and we ordered a tortilla Española, which was basically a potato omelet, croquetas, and a plate of jamón.

Archer took a long pull from his beer. "Well, everything has always been very easy for her. I don't think she's ever given any thought to her life as her own person."

"I think most people probably feel that way," I said, but I was thinking of myself now, how I'd been so hesitant to disrupt the status quo, going so far as sneaking around behind Etta's back, oscillating between caring too much and then not caring at all, but it was nice today, being with her. I'd been silencing the thought since she left, but now that we were reunited, perhaps I really did miss her. "Maybe she'll do something with this digital art stuff?" I said.

He pitched an olive pit into the porcelain dish between us. "I hope so. I've been trying to talk to her about it, but you know how she is."

There was a moment between us, something percolating. I wanted to say I was sorry for everything, for what had happened at the Ubi Dub party. Instead I said, "But also, this thing with Erik." Archer raised his brow. "It put her over the edge."

Archer eyed me knowingly and I knew I'd messed up. "So that's why dinner was canceled."

"No," I said, "no, she's sick."

"Ren." He smirked. "She's my sister. You don't think we know each other's tricks by now?"

I took a deep breath. "Okay, fine. But this stays between us."

"Who would I tell?"

"You know what I mean. He texted her last minute that something came up. She was really upset. She talked about him all day. It was…sad. I don't know. I had a bad feeling. And when he told her he wasn't coming…" I trailed off and thought of a line from *The Bell Jar*, how if you never expected anything from others, you could never be disappointed.

"I guess she expected too much," I told him.

"Etta does that sometimes," he said.

"Does what?"

"She's too optimistic."

"That's funny," I said, "she kinda said the same thing about you."

I tried to smile, but my mouth felt stuck. I noticed there was no music playing, just the melodic sounds of voices speaking in other languages and clinking glasses and silverware, an espresso machine humming behind the bar. Though I could hear the buzz of an AC unit, the open windows funneled humidity into the room, and I felt as if I was breathing stale air.

He said, "Maybe it would have been different, better, if she'd just been a photographer, like she wanted."

I laughed. "Wait—what?"

Archer cocked his head to the side and drank his beer. "Etta? Wanting to be a photographer? You didn't know?"

I couldn't gauge whether he was joking. "No," I said, drawing it out, "I did not know this. Sorry, are you serious?"

Archer held up his hand, as if taking an oath.

"So what happened?"

"I think she realized that in order to pursue it, to get *good* enough, it would require a lot of dedication, and possibly sacrifice, and she wasn't ready for that."

I pictured Etta's Instagram, her perfect posts and flattering color palettes, how everything was "just so"—it was probably the closest she'd get to being a real photographer, curating an ideal. Still, I felt betrayed in a weird sense that she had never told me she'd wanted to do that, *be* someone else. There were things we kept from each other, no matter our purported definition of closeness.

"Did your parents know?" I asked. "Maybe they could have helped?"

Archer examined the label on his beer. "Maybe, but I don't know if they necessarily believed in her. That she was 'good' enough." He paused. "I realize how terrible that sounds."

"Can't say I'm shocked."

Archer chuckled. Then he twisted around in his chair, toward the windows behind us.

"Are you looking for someone?" I asked, and his gaze shot back to me.

"No, sorry. Sorry." He placed his hand on mine across the table. "I'm here."

"Archer," I said, "I wanted to say I'm sorry." He made a face, as if insinuating he didn't understand, and I said, "When we were arguing about whether to tell Etta. I was an asshole."

He shifted in his seat and the server returned with our plates of food, another beer. Archer served me first, and after a moment, he said, "I won't lie—I wasn't happy. And I still don't entirely understand your rationale, but I guess if you aren't ready to tell her, or think it's too soon, we can wait."

"Well, do you think it's too soon?"

"No," he said, "but it is her birthday, and I also know how she is. Maybe she'd be pissed we robbed her of attention or something."

I brightened instantly with relief. "Okay, yeah, that's what I was thinking, too." He reached across the table again and wove his fingers with mine. We agreed we would figure it out in New York. That things always solidified in the fall.

"So," I said, "how were your meetings today?"

He bit into a piece of bread. "Good. Great, really. They're excited to work with me, and Astrid thinks it's an opportunity to tap into more clientele abroad."

"Archer," I said with a smile, "please speak English."

"So the laws here make it easier for collectors to acquire art in Europe, to really build their collections." He rubbed his beer bottle between his palms and I waited for him to continue. "The people who buy art here, who collect art, they're on another level. It's kind of intimidating, and there's a lot of pressure, but I guess it's also...exciting. To even enter the conversation of art that's 'worth' something."

"Too much expectation," I said, "breeds disappointment."

"You're pragmatic. I like that about you."

"I don't know if I'd call it pragmatism as much as my own paranoia but—" I held his gaze "—I'm really happy for you."

"It's a shame honestly," he said, "that you can't see more of the city while you're here. There's so much art, culture. I mean, I can't believe Etta took you to La Rambla."

"She said it was like Times Square, but I think Times Square is worse. At least you can walk on La Rambla. At least there's... trees. No flashing billboards that blind you and distort your sense of time. I don't know, Times Square is..."

"Hell," he said definitively.

I nodded. "Hell."

"But I'm sure she took you to La Sagrada Família?" I shook my head and his eyes went wide. "It's around the corner," he said. "You can see it from her balcony."

"I wouldn't know. I've only been here for twelve hours."

After we ate and Archer paid the check, he led me around the block, down another street, and there it was: La Sagrada Família. I'd seen the pictures, of course; the church was practically synonymous with Barcelona, its tall spires twisting to the heavens.

At night it glowed yellow against a sheet of black sky, towering above all the other buildings around it, but it was protected by a fence barring anyone from getting too close.

We stood on the opposite side of the street as Archer went on about how it was perhaps architect Antoni Gaudí's most famous work. "Well, that and Park Güell," he said.

I pointed to the spires and what appeared to be ladders running parallel between them. "It's still under construction?" I asked.

"Over one hundred years," Archer said. "And still not finished. It's kind of haunting, right? How it looms over the city, almost like it's watching us."

I lifted my face toward the sky and felt extremely insignificant. A group of Italian tourists had congregated nearby, snapping photos with their phones, and I wasn't sure what came over me, but I dashed across the street, narrowly avoiding traffic as the light changed. Archer called after me, the sound of my name rivaling the chorus of car horns.

I ran my fingers along the grooves in the fence barricading the entrance to the church. Yet another world from which most were barred entry.

From behind, Archer slipped his arms around my waist, spun me toward him and kissed me.

He whispered into my hair, "Are you coming back with me?"

I laughed. "Your hotel is by the beach."

"With a king-size bed..."

I laughed again, but if I'd learned anything in the past twelve hours in terms of the city's geography, the beach and therefore his hotel were not close to Etta's. A twenty-minute cab, at least, maybe more with Friday night traffic.

"I don't know," I said. "I probably shouldn't." I thought of Etta in her apartment, roused from a possibly Ativan-induced slumber, delirious, wondering why I'd been gone so long, but then knowing exactly why.

It was as if Archer could read my thoughts. His eyes floated behind me, in the direction of Etta's apartment blocks away.

He pressed his lips to my forehead. "You're a good friend," he said, and I thought, *No, no, I'm not.*

28

Archer was right; the boat was not a boat. It was, indeed, a mega yacht. Four decks, like the tiers of a cake, with two pools and a hot tub, a helipad and staff in pristine white uniforms floating mimosas on trays and shots of green juice and bottles of champagne costing more than my rent. Etta in a Missoni crochet dress and bikini and cat-eye sunglasses, and Lizzie in one of those giant sun hats, looking like a wannabe movie star. Me in a pair of K.Jacques sandals that Etta allowed me to borrow because they matched my cream-colored cover-up that now seemed conservative in comparison. Astrid on a lounger in the shade, decked in a white jumpsuit, sunglasses perched on the bridge of her nose, texting on her phone, pretending the rest of us didn't exist.

Lizzie, Etta, and I were sitting at a banquette when Lizzie turned to Etta and asked, "How much longer?"

Etta whipped out her phone, scanning her messages. "He claimed five minutes."

"That was five minutes ago," Lizzie said.

"We can leave without him," Etta told her.

From across the deck, Astrid said, "No, we can't, actually. Archer and I have things to discuss."

Lizzie's voice dropped an octave. "I'm seriously going to toss her phone into the fucking Mediterranean, so help me god." She gulped her mimosa and Etta and I exchanged glances as she got up and walked over to Astrid.

All around us, a staff of twelve lined the perimeter, paid to be simultaneously attentive and aloof, anticipating our every need while also avoiding eye contact unless prompted. A reminder, still, that our actions were being documented, that we were under surveillance.

"Sorry I was such a party pooper last night," Etta said.

"It's fine."

"I mean, it's not. You flew all the way here and I promised you a good time."

"Don't worry about it. I was tired anyway. Are you feeling better?" I asked.

"I always feel a little weird after I take Ativan. Knocked me *the fuck out*, but yeah, I'm okay. Better than last night, for sure."

"Have you heard from Erik at all?"

She squinted into the sunlight. "He called me a few times, probably to apologize, and he wished me a happy birthday this morning."

"Well, that was nice."

"It's not like it was sincere. It's obviously just his guilt talking."

A pause. "Maybe. Or he really was sorry? He knew he messed up?"

Etta touched her cheek. I could see a pimple underneath a thin layer of tinted sunscreen, a flat red dot working its way to the surface. "I don't know," she said. "Sometimes, people aren't deserving of our forgiveness. You know?"

I swallowed a mouthful of champagne. "Yep," I said. "Completely."

When Lizzie slumped into the banquette, she seemed agitated, motioning to one of the servers to bring more drinks.

"So wait," Lizzie said to Etta, "who is this friend of yours that's coming today?" She adjusted the brim of her hat so I could make out the subtle arch of a brow, and I thought, *What friend?* Etta hadn't mentioned another friend to me.

"No," Etta laughed. "It's not like that. Her name is Sofia. She's from Barcelona."

Lizzie mouthed *Ooooh,* and Etta pressed her fingers to Lizzie's cheek and made a kissing face. "She's fun. You'll like her."

A moment later Archer barreled up the stairs of the yacht in swim trunks and a T-shirt. "I'm sorry, I thought I set an alarm," he said.

Lizzie said, "It's lucky you're attractive."

Archer pushed his sunglasses up his forehead and rubbed his eyes, which were puffy. He said it was nice to see Lizzie, too, and then, noticing Etta, leaned over the banquette, slipped his arm around her back, and kissed her on the cheek. "Hey, happy birthday," he said. "You feeling better?"

"Good as new," Etta said.

"Bad paella. That'll do it."

Etta studied her nearly empty glass of champagne. "Hmm, yeah, just needed to sleep it off."

He rubbed the knob of her shoulder. "Glad to hear."

"So what did you get into last night?"

"What do you mean?"

"You look dead," she said. "You sleep at all?"

"Thank you, so kind. Not really, I was out late with a friend."

"You went to the clubs?"

"No, just a bar," he said, "near my hotel."

"Oh," Etta said, but she seemed unbothered.

I was concentrating on a puddle of water on the deck as Archer's eyes landed on me.

"Hi, again," he said.

I gave him a small wave.

"I didn't realize you knew Ren?" Lizzie said, and Etta was quick to say, "We all had breakfast together yesterday."

Lizzie nodded to herself. "Uh-huh."

Astrid spotted Archer and called to him. "Excuse me," he said, and when the three of us were alone again, Lizzie clicked her tongue.

"Um, okay, what was that?"

"What was what?" Etta asked.

Lizzie threw her gaze over her shoulder, toward Archer, then in a low voice said, "Did you not pick up on Archer's energy?"

"Um, what energy? He looked hungover?"

"Archer was all—" Lizzie batted her eyes dramatically "—at Ren."

"What?" I said. "No, he wasn't."

In a singsong voice, Lizzie said, "I don't know," and wriggled her fingers at me as if she were an oracle.

Etta was watching closely, so I smiled, pointed to the champagne in front of us and asked Lizzie if I could have some more?

"Take, take," Lizzie said. "Please, it's all yours."

———

We'd set sail an hour before, cruising from the port toward the open ocean, turquoise and glittering like a jewel in the hot sun, when Etta summoned Archer. So far, he and Astrid had spent the entire time in conversation, and Lizzie had drunk at least four mimosas, eventually asking for her own personal bottle of champagne for "self-service."

Archer flicked his head toward the sound of his name and said something inaudible to Astrid before getting up and walking over to us.

"What's up?" he asked.

"Have you met my friend?"

Sofia was twenty-two. She had thick brows framing big brown eyes with the longest eyelashes, bow-shaped lips, and straight brown shoulder-length hair that seemed to refract light at every angle. Which is to say, she was gorgeous.

I brought my champagne to my lips as Archer introduced himself and shook her hand. Sofia was blushing, I noticed, but then again, Archer was nice to look at; perhaps blushing was a normal response. She said in her adorable accent, "Etta has told me about you. It's great to meet," and I imagined what would happen if she were to fall overboard.

"Has she?" Archer said, his eyes on Etta.

Etta added, "She's an artist, too. Well, a painter specifically. I thought you two might have a lot in common."

Archer focused again on Sofia. He seemed genuinely interested, and I remembered how kind Archer could be, pleasant to a fault. "Really? What do you paint?" he asked.

Sofia gestured with her hands. "Etta, how do you say, embarrasses me? In the spotlight?"

"You're putting her on the spot," I interjected. Archer and I traded quick looks and I could feel my mouth twitch in agitation.

Sofia turned to me. "Thank you!" she beamed, and to Etta, "Yes, you're putting me *on the spot*. I'm not like your brother. I'm a beginner."

Etta brushed her shoulder. "Stop that. You're incredibly talented. Archer, you should see her watercolors." She rolled her eyes, as if to say, *Positively orgasmic.*

Sofia burst into a fit of nervous laughter. "Etta, please."

"She's getting her own show," Etta said, as I chugged my champagne.

My phone vibrated on the table. Natalie. Always Natalie, the Wi-Fi an invisible string tethering me to her across the Atlantic.

Archer nodded his approval. "Congratulations. Where?"

I bit the inside of my cheek as I read Natalie's messages, jumbled words on a smudged phone screen.

"A *small* show," Sofia corrected. "In a uh, little gallery in Barri Gòtic. Not until November, though."

Lizzie flexed her neck at Archer. "Aren't you doing some show in Barcelona? Isn't that the whole reason you're here?" She burped softly into my ear; it smelled like onion.

Archer said, "Yes, it's looking like it, but not until next summer. Etta told you?"

"Astrid," Lizzie said with a smile.

"Sorry," Sofia said, "you are showing in Barcelona?"

"I am," Archer told her, and Sofia's face lit up like a Christmas tree, all the trimmings and a star on top, to boot.

More champagne, I thought, motioning to Lizzie as she topped off my flute. My head felt light and my temples thrummed.

Etta's eyes flitted between Archer and Sofia. Then she stood and placed her hands on Archer's shoulders, moving him so that he was sitting next to her. "You two should talk," she said. "I'm going to take a dip in the pool."

Archer's gaze followed Etta as she ascended the stairs to the upper deck and Sofia shifted toward him. When his eyes settled on mine, I stood, too.

"Lizzie," I said, "can you tell me where the bathroom is?"

She pointed at one of the staff. "He can show you."

The nearest restroom was located down a short flight of stairs. The attendant noted an elevator across the hall and said I also had the option of taking the lift back up, if I wanted, if I was "too tired" to take the stairs again, and I laughed before realizing he wasn't joking.

"Thanks," I said.

Of course, the bathroom was occupied. I knocked and waited, knocked again, thought of Archer and Sofia and all their mutual interests, their conversation evolving while I fled the scene, and wondered if Etta had, in fact, suspected something, if she was playing at control, or if she was simply being a good sister, fixing up her recently single brother.

Natalie's emails continued to arrive in quick succession, one after the other. She asked if I could send her a document; she was using it as a template for some new business proposal. Never mind that it was Saturday, that I was thousands of miles away, in the middle of a literal ocean on a boat with alarmingly excellent

Wi-Fi. I scoured my emails to find the elusive PDF, hidden in an endless thread of messages from last December. This it? ☺, I said, attaching the document, though I wanted to say something more like, *Here it fucking is, the document is saved on the server, I don't know why you couldn't just find it yourself; it's right there.*

I knocked on the bathroom door again, rapping my fist harder and harder until it started to throb. When it swung open, there was Astrid.

My hand flung to my mouth. "Oh my god, I'm so sorry," but she was the picture of calm.

"Hi, Ren. How are you?"

"Good," I said.

"You flew all the way here for Etta's birthday?"

I nodded. "Yep."

"Nice friend." She peered at me, as if inspecting me. Was she waiting for me to say something, to admit whatever it was she suspected? That yes, my being at Archer's apartment months ago was exactly what she thought it was?

"So how are you?" I asked.

Astrid said she was fine, but jet-lagged; she'd been traveling so much. She didn't know what time zone she was in anymore. "Dubai, Hong Kong, back to New York, now here. I'm a mess."

"Yeah," I said, "I'm dying right now and it's only been a day."

She asked how long I was here for and I told her until Monday and she said, "I mean, that's quite a trek for a weekend. I won't do quick trips overseas unless the return is really excellent," and winked.

That smile, I recognized it, sewn into her face. A smile that said, *I know something. I have something over you.*

She went on: "So I'm sure you must know how excited Etta is to have Archer here."

I laughed. "Yeah, I think this is her dream, having the two of us to herself for a whole weekend."

Astrid pushed her tongue against her cheek. "Right, and then all fall, too."

I smiled back at her. "Sorry?"

"Well, starting in November, technically. We're sorting out logistics."

I didn't want to admit I had no idea what she was talking about, but I had no idea what she was talking about, and then I remembered. "Wait—yes. For the show. Etta mentioned."

"No, not just the show."

Above us, a remix of "Despacito" thrashed through the speakers, but Astrid's voice was clear when she said: "He's been trying to transition out of New York for some time."

Astrid considered her phone, this conversation, the details, all background noise to her.

"Oh, oh, you mean Archer is moving?" I could barely get the words out.

After a moment she said, "Looking like it."

I managed to say, "It'll be good for Etta, I'm sure. Having him so nearby." But something crackled in my ear, escalating into a screech, like nails on a chalkboard amplified by a thousand. The entire left side of my face throbbed. What was happening? *Sonic warfare*, I thought, *North Korea*. Archer and Sofia would die in each other's arms and I would be stuck down here, alone.

Astrid said something, gesticulating behind me. I turned around: an in-wall speaker.

"Are you all right?" she asked, though my ear was ringing and it sounded as if we were underwater.

"Fine," I said. "It was just really loud. I wasn't expecting that." As I smiled again to show her just how *fine* I was, Natalie's name lit up my screen. I ignored her call. She'd assume the Wi-Fi was spotty; she didn't have to know the truth. No one did, that was the thing, this whole weekend was one complicated charade.

Astrid started to respond when Lizzie's head came into view above us, a full moon craning over the opening in the stairwell.

"Astrid," she hissed, "what the fuck?"

THE ART OF PRETEND

Astrid smiled beatifically and promised she would be up in one second.

Lizzie glared at the both of us. "Fine," she said.

Astrid shifted her focus back to me. "Does Archer plan on giving her the painting today?" she asked.

"What painting?" I was still in a daze, rubbing the side of my face. Natalie texted me; the document wasn't opening. Could I send it again?

"The painting you said he was making for her." She paused. "For her birthday?"

I couldn't even keep track of my lies anymore: the painting, the supposed reason why I was at Archer's studio months ago. I launched into a frenzied "Oh, right. Um, no. The painting is in New York. I don't think he wanted to travel with it."

"So you'll ship it, then," she said.

"Sure, I guess."

"Well, you'll just want to be careful shipping art overseas."

"Uh-huh."

"Things can get lost."

"Of course."

"Damaged."

"Hmm."

"Maybe you want to give it to her when she's next in the city, as opposed to risking it?"

"Honestly, I'm not really worried about it," I clipped. "We'll figure it out."

Astrid stepped back, considered me for a moment. I was sweating, delirious.

A door swung open down the hall. "Otto!" Astrid said, beaming, as if she were an actress and his arrival her stage call.

He wore a linen shirt, perfectly pressed khakis, loafers, and a baseball cap. "Beautiful day," he said.

Astrid nodded. "Stunning."

His voice, I recognized. That thick Russian accent. He stepped closer, hit the down button on the elevator. This was the man from the Ubi Dub event. The same man who had pinched my ass, whom I'd wrongly assumed to be a finance-dad from Connecticut on a lone night out.

I didn't know what came over me when I said, "Nice to see you again." Was I pining for acknowledgment, to prove my relevance to Astrid, that I belonged here, too?

He studied me from under the brim of his cap. Of course, he said nothing. He didn't remember me, just another stranger on his yacht. The three of us stood in silence, until the elevator doors parted and Otto disappeared behind them.

Astrid bowed her head, the image of grace, but I saw it, how she was wringing her hands.

"Lizzie's father," she said once he'd gone. "This is his yacht, you know."

"I know," I said softly. "I know."

In the bathroom I splashed my face with cold water until my cheeks turned bright red, then poured an entire bottle of Bulgari body gel down the toilet because I could.

———

We were bobbing in the water, our heads like buoys, each of us drunk and sunburnt. Lizzie had sweated off her makeup, her sun hat becoming more crooked the more she drank, her arms drooping over her limp pool noodle. Etta and Sofia were discussing the Barcelona terrorist attack last month; Etta said classes were canceled for days. Lizzie butted in, comparing it to 9/11, and Etta was adamant that it wasn't "quite" like 9/11. Archer suggested that everyone remembered things differently, and not to discredit one person's account, and I found myself rotating away from him. His confidence, his assured way of existing in the world. The way he tilted his head in conversation, or knitted his brows together and nodded when you said something really interesting; how he made you *feel* like everything you said was interesting. The raspy quality of his laugh; the nervous, endearing habit of clearing his throat.

He had lied to me.

Seated across from one another at dinner last night, I'd asked about his meetings and he hadn't mentioned he was moving. No. He was leaving, he was leaving, and he had said nothing at all.

Something pinched my waist in the water and I yelped. When I twisted around, I realized it was him, winking at me as he paddled away.

Etta shot me a look. "What's wrong?"

"Nothing," I said.

"You just screamed. Was it a jellyfish?" She glanced around, paranoid.

"No, no. I thought something bit me, but it was just Lizzie's noodle."

Archer was already swimming back toward the yacht. Sofia watched him go. I decided I couldn't hate her; we were both foolish.

———

After, as we ascended the stairs to the first deck, there was Archer, holding a tiered cake with raspberries and pale pink frosting and sparklers. He and Astrid ushered us into singing "Happy Birthday" and Etta cupped her hands over her mouth, as if she'd temporarily forgotten it was her birthday at all. She migrated toward Archer and the cake, and as we all gathered around her, Archer's eyes drifted to mine. He smiled as he sang, dipping his chin at me as if he were trying to signal something, and I ignored him, just mouthed the words because actual singing activated some emotional reflex that made me want to cry. Etta blew out the candles, then grabbed my hand and pulled me to her side so that I was nestled between her and Archer. She looked to me, and then Archer, said she loved each of us, and thanked us for making this day so special.

29

That night Etta and I ate dinner at a Michelin-starred restaurant, three hours and a five-course tasting menu. Etta picked up the tab, and I offered to split it because I felt awkward. After all, it was her birthday, and shouldn't *I* have been treating *her*? But she laughed, and wouldn't let me see the bill. "You being here is your gift to me," she said.

Around eleven we returned to her apartment. Etta changed out of her dinner dress and into a red halter jumpsuit and sky-high platforms, her "dancing shoes," she told me. She decided I should borrow a light pink Hervé Léger dress that was so pale it was almost white and which made the act of sitting and standing especially difficult. "But you look hot," she said, and I shrugged. I didn't feel hot; I felt dehydrated and amoral.

I practiced sitting on the sofa, shimmying my body onto the cushion, as she arranged a plate with flatbread and another with olives on the coffee table.

"Are you expecting company?" I asked.

"Sofia," she said. "She lives around here. We'll cab to the club together."

"Oh. Fun."

Etta topped off her glass with more wine and asked if I wanted a refill. "Okay," I said, though I didn't need any. I was still drunk from the yacht, from dinner, my sobriety a thing of the past.

Etta sat beside me and studied her phone. "Archer says he'll meet us there. I guess he joined Lizzie and Astrid for dinner and they're running late. Kind of annoying. He said he couldn't make my dinner because he had to 'catch up on email.'"

"But aren't Lizzie and Astrid flying back to London tonight?"

"What are you talking about?" she snapped.

I tried again: "I thought I heard her tell Sofia that. I didn't realize they were doing dinner, too."

"Yeah, well, it probably turned into a work thing. It always does with Astrid."

"Oh," I said. "So what *does* Lizzie's dad do exactly?"

"What do you mean?" she asked, but she sounded less hostile now.

I shrugged. "I don't know, that was a pretty nice boat. Yacht."

Etta sipped her wine and relaxed into the sofa. "I'm not sure, exactly. He's like, an oligarch."

"A what?" I was expecting her to say he had a hedge fund, or a patent, something remotely normal, but again, I was wrong.

"He's a big deal in Russia, and London. He knows people. I don't fully understand it except that he's very, very wealthy."

I considered informing her of my run-in with Otto at the Ubi Dub event and decided against it, because that would've illuminated the fact that Archer was there, as well. Not that any of it mattered, because he was moving. Etta would get what she wanted without even trying.

"So it seems like Astrid has Archer working really hard these days," I said.

She was still scrolling through her phone. "I think the reception of his last show really fucked with him. Now he's obsessed with this idea of a 'second act.'"

"He told you that?"

"He doesn't have to. I just know."

"Stressful," I said. I reached for an olive on the table, but when I popped it into my mouth, my teeth struck its pit.

Etta scooted closer. "Should I post this one or this one?" she asked, alternating between two seemingly identical photos of her on the yacht, the line between the pool and the azure Mediterranean blurred so it created an illusion of Etta commanding one large body of water.

"That one," I said, pointing to the first. "I like that you're smiling."

She inspected her screen. "Hmm, I think I prefer the other one. My hand looks kind of weird, like a claw."

I cracked a flatbread in half and granules of salt fell to the floor.

"Posted," Etta said. "I wonder if Erik will like it. Fucker. He feels so bad, of course, but I'm ignoring him. He deserves it."

I decided to change the subject. "So Sofia is cool."

"Isn't she? She has great energy."

"Yeah, she does." I paused. "She seemed to like Archer."

She raised her eyes to mine. "Ha. I had a feeling they might hit it off."

"And perfect timing, right?" My vision was becoming swimmy, I knew I should probably slow down, switch to water, but I kept drinking, my stop button no longer functional.

Etta was newly serious. "I don't think I'm following."

"Well, Astrid mentioned that Archer was moving here. On the boat. Yacht."

Etta was quiet. I could hear a clock ticking across the room, the steady clicking punctuating the silence.

"Yeah," Etta said finally. "It's a little crazy."

"So he *is* moving."

"That's the plan. I know he was looking at places earlier this week. I mean, we could never live together."

She laughed and I laughed, too, but I felt like I might be sick.

Etta sipped her wine demurely, broke off a piece of flatbread and gnawed on it. "I like my space," she said, "but I guess it would be cool to have him here."

I nodded heartily. "So it wouldn't be weird for you? If Archer and Sofia...you know."

Etta smirked. "What?"

"You know, hooked up."

"Well, she's not like my *close* friend. I doubt we'll stay in touch once I leave." Etta's eyes traveled back to her phone, and I thought I should tread carefully. I was asking direct questions, trying not to appear obvious. "I don't really think it would mean anything anyway, if they did. Just good old-fashioned fun," she added.

Good old-fashioned fun. Was that how she might frame me and Archer?

"And he seems over Jane," I said.

Etta kissed the glass to her lips. "How do you know about Jane?"

Shit, I thought. "You told me," I said.

"I did?"

"Yes?"

Of course, I'd learned this news in Amagansett, at Archer's dinner party. Etta had never mentioned it.

"Huh," she said. "I must have forgotten." The doorbell rang, and Etta blinked, as if awaking from a trance. "That must be Sofia," she said, and got up to answer the door.

———

We cut the line at the club, navigating to a round table in an elevated section behind a red velvet rope. The space was huge, like a warehouse, and packed, everyone bathed in a lurid purple light, the smell of sweat and liquor and that faint powdery, almost chemical scent of the fog machines. Scantily dressed women danced burlesque on circular platforms and a DJ commanded his throne in sunglasses and a black T-shirt that said "WEIRD" in cursive font. Revelers flailed their limbs on the dance floor, and every so often, the DJ would single you out, you'd swear it, that *you* were having a moment, but the fact was you were only another face in the crowd, a stranger he would never remember on a night like any other, that to you, was nothing short of "extraordinary."

At our table Etta dug an empty glass into a bucket of ice, then proceeded to fill it with chilled Grey Goose, adding a splash of cranberry. We didn't need to drink more, but Sofia and I followed her lead.

Etta's face was lit by the blue glare of her phone screen as Sofia shouted in my ear over an Avicii remix that was big right now. "I *never* go out to the clubs," she said.

"Really?" I shouted back.

"Yes. This is—" she stuck out her tongue, flailed her arms "—too crazy for me."

I nodded; she was, in fact, supremely cool and fun and self-deprecating in all the right ways.

"So Etta's brother," she said, still screaming in my ear, "he's cute, no?"

"Yeah," I said, trying on nonchalance for size. This was what I wanted, right? For no one to know?

Sofia inched closer. "Etta tells me he might be moving here?"

I swallowed a mouthful of vodka that burned like gasoline. "What?"

She shrugged, her mouth now brushing against my ear. "Something with his work. I'm not sure."

I peeled myself away, watched as she drank her vodka cranberry. Then I looked to Etta, who had since graduated to bopping her shoulders to the music even though it lacked a true beat.

"I have no idea," I said to Sofia. "I barely know him," and I was telling the truth.

When Archer arrived, it was well after one. He apologized to Etta, dinner went long, but she was in a good mood and said, "It's fine, you do you, Archer. I'm just happy you're here."

He laughed to himself, then touched his hand to her forehead as if he was taking her temperature. She gazed up at him with adoration, it was almost sickening, then motioned for him to sit between her and Sofia. Etta and Archer spoke, their heads bowed; she was laughing loudly as Archer fixed himself a drink from the buckets of alcohol on the table.

He shifted toward Sofia, sliding his arm across the top of the booth, giving the impression of a shared closeness. Etta was simultaneously texting and shimmying and I had no one to talk to, so I kept drinking, trying to seem occupied. Sofia laughed into her shoulder; Archer's face was too close to hers. What were they talking about?

I tugged on my dress, pulled down the hemline. I didn't want to be here, but then something cold and hard smacked me in the face before falling into my lap. Ice. Etta had thrown ice at me. "Are you there, Ren?" she asked, waving her hands.

"I'm here," I said, and smiled wide.

"Don't tell me you're tired."

I gestured to my drink. "Why do you think I'm drinking Red Bull?"

Etta searched her purse, then pressed a little yellow pill onto her tongue. "This is better," she said.

"Where did you get that?" Archer asked. He seemed concerned.

"A friend," Etta said. "Why, you want one?"

"I'm good," he said.

"Oh, like you didn't used to do the same thing. Ren? Can I interest you?"

Archer and I locked eyes. "No, thanks."

She stuck out her tongue, rinsed her mouth with her drink, and exhaled loudly for effect.

"Any word from Erik?" I asked. She stared at me blankly, so I thought she couldn't hear. I shouted this time, "ANY WORD FROM ERIK?"

"No," Etta said. "Ren, not now."

But it was too late; Sofia swung her whole body toward her. "Wait, sorry, Erik?"

"No, no Erik," Etta said.

"This is Erik from school, right?" Sofia asked, alternating glances between me and Etta.

Etta shook her head at the exact moment I said, "Yes," and her eyes told me I had fucked up.

"I just figured…you posted that photo? Did he like it?" I asked, and at that, Etta stood and announced she was going to find the bathroom.

I had gone too far, I knew, but it felt oddly good, watching her squirm a little.

After she'd gone, Archer asked, "What's going on?" as if we might enlighten him.

"I have no idea," I said.

Sofia spoke slowly. "The only *Erik from school* I know is married. He lives outside the city with his wife and daughter."

"He's married," I said, flatly, and Sofia nodded. "Fuck." Etta had done it again.

"You think something was going on between them?" Sofia asked.

"No," I lied.

"Should you go find her?" Archer asked me, and I thought, *Now you want to play the hero?*

"She just said she had to use the bathroom," I said.

"Well, she seems upset."

"So you're accusing me of upsetting her?"

"No, I just thought you might be able to talk to her. You seem to know what's going on."

I wanted to say, *You think you know everything, don't you?* but I couldn't, because all of this was my fault, really. My fault for not wanting to tell Etta about us. My fault that I'd now ruined her birthday. I should have gone to find her, to apologize, to explain myself.

I did none of this. I got up.

"I need air."

I pushed my way through the crowded dance floor and up a flight of stairs to a porch, where people sat on white leather stools around circular tables, smoking and speaking in different languages. The music from inside the club drifted outside, but at least you could hear your own thoughts. I tried to catch my breath, but my heart was beating too fast and, looking out at the beach, the black water bleeding into the black horizon, it all seemed pointless.

So I'd outed Etta for her secret relationship; the irony wasn't lost on me. I was chewing my bottom lip so hard that I tasted blood, and my hands trembled as I pulled out a chair at an empty table. A man with long hair asked if I had a lighter.

"No," I said, but I must have shouted it, because he backed away with his hands above his head.

A moment later I heard my name, and there was Archer hovering above me. "What happened in there?" he asked.

"Oh, you mean that I basically exposed Etta for sleeping with her married professor?"

Archer was silent.

"Yeah," I told him dryly. "Happy birthday, Etta."

Maybe now he would leave me alone. I steadied my gaze on the beach, vaguely aware that he was still watching me.

He sat on the empty stool beside me. "Are you planning to come back inside?"

I crossed my arms. "I don't know."

"You don't know."

I shrugged. "Nope."

"Okay, so we're just going to sit here," he said.

"Guess so."

"Darn, wish I'd brought a book."

From the corner of my eye, I saw that Archer was smiling. My attempt at defiance had delighted him. I was about to say, *Fuck you, it's not funny*, but it came out as, "Where's Sofia?"

He glanced over his shoulder, toward the club. "Inside some-where. She saw people she knew." He was painfully oblivious as he leaned in. "Are you sure you're okay?"

Was I okay? I laughed. Asking someone if they were okay was the equivalent of saying you were sorry when someone died. You meant well, but the gesture was meaningless, empty. It would change nothing.

"Ren—" Archer started to say, and I told him, "I'm just going to text Etta." But as my fingers explored the inside of my purse, my phone wasn't there. "Do you have my phone?"

He checked his pockets. Nothing.

"Shit," I said. *"Shit."* I emptied the contents of my bag onto the table: a credit card, my license, a lipstick, and Starbucks punch card, a crumpled Duane Reade receipt. A chill swept through me, then the tears came. "Fuck," I said. "My phone is gone."

Archer was calm. "Maybe you left it at our table?"

"I didn't take it out of my bag."

"Are you sure?"

"Yes, I am *sure.*"

"All right, well worst case, you can get a new phone, or a temporary one or something. We can figure it out in the morn-ing. When are you flying back again?"

I shook my head forcefully. He didn't get it. It wasn't just my phone.

"When were you going to tell me you're moving?" He said

THE ART OF PRETEND 293

nothing, and I thought I might explode. "Astrid told me," I said, "earlier, on the boat, *yacht*, whatever. She thought I knew. But luckily for you, Sofia also knows, so now you can be together. Hooray! I'm sure Etta would approve."

Archer burst into laughter. "Ren, what the hell are you talking about?"

I wiped the snot from my nose; the jet lag, the emotional exhaustion, it was all catching up to me. "Just stop," I said.

His expression didn't change. "I am not moving."

"Yes, you are."

"No, Ren, really."

I blinked, could feel the tears trickling down my cheeks. "You're not?"

"Nope."

"But why would Astrid say you were?"

Archer placed his hands on the table. "Well, if we're being up front, there was a time where I was considering it, moving, I mean, earlier in the summer, after the reviews ran. We thought a change of scenery might be a good idea, creatively, but then I realized I would be running away. Besides, I don't want to uproot my life. Not now anyway."

"But Etta said you were checking out apartments."

"Astrid and Lizzie are looking to buy a place, as an investment."

"I hate myself," I said quietly. "So you and Sofia…"

"Ren, really?"

"I don't know, you guys seemed pretty into each other on the boat. *Yacht.*"

"She's an artist. I was being polite."

"It didn't seem that way."

Archer's eyes crinkled as he smiled. "The person I like lives in New York, though she is occasionally self-destructive and paranoid and asks me to keep things from my sister, but…here we are."

I attempted a laugh, but it came out sounding as if I was winded.

"I'm sorry," I said.

Archer stood, holding out his hand. "Come on. Let's go inside."

"But Etta hates me," I said.

"She doesn't hate you. You're drunk, and so is she. Just say you're sorry and it will all be okay."

———

Archer gripped my hand and guided me into the club. Everything would be fine. So what if I didn't have a phone? I'd apologize to Etta and she and I would have an overdue heart-to-heart, and then we'd dance into the wee hours of the morning and get falafel from one of the carts outside as the sun was rising, and it would be like the old days, just like New York.

In the middle of the dance floor, a group of men blocked our way and I was pushed against Archer's back. His shirt was damp and smelled like smoke, but also faintly sweet. He pivoted so that he was facing me now, when a horde of girls streamed past, shoving me into him again. We were both laughing, and I tilted my chin up to his, the mist from a fog machine obscuring us from one another, as if we were in a dream. When the smoke cleared, his mouth found mine; his lips on my lips, his hands in my hair. The girl he liked lived in New York, he'd said. That girl was me.

I pulled away, pressed my palm against his chest and smiled, nudging him back in the direction of VIP, where Etta would hopefully be waiting for us, where I could say, *I'm sorry, I fucked up, I love you, happy birthday.*

But she wasn't waiting. She was watching.

How long had she been standing there, behind a man with a single hoop earring? Based on her expression, long enough to have seen us. We'd let our guards down, assumed a congested room granted us anonymity.

We were wrong.

It wasn't supposed to be like this. That was the first thought I had, what I would tell her, but she took off, so that Archer and I had to practically plow over people in pursuit, up a flight of stairs, past coat check, and out onto the street, where the tall palm trees were skeletal against a black sky and the line for entry snaked around the block. Tourists screamed incoherencies, a girl vomited into a gutter while a friend held her hair. Men sold long-stemmed red roses, whistling at club-goers as they passed.

Archer shouted after Etta, but she continued walking at a clip, her arms crossed at her chest.

"Etta," he said. "Where are you going?"

Finally, she stopped and spun around. "What *was* that?" she asked, but she didn't seem so angry, I thought, only alarmed. Maybe it wouldn't be so bad, telling the truth.

I took a deep breath. "This wasn't how you were supposed to... We wanted to tell you."

That was apparently the wrong thing to say.

"Wait—how long has this been going on?" We were both silent. "What, since I left? *Before?*"

"No, not before," Archer interrupted.

Etta threw back her head. "Holy shit. This wasn't what I meant when I asked you to look after her, Archer. This is *insane.*"

"I mean, it's not that insane," Archer said.

Etta was glaring at us now. "Fuck both of you," she said, and took off again.

Archer jogged after her and tugged her by the wrist. He was bigger than her, and when she bent to him, her eyes were wild.

"Etta," Archer said, gesturing to me, cowering several feet behind him. "Ren is your best friend. This isn't fair."

She didn't speak, but her mouth trembled, as if she was ascertaining what to say. After several seconds she said, "You stayed in my apartment all summer, Ren. You said *nothing.*"

"I'm sorry," I said to the sidewalk.

She was walking toward me now. When she was inches from

my face, when I could smell the vodka on her breath, she aimed her finger at me. "You are pathological."

I said nothing. She was right. For months I'd lied to her because I was afraid I couldn't have them both, that there was no world where Archer, Etta, and I could happily coexist. I was afraid that she would take Archer away from me, that she *could* take him away from me. I was afraid I would end up alone.

I tried to apologize again. "Etta," I said, but the words didn't materialize, and it didn't matter anyway because Etta had cut the cab line and was sliding into the backseat of an idling car. She slammed the door shut and the cab drove away.

Archer and I stood in silence, and a bald man selling red roses by the stem asked if Archer would like to buy one, for his "pretty lady, his *novia*." We just looked at him.

30

I was still wearing Etta's dress and heels when the cab pulled up to her apartment the next morning at nine. The door was unlocked, as if she was expecting me. In the living room, Dua Lipa's "Be the One" played on speaker, but there was no Etta.

I found her sitting on the balcony, an ashtray and a pack of cigarettes on the small circular table beside her. Etta only smoked when she was drunk or livid, so I knew she was still fuming. She wore a bathrobe and her eyes were red, her skin pink and raw.

I stepped out, closing the door behind me. She didn't look at me.

"Hi," I said.

She dragged on her cigarette, twisting her head in the opposite direction.

"This is quite the view." And it was—in the distance, I could make out La Sagrada Família, its spires pricking the porcelain sky.

Still nothing.

"So you're just going to ignore me?"

She blew plumes of smoke into the air. "Where did you sleep last night?"

I hesitated, slipped off the heels. The tile was warm beneath my feet. Of course, she knew the answer, but she wanted to hear me say it.

"Ha," she said when I didn't respond, "got it."

"We wanted to tell you," I said. "It's my fault. I was afraid you would react like this."

"Like this," she repeated, flicking ash into the tray.

"Well, you know, that you'd—"

"Feel betrayed? Used?" she asked, whipping her head toward me now.

"I can understand why you're upset," I said.

"I've been gone three months. Three months. And all the times we've spoken, you never said anything. Not even a blip."

"Well, how would you have reacted if I told you?"

Etta paused. "I still would have found it weird."

"Exactly."

She raised her hand, the cigarette perched between two fingers. "No, don't. You still found it so easy to lie. It's honestly terrifying."

"I didn't find it easy. I hated it. It made me feel sick."

But she didn't care. "I don't need liars in my life. I don't need friends who use me and then try to play the victim."

"I didn't use you," I said.

"I was good enough for everything else, right? The dinners? The trips? The parties?"

"Oh my god, Etta. Really? You think that's what this is about?"

She narrowed her eyes. "It was always what I could do for you."

"Jesus, Etta. Friendship is more than things. It's more than buying people."

"Except you liked being bought, right?" I'd given her free

ammunition. "You like living in my apartment, too. Don't pretend you're above it."

"I didn't want to live there," I said. "You made me."

Etta nodded to herself, smiled privately. "I didn't make you do anything."

My stomach soured, a nauseous pit burning at its core. Sure, maybe I didn't mind living in Etta's apartment, if we were being honest—it was beautiful and comfortable and anyone would have felt the same—but this was about more than that. The tectonic plates of our friendship had shifted underneath us, shaking the ground we stood on. In her absence, I realized, I had gained something over her, outsmarted her, even. I wasn't as weak as she'd thought.

I inhaled deeply, but my jaw was clenched. "This feels like it's about more than Archer." Etta scoffed and I went on: "You like controlling me, and if I'm with him, you're afraid I might actually be your equal or something."

She laughed now, practically choking. "Sorry, what?"

I crossed my arms. "Just what I said."

"No, no. The fact you even *think* that's a conscious thought I've had," she said, but I saw how red her face was and I kept going.

I thought back to our chat at the beach the other day, when I'd tried to tell her about the latest development with my mom, how she'd retracted her hand, how she'd rejected the conversation altogether. How on some subliminal level, this dynamic was just how she liked it, exercising control over what we talked about, determining who could hurt more.

"You're scared that I don't need you anymore," I said. "That I'm not broken."

Her eyes cut to mine, like daggers. "You're not broken? Oh, because now you have Archer to make you feel better, right?"

I dug my foot into the grooved tile on the balcony. "You were trying to set him up with Sofia. What's the difference?"

"The difference, Ren, is Sofia isn't my real friend, and you lied. Are you sure this doesn't have anything to do with me leaving you? You were acting out?"

I was stunned. "You think I'm with Archer because I'm acting out."

"I mean, yes. For attention."

"Wow."

Etta shrugged and returned to her cigarette, sucking in the hollows of her cheeks.

"Archer told me you wanted to be a photographer," I said. I waited for a reaction, but there was none. I stepped closer; I was angry, but I felt like I could salvage the situation, play to her sympathies. "He worries about you," I said. "He talks about you *all the time*. And you can't hold it against him just because your whole life is dictated by your parents."

"Oh my god," Etta said. "That's what he tells you?" But I thought I had her then, the facade cracking.

"Why can't we just…move on?" I said. "I mean, it's out in the open now." Etta crossed her legs, took another long, luxurious drag of her cigarette. "I'm sorry about what happened with Erik. And I'm sorry for lying." I placed a hand on her shoulder.

She shook me off. "I've just done so much for you, Ren. I mean, I *made* you."

"You made me?"

She was ranting now, speaking with her hands. "You came to New York, just like, *oblivious* to the world, needing my guidance. I mean, I guess not much has changed. You wore my clothes this entire weekend."

"You offered."

"You didn't refuse. You're like a vampire. You drain everything and everyone around you, and you'll do the same to Archer if he doesn't see through you first."

I could feel the tears stinging my eyes.

"Did you even wonder what happened to Jane?" Etta asked. "He got tired of her."

I knew what she was getting at. That I wasn't good enough, special enough. That Archer would treat me just like all the others,
an object he could dispose of when the next best thing, the next
wide-eyed girl, came along.

When I opened my mouth to speak, I tasted salt.

"You know, Etta," I said, "sometimes, I think I hate you."

I thought I could make out a hint of a smile as she smoked
the last of her cigarette, and a part of me wondered if she was
secretly proud of me. When I realized she wasn't going to en-
gage further, I said that maybe it would be best if I moved out
of her New York apartment.

She stood and said she assumed that was a given. Laughing
softly, she pushed her way past me. "It's funny," she said before
stepping inside, "how much you worship him, but I guess it's
just your pattern."

"My pattern?"

"Well," she said, "you used to do the same with me."

───

I stayed at Archer's hotel again that night, and managed to get
on an early-morning flight out of the city the next day.

At seven we slid into the backseat of a cab—Archer said he
would accompany me to the airport, even though he would be
in Barcelona a bit longer.

The driver was especially cheery. "Did you enjoy your trip?"
he asked.

"Oh. Yes," I said. I could make out my reflection in the rear-
view mirror, my puffy eyes and forced smile.

"Excellent," he said, then turned up the music.

I angled my body toward Archer, who was staring out the
window. "Thanks for coming with me," I said.

"Of course."

I positioned my hand in the empty seat between us, counting
the seconds until he acknowledged it, but he never did. The si-

lence was making me anxious, fueling the thoughts on loop in my mind, my conversation with Etta on repeat.

"When do you leave again?" I asked. I already knew the answer, but was straining for small talk.

He ran his fingers through his hair, his gaze still fixed on the passing scenery. "Wednesday. Or maybe Thursday. I have to check."

"More work stuff?"

Archer sucked at his teeth. "Always."

I was trying to be normal, trying to forget about the denouement to the weekend. Had it been worth it? Did Archer ask himself the same question?

"Will you see her?" I asked. "Before you go?"

Her meaning Etta. I couldn't bring myself to say her name.

Archer's eyes fell to his lap. "Doesn't seem like it. She hasn't answered any of my calls, or texts."

"I'm sorry," I said quietly.

"We're both at fault, right?" He finally faced me, and I noticed how tired his eyes seemed, almost sunken in, the stubble around his chin, the exhaustion from the weekend marking him. I waited for him to say more, but he scrolled through his phone instead.

Archer was right—we were both at fault, and though Etta probably felt she'd lost, I hadn't exactly won, either. No, I felt empty, uncertain. What version of New York would I be returning to? Etta was gone and had been for months, but now her absence seemed more weighted; and Archer, well, there was no promise of what might happen when he came back to the city. Perhaps it would be just as Etta had warned: he'd grow tired of me. Maybe he was growing tired of me already.

But then he reached his hand across the empty middle seat and squeezed my knee.

"It'll be okay," he said, and I nodded. Empty reassurances were still reassurances.

In the window I could just make out La Sagrada Família, the church like a sandcastle, melting to the ground.

31

All the lights were off in the East Village apartment. There were dirty dishes stacked in the sink, water glasses and wineglasses on the coffee table, their rims stained red. I ordered Chinese and ate in the dark, watching the shadows travel across the walls, then fell asleep on the couch and woke up at 3 a.m. to incoherent screams across the street. Abdul still wasn't home as I got into bed, and when I woke up again three hours later, I didn't know where I was, only that my chest hurt. I couldn't fall back to sleep, and so I stood outside the Verizon store in Midtown at opening to get a new phone before work.

When Verizon restored my phone, there were no new messages. I'm not sure why I'd expected to hear from Etta, that she might proffer me with an apology, admit she'd overreacted.

I'd told her I hated her, and she'd known I meant it.

32

Archer had landed last night, and I was supposed to see him later. I started to text, **What time should I come over?** when Natalie's voice cut across the room. She was hugging the entrance to the long hall leading to the executive offices, arms crossed.

"Jeff, can you chat for a second?" she asked.

"Of course," Jeff said. He whispered that he would meet me in the kitchen after.

I waited for him, scrolling through Instagram in the meantime. Over the past few weeks, Etta had amassed an additional three thousand followers, her posts clearly drafted by the underpaid office-dwelling employees of brands with whom she partnered, like the line of matcha with so-called aphrodisiac effects. All she had to do was copy and paste; it was easy, just how she preferred.

After ten minutes, however, Jeff emerged from Natalie's office and marched to his desk. He stood there for a moment, hands on hips, surveying the room, then lifted his eyes.

"What did Natalie want?" I asked, toggling my computer

mouse, skimming my emails. There was a new one from Roger, sent fifteen minutes ago.

Jeff opened and closed a drawer; actually, he slammed it.

"What are you doing?"

"I got let go," he said.

I laughed. "Okay, no you didn't."

"Oh, but I did," he said, dropping a tube of hand lotion into a canvas tote, a forgotten gift from one of the grab bags at our annual holiday party. The evidence of his impending departure was littered all over his desk: Listerine strips and two bags of Goldfish, pencils and Post-it notes and gel pens and lip balms. He was cleaning house. He was leaving me.

"But what? Why?"

He shrugged. "Company finances are bad. She said it was a *tough* decision." He considered me. *"Tough decision,"* he repeated, this time in air quotes.

It took me a second to respond, to understand this was, in fact, not a joke. "I feel sick."

"Don't," he said. "I'm fine. I just want to get out of here."

Jeff sifted through the rest of his belongings before I called the elevator and hailed him a cab. He fell into the backseat, tipped up his chin, and I'd wanted to say, *Take me with you,* but that would have been melodramatic, so I closed the door.

"I'm going to get very, very drunk," he told me through the open window.

From the bench outside the office, I watched as his taxi crept down Seventh Avenue in midday traffic. The construction across the street was stalled, an empty forklift, scaffolding, and blue tarp blowing in the wind. It looked haunted, like a project that might never reach completion.

A message from Natalie pinged on my phone; she needed me in her office, and I thought, *I'm next.* Except I didn't even care. I decided I would be grateful. I'd thank her, say, "I was waiting for this to happen because we both know I don't have the courage to do it myself."

Archer would be happy, that was for sure. We'd celebrate and he'd remind me that I was free, and wasn't this what I'd wanted all along?

I paced down the long hall to Natalie's office and knocked twice. She was sitting at her desk, head in her hands. "You can shut the door," she said.

I lowered myself into the chair across from her, clasped my hands neatly on the desk, steeling myself for whatever was about to unfold. Regardless of the outcome, I was ready. I was stronger than I thought. *This, too,* I kept repeating in my head, half a twisted little mantra. *I could handle this, too.*

Natalie wrenched her monitor, rotating it in my direction. On the screen was an article published in *The New York Times.* The headline read: "You Otto Know: How Otto Semenov Does His Laundry." Roger's name was in the byline, his black-and-white photograph taken twenty years ago, when his hair was still black, his jaw chiseled.

Natalie stared at me, unemotive.

I asked, "What is this?"

She was eerily calm. "You are on the email, Ren. Roger sent it to us."

The email Roger had sent me a half hour ago. I quickly checked my phone and there was his message. The subject read, "Overdue," addressed to me, with Natalie in copy. In the body of the email was a link, and above it he'd written a cryptic message: *My swan song.*

Several seconds passed and I struggled to gauge what was happening. Natalie clicked her tongue and said, "Mind explaining what the hell sort of event coverage this is?" I examined the screen. "Well?"

"I'm looking," I snapped. "I don't know."

She slammed her hands on the desk and I jumped. "*I don't*

know isn't cutting it, Ren. We need to get ahead of this now or we risk losing our client."

She spoke like it was life-or-death and I wanted to scream, *None of this even matters*, but then I thought, *This, too. This, too.*

When I wasn't reading fast enough, she began to summarize. "It's an exposé on this Otto character. He's Russian royalty apparently."

I thought back to what Etta had said, how he was some sort of oligarch. His gargantuan yacht, the sheer scale of his life and wealth, how abnormal it all was.

Natalie went on: "It's about his dirty money and how he cleans it through laundering art."

I wasn't following. "So what does this have to do with our client...?"

"Well, that's just it," she said. "It doesn't, except the launch party is mentioned as the location of where Otto was seen chatting with one of his dealers. The whole thing reads like some TV drama, it's *unbelievable*."

"Dealers," I said, as if confused. I was thinking of the skinny guy who lived in Chinatown, the NYU dropout who sold Etta coke, then became her sort of boyfriend one summer before being cast aside like an obsolete object.

"Art dealers," she quipped. "It'll raise questions of Ubi Dub's possible involvement, and the client is going to lose their shit if we don't figure this out."

"Sorry, what?" I asked.

She jabbed her finger against the screen. "Read. Fast."

I tried, but it was as if a bomb had detonated in my brain, the words all jumbled. What I gathered was that Otto was suspected of laundering hundreds of millions of dollars in art and antiquities, essentially cleaning his dirty money, and he probably would have gotten away with it were it not for a disgruntled French buyer tipping Roger off earlier this summer, when Otto's dealers sold him a Chagall, and then a stolen Rothko at a gross markup, pocketing a hefty profit. The Chagall in question? None other than *Circus Horse*, the same painting I'd admired at Lizzie and Astrid's duplex. His dealers used Otto's yacht to travel between European ports.

The next line is where my breath caught. Otto's dealers? An "aspiring artist" named Archer Crofton and an Astrid Banks.

Barcelona, Mykonos—had all these trips been linked?

"Are you done?" Natalie asked, and I looked up, my vision swimmy.

"I had no idea he was writing this. I don't even know what he's talking about."

And there was still that possibility, despite decades of reporting and prestige and experience, that Roger was wrong.

Again, Natalie pointed at the screen, scrolling past where I'd stopped reading. "So you don't know this guy?"

Her middle finger smudged Archer's face; it was the photo David had taken at the launch party. Archer with his half smirk and flushed cheeks. His sneakers weren't even properly laced, and yet I was supposed to believe he was an accomplice to a massive money-laundering scheme? I almost laughed out loud.

"No," I said, because the Archer I knew and this other Archer were two different people.

Natalie bent forward and I flinched. "But I saw you talking. At the event."

I thought fast. "He asked about the specialty cocktail."

She zeroed in on me. I felt the sweat snaking down my spine. After a moment she swiveled the monitor back toward her and tucked her phone between her ear and shoulder. "I'll deal with Ubi Dub's team. Hopefully they haven't seen the piece yet, so this should be fun. What a shitshow."

"Can't we just ask Roger to pull the piece?"

She inspected the screen, punched the keypad on her phone. "Well, no. He can technically run whatever he wants as long as it's factually correct. He does have editorial discretion…"

"Right," I said. The reminder that publicists only had so much control, that writers could still write whatever they wanted.

I could hear the phone ringing on the other end, but no one answered. Natalie left a message, sounding uncharacteristically chipper for the circumstances. "Gimme a quick call when you have a second! Thanks!" she said, then started texting on her phone, presumably a similar message.

"I'm sorry," I said.

"For what?" she asked, not kindly.

Maybe she was expecting a confession, or waiting for me to crack under pressure, but I had become like glass. I could endure sudden changes in temperature and survive. I opened my mouth and Natalie's eyes were impatient and I said, "Just everything."

Natalie sighed, told me I could go, that she would take it from here, and I stood to leave, but when I reached the door, our meeting felt unresolved. I turned back.

"Natalie?" I asked. "Sorry, was I just fired?"

She sighed again. I was exhausting her. "Did those words come out of my mouth?" I hesitated and she flattened her hands to her desk, newly sympathetic. "Listen, you didn't let Otto and that Archer character into the event, and that's why we're in this mess. That one was all Jeff."

"Jeff?"

"He was at the door."

He was at the door. I could feel a lump in my throat, expanding. When Natalie had spotted Otto and his friend, she'd asked if I recognized them, then who was managing the door, and I'd said Jasmine. But had I also mentioned Jeff? I couldn't remember.

"It wasn't Jasmine?" I asked, feigning calm.

"He was managing her," she said, simply.

If I was an honest person, I would have insisted that it had, in fact, been my fault. That *I'd* allowed Otto and his friend inside, not because they deserved to be there, but because it was easier to let them walk all over me. *The door girl on a power trip,*

Otto had said—what power trip? I said nothing then, and I said nothing now.

This, too, I kept repeating as I walked back to my desk, but my hands were shaking.

33

My swan song. I read Roger's email, its single line, again and again on the train to Archer's. I analyzed its meaning—"swan song" was a final bow before curtains closed. "Swan song" implied "one last dance." The last piece before he retired. Roger's parting gift; his "fuck-you" to his editors, to the people who had forced him out. A pure power play. People would do almost anything to guarantee their importance, to secure their stake in the world. I should have known that by now.

———

Archer hunched over his desk, a canvas gleaming on the floor, its paint still wet. A cracked window drew a cool breeze into the studio, rustling papers beneath a paperweight, and soft, early-evening light Tinker-Belled across the floor.

I stood there, waiting for him to say something, anything. He had returned to the city late last night and it was the first time I'd seen him since Barcelona. Did he not know about Roger's article? I could have asked, of course. Could have demanded answers, put him on the spot.

"How was your day?" I asked instead.

"Um, fine, mostly. I've been working—" he inched his neck toward the canvas on the floor "—and I drank too much coffee, so I've been kind of...on edge."

"Hate the caffeine jitters."

"Yeah," Archer said, before turning around again.

"Can I grab a water?" I asked.

He extended his hands in grand gesture. "Help yourself."

I walked across the room, opened the mini-fridge, and took a bottle of Voss, twisted it open. My motions were robotic and strange. I could feel him watching, registering my anxiety.

"So Jeff was fired," I said.

"Oh. That's a shame. What happened?"

Well, I allowed Otto into the Ubi Dub party, you know the one, where you thought it looked like I was having fun? But Jeff was blamed and now he's lost his job, and I'm exhausted, and does anyone tell the truth anymore?

I cleared my throat. "He messed up. He let some people into an event that didn't belong."

Archer reached for a roll of paper towels on his desk, tearing off a sheet and scrubbing at the paint on his forearms. "Must have been a pretty big slipup, if it cost him his job."

I shifted on my feet in front of Archer's bed. "Yeah, well, I was kind of jealous, at first. That he got let go. After I found out, I was ready to quit, honestly. It all just feels so—" I held his gaze "—pointless."

"So did you?" he asked.

"Did I what?"

"Quit."

"No, of course not."

"Yeah, I guess that's not realistic, right? I mean, if you're going to quit, you have to be serious about what's next. This life, this work—" he considered his studio, his surroundings, and the fact that neither of us was addressing the article made my stomach churn "—it's not for everyone."

"Yeah," I said, lowering myself onto his bed, "maybe not."

Archer pitched the used paper towel into the waste bin and tugged open a drawer. I noticed his copy of *The Catcher in the Rye*, still on his nightstand. As I grabbed it, a sheet of paper slid out, floating onto the floor. Printed on it was the image of *Circus Horse*. The girl in the circus ring. The minstrel, and the dragon.

I held it up to the light. "What is this?" I asked.

"Oh, that's the Chagall you liked. Remember? *Circus Horse*?"

I examined it more closely. "Why do you have a picture of it next to your bed?"

He was quiet. "I don't know. Forgot it was there, to tell you the truth."

To tell you the truth. Well, I needed to hear the truth.

"So you weren't planning to sell this to Otto? Or do you have another buyer?"

"What do you mean?"

I folded the paper in half, down the middle, saw that my hands were trembling again.

"*The New York Times* has a really extensive readership. In the millions." A pause. "I read about it at work. Our client was mentioned. Well, just barely."

Archer stared at the floor, rubbing his cheek. For a moment I thought he might never lift his head again, and why would he when he could take the easy way out, evading me, my inevitable questions. Then he looked up. "This summer," he said, quietly at first, "after those reviews ran, I was in a bad place. Full of... doubt. A lot of artists, they have a benefactor, like someone who pays for them to work or study. Who supports them, essentially."

"Oh," I said. "Otto is your benefactor."

He nodded.

"So you needed money?"

He said nothing and I tried again.

"You *didn't* need money…"

"No, I—" He stopped, collected himself. "Initially, it was good between us. He liked what I was working on, felt it was going in the right direction. He knows a lot of people, Otto. He can be very persuasive, you know? Influential."

I shook my head. I didn't know.

He tried again: "He donates a lot of money to a lot of causes, knows a lot of people, like I said. People that wouldn't want to get on his bad side. It means something, his opinion. I felt protected. Like I wouldn't have to worry about the bad reviews anymore. At least, that's what I thought."

So Otto's clout had briefly shielded Archer from the harsh realities of the art world. How ironic, considering Roger still wrote his story anyway.

Archer went on, said Otto made the right introductions with buyers and gallerists, that their relationship was the change in tone his career needed, that Otto "validated" his work within a circle where his approval mattered. I recalled Etta's words about Otto's power, his connections, how he owned New York and London and knew a lot of *very important* people.

"And?" I said. "What happened?"

Archer paused. "He wanted paintings in return, kind of like an exchange."

"*Your* paintings?" I asked.

"No," Archer said. He wasn't looking at me anymore. "Not my paintings."

"So what kind of paintings, then?"

He snapped toward me, my question apparently asinine. "You already know, Ren. You said you read the article, right?"

"I mean, I was hoping—"

"You were hoping what?"

"That Roger was wrong," I said softly.

Archer laughed, a cruel sound. "Yeah, well, you and me both.

Otto's generous, but he's not *that* generous. I needed to pull my own weight."

"Pull your own weight?"

He absently twirled a brush in a can of paint on his desk, as if trying to appear casual. "Otto's involved in some...precarious business situations, but we were smart, had a good system. Buyers would purchase art from his collection, and vice versa, and we would legitimize Otto's finances through these sales."

"His collection?" I asked.

"Well, he obviously has an extensive art collection, but we found him other works, too. Mostly from private sellers, some through auction houses."

"Some stolen?" I asked. He didn't like that, my probing. Months ago, Jeff had labeled him as "cagey," and maybe he wasn't wrong.

"We didn't 'steal.' That Roger guy is hyperbolic. The owners didn't even want that Rothko anymore."

That Rothko, as if everyone had one.

"So that was how you cleaned his money," I said. "Shuffling paintings around?"

"It was foolproof," he countered.

I didn't respond.

"It wasn't *all* bad, Ren," he croaked. "I'm not some criminal."

"But it's illegal...what you did."

"Not all of it."

I stepped back, could feel my mouth folding into a frown. "What are you talking about? Of course it is!"

"Okay, the laundering, yes, sure," he said, gesticulating now. "But the sales, the sales aren't illegal. They mainly happen overseas, at the free ports." I asked for clarification and he said, "They're glorified storage units. It's just a place where people can protect some of their assets from being taxed. It's very common in these circles." He leaned in for emphasis. "And technically legal."

A pit in my stomach. "So that's why Astrid wanted you to move."

Archer said nothing, and I thought, *I am an idiot.*

"The show in Barcelona," I said, "was that just a lie, too?"

"No, of course not. I don't know about that now, though, if the gallerists will still want to work with me after this."

"I saw him," I blurted. "On the boat. *Yacht.* Whatever it's called."

"Saw who?"

"Otto. He's the same guy you were speaking with that night, at the Ubi Dub event. He's not a friend of your parents', is he?" A wave of nausea rolled through me, remembering Archer had commented how "random" it was running into him, and in return, I'd joked that Otto was stalking him. "Wait—did you *tell* Otto to meet you there?"

Again, Archer was silent.

"Oh my god. Jeff lost his job because of this, because of *you*," I said, but I didn't clarify that it was, in fact, my fault, which was apparently fine, because Archer didn't seem to recall those finer details.

Outside, a siren wailed, until it became a strained, distorted sound that thinned altogether. But it was the sound of my laughter that surprised me most.

"How'd you do it?" I asked.

"I just told you everything, Ren."

"No. Lie like that. I mean, all the shit you said. How you didn't want your parents' help. How god forbid you were anything like Etta. That your 'art' was worth its risk, the discomfort. Did you mean any of it?" My eyes landed on his copy of *The Catcher in the Rye* and I again seized it in my hand. "Holden Caulfield is a compulsive liar, you know that, right?"

"Ren," he said, "I am not Holden Caulfield."

"But you've been lying. This whole time."

"I haven't. Everything I told you—I meant it. Things just got a little complicated. I'm not perfect."

I flailed my hands, couldn't stomach his delusion. "Why didn't you just ask your parents for help?"

He laughed. "Oh, yes, because everyone loves a narrative about rich kids being funded by their parents."

"What about their connections? Their friends, their...parties?"

"It wasn't enough."

"So if Otto's been detained in London, then why are you here? Won't you go to jail?"

Archer crossed his arms, globs of wet paint dripping onto the floor from the brush he was still holding. "You want me to go to jail."

"Of course not. But I want to know why you're here, sitting in this apartment, acting like everything is fine and you're—" I motioned to the floor, the drying canvas "—painting like you did nothing wrong?"

"Because there's nothing else I can do. It's out of my control!" he shouted. I continued folding the corners of the *Circus Horse* tear sheet, making little creases out of nervous habit, and Archer softened. "Sorry. I didn't mean to get excited. I don't... I can't keep thinking about it. My parents are dealing with the lawyers now. Hopefully this will all sort itself out."

My eyes gave me away, splintering as if to say, *Your parents? Are you kidding me?*

"Don't," Archer said, wagging his finger. "Don't go there, with your...judgment."

"I'm not," I said, because the truth was that despite their imperfect familial dynamics, I was jealous. Jealous he could rely on Plum and Warren, that they would support him when he needed their help. A month ago he'd said his parents weren't exactly good people, and yet, they still met the definition of unconditional love.

"You think I'm enjoying this 'attention' right now, that I've basically reassured everyone who's ever doubted me what a joke I really am?"

"I don't think you're a joke," I said, but I could tell Archer didn't believe me. "I just, all you've talked about is the impor-

tance of your work. The 'trances' you're in when you're painting, and like, wouldn't *I* be more inspired if I went out into the
world and 'experienced' things? When really, it's all about being
in the right place, at the right time, with all the 'right' people."

"Yeah," Archer clipped, "and you want to be one of them."

"What?"

"Etta called me," he said, "after you left."

"You said she wasn't answering any of your messages."

"She mentioned the money she left you," Archer said.

"What money?"

"A check for your rent or something, that you never acknowledged it. Or thanked her."

Months ago, at Lizzie and Astrid's apartment, Etta had offered to pay my rent, and I'd rebuffed her generosity, thought it
excessive. Regardless, there was no check. Archer had bad information, and whatever saintly image Etta had tried to culti-
vate was a lie.

"Archer," I said, "I really have no idea what you're talking
about. There is no check."

He paused. "She warned that you were using me. That it was
your 'thing.'"

"And you believe her?"

"I don't know," Archer said, shrugging, deflective, and I felt
as if they'd conspired against me. That I had always been set up
to fail this way.

"Why would I be using you?"

"Access, I guess."

"Access," I laughed. "Access to what? Your—" I threw my
arms up "—studio? Your twin bed?" Archer said nothing. "If
I was using you, then why would I have confided in you about
my mom? I let you into the most painful, the most…shameful
part of my life."

"For attention, I don't know."

"You think I did that for attention," I said. The same reason Etta claimed I had gotten involved with Archer in the first place. What was she doing, projecting onto him? I knew these were Etta's words, not his.

But he wasn't watching me anymore, was so passive, so unaffected, he rivaled his sister. After a moment Archer placed the brush in a jar of murky water, then picked up a pen, playing with its cap so that it made a popping sound.

"Did you talk to Roger?" he asked.

I narrowed my eyes at him, sure I was mishearing.

"I saw you chatting that night, at the Ubi Dub thing. Maybe you knew something. Tipped him off."

"Wow," I said. "I had no idea what you were up to, and if I did, you really think I would have trusted *him*?"

I tore at the sheet of paper with that same stupid painting. *Circus Horse*, and that was exactly what this was: a circus. I'd hoped that if I was good enough, smart enough, pretty enough, I'd frame myself as indispensable, "worthy." Etta had accused me of this, called out my obvious wanting, and perhaps she was right. I thought I'd master the tightrope, lasso the horse, charm the crowd, but the crowd was too fickle, the ambiance chaotic, and despite my best efforts, I would never win. My efforts were pointless, and I'd wind up alone anyway.

"You're a hypocrite, Archer. You claim not to want your parents' handouts and then look what you did. It's pathetic. You think *I* use people?"

He threw the pen across the room and I jumped.

"At least I go after what I want," he shouted. "I care enough to take these risks."

"Oh, that's good. I hope you tell yourself that. That these are *risks*. Your parents would have helped you from the beginning, if you just asked. You are the favorite, after all."

"And you?" he said. "You have this knack for focusing on what you lack, and then you do absolutely nothing about it. *That's* pathetic." He strode toward me, pressing his face into mine. "No one is going to make your life what you want it to be, Ren, except you. So stop being a coward and *do* something about it."

Looking into his eyes, I saw I *was* pathetic. My gross optimism, my childish belief that things would simply "work out." Except they never worked out for me. Maybe for Etta and Archer, but I wasn't one of them. Even now, Archer would likely emerge unscathed, his parents talking the talk, assuming the heavy lifting. He'd be spared the true pain of his consequences, and I couldn't hate him for it. It was simply his birthright; and mine was, what? I didn't know; what I did know was the pressure of an invisible weight knocking into my chest, grinding into my heart.

Seconds passed, the tension suspended like a storm cloud. Archer's pulse throbbed in his neck in rhythmic pentameter.

I whispered, "I was trying. I chose you over Etta, because I thought you were different."

Archer pulled back. The light on the floor had dissolved like the tide and we now stood in the near dark.

"I don't know," he said finally, flapping his hands at his sides. Like he'd given up. "Maybe we're just too different."

On the desk, Archer's phone rang three times until he answered. "Hi," he said, turning his back to me, his tone silky, smoothed of our conversation's rough edges. "What did the lawyers say?"

An electric current coursed through me as I grabbed my things, waited for the elevator in the hall. *Maybe we're just too different.* Maybe he was right.

A single bulb flickered, as if it might go out at any second, and it was funny, how the words came to you after the fact. All the witticisms that arrived after the argument, after you'd left the room, after somebody slammed the door and the moment and all its gravity had dissipated.

But it didn't matter, what I could have said. I was already gone.

34

I walked the city streets aimlessly. It didn't help that my phone lit up every other minute with a message from Natalie, updating me on the Ubi Dub fiasco, dialing me into a present I was trying to escape. His team had drafted a statement, but our client opted for a reactive response, meaning we would practice silence unless asked. *Sounds familiar,* I thought, feigning ignorance a perennially effective strategy.

After an hour, my feet throbbing, I wound up in Washington Square Park. Though it was the end of September and the leaves were beginning to change, it was unseasonably warm, the air like bathwater. As the sun set, a group of teenagers attempted tricks on their skateboards, and on a small patch of green, a father passed a soccer ball with his son. There were a few families, their children confined to strollers, the regulars gathered around chessboards, swapping stories and conversation, and me.

As I lowered myself onto a bench, I could see the skin of my heel starting to peel, pink like a newborn, touched the area to feel the sting. A pair of eyes on me then—that acute sensation

LAUREN KUHL

you were being watched. Across from me was the same girl from summer, with her freckled shoulders, her book, her attitude. I remembered how she'd observed me and Archer. At the time, I suspected she'd envied me, whatever she believed Archer and I "had," but I'd envied her, too, not her solitude, but her relationship to it. I envied how comfortable she was being alone. Well, I was alone now, too.

I was starting to believe that Etta wasn't so wrong, about my *pattern*, how easily I resorted to "worshipping" others, ogling their lives, trying to slot myself in like a piece in a board game. First Etta, then Archer, now this stranger. Perhaps a person with more self-conviction would have recognized the red flags, would have noticed that Etta had a tendency to demand attention, dial up the charm when her personal life was at a deficit, then rescind affection when no longer convenient for her. Would have noticed that Archer was too good to be true. After all, he was Etta's brother.

Not that I was so innocent, either.

I received another message from Natalie and knew what I needed to do, what I should have done hours ago. I asked if she could talk. She called less than three seconds later.

"Yep?" she said, and I launched right into it.

"Hi, I'm sorry, I know you've had a day, but I need to tell you something. About Jeff."

Silence. "Yes...?"

I scraped the soles of my sneakers against the pavement. "Um, I know you said you fired him because he let Otto and—" I could just barely say his name out loud "—Archer Crofton into the Ubi Dub party."

"Ren," she sighed, "I get he's your friend, but I can't rehash this with you."

"No, I know. Of course. It's that I—well, Jeff didn't actually let in Otto and Archer. I did."

A few feet away, the girl was now laughing with a bearded

man. So she wasn't alone. Ironic, I thought, how we'd switched roles, except I wasn't comfortable with my solitude. Even now, I'd found a way to interrupt it by calling Natalie.

"That's impossible," Natalie said. "He was managing the door."

"He went to Duane Reade to get stuff for Ubi Dub's rider," I explained, "and I was covering for him. It was just me and Jasmine. I'm sorry, but yeah, I wanted to clarify the situation."

I was about to lose my job, but I couldn't allow Jeff to take the fall, not when it was my fault.

"All right," Natalie said, "well, that's admirable of you. Is that all?"

"So do you think it's possible to give Jeff his job back? Or something?" I wasn't sure what that *something* was but I was trying to be gentle, tactful.

Another sigh. "Can you keep a secret, Ren? Between us, we were planning on letting him go anyway. What happened just gave us the validity to move forward. Firing employees is a real bitch these days with HR."

"Oh."

"On a separate note," Natalie said, "can we discuss the outreach strategy for the jewelry launch? Put some time on my calendar for tomorrow?"

Another launch, another strategy. It was back to business, this conversation ultimately meaningless. Jeff was just a number and soon, Natalie would forget his name, find someone to replace him.

She obviously didn't care about what I'd done, my carelessness. I'd judged Archer for believing himself beyond consequence, his parents for sheltering him and Etta from any real hardship, but now, here I was, skirting punishment myself. Except I'd sought the consequences, right? And that counted for something? I'd opened my arms to them, practically begged for retribution, and yet, the universe had granted me a free pass I didn't deserve.

"Ren?" she asked when I hadn't responded. "The strategy? Can we talk tomorrow?"

"Okay," I said. "I, um, I actually drafted something already, thought it might be helpful."

"Amazing," she cooed, "I was hoping you'd say that."

I understood then, why Natalie liked me, because I was a people pleaser, desperate for recognition, struggling to fill a perennial void. But what would happen if, and when, I stopped being useful to her? Would she write me off, too?

"You okay?" she asked then, sounding oddly maternal. "About your friend?"

"Yeah," I lied. "I will be."

"I don't expect you to understand this now, Ren, but someday, you will."

"Understand what?" I asked.

I could hear the smugness in her tone. "That you have to trim the fat."

When we hung up, I studied my phone in my palm. I'd tried to confess, tried to save Jeff to no avail. I was an aspiring writer who never wrote, whose words didn't matter. An insufferable people pleaser in pursuit of a reward for all my good behavior. I recalled the sense of accomplishment when I'd rescued Roger from Jasmine's ignorance at the Ubi Dub event, though of course, I would fuck everything up shortly thereafter. But my people-pleasing seemed to be a symptom of a greater issue: just how much my mom's leaving had affected me. I'd been avoiding it, finding ways to dull the ache, and Etta's and Archer's and Natalie's validation was one of them.

I queued up a new window on my phone. The same set of digits arranged themselves neatly on the screen. There was the chance the number belonged to someone else, but what if it didn't? What if she was waiting to hear from me, pining for the sound of my voice after all these years, hoping I'd want to hear hers, too, to start over, to begin again?

My thumb hovered over the number and I pressed "Call." It rang once, then twice, as I considered what I would even say. *Hi, it's me, your estranged daughter?* It was illogical, but so was everything else in my life. I'd spent an afternoon cruising the Mediterranean on an oligarch's yacht; calling my mother seemed perfectly normal in comparison. Maybe I could even recount the details of what happened, and she'd listen and dole out advice, sprinkle our conversation with equal parts tough love and optimism.

Across from me, the young boy kicked the soccer ball to his dad for the last time. The man shouted, "All right, bud, that was a good one," as he extended his arm, the boy grabbing his hand as they left the park. Meanwhile, the phone continued to ring, and I recognized that it didn't matter if she was avoiding my call, my own unfamiliar set of digits displayed on her screen. It didn't matter because she wasn't picking up, didn't care enough to identify the voice on the other end.

Hey, it's Susan, she said. *Leave a message and I'll get back to you.*

It was her. She sounded cheerful, fine, happy.

A long beep sang out.

I hung up.

———

It was bold returning to Etta's apartment, I knew, but I couldn't sleep and had hoped to find Ambien in the medicine cabinet. It was just after eleven, and to my relief, the doorman seemed unaware of any strife between me and Etta. He only smiled as I requested the elevator key. A painless transaction.

The apartment was dark apart from a faint bluish light stretching across the floor, the same neutral furniture, everything eerily untouched like no time had passed. I marched to the wing of bedrooms, first checking Etta's bathroom, but all I found were Q-tips packed into an empty Diptyque candle, an unopened bottle of Claritin, and a YSL lipstick. Strange—

didn't she have an excess of prescriptions for every ailment? My efforts were similarly futile in the guest bathroom and half bath off the main hall. I tried Etta's bedroom, but her nightstand drawers were empty, too, apart from the box of condoms Archer had unearthed months ago, back when my actions were still buffered by my own ignorance.

In the kitchen I emptied drawers full of notepads, old grocery lists written in a scrawl I didn't recognize—perhaps belonging to Cora the house cleaner or an old boyfriend of Etta's, I wasn't sure—an extra set of keys, an assortment of lip balms. I gathered she must have taken all her pills and potions with her across the Atlantic, and maybe I didn't deserve sleep, only a fitful six hours of nightmares and restlessness, so I slammed the drawer shut. I would return to my apartment empty-handed, forced to settle for Advil PM, except then the drawer bounced back open. I tried again; it still wouldn't close. Something was caught. I stuck my hand as far as it could go, groped around, and uncovered a checkbook.

Archer had claimed Etta left me money for my rent. Surely he was wrong, and Etta was lying.

But as I flipped open the checkbook, there it was. Still attached to the booklet, dated June 11, 2017, signed by Etta, twenty thousand dollars. And made out to me.

Why hadn't she said anything all these months?

Twenty thousand was pennies to Etta in the grand scheme, but still, I understood the price of such a gesture, its meaning. I thought of the cab driver Etta had bribed with a wad of cash, and how Archer had funded the birthday party of a kid he didn't even know. At the time, I thought he was being generous, but it could have been more than that, just another self-serving act meant to lessen his own guilt. And now, this thin slip of paper in my hand. How money was power, and power was the only currency that would ever really matter.

PART FOUR

OCTOBER–DECEMBER

35

Etta sat in a booth at the back of the restaurant, a cozy place with subway tile walls on the Lower East Side that had just opened and where it was, according to *Grub Street*, "impossible" to secure a reservation unless you knew someone. Unless you were Etta. She wore a black turtleneck, thin gold hoop earrings, and almost no makeup. There were no overly cheerful hellos between us, no "I've missed you's."

I was relieved; such behavior would have been fake, even after I'd extended an olive branch and called to apologize the morning after I'd found the check. She had granted me five minutes of her time, mostly consisting of me reassuring her that I didn't know about the check. "Honestly," I said, and she'd laughed, because it was ironic that she would choose to believe me now. She had wanted to know why I'd returned to her apartment in the first place, and I told her the truth: that I was hoping to find Ambien. That earned another laugh, even if it was colored by spite. She didn't mention Archer, and I didn't ask. "I appreciate the call," she had said, then hung up. Weeks passed with no contact, so I was surprised when she asked me to dinner. She would be in the city for the weekend and could meet Friday night, if I was free?

"So I heard the duck is supposed to be good here," she said. "Do you like duck? I can't remember."

I folded my napkin on my lap, in a moderate state of shock that we'd arrived at this moment. "Yeah, duck," I said. "That's fine."

Etta closed her menu and placed it on the table. "I also ordered us the crudo to start."

"Sounds good."

She nodded, and it felt like we were a couple trying to remediate after we'd slung the most hurtful insults at one another.

"So," I said, absently gazing at my menu, "you're here for the weekend?"

"Until Tuesday. With everything going on, I wanted to come home. I just couldn't leave right away, with classes."

"Of course," I said.

The press had been all over Archer and Otto. I considered texting Archer, once, to see how he was doing, but then flashed to our argument and all the insults we'd slung at one another, and making contact felt pointless. I wondered if Etta knew what had happened between us, if she was secretly pleased by the dissolution of our relationship. If so, I couldn't blame her.

We both examined the other. Etta seemed different, older somehow, more weathered, or maybe it was the jet lag.

"But things are good with you?" I asked.

Etta gave a little laugh. "All things considered, yes. School is good. Barcelona has grown on me. I'm no longer in the throes of an existential crisis. Twenty-six is still young." I couldn't tell if this was sarcasm, but it seemed honest. "So I want to thank you," she said, "for calling me. I know that must have taken a lot."

"Yeah, well, I felt terrible about how we left things."

She tucked a strand of hair behind her ear and I noticed a new gold tennis bracelet, diamonds winking at me from across the table.

"That's gorgeous," I said. "Is it new?"

She admired it, holding it up to the light. "A belated birthday present from Plum."

"Well, it's beautiful," I said, and Etta shrugged.

"I know the Archer thing must have been a shock," she said. The words caught as she chewed her lower lip, and I was crumpling my napkin in my lap. She leaned in. "How are you? Handling it all, I mean?"

"I'm okay," I said.

She leaned even closer. "I heard some journalist tried to interview Jane. I guess they assumed they were still dating. So awkward."

"Huh, yeah, that is awkward."

"Did anyone try to speak with you at all?"

"No," I said, my voice suddenly small. "I never heard from anyone."

"Well, you're lucky. I was fielding requests left and right, mostly randos sliding into my DMs. Plum and Warren have spent the last month dealing with it all, and Archer is holed up out east. I'm going to see him tomorrow. He's not doing so well, I'm sure you know."

I didn't know. I pictured our argument. How his voice broke when he tried to convince me he wasn't a criminal, how he avoided eye contact while explaining the details of his summer working for Otto. I banished the memory from my mind. I would refuse to feel sorry for him.

"Yeah," I said, "I can only imagine how stressful this must be for your family." I reached for my water, the ice knocking against my teeth as I drank. "How are *you* doing, though? What else is going on?" I wanted to hear about Barcelona, and parties, and Sofia. I wanted to talk about things of no real importance. I wanted to drink wine and pretend like we were college students, that things were like they'd been.

But she pursed her lips, and her face crumpled, rippling like a wrinkled sheet. I slid next to her in the booth and she rested her head on my shoulder. I locked eyes with a server who had been about to stop by our table and recite a list of specials, I was sure. He turned back around when he saw the scene unfolding. After a minute Etta seemed to calm down. I returned to my seat and she wiped her eyes with the back of her hand.

"I'm sorry," she said. "I haven't really processed it, I guess. You're the first person who asked how I was and…yeah. It just hit me."

"I really had no idea," I said, "what he was doing."

"No one did."

"I would have told you."

She smiled through her tears. "You sure about that?"

"No," I said, and Etta laughed. "But everything will be okay, I'm sure?" I asked. I envisioned Plum and Warren, running some sort of covert operation from their Amagansett compound, making calls and bailing Archer out.

Etta played with the gold strand on her wrist, eyes searching the room, as if she couldn't decide where to commit her gaze. "I mean, it seems bad now, but once we get over the initial shock and maybe some legal ramifications, it should be all right. No one is going to jail." She smirked. "Come on, Otto? In jail? His lawyers are sharks. The questioning in London is just a formality so people feel like he isn't getting off so easily."

"And for Archer, too?"

Etta mimed for me to lower my voice, then whispered, "The same thing. It'll blow over. It has to." She stopped. "Sorry, did he not tell you any of this?"

"He started to. We got into an argument."

"When? About what?"

I thought, *You. His hypocrisy. How pathetic I am apparently.*

I drank my water. "Everything. It was just after he got back from Barcelona. He didn't say anything?"

"No. So wait, did you break up? Sorry, that came out wrong. I wasn't like, rooting for that to happen or anything. I just—"

she winced "—is it fair to wonder if you did? I never knew how to refer to you guys, or like, what you are. Or, were."

"Well, it doesn't matter anymore. I'm pretty sure it's done. I feel really stupid."

Etta would like that, me admitting my own mistake, after what I'd pulled in Barcelona. It was all coming full circle, my penance in acknowledging that Archer was the wrong choice, that I was sorry. So very sorry. Still, I found myself refusing to say those words because I didn't want to see it: the look of triumph that would register across her face. The personification of a thousand "I told you so's."

She reached her hand across the table and spoke slowly, firmly, like a stern yet caring teacher. "I try to remember that there's nothing we could have done to stop him, you know? Archer is an adult. He makes his own choices. And we all do things, say things, that we wish we could take back." She squeezed my hand twice.

"Yeah," I said, and squeezed her hand, too, "I know what you mean."

———

Etta ordered a bottle of Cabernet that we nearly finished before the duck arrived. I was dipping the crust in my wine, my head heavy and cheeks warm, as I told her about what happened at work with Jeff, that he made being there tolerable, and Natalie only liked me because I was a people pleaser.

"You're not a people pleaser," she said.

I suppressed a smile. "No, I think I am."

"Well, would a people pleaser tell their best friend they hated them?"

Shame splintered my face. I'd told her I hated her, had, in effect, chosen her brother over her, and now here we were, breaking bread and drinking wine and laughing as if nothing had happened.

I lowered my head. "No, but they might throw their work husband under the bus in order to save their own ass."

"But you still did the right thing, Ren. You told your boss."

"I don't know," I said, dragging a piece of bread through a pool of olive oil on my plate. I knew we were drunk, our conversation becoming progressively more vulnerable, even sentimental. "It doesn't matter. He was still fired."

"What's he up to now?" she asked.

"Looking for a job. On unemployment in the meantime." Etta grimaced, the concept likely invoking some mundane plebian image. "But I am sorry. For when I said I hated you."

Etta relaxed into her chair. "I mean, I'm not going to lie, I was *pissed* at first. I called Archer and was like, freaking out. But then I realized I would have probably hated me, too. I just wasn't... I wasn't aware of my behavior, all these years, how it might have come across. I know I can be a bit much sometimes, too selfish, self-involved..."

"Archer said that you accused me of using him."

I waited for the moment of impact, for Etta to say, "I didn't mean it."

Instead she told me, "I was angry, and I'd lost control. I mean, I also wrote you that check, and you didn't even say thank you. Not that you had to or anything, but I felt disposable, Ren. I *did* feel like you used me."

I took a breath. "I didn't know about the check, Etta."

"I know," she said, blithely. "I believe you. I must have—" she waved her hand, fluttering her fingers "—thought I told you or something. It's fine. It's whatever."

But was it *whatever*?

Etta pressed her hands together, as if in prayer. Then she looked up. "I mean, it was pretty shitty what you did. Like, really shitty. Really fucking shitty."

"I should have told you," I said, "about Archer from the beginning."

"Yeah, but then what?" I was about to answer before I realized it wasn't a question. "I would have freaked out, and you would have stayed with him anyway. Right?"

I said nothing, watching as she drummed her fingers on the table; her wrists were bony, her cuticles uncharacteristically gnarled.

"I think sometimes, Ren, and don't take this the wrong way, you do things in spite of what other people want." She laughed a little. "You're a closet rebel. Deep down." I was about to ask, *What are you talking about?* but Etta continued speaking. "I mean, I am, too. I like to go against the grain, stir the pot. It's just how I'm wired."

"I don't know if I'd call myself a rebel."

"But look at what you did with Archer." She tore a piece of bread, buttering it as she spoke. "Sorry," she corrected, "I'm not attacking you. It's a compliment."

"It is…"

She nodded. "It means that at the end of the day, you have it in you. To go after what you want."

I topped off my glass. My head felt weightless, as if it were separating from the rest of my body. Etta gnawed at the bread, covering her mouth with her hand as she chewed, but I knew what she was implying: that I'd gone after Archer. That perhaps I was always *going* to go after Archer. I considered the years of knowing him through Etta, how he only knew *of* me. Even that night at the Brooklyn loft party, he'd had to ask my name twice; to him, I was "Etta's sidekick," my presence limited to a supporting role. Until I stepped out of the frame she and I had shared. Until I reassured him I was my own person, too. That I existed beyond Etta's shadow.

"And I don't know," Etta said then, "maybe things happened exactly as they were meant to. Maybe we needed this time apart. To better appreciate one another. I know I definitely took you for granted."

I shrugged, finding it suddenly hard to look her in the eye. "Yeah, I guess it's easy to take things for granted when it all becomes too guaranteed." A pause. "You really didn't know what he was doing?"

Etta crinkled her forehead. "No, I already told you."

I hesitated. "So there was a night, this summer. I didn't think anything at the time, obviously, but we stopped by the gallery. He said he had to get something. It was after-hours…he was digging through locked drawers." I stopped, heard how bad it sounded now, out of context.

"You think he was up to something," she whispered.

I stared past her toward the restrooms in the back of the restaurant, the kitchen door swinging open and shut. "Sometimes, I reread the original article, because a part of me is still convinced I made all of this up. Apparently some of the paintings were stolen? Like, a Rothko?"

"There are plenty of Rothkos in the world. You're going to have to be more specific."

"I don't know, it's just in the article. I guess they were laundering some really famous pieces of art. I don't fully get it."

Etta was visibly annoyed. "Can you please lower your voice?"

I should remember my place, I thought. Archer was still her brother, and I was intruding. Still an outsider.

"Sorry," I said, gulping my water. "Forget it. It's not important."

She softened. "No, it's okay."

But it wasn't. None of it was okay. I pictured Archer, in Amagansett, painting in his studio, thinner than normal, eating sad, silent dinners with his parents who did their best to reassure him he was still great, still their golden boy, still the favorite.

"It's good your parents are with him," I said.

Etta poured water from the carafe on the table into both our glasses. "What do you mean?" she asked.

"You said Archer was out east. I assumed your parents…"

Etta looked perplexed. "Are they not with him? At the house?"

She shook her head. "No," she said. "He's been there by himself for weeks."

36

Paul drove us to Etta's apartment. She was exhausted from traveling, and yet in the kitchen, she selected a bottle of Chablis from the wine cooler and uncorked it, pouring us each a glass. I was starting to sway back and forth as Etta sipped her wine and thought that if I drank more, I'd probably pass out and perhaps that wasn't such a bad thing, when Etta said, "I've actually been thinking a lot," and I was suddenly sober.

"About...?"

"It was ignorant of me to think that you weren't damaged from everything that happened, with your mom, your family, I mean."

"But you knew I was, Etta." My damage was perhaps the very reason she was drawn to me. "You were scared I didn't need you anymore. Remember? What you said in Barcelona?" Had she forgotten how she'd accused me of not needing her because I had Archer to make me *feel better*?

Etta considered my words. I noticed her lips were chapped, flakes crusting in the corners.

"Well, you didn't need me," Etta said. "Archer *was* my re-placement."

She wasn't wrong, that she had left and I'd run to Archer. But she'd also told Archer I *used* him. *Had* I used Archer to feel better? To forget about my missing mom, my emotionally distant dad and sister? To feel the sting of Etta's absence less? Is that what all relationships were, a simple exchange? And had Archer needed me that way, too? A good distraction from his bad reviews, from his shady extracurricular activities?

"I did need you," I said to Etta, "but you were gone, so..." I flapped my hands by my sides and Etta lifted her chin toward the ceiling, as if collecting her thoughts.

"Regardless," she said, "all I'm saying is I didn't get it, and I don't know if I ever will, but I am sorry. I should have..."

"Should have what?"

She squeezed her eyes shut. "I'm just... I'm sorry."

I couldn't believe it. She had said those two words. *I'm sorry.* I'd waited for this apology, *prayed* for it since Barcelona, optimistic that Etta would manage to come around. I'd imagined feeling elated and glorified and wholly, fully satisfied. But now that she'd done it, I felt oddly disappointed. Empty. "Thanks," I said.

She swirled her wine. "You know, it was really sad coming home to an empty apartment. You're more than welcome to stay here again." She raised her glass. "Only if you want, of course."

I said I would think on it, and Etta smiled. She drained the rest of her wine, depositing the empty glass into the sink. Then she started toward the living room, down the little flight of steps, flicking on lights as she moved about the apartment. "Is it okay if I take a quick shower?" she asked. "I flew commercial today—I feel so dirty."

"Sure," I said.

Etta shouted from the hall that she would only be five minutes, and I told her it was fine, she could take a longer shower, I didn't care. But it seemed like she was eager to please me, like she was walking on eggshells for a change. Etta choosing her words carefully, asking if things were *okay*. Was it *okay* if she took a quick shower? That I could stay here, only if *I* wanted. Was it possible I held the power, even if temporarily?

I set my wineglass on the coffee table and listened to the gentle prattling of water as I sank into the sofa, my eyes fluttering, all the muscles in my body humming to stillness, when my phone buzzed on the cushion. For a second I thought it could be Archer. I wondered if he knew I was with Etta tonight, that we'd gotten dinner.

If he thought about me.

But it was Jeff.

"Want to come over?" he asked. "I'm so bored. I'm losing my mind."

Weeks after his firing, the monotony of his days was clearly chipping away at him. "I'm actually at Etta's." He didn't believe me and I whispered as I stood again, pacing around the apartment. "No, really."

"But Etta's in Barcelona? And hates you?"

"She's here for the weekend. She's going to see Archer. I think we made up, I don't know. We had dinner together." I felt hopeful. "Do you want to come here?"

"Wow," Jeff laughed. "An invite to Etta's."

"Is that a yes?"

He didn't answer for a moment, and I drew a smiley face in the film of dust on the window behind me. Outside, the blue-gray of the Hudson, New Jersey across the water, and the cobblestone streets below.

"I'm just thinking," he said, "about the last time I was there. And Archer was stealing shit from right under our noses."

"Jeff, I don't want to talk about Archer or the article or any of it. I'm sorry. I can't."

"It's not in the article," he said. "You don't remember?" In my mind I answered no, but in fact, I said nothing. Jeff con-

tinued: "When he came over to collect that painting or whatever." I was trying to locate the memory. "You made me hide
in Etta's bedroom."

"Oh, right, yeah. But um, no, that was his painting."

Jeff's voice dropped an octave. "Are you serious?"

I checked down the hall to ensure Etta was still in the shower
and not listening to our conversation. She was singing, ignorant. When I turned back around, any relief I felt vanished. The
painting Archer had taken months ago, he'd said it was his, that
he'd sold it, and I'd never doubted him. But what if Jeff was
right? What if it hadn't been his?

Roger had written about a stolen Rothko in his article. The
sellers would have needed authenticity papers; you couldn't just
"off-load" a painting without proof of its legitimacy. I told Jeff
to hold on, opened the article again on my phone, and in a new
tab searched the name of the Rothko painting it referenced.

"Well?" Jeff asked.

I couldn't speak. Blinking at me on the screen were hundreds
of identical images. Hundreds of identical images of the very
painting that had once been on display in the hall outside Etta's
bedroom. It was a Rothko, worth millions. Archer hadn't expected me to know the difference.

But the authenticity papers, I thought, and then I remembered
our little field trip to the gallery after the MoMA. He was ri-
fling for a slip of paper in a locked drawer. What if it belonged
to the Rothko? Or what if he found the papers that weekend
in Amagansett, when he knew his parents weren't home? My
head spun with questions, and a part of me understood I might
never have all the answers.

"Ren?" Jeff asked. "Are you alive?"

"That was the Rothko," I said. "The painting Archer took.
That was it." My breath caught in my throat, like yarn snagging
on something sharp. "You're right."

"Oh, shit."

"Wait. Jeff. Did you tell Roger?"

"Tell him what?"

"You know. About when Archer came by the apartment. When he took the painting."

"No, no, I didn't *tell* Roger. I don't even know him?"

I chewed the inside of my cheek. "I'm sorry, it's just weird. You were the only other person who knew."

"Are you sure?" Jeff asked. "I mean, maybe Archer told someone. Didn't you say he had like, an art dealer he worked with?"

"Yeah, but she was in on it." A pause. "Maybe it was Priest?"

"Who the hell is Priest?"

"I don't know, I don't know anymore. I wish I could turn off my brain sometimes. I shouldn't even care, it has nothing to do with me." The shower stopped running. Etta, I thought. Etta was the only other person who knew. She'd noticed the vacant wall when we were on FaceTime; she'd asked about the painting and I, not suspecting anything, had told her Archer had come by to pick it up. Except she knew it didn't belong to Archer; she knew it was a Rothko, just like she knew the Pollock wouldn't fit on the wall outside her bedroom because that wall was *too narrow*. Etta didn't miss the fine details.

She clicked open the bathroom door and the nausea I'd tried to suppress reasserted itself. I hung up on Jeff without saying goodbye as Etta padded into the living room. She had wrapped herself in a towel and wrung out her wet hair, twisting it between her palms like the ends of a rope.

I was quiet, staring at the floor.

"Are you okay?" she asked.

"Tired," I lied.

"*You're* tired? Excuse me," she laughed, "did you fly all the way from Spain?" She smiled and I looked away. "Should we watch a movie?" she asked.

"Etta," I said, gathering my breath, "that painting that used to be in the hall." I pointed behind her, to the hall from which she'd just emerged, and she followed my finger.

"What about it?"

"That was a Rothko, right?"

She shrugged. "I don't know, I don't remember? I haven't been here in ages."

"So it wasn't Archer's, then."

"What?" she asked with a laugh.

I hesitated. "How did Roger know Archer had stolen a Rothko?"

She spun toward me. "Who's Roger?" she asked, and I knew she was deflecting.

"You were the only person I told that Archer took that painting. Months ago. When he stopped by and I said he'd just sold it?" Etta watched me, indifferent, and I realized I was gripping my phone so hard that my knuckle had turned white. "Were you helping him, too?" Etta stood there, still twisting her hair. Beads of water dripped onto the floor, leaving a sheen on the wood, and I thought I might explode. "Etta!" I said, flailing my arms. "Come *on*."

I was done playing coy. It had gotten me nowhere.

She shot me a look, said, "I didn't mean to, okay?" and I almost choked.

"You *didn't mean to* what?"

She sat on the arm of the sofa and crossed her legs. "That night at Lizzie and Astrid's, after Archer's show, I was angry. I was angry about leaving, angry that Archer was parading around. Again. That I had to go to Barcelona, and he could just stay here. And so I introduced myself to Roger, after you told me who he was—" I'd forgotten this part, how Etta had asked about him after she saw us speaking, and wanting to impress her, I'd regaled her with the details of his importance "—and he said, let me get your email. And I wasn't thinking. I thought I was just like, making a connection."

"So what did you tell him?" I asked.

"I said I was Archer's sister, and then I...probably told him too much."

"Oh my god," I said.

I thought back to that night, what felt like ages ago. How Etta drank too much, then locked herself in the bathroom, needing me to help get her home. Was she managing her guilt, the knowledge that she'd messed up in some unforgivable way?

"But I didn't hear from him for a while," she was quick to add. "I was in Barcelona, and I thought, 'This guy forgot all about me, thank god.' Then in September, he emailed me. Before you came to visit. He was asking all these questions."

"Why didn't you just ignore him?"

"Because it was too late, Ren! Jesus. He already knew everything from when we spoke at Lizzie's." I said nothing; she continued: "So when he heard about a Rothko that had changed hands, he knew its previous owner was my father. I guessed Archer had the authenticity papers and everything and... I confirmed it used to be at my apartment. And that Archer had taken it."

I lowered myself into the adjacent armchair, both of us resuming our designated seats. Etta lounging on the sofa and me, across from her, just like when she'd finally admitted she was moving, and I'd sat there, nodding and smiling, when I wanted to scream.

"But your parents," I said, "wouldn't they have realized the painting was missing?"

She was silent for a moment, and I understood what she was thinking before she could say it.

"Ren, you know they don't come here. I mean, maybe it's possible they knew what Archer was up to, but..." She trailed off, gnawed at a cuticle. "We don't talk about those sorts of things."

"So you knew," I said, "what Archer was doing with Otto."

Etta threw back her head. "Of course. He's my brother. I can tell when something is off with him, as he can with me."

I recalled how Etta had seemed especially interested in my brief encounter with Astrid months ago. I'd panicked that it was because Astrid had seen me at Archer's studio, and what did Etta know? When really, it was never about me. It was always about Archer and what they were doing behind the scenes.

"Lizzie knew, too," I said, "didn't she."

"She isn't exactly ignorant about where their money comes from."

"But why didn't you tell your parents? Maybe they could have, I don't know, threatened Roger, pulled the story? I'm sure they know people there?"

Etta ran her tongue along her teeth, but she wasn't looking at me anymore.

"Or did you not *want* to tell them? Because maybe a part of you *wanted* this to happen."

"I couldn't tell them, Ren," she snapped.

More excuses. I folded my arms across my chest. "Why?"

Her gaze dropped to the floor. "Then they would have known it was my fault."

I examined her tennis bracelet again, the gift earning a different meaning now that Etta could be the favorite, winning her parents' affection at the expense of her brother. That would always be their sibling dynamic. It wasn't about love or loyalty; it was about power. Who had more of it, who had less, who mattered more. And while Archer wasn't perfect, Etta suddenly seemed more calculated, conniving, pushing a normal sibling rivalry one inch too far.

I recalled Etta's behavior in Barcelona, how she'd opened up to me, explained her fears of mediocrity, and I'd felt sorry for her. But it was all a ruse. She'd played into my sympathies, once again, then convinced me *I* was a terrible person for hiding my relationship with Archer. And that was *our* dynamic—a cycle of reassurances and rejections. Even now I was sure she hoped I would ameliorate her of her guilt, that what she did to Archer was okay, just like I had needed her forgiveness.

Were we more alike than I'd wanted to believe?

"You can't say anything, Ren. To anyone. To Archer." Etta paused. "Especially Archer."

I wanted to remind her that Archer and I were done and she was a coward. That she was a coward for not trying to be a photographer, for hurting her brother to make herself feel better. But that would have made me a hypocrite.

"Ren," she said again, this time with more urgency. "You can't say anything. I mean it."

"I won't."

"Promise me."

I nodded. I wanted this day to be over. "Okay, fine."

"Say 'I promise.'" Her eyes were wide.

"I promise."

Satisfied, Etta stood, took a deep breath. She dragged her fingers through her hair, winding the stray pieces into a tiny knot that she dropped to the floor.

"It's just interesting," she said.

"What is?"

She cleared her throat. "If you're so done with Archer, then why do you care so much?"

"I don't. I just hate being lied to."

"Yep. Well. I guess we're even, then."

———

It was thoughtless, my exit. Etta went to change and all of a sudden, I came to in the elevator and my palms were slick and my chest hurt and the doors had closed, sealing me inside. I saw my reflection flashing back at me in the mirrored walls, warped as if in a fun house, and I didn't recognize myself.

Outside, the air was sharp. I walked north until I hit Canal and Sixth, making a right on Grand and meandering through the narrow streets of Nolita, the restaurants and bars on Elizabeth Street warmly lit and packed with people, and I wondered how many lies would be exchanged between dinner companions. My head felt clouded, my mouth dry. I was drunk, and now I was hungover, my skull throbbing, and as if by muscle memory, I wound up on the corner of Bowery and Houston, heading toward the East Village.

It was outside the Whole Foods that I noticed my phone was ringing, that Etta had called six times. I halted at the crosswalk and stared at the screen, waiting for her name to appear again, which it did on cue. I declined the call, stopped into a bodega on Second Avenue, where I got a big bag of gummy bears and a liter of water. Then I hailed a cab.

The red gummy bears were Etta's favorite, but they were mine, too, so I made a point of searching for all the red ones. I ate them in quick succession, shoveling them into my mouth. I wasn't paying attention when the driver slammed on the brakes. I pitched forward, my head smacking into the partition, and swallowed half of them, spitting the rest into my hand, their tiny mauled bodies and red dye number whatever bleeding into my milky palm. All around us, a chorus of beeping horns, and in the windshield, a man banged on the hood of the car. He was screaming, the driver was shouting, and my ears were ringing.

The driver shook as he gripped the wheel. He had run a red light. I touched my head. There was no blood, but it ached just below my hairline. In the chaos, Etta called again. She wouldn't stop until I answered, and I could only evade her for so long, so this time I picked up. She was panting, and I pictured her running barefoot through the streets of Tribeca in a bathrobe, her hair a wild tangled mess, yelling my name. But I heard a television in the background; she was at her apartment, safe and sound, probably wearing one of her matching silk lounge sets, and I was the one with a potential low-grade concussion in a cab fleeing my self-inflicted problems.

She wanted to know where I was. I scanned my surroundings; the light had since turned green and we were moving again, past the now-resolved mayhem. No one was hurt. The man from the crosswalk would go on with his life, a little shaken, arriving at his next destination where he'd recount to his partner or friend or roommate that he'd almost just died, like, *really* died, and it was entirely possible that no one would believe him. Or care.

"Ren?" she asked, when I didn't answer.

"Sorry," I said, "I just needed air."

"Well, are you coming back?" She laughed, but I caught the fissure in her voice.

I mouthed to the driver to please pull over. He said he wouldn't turn off the meter and I shouted, "I don't care!" Etta asked, "Wait, what?" and I said, "I wasn't talking to you," as I rolled down the window and stuck my head through the slat, gulping the tangy fall air, but all I could think of was the traffic light, how the world worked in metaphors. Believing it was your chance, your break, but you still had to yield because there were rules.

Even if they broke all the rules, the world would continue to bend to people like the Croftons. That would never change. I thought I could spite them by leaving, but it was me stuck paying for a cab, me who had hit my head, me who'd choked on a dozen red gummy bears. And Etta, she was fine. Unscathed. Like she always was, like she always would be.

"Yeah," I said, "I'll be back soon."

"Okay, good, I was worried. You seemed upset."

I examined my hand again. The sticky and masticated gummy bears. The red coloring staining my palm like blood. I discovered a handful of napkins in my purse and cleaned up the mess.

37

Jeff's replacement was a woman named Petra. I knew it would happen, eventually, that they would find the "new Jeff," but it had happened quickly, almost like a rebound relationship, one partner insisting they were fine and ready to begin again when the wound was still raw.

To celebrate her first day, we took Petra to lunch at an Italian place a few blocks from the office and frequented by the banking set. We sat next to a table of Italian businessmen in expensive suits drinking red wine, and Petra regaled us with stories of her time living abroad between bites of her vitello tonnato, occasionally adjusting her posture and tucking her black bob behind her ears. Natalie kept trying to catch my eye over the top of her water glass, as if to say, *Isn't she incredible? An upgrade, even?*

On the walk back to the office, I noticed the trees were bare, their branches like emaciated limbs hanging overhead. It was, after all, early December, the sky gray, as if it wanted to snow. My nose was running and I wiped it with the back of my sleeve. Natalie pulled me aside when Petra stopped to take a phone call from a possible new client and whispered, "She knows you're going to shadow her."

I stopped, but Natalie continued, and I was forced to catch up. "What do you mean?"

"Petra has a lot of great experience. I thought it would be good for you to have someone to look up to at the office, besides me. We have a new business lead," she went on, "in Austin. It's not sexy, per se, but it's tech. Female-founded, female-led. A big retainer. They're looking for a team of powerful women to be their agency of record. I want you and Petra to draft the pitch deck. She'll lead, of course, but I told her you're ready for this. Then if things go well, we'll hopefully have the chance to fly out and present in person."

"We?" I asked.

Natalie smiled and gave me a nod. There was a scrap of spinach lodged between her front teeth and I knew I wouldn't tell her about it.

"I'm excited for you, Ren," she said. "Soon, you'll be bringing in your own new business leads. That's the next step for you anyway."

My review was slated for next week, where I'd lie about all the ways in which I saw myself growing at the company in exchange for a title change and paltry raise. But to Natalie, everything and everyone was replaceable.

When Petra hung up, she turned around and said she had great news. I strained to listen as they walked ahead of me, the conversation just beyond my grasp, then ceased caring altogether. I felt my purse vibrate, and searched for my phone. The name on the screen caught me off guard.

"Ren," Natalie said. She had stalled at the corner. "Mind stopping by Starbucks? Petra and I have a two o'clock to discuss post-event outreach for Basel. You can listen in, might be good for you."

"Uh, sure," I said, and glanced at my phone, still buzzing in my palm.

Natalie gave me the company card. "Two almond milk lattes. Mine with an extra shot. And get yourself whatever you want, too."

I nodded, and when they were far enough up the street, out of earshot, I answered.

"Hey, is now an okay time?"

My hand flew to my chest, tightening at the sound of his voice. The last we'd really talked was that night in his apartment over two months ago.

"I'm at work," I said.

"Oh. Of course, sorry. I should have figured. I can try you later?"

"Well, I have a few minutes before my next meeting." I cringed at my self-professed importance, a stark contrast with the company card in hand, the coffee order dictated only moments earlier.

"I'll be quick." A pause. "How was your Thanksgiving?"

"Fine," I said, "I went to my dad's."

"Really?"

"It was us and Shari. Her daughter was with her dad."

"Shari…his girlfriend, right?"

"Yep."

"And it was okay?"

"Surprisingly. A little weird, but…yeah, Shari's cool. Dad says he's going to visit me in the city. So we'll see."

"Well, I'm happy to hear that."

I waited for Archer to continue, and when he didn't, I asked what he wanted to talk about.

"Right, sorry. I'm not sure if Etta told you, but things have kind of mellowed. With the whole situation, I mean."

"No, she hasn't mentioned anything," I said, though she had, when we last spoke two weeks ago. She seemed more relieved than genuinely happy, for obvious reasons, but I wouldn't tell him that.

"I wasn't sure. I was glad to hear things are better between you two."

"Yeah," I said, but I suspected that it would never be the same with Etta, the distance between us a strange blessing now, escorting each of us to our real lives, whatever they were. She had started dating someone new in Barcelona, and her influencing gig seemed to be taking off; a hard seltzer company would pay for her to attend a music festival in Berlin and support their brand.

"So anyway, I'm sorry it's taken me so long to get in touch." Archer cleared his throat. "I said some pretty horrific things that night that I didn't mean."

"Really? Because it felt like you did."

"I was projecting," he said.

"You were projecting when you accused me of going behind your back with Roger?"

"No. I was just being an asshole."

"Well, at least you can be honest about that. It's a start."

Archer laughed, his voice bellowing into the phone, and I realized I was smiling and then frowned for effect, though he couldn't see me.

"Okay, I deserved that."

"And were you also projecting when you told me all I did was complain? That, what was it? I focused on what I lacked, then did nothing about it?"

"Ah, that was harsh, yeah."

"But you meant it."

He was silent for a moment. "I just want you to push yourself. Don't settle."

"That's quite a line."

"It's not a line," he laughed.

Across the street, a man stood on a Genie adjusting holiday

wreaths on the glass windows of a gray office building. I flipped the credit card between my fingers and kept walking.

"That's good news, though," I said, changing the subject.

"What is?"

"About—" I lowered my voice "—the situation."

"Oh, yeah, I'm lucky. Looks like they don't have enough of a case, and I'm pretty much off the hook."

"Sounds *very* lucky," I clipped. "I hope you're not still working with that guy?"

"No," he said, emphatically. "No, that's done. I mean it."

I wanted to believe him. "Hmm."

"Yeah," he continued, "I'm trying to stay positive, with everything. It'll take some time, rebuilding. I'm a lot like Lazarus, rising from the dead."

"Not like you haven't done it before."

A siren wailed, growing louder, closer, and within seconds, an ambulance sped past, its red lights flashing.

"Jesus," I said, clutching the phone to my ear. "Freaking Midtown."

"Ah, you're still in Midtown." He laughed. "I miss the sounds of New York."

"Wait, are you...are you not in New York?"

"No. I'm in London. I guess I should have led with that."

"Oh." London. Lizzie was in London. Astrid, too. And Jane. Something melted on my hand; it was beginning to snow. "Permanently?"

"No, no. Here dealing with some final legal things. I'll be back soon."

My heart fluttered and I thought, *Stop*. "Ah," I said.

"Listen, Ren. I, uh, I'm calling because I wanted to say I'm sorry. For everything."

"What's everything?"

"For lying. For the things I said that were completely unfair and untrue when you were nothing but kind and supportive.

I could have trusted you, and I wish I'd let you in more, but I couldn't, because then you would have been involved, and I didn't want that. You being implicated in my shit."

"Hmm," I said again, but my eyes were stinging and everything hurt. "Well, I'm also sorry. I made quite a mess this summer."

"Is it fair to say I made a bigger one?" he asked, and I strained to laugh. "I really—I really miss you."

Months ago validation from Archer was all I'd wanted. So much so that I'd lied to Etta, to everyone in my life, to myself, about how badly I craved it. And now that I'd had it, what did it mean?

"I'm going to Austin," I blurted.

"Oh." The word caught. "For good?"

"No. For a business trip," I said, though I didn't know if this was true. Still, it felt dramatic, like the right thing to say.

"Ahhhh. Nice," he said, and I thought I could make out relief. "That's great. Congratulations? Should I be congratulating you?"

"Sure, yeah, why not." We both laughed and I wiped a tear from my eye and told myself it was from the wind.

"Hey, I'll be in New York in a few weeks, for the holidays. If you're not in Austin, maybe we can get a coffee? Catch up?" I didn't say anything, just watched the traffic slur to a stop. I examined my other hand and saw that it was red and raw and dug it into my coat pocket, sniffled because my nose was running again. "As friends, of course," he added.

"Friends," I said, flatly.

"Yeah. Would that be okay?"

A calendar notification blared on my phone. It was 1:59; Natalie and Petra would be expecting their caffeine fix.

"Archer," I said, "I actually have to go. I'm running late for a call."

He was apologetic, said of course, I didn't have to let him know right now; he realized he was asking a lot on such short notice, and after he'd all but fallen off the face of the Earth. But he would text me, he promised, if that was okay, when he was back in town.

"Okay," I said, but I doubted I would hear from him again. It was like old friends from past lives running into each other and swearing they'd meet for a drink, then neither of them following through with it.

It was 2:01 now. I started to text Natalie a bible of excuses about why I wasn't back yet: a long line at Starbucks, they'd messed up her order, forgot the extra shot. All lies, but I was tired of pretending.

"Ren?" Archer said. "One last thing."

"Yeah?"

"I lied. I'm not in London."

Wind rattled the windows of the Lenwich at the corner and I hugged my arms to my chest. "What do you mean…?" I asked.

"Turn around."

EPILOGUE

Boxes in the windows blocked the sunlight so that Jeff's apartment was unusually gloomy for a Saturday afternoon in mid-April.

"You ready to move?" I asked him.

Jeff kicked his legs up on the coffee table. "It's only around the corner. I'm not sure that even constitutes a 'real' move."

I touched his arm. "It still counts. A move is a move," I said, as I got up, stepping carefully over the boxes, the scissors on the floor, hunks of masking tape, and stuffed a box of elaborately designed hookahs with newspaper.

"Fucking landlord has some nerve selling this building," Jeff said. "Who does that?"

"I don't know, a landlord?"

Jeff sighed. "So any gossip from the old office?"

"I hardly talked to anyone there except you. Why would I be in the loop now that I don't even work there?" I walked to the kitchen, filled a glass with water from the sink.

Jeff laughed, shaking his head. "I still can't believe you quit."

"The proper word is *resigned*, but yes—" my eyes flashed to his "—it's officially the end of an era."

Jeff asked me to recount the details of my resignation again, as if it were a twisted bedtime story for jaded adults, and I rejoined him on the couch, deciding I would indulge him.

"It was a Friday in March. I knocked on the door to Natalie's office, and I told her I needed to speak with her. Then I sat down, said I was ready to move on, and that I would be giving her my two weeks. She was upset, obviously, because I was supposed to pitch with them in Austin." Jeff was practically on the edge of his seat. "But then she said, 'That won't be necessary, you can leave today,' and so I packed up my stuff, and Jasmine—"

"Fucking Jasmine," Jeff said.

"Jasmine asked if I'd been fired. And I said, 'People can quit, you know.' But I feel like Natalie told everyone I was laid off, because I was getting texts saying they were 'sorry to hear.'"

"That's more than what I got," Jeff said. "I was just—" he flaunted jazz hands in the air "—*poof*! Forgotten."

"You were too good for that place," I told him, but I was thinking how I was complicit in his firing and I'd never be able to tell him the truth.

"And you like the new job?"

I'd started work at an ad agency last month; it was better than working for Natalie, or maybe that was only because I was still new, the office's flaws not yet apparent through rose-tinted glasses.

"It's fine," I said. "Did I tell you I signed up for a writing class? We meet on Wednesday nights. Everyone is so talented and smart, and…" I stopped.

"And so are you."

"Eh, not really," I said, but then I remembered how Etta had chastised me for refusing to accept a compliment. "Thanks," I told him. "So how's the new PR gig treating you?"

He shrugged. "It's not as soul-sucking. My boss is cool. You would like him."

I gave a little laugh and Jeff asked, "What?"

"It's just funny—I didn't realize you liked PR that much? Enough to stay in it, I mean."

"Like it's so different from an ad agency?"

"Touché," I said.

I checked my phone, though there were no messages, and Jeff scrolled through Instagram on his. "Sorry, what?" he asked, examining his screen. "Etta has hashtag content partners now?"

"Yeah, seems like she's doing very well."

"Speaking of," he said, "I think I saw Archer last week."

I had that quivering sensation in my chest, like butterflies but also like my heart might stop beating at any moment.

"Did you? Where?"

"I *think* I did," he said. "Crossing Canal. He was with a woman in a pantsuit. She was very—"

"Oh," I said, deflating. "That's probably Astrid, his art dealer."

"Figures."

He turned to me. "Sorry, was that insensitive?"

"What was?"

"Bringing him up. I can never tell if you'd rather pretend he didn't exist, or if you like, want to talk about him."

I waved my hand in front of my face. "I mean, obviously it was a shock when everything happened, but yeah, I'm fine. I'm good. He called and apologized and we will just leave it at that."

Jeff held my gaze so that I looked away.

"It's just weird that nothing really happened," he said. "After that whole thing."

"Hmm, well, if anything, Roger's story just gave them free PR."

Jeff glanced at his lap. "Proves my theory that there's no such thing as bad press."

"Ha," I said, "Etta kinda said the same thing."

Outside, someone screamed, followed by peals of laughter.

"Do you miss her?" he asked.

"Who? Etta?" He nodded. "Jeff, she isn't *dead*."

"It's just a question."

Did I miss Etta? Of course I missed her, in the way we were all nostalgic for any part of our life that had ended, but too much had happened between us to keep pretending. Still, I kept my promise that I wouldn't tell Archer she'd sold him out to Roger. I had no intention of betraying her any more than she'd betrayed Archer, or me. And in a twisted way, honoring a secret could be almost as virtuous as telling the truth.

"Sometimes," I said. "I don't know, I'm too nostalgic. It's like I only remember the good parts."

"Oh, not me. I remember the bad."

I squeezed Jeff's shoulder. "I know you do."

"You're less cynical than the rest of us."

"Well," I said, "I don't know if that's necessarily true."

"Oh, she's humble, too!" Jeff called over his shoulder as he crossed the apartment to the kitchen, and I rolled my eyes for dramatic effect, though he wasn't looking at me. He opened the refrigerator as my phone vibrated softly on my lap. I ignored the call.

When Jeff plopped beside me again, I angled my phone toward him, now open to a dating app. Jeff's eyes landed on my screen before traveling to my face, then back to my phone.

"An accountant?" he asked, smiling wryly.

"I mean, he's definitely a tool. Look at the picture of him on that ski trip. Where is his shirt?"

"Ren. You were once involved with an art launderer."

"Accomplice," I corrected. "Accomplice to an art launderer."

"Same thing."

I stole another glance at my phone, the shirtless skiing accountant, chuckled, then dropped it into my purse.

"He asked if I was free tonight. Feels a little last-minute, though."

Jeff perked up. "No, no, it doesn't. Go!"

"You won't be mad if I leave?"

"Of course not." A pause. "I've forgiven you for worse things, haven't I?" and I wondered if he somehow knew it was my fault he had lost his job, but I wasn't about to ask. Instead I said, "True," and smiled.

———

Jeff thinks that I'm going to meet the accountant for drinks, and a part of me entertains the possibility, of what our evening might entail. Whether he would choose beer or wine; if he prefers white because red stains your teeth and his teeth are so pristinely pearly he can't put his vanity on hold for two hours. Except when I leave Jeff's apartment, that tightness in my chest returns. It's guilt. Guilt that I can't tell him everything, at least for now.

After all, pretending is an art and all art comes at a price.

Ironically, Archer's involvement with Otto has been a good thing for his art: it means that he is still the talk of the town, a curious wunderkind. People want to analyze his choices about why he did what he did, and he won't give anyone a straight answer, and the reality is, there is nothing people love more than a mystery. Uncertainty is like catnip for the discerning because it keeps us guessing, always. Archer had compared himself to Lazarus, an observation he liked so much that he mentioned it in a recent profile piece, where he spoke at length about trying his hand at sculpting, how he was learning to meditate, and the writer commented that a new medium might match a new narrative, that people are invested in this idea of new beginnings.

As for my new beginning, whenever I feel unsure of my place, I remember the night Etta left me at the Brooklyn loft party almost a year ago. How I'd panicked, stalling in the kitchen, willing her to appear.

And how in the end I'd found my own way home.

I think about Eve Babitz a lot these days. She had an interesting life, a life she could write about. Maybe one day, I hope, I can do the same, if I keep up, if I play along.

———

My phone rings again and I pause at the end of the block to answer it. "I'm across the street," he says, and then he is shouting, "Over here!" and waving his hand. He's smiling through the open window.

I make a run for it while I still have the light; on the sidewalk, a couple argues over coffee at a café and there is a black Lab fighting against the pull of its leash.

I tug open the door and slide in beside him. He kisses my cheek.

"Hi," Archer says.

The window glides shut.

★ ★ ★ ★ ★

ACKNOWLEDGMENTS

I started dreaming of this story and what it might look like ten years ago. A pandemic, career change, and countless drafts later, to see it come to fruition is just that, a dream. I am grateful to many, many people for making it possible.

To Abby Walters, who understood *The Art of Pretend* from the beginning and held my hand along the way. To the team at Graydon House and especially Melanie Fried, whose enthusiasm, attention to detail, and dedication means everything—you have made *The Art of Pretend* better. And of course, to Austin Denesuk, my dear friend, one of my first readers and now agent. Thank you, thank you, thank you. Next up, world domination.

To my friends, who supported me while I was still "writing with the door closed," especially Betsy Chester, who makes me feel less crazy and somehow always knows the right thing to say, and Alyssa Hollander, my trusted reader and honorary muse. To Matt Leonard, my very own Jeff and one of my most favorite people, and Emelie Pierpoint, my eternal work wife. It is such a joy when work friends become family—I count my lucky stars that our paths crossed.

To my parents, who have been listening to my stories since I could talk (and draw on Post-it notes), thank you for encouraging me to dream. Special gratitude to my mother, who read every draft, who showed me patience and kindness and always encouraged me to keep going. To Sarah, for your humor and being the wisest soul at the tender age of eighteen, and John, who, even at the point of publication, is still unconvinced this book is real.

I am the luckiest.

DISCUSSION QUESTIONS

1. Discuss Ren and Etta's relationship. What does Ren gain from Etta, and vice versa? Do you think this type of friendship can still be genuine? How is their dynamic different or similar to Ren and Jeff's?

2. Did you feel Ren was justified in hiding her relationship with Archer from Etta? Why or why not? Have you ever withheld a big secret like that from a close friend or loved one?

3. In the novel, certain characters pay the consequences of their actions, whereas others don't. Discuss how wealth, or the lack of it, defines how much power one has. What kind of power does Ren seek? How does she try to get it?

4. Did you understand the compromises Archer made for his career? Why or why not? Were you surprised by them?

5. Compare Ren's friendship with Etta and her relationship with her boss, Natalie. How are they similar and different, and how does each evolve over the course of the novel?

6. How are Ren's relationships informed by her mother's abandonment? Do you think she'll ever fully break away from its shadow?

7. Discuss the novel's ending. Why do you think Ren chose to be with Archer? Was it a decision purely motivated by love, or by something more complicated than that?

8. Having now read the book, what does the title, *The Art of Pretend*, mean to you?